DEATH IN SUMMER

DEATH IN SUMMER

Michael THEURILLAT

MANILLA

First published in Germany in 2006 by Ullstein Buchverlage GmbH, Berlin

This paperback edition published in Great Britain in 2018 by Manilla Publishing,
80–81 Wimpole St, London W1G 9RE
www.manillabooks.com

A CIP catalogue record for this book is
available from the British Library.

ISBN: 978-1-78576-724-1

Also available as an ebook

1 3 5 7 9 10 8 6 4 2

Typeset by IDSUK (Data Connection) Ltd
Printed and bound in Great Britain by Clays Ltd, Elcograf S.p.A.

Manilla Publishing is an imprint of Bonnier Zaffre,
a Bonnier Publishing company
www.bonnierzaffre.co.uk
www.bonnierpublishing.co.uk

But worst: to be denied
a death in summer,
when all is bright,
the earth soft beneath the spade.

Gottfried Benn

Chapter 1

The man stepped onto the green and picked up the little white ball; he had never played golf in his life.

He wore rimless glasses and thin latex gloves, as is the custom for police officers working in forensics. It was the first time he had ever held a golf ball. He marked its position with a little wooden stick and placed the ball in a clear plastic bag.

It was the first find of the afternoon, except, of course, for the body lying 150 metres away. Inspector Eschenbach had received the call about the dead golfer just after his lunch break. He had been sitting in front of the mountain of files he had been putting off for days. Next to him sat the cup of espresso he had bought from the Starbucks café that had just opened.

'Male. Mid-fifties. Shot dead at the fifteenth hole,' said Elisabeth Kobler, police chief for the canton of Zurich, when she called to brief him. 'Drive over and take a look at the crime scene. I've come to see Councillor Sacher about this brawl on Limmatplatz. Might be along later.'

'All right,' he grumbled. 'I'll take care of it.'

The espresso was awful, he thought – much too sweet, and the oversized Styrofoam cup only made matters worse.

'And remember, Eschenbach. That club's a fancy place. Full of poshos. Make sure you wear a tie . . . and keep it *on the DL*.'

'Of course.'

'OK, see you later.'

'Later,' he mumbled and hung up.

'On the DL' had become Kobler's phrase of choice in recent weeks. After the press had put pressure on Kobler due to some suspected misconduct in the police force, it was imperative that everything remain 'on the DL'.

It would be difficult, he thought, to keep the news that a golfer had been murdered at a swanky golf club on Lake Zurich 'on the DL'. And he hated Americanisms.

He opened the cupboard and took out an orange Hermès tie – a gift from his daughter for his fiftieth the month before. He put it on. 'Poshos,' he thought. He found he had tied it too long, so that it dangled over his waistband; he loosened the knot and tried again. He looked at his reflection in the shaving mirror on the cabinet door and wondered whether things would change now he was fifty. Would life be grimmer, older, or greyer from now on? Perhaps it would be all three.

When he had taken up the role as chief of the Criminal Investigation Department, aged thirty-eight, Eschenbach had been the youngest chief in the history of the Zurich CID. In the intervening years, his dark-brown hair had grown lighter, he thought, at least at the edges. He had hardly any grey hair. He would have preferred it the other way around. He pulled a face in the mirror, then shut the cabinet door.

He would not need his gun – that was something. It occurred to him that he had left it with the gunsmith and should give him a call. He hated the thing; he preferred thinking rather than shooting any day. Perhaps it was because he could control one better than the other.

He took his jacket off the chair, slipped it on and left his office. On the way, he met Claudio Jagmetti, the trainee from the police academy who had been assigned to him for the summer. He asked him to type up the corrected report on his desk. Then he took the stairs down to the underground garage and got into his car.

Eschenbach crossed Bellevue and headed towards Bürkliplatz with Lake Zurich on his left. The white sails of the boats reflected the sunlight and behind them stood the Alps: majestic, topped with a permanent dusting of snow. Against the deep blue of the summer sky, they painted a picture in blue and white. Blue and white, he thought, the colours of Zurich.

It was early July, and for weeks Zurich had been sweating in temperatures more commonly found in the southern Alps. He loosened his tie, then took it off altogether. Beads of perspiration were forming on his brow. At the lights, he leant over and pulled his Brissagos out of his jacket on the back seat. Eschenbach loved the knobbly cigarillos from Ticino, the Italian speaking part of Switzerland. They helped him think. He lit one and thought of Corina. She and Kathrin had gone to The Engandine Valley to stay at his in-laws' apartment. They had left three days earlier than expected – because of the heat, the summer holidays had started early. All because of a measly thirty-eight degrees in the shade. Wimps, he thought. All of them.

Eschenbach had promised to drive up at the weekend and visit them.

There was little traffic on the road along the lake. Eschenbach made good time and reached the gates to the golf club in twenty minutes. Plane trees lined the well-tended gravel path that led up to the clubhouse. Eschenbach parked his Volvo next to two dark-blue luxury cars, got out and noticed that his light-blue shirt was clinging to his back, sodden with perspiration.

Across from him, two elderly women in cream plaid outfits were getting into a golf buggy. Burberry. He knew the brand. His daughter had a similar blouse, of which she was immensely proud. It had been a present from Corina. Plaid was *mega*, or so he had been informed, *totally sick*. Eschenbach found the pattern ridiculous, somehow old fashioned, and he vaguely remembered his grandmother wearing something similar.

He swept away the cigarillo ash on his beige trousers. The ladies in plaid were eyeing him with suspicion. He greeted them cheerily and – unfazed by the snootiness he had encountered the minute he stepped out of the car – walked up the steps to the clubhouse. He stuck his half-smoked Brissago in the brass pot near the entrance.

'Are you a member?' asked the woman at reception in a hushed tone.

'Inspector Eschenbach,' he said. Then, more quietly: 'Zurich CID.'

The young woman shrank back, horrified, but composed herself at once. Eschenbach leant over the smooth, varnished counter and whispered, 'I'm here about the dead golfer.'

'Yes, I know.' The woman's nasal tone transformed into a conspiratorial whisper. 'It's simply awful. I'll call Mr Aebischer. He's the manager.'

'Thanks. I'll wait outside.'

Eschenbach recovered his cold Brissago from the brass container, lit it and stepped out into the sunshine. It was warm and summery outside, but he felt a chill. Was it the beginning of summer flu? Or some sense of rising unease? The golf bags standing in front of the clubhouse looked like silent guard dogs.

He waited.

The hedges were neatly trimmed, and footpaths stretched across the green with utmost precision. The grass was a uniform green. It gave Eschenbach the impression of a shaggy bear primped and clipped like a poodle.

He took a drag on his cigarillo.

'Inspector?' A scrawny man in a blue blazer hurried towards Eschenbach. He introduced himself as the manager of the golf club. In a series of convoluted sentences, he described what had happened. The first thing that Eschenbach was able to make out was that somewhere on the green, in between two holes, lay a dead man.

Eschenbach listened to his wild theories about stray bullets, the army, and young marksmen mixed with fears about the possible damage to the image of the club and to golf worldwide.

It bored him. He was craving a cold beer.

'Can I get something to drink?'

Interrupted mid-flow, the scrawny man in the blazer looked as if he had just been slapped in the face.

'I'll get you a glass of water and then we can drive to the fifteenth hole, where the body is. Your colleagues have been at work for over an hour reconstructing the crime scene.' His last sentence seemed to bear a taunting undertone.

It was just before half nine when Eschenbach concluded his investigations on the golf course. He felt tired and drained.

His people had cordoned off the golf course in time to stop the minibus from Tele Zurich, which arrived with two camera crews. He could understand why the media were so annoyed by this. Club members' cars were stopped as they made their way home through the chaos, cameras clicked at tinted windows.

'If you don't get out of the way, I'll run you down!' snarled an old, balding man with a bright red face through the gap in the window of his Jaguar. Further back, a Mercedes S-Class sounded its horn.

Cows grazed peacefully behind the electric fence, undisturbed by the spectacle.

The terrace of the club restaurant, which offered a wonderful view of Lake Zurich and the Glarus Alps, was still a hive of activity. Eschenbach sat down at a free table and ordered a beer.

A few of the guests eyed him furtively. Others were friendly, offering a greeting or even a wave. They had been questioned about the incident and their names had been recorded. They seemed to be relieved that the ordeal was over.

This was the type of place where the sensationalism that often arose unchecked in such situations, hampering police investigations in the process, was discreetly concealed beneath the guise of genteel indifference. The guests whispered quietly to one another at their tables. They prophesied the end of golf as they knew it and speculated about the perpetrator and possible motives. The club management were serving delicious appetisers and champagne in delicate glasses. They seemed to want to make up for the events of the afternoon and help their guests to relax.

Eschenbach felt out of place. Everyone who visited the club was running from something. From boredom, stress or depression. Sadness. Overwork. Joylessness. Lovelessness. Anaemia. Low blood sugar. Cold hearts. Heart attacks. They were exiles from a tragic continent, where the superficial was prized above all else.

Why would someone murder Philipp Bettlach? Eschenbach stared at the lake and wished the whole thing was over and done with already. Drawing to a close, like the day itself. He knew that, in reality, it was just the beginning. There would be the interrogations at HQ, the press to deal with, and the lies from people making their false confessions.

He paid for his beer and followed the gravel path back to his car, all the while looking out at the lake, lost in thought. It would be a clear summer night.

Eschenbach could quite clearly make out the navigation lights of the ships coming in to dock. Red for port, green for starboard. He knew them well. Now and then, when work allowed, he would take his friend's old fishing boat out onto the lake. It had little to do with fishing; it was simply an excuse to do nothing at all. He found the nylon wire too fiddly and he couldn't make head or tail of bait, spoon lures and flies. He liked nothing more than to read the paper and go for a swim. Sometimes he simply lay on deck, letting himself be rocked by the waves, looking up into the sky where the clouds chased after one another.

On the journey back to Zurich, his mind replayed the few hours he had spent at the golf course. He had a dead golfer, who, according to details provided by the club management, was fifty-six years of age, vice president of a Swiss bank, and well liked by all. He was happy, divorced, had no children and no enemies. Why would someone have wanted to shoot him? And why there? Why then?

The shot must have been fired from a considerable distance, otherwise some trace of the killer would already have been found. Eschenbach suspected he had used a long range rifle.

The people from forensics would resume their search the next morning, in better light. They would turn over every blade of grass as far as the Alps if they had to.

Eschenbach pondered the case. The golf course was surrounded by a seemingly endless chain of hills – and like in a gigantic haystack, the needle was nowhere to be found.

Feeling discouraged he drew on his Brissago and blew the smoke through the open window in short puffs, out into the balmy summer night.

If he had no clue as to the distance from which the shooter had struck, he must at least try to form a clearer idea about the direction from which the bullet had come. He had to find out at what angle the bullet had entered the victim's head. He also had to ascertain how the golfer had been standing when the bullet hit. What position had Philipp Bettlach's head been in and how had his body been aligned? It's too complicated, thought Eschenbach. It'll be impossible to reconstruct. But he knew he must.

Chapter 2

As Eschenbach made his way towards Bahnhofstrasse at 7.30 the following morning, it was already a warm summer's day. He had yet to put on his jacket, which hung casually over his right shoulder.

The crisis meeting he had just left made him feel positive for the rest of the day. Now the operation was running full steam ahead. He was used to the mad rush that followed a murder. It was like a crackle of electricity that energised the otherwise inert police force and set it blazing with light.

In his light-grey trousers, fresh sky-blue shirt – which he wore without a tie – and his sunglasses, he looked more like an Italian tourist than the head of the CID.

Perhaps this was due simply to the city where he worked. In Florence or Rome he could have passed easily for an inspector, maybe even a bank manager. Here in Zurich, the metropolis of money, bankers wore dark suits, even in summer. They did it more out of the conviction that this was the proper way to dress than vanity.

The coffee bar on St Anna-Gasse had already set up its tables and chairs outside. Eschenbach sat down, stretched his legs and ordered an espresso.

When the inspector climbed the steps to headquarters scarcely an hour later, he had some idea of what might await him.

The officers at the entrance greeted him pleasantly; they stood with their arms wide, attempting to keep the camera crews, photographers and journalists at bay. It was a storm of noise, questions flying everywhere. Eschenbach acknowledged them, unsmiling. 'The press conference is at 9.30,' he shouted. Then he disappeared inside.

On the third floor, chaos reigned. The telephones were ringing constantly, and officers were running with unusual urgency through the open-plan office, which was divided by partition walls. A sketch of the crime scene hung from a large pinboard; coffee-stained paper cups lay scattered throughout.

In the midst of the chaos stood Rosa Mazzoleni. She had keen, brown eyes and a sturdy figure, and had been Eschenbach's secretary for over ten years. A pair of reading glasses dangled from her neck on a gold chain and her short black hair gleamed. Rosa enjoyed the chaos; it reminded her of Naples, her home town, of the traffic and the way people did business south of the Alps.

When the inspector arrived on the third floor, his secretary initially made no move to greet him. She pulled a face and waved her right hand at him, then pointed towards Eschenbach's office. 'She's already in there . . . she just walked straight through. She's been on the phone for over half an hour.'

His office door was ajar and, through the gap, Eschenbach could hear the voice of Elisabeth Kobler.

'But you must understand that we cannot comment on possible suspects so soon after a crime.'

Silence.

'No, we don't. The press conference is at half nine. OK,' she said, and finished abruptly.

Eschenbach opened the door to his office. At once, Kobler took her feet off the desk and made to slip them back into her dark-brown loafers.

'You can leave your shoes on next time,' he said, grinning.

'Bloodthirsty hacks!' Kobler was annoyed. 'What do you think you're doing, Eschenbach? You can't just leave me hanging here. The phones have been going since half seven. I've yet to see a report and you've only just got in!'

'Nothing's come through yet. We know he was shot, possibly with a long-distance rifle. So, my guess is either a lunatic sniper or a professional marksman.'

'Like the one in Washington, DC, who shot thirteen people? You're telling me we've got one of those on our hands?'

'So far, all we've got is a body. I assume that's it for the moment.'

'And now what do we do?' asked Elisabeth Kobler, visibly relieved not to have missed any important developments.

'Dr Salvisberg is examining the body. I think we'll know more by lunchtime. After that, I'd like to arrange a reconstruction with him and a golf pro.'

'A golf what?' Kobler raised her eyebrows.

'A golf pro, you know . . . a golf instructor.'

'I don't play golf.' She stood up.

'Me neither,' he said, passing Kobler her jacket from one of the chairs.

Without another word, she went out into the corridor and down the stairs, where a ravenous crowd of journalists were waiting in the large conference room.

The press conference went better than expected.

Kobler held back and left the talking to Eschenbach, who knew, in his stolid, casual way, how to make a molehill out of a mountain.

'One last question, then that's all for today,' he said, pulling a cigarillo out of his jacket. A smoking ban had been in place at HQ since the first of January; it was obvious he wanted to get going.

'Are you expecting the killer to strike again?' The question came from a young female journalist, working for the *Zürcher Tagblatt*. Eschenbach had never seen her before.

'We are not assuming that for the moment, though of course we can't know with any certainty.'

There were another two queries along the same lines, then Eschenbach dismissed further questions. He looked at Elisabeth Kobler and they nodded at one another. She took over, thanked everyone for coming and brought the conference to an end.

'You should have been a lion tamer,' said Kobler, when they were standing outside in the hallway. She seemed visibly relieved and in good spirits once again. 'Do you really think he might strike again?'

'Did I say that?'

'No, but you were thinking it,' she added quietly and placed a hand on Eschenbach's shoulder.

'I just hope that no one else can read my thoughts. Otherwise we'll have a serial killer on our hands before we've even a scrap of evidence.'

'Good luck,' said Kobler as she walked towards the exit, before leaving the building through the revolving doors.

Eschenbach took the stairs to the third floor. Rosa Mazzoleni was so engrossed in her computer screen that she hardly noticed as he scurried past.

He went into his office, closed the door behind him and lit the Brissago that he had held in his hand the whole time.

Smoking in private offices was neither banned nor permitted. The final decision on the matter was taking a while. Two executive members of the government were heavy smokers, so there was nothing to fear for the time being.

Deep in thought, Eschenbach opened the window and blew smoke out into the muggy summer air. He was reluctant to go outside, now that the sun was shining ever more strongly, but he had to get to the golf course. He had no time to lose.

He asked Rosa Mazzoleni to call Pathology and connect him to Dr Salvisberg. He was rarely around at this time of day. In addition to his work with the police, Salvisberg lectured on forensic medicine at the University of Zurich, marked his students' seminar work and wrote reports for the Swiss Tropical Institute, the pharmaceutical industry and God knows who else. 'When you're surrounded by dead people, you have to work hard to stay among the living,' Salvisberg had once explained.

Rosa Mazzoleni got through to Pathology immediately.

'Dr Salvisberg, Eschenbach here – not disturbing you, am I?'

'Never, Eschenbach. Would you believe it, you've caught me in the freezer.' He sniggered quietly.

'Do you play golf?' asked the inspector.

'Goodness, where would I find the energy for that? I cut up bodies all day, and then there's the stress of dealing with these damn students.' Salvisberg sighed. 'My students are currently evaluating my performance as a lecturer ... Can you imagine ...?'

Eschenbach laughed.

'This is the latest thing from management – it's an absolute turd of an idea,' he continued. 'They've got shit-for-brains, I'm telling you ...' He ranted about education policy, both Swiss and European, and griped about the university administration. 'They've got more dead brains up there than I've got in Pathology.'

He finished with a description of the dementia he believed was raging worldwide. He was losing hope, he said: 'Luckily I've still got the reports. At least they pay properly.'

'Then it's not half as bad as you say,' joked Eschenbach.

'What do you mean "not half as bad"? It's ghastly.' And, after a brief pause, 'What were we talking about?'

'Golf,' replied Eschenbach.

'As a cure for dementia?' Salvisberg laughed at the top of his voice. 'I have better things to be doing with my free time.'

'What's better than golf?' asked Eschenbach.

'Fishing!'

'Oh, you're into fishing.' For Eschenbach, anything was more interesting than golf. But he never would have guessed Salvisberg would be into fishing.

'Of course. Fly fishing,' replied Salvisberg, noting the irritation in his colleague's voice. 'Why don't you come along? I've been fishing on the River Sihl for years. It's peaceful and sheltered. And there's not a soul to be seen.'

'Just like Pathology, then – no souls there either.'

Salvisberg sniggered again. 'Exactly. And there's no one to complain about poor treatment.'

'Let's be serious for a moment, Salvisberg. Have you got any ideas on the angle the bullet went in?'

'I can show you approximately where. Not on the victim's head, of course, there's not much left of it.'

'I see.' Eschenbach grimaced. 'Could it be reconstructed on a dummy?'

'Yes, of course. Come by. Bring a mannequin.'

'You may laugh, but that's the plan. I can't come myself though. My assistant, Claudio Jagmetti, will have to do it.'

'I look forward to it.'

'And please, Salvisberg, be nice to him. He's a good boy, fresh out of the police academy, and I'd like him to stay with us for good. There are enough traumatised police officers as it is.'

'Sure, I'll send over that report, then. Speak soon ... and come fishing some time. I'd like that.'

'Maybe ... speak soon.'

Eschenbach put the phone down and pressed the button on the intercom to speak to Ms Mazzoleni.

'Send me Jagmetti, when you see him.'

'Will do,' came her crackling reply through the loudspeaker. 'What was that with Kobler, boss?'

'All good. I think she managed to control herself.'

'It's horrible, what the papers have been saying about her recently,' her voice crackled again.

Eschenbach didn't respond. He took a brief look through the signature folder and signed it as required. Then he stood up, picked up his jacket and left the room.

As Eschenbach walked along the corridor towards the stairs, he came across Claudio Jagmetti.

'Sorry, boss. I was at the dentist.'

'Oh, I completely forgot,' said the inspector. 'Come with me ... and for God's sake, stop calling me "boss".'

Without exchanging another word, they walked side by side to the exit. The summer heat hit them as they stepped out of the cool, air-conditioned foyer.

The café opposite was serving lunch to its first customers who had found themselves a comfy spot in the garden, amid the terracotta pots.

The two police officers crossed the street and found seats at a small green bistro table. Eschenbach explained that he wanted to reconstruct the golfer's murder at the golf course. 'We'll need a life-size dummy with a movable head.'

Jagmetti eyed the inspector disbelievingly.

'Get a dummy, ideally from a department store, and then take it to Salvisberg in Pathology. He'll know you're coming.'

'Will do,' said the young police cadet, noting everything down neatly in a small square notebook.

'Then drive over to the golf course – it's called Lake Zurich Golf Club – and arrange for a golf pro to join us.'

Jagmetti nodded.

'Do you know what a golf pro is?' asked Eschenbach.

'Someone who knows how to play golf?' replied Jagmetti, as if he didn't understand the question.

'Exactly, a golf teacher,' explained Eschenbach. 'We'll need him from three o'clock.'

'OK, consider it done,' said Jagmetti, proud to be involved in such an important case.

Eschenbach placed the money for the drinks on the table. They stood up, left the café and made for the exclusive shopping avenue Bahnhofstrasse, before going their separate ways.

The inspector was curious to see how Jagmetti would set about his vaguely formulated task. As he walked, he began to wonder whether he had explained himself properly. He was surprised that the young police officer hadn't asked any questions or expressed any concerns. It wasn't in keeping with his past experience of trainees.

Chapter 3

The offices of Zurich Commercial Bank were on Rennweg, one of the most beautiful streets in Zurich. The entrance was flanked by sandstone columns on either side and a solid glass door offered a glimpse into the main hall.

In place of a doorknob, there was a bronze lion's head. Into the lion's den, thought Eschenbach, as he gripped the bronze head and went to enter. Yet the door opened of its own accord, as if pulled by a ghostly hand, and he was greeted by a draught of pleasantly cool air.

The dark brown of the polished oak floor and the light reflecting softly on the white walls gave the room a simple elegance.

To his right stood a Giacometti statue on a plinth, almost two metres high. Despite its slender silhouette, the bronze sculpture seemed to invade the whole space.

A plump blond woman – a charming contrast to the Giacometti figure – sat smiling behind the reception desk.

A metallic clicking behind him made Eschenbach jump – an old reflex – and he turned around. He relaxed when he saw that it was just the door closing after him.

'Can I help you, Mr . . .'

Eschenbach turned again and walked over to the woman, who was still smiling.

'Eschenbach, Zurich CID,' he said, showing her his badge. 'Dr Bettlach is expecting me.'

'Ah.' She picked up the telephone and dialled an internal number. She spoke briefly to the person at the other end of the line and replaced the receiver.

'Come with me, Inspector.' She stood up and accompanied him the few steps to the lift, before holding a magnetic card up to a small Perspex plaque. Then she pressed the button for the top floor.

Dr Johannes Bettlach was a large, gaunt-looking man. His grey hair, combed severely back, shone almost white in the sunlight and was longer than one might expect for a bank manager. Beneath his strong brow sat strikingly pale eyes, ensconced in two dark sockets. His features were stern, but not unfriendly.

He walked slowly across the room towards Eschenbach.

On the walls hung large-scale contemporary art pieces and behind the desk a bookcase, packed with books, reaching as high as the stucco ceiling. The room was not what Eschenbach had expected of a Swiss bank: the books, the dark wood floor, the Buddha sitting enthroned upon a cigar box, propping up a stack of books, the bronze ballet dancer hovering in a seemingly weightless pose next to the telephone.

The inspector was familiar with the banks along Bahnhofstrasse: the marble halls with barriers of bullet-proof glass, and the plush carpets in grey or anthracite covering the directors' floors, creating an air of detached elegance. He knew them from some of his previous investigations. But this place was different.

Dr Bettlach took Eschenbach's hand in his and gave it a light squeeze. His hand was warm and, despite the sudden intimacy of the gesture and his lack of familiarity with the person performing it, Eschenbach didn't find it unpleasant.

He was reminded of his passing out ceremony at the Church of St Francis when he became a young lieutenant in the Swiss Army. His commander, Colonel Nydegger, had looked deep into his eyes as he shook his hand.

It had been a moment of celebration, a moment that lived on inside him long after the fact.

With that handshake *le motto* had found its way into the moral values of the young officer, like a spark of good middle class ethics. It came back to him again now, in this curious situation in Dr Bettlach's office.

The two men stood looking at one another for a short while. Neither spoke until Dr Bettlach's quiet, cautious voice broke the silence.

'Shall we sit?'

Dr Bettlach indicated a leather armchair. Eschenbach promptly sat down and felt the black leather receive him as a great sense of weariness descended. He closed his eyes for a moment, then opened them again. 'I couldn't reach you yesterday. It's . . . I wanted to inform you in person.'

'I know he was shot . . . at the golf course.' Dr Bettlach looked at Eschenbach with his pale eyes. His gaze wandered to the window, then outside, before becoming lost somewhere amid the roofs and chimneys opposite.

The ornamental geraniums hanging from the balconies' wrought iron bars in grey slate boxes, their vermillion petals dancing in the sunlight, did nothing to counter the sadness in his eyes.

'Yes, that's what happened,' said Eschenbach slowly.

'Do you know who did it?'

'No. The investigation is under way. We're . . . we still don't know.'

'Philipp was my brother, my younger brother.' Dr Bettlach's gaze, which had returned to the rooftop gardens as he spoke, drifted again. 'It is so sad, it's all so immensely sad,' he continued. This time, his eyes remained fixed outside and his thoughts seemed far away, lost amid the geraniums, the ivy and the horizon, between the midday sun of July and the dark shadows of grief.

'Who could have wanted to kill your brother?' Eschenbach slid forward, as if to shake off the melancholy that seemed to have wrapped itself around every inch of the room like black seaweed.

'I don't know, Inspector. I don't know.'

Eschenbach loosened his collar, undid his top button and took a deep breath. Had he put on weight? His voice was hoarse. He cleared his throat. 'Why don't you tell me about him? What sort of person was your brother? What was he like? Tell me about his friends, his wife, his family, relationships. Everything.'

Dr Bettlach noticed Eschenbach's attempt to throw off the air of gloom and he began, slowly, hesitant at first, then with increasing fluency, to talk about his brother.

Eschenbach interrupted him briefly to ask if he could use his Dictaphone, to which Bettlach agreed with an absent-minded nod. The inspector placed the recorder on the table to ensure that his interviewee could see it.

As Dr Bettlach spoke about his brother, describing his personality and his quirks, he switched – at first occasionally, then with increasing frequency – between a sombre past tense and a more cheerful present. 'Was' became 'is', 'had' became 'has', 'could' became 'can' until at last it seemed the dead man was alive again.

Bettlach spoke in a calm, sober tone. He seemed to select each word carefully, gave every pause its full weight. When his secretary came to give him two notes and inform him that he needed to return some calls, he didn't seem remotely interested. And later, when they were served espresso and amaretti, he seemed hardly to notice.

Eschenbach had just ejected the cassette from the Dictaphone and went to insert a new one, but realised that he hadn't brought a second cassette with him. Instead he turned the device off.

'Philipp was bright, quick-thinking, he had a sunny disposition. When he laughed, he had the whole world at his feet.' Bettlach took a sip of coffee, stirred it and was quiet for a moment. 'It's hard, when you're sixteen years older,' he continued. 'I can still remember holding him in my arms when he was a baby. He seemed like a creature from another world.' He smiled. 'The age difference was harder for him than it was for me; he used to shout at me as if he couldn't accept the fact that I was his older brother.'

Eschenbach sat quietly, expectant.

'When he was small, it was relatively easy, but as he got older, he realised that I was ahead of him and had already done everything that he wanted to do, and for a time he turned against Mother and me. He broke all the rules. He would be out night after night – no one knew where he was. When the phone rang at four in the morning, we knew he had been picked up somewhere because he was drunk, or on drugs, or had stolen something. The police stations became familiar with him after a while and it was equally clear who was picking him up and who had to pay for the damage he had caused.' Johannes Bettlach stopped and bit into an amaretto he had taken from his plate. He chewed and went on: 'It was a hard time for Philipp . . . and for our mother, Adele, of course,' he added. 'To me, it seemed he had only started all of this because he knew how much I deplored it, and because I had never done these things myself. It was a desperate attempt to better me.'

Eschenbach wondered whether he would see things the same way if it were his brother. He had no siblings.

'And when I stopped getting angry – when I no longer found the night-time trips to the police station embarrassing, because they had become as much a part of my day as brushing my teeth, that's when Philipp stopped. It had lost its appeal.' Johannes Bettlach smiled. 'But I think that's normal for brothers. Later on we became friends.'

Eschenbach was astounded by the way Johannes Bettlach spoke about his brother. It wasn't one-sided or short on detail. He spoke with distance but lovingly, warmly, rounding out his brother and bringing him to life. It was both happy and sad all at once. It reminded Eschenbach of the way a mother speaks about a child who is dearest to her because it is different and more difficult than the others.

'It's not much, I know. I've no clues as to how to help you with your inquiries . . .' Bettlach passed a hand through his hair, turned to Eschenbach and looked at him with his blue eyes.

'A start . . . it's a start,' said Eschenbach, clearing his throat. He was thinking about what Bettlach had said. It occurred to him that Bettlach had spoken at length about his brother's childhood and teenage years but had hardly mentioned his recent life. This was a peculiarity that Eschenbach often observed in older people. According to the report, Philipp Bettlach was fifty-six: there must have been more to him than youthful rebellion and friendship.

'Could you tell me a little about your brother's family circumstances? Who did he live with? Did he have children?'

'No,' replied Bettlach plainly. Then, somewhat hesitantly, he added, 'He was married once . . . it's over twenty years ago now. Her name was Eveline. A nice girl . . . but they weren't right for each other. They separated a year later. He had lived alone ever since.' He hesitated again, then added: 'He had a number of acquaintances.' Bettlach smiled. 'But that's . . . that was his business. I didn't get involved.'

'And he worked for you, here at the bank?' asked Eschenbach.

'Yes, he was head of the marketing department and dealt with our foreign customers. He was very popular.'

At that moment, there was a knock at the door and the slim woman who had brought in the messages and the coffee stepped into the room.

'Mr Trondtheim is here and would like to speak to you,' she said to Bettlach.

'I'd like to take a look at Philipp's work space,' said Eschenbach. 'And get to know his closest colleagues.'

'No problem. Ms Saladin will show you everything.'

The inspector slipped his Dictaphone into his jacket pocket and stood up. 'And if anything occurs to you, you can reach me here any time . . .' He gave Johannes Bettlach his card with the address and telephone number for headquarters. 'My number's on the back,' he added.

Johannes Bettlach considered the seven-digit number written in a sweeping hand on the back of the card.

'I'll escort you down, Inspector,' said the woman kindly. There was a sing-song quality to her accent.

'Are you from Basel?' he asked.

'Can you tell?'

There was no question about it.

The inspector turned again. He wanted to say goodbye to Bettlach.

Bettlach had opened the window a crack, paused for a brief moment with his left hand in his trouser pocket and his right on the handle of the window. Then he walked over to the inspector, held out his hands – first his right, then his left – and the two men took their leave of one another just as they had greeted each other not long before.

Eschenbach saw the age spots on Bettlach's hands and the melancholy in his eyes. Despite the sun, despite the warmth of his gestures and the friendliness in his voice, Eschenbach sensed a deep sadness emanating from the man.

Philipp Bettlach's office was very grand for a man who had only been vice president of the bank. It was large and bright, and did not give the impression of a place of hard work. Eschenbach was reminded of the magazine *Good Living* and he tried to work out how many times his own office could fit into the space – two or three, perhaps.

'Mr Bettlach had the furniture specially made in Italy,' said Constanze Rappold.

Eschenbach nodded.

She had introduced herself as Philipp Bettlach's *personal assistant*. She said this in English, with a German accent. She wore a neat, navy-blue outfit, like Bettlach's two other colleagues.

'Could you tell me a little about his duties?' asked the inspector. He had picked Constanze to interview first and sat with her at the oval conference table in the manager's office.

'I assume Dr Bettlach has told you that we are not allowed to divulge the names of clients.'

'I don't want names . . . I just want to know what Mr Bettlach's duties were.'

'Clients.'

'What does that mean?'

'I can't . . . I can't divulge the names of any clients.'

'Jesus Christ!' Eschenbach had to stop himself from crying out. Was she really this stupid, or was she just pretending? 'I mean, did he oversee clients, visit them, was he responsible for acquiring clients? Did he carry out stock exchange transactions for them or pick their children up from boarding school? I don't know what the job would entail . . . I'm a police officer.'

'He did all of that . . .'

'Care to be any vaguer?'

Her mouth twitched; she seemed to want to say something, then tears appeared in her eyes. She began to howl uncontrollably and hid her beautiful face in her hands.

After a while, she calmed down and Eschenbach carefully brought the conversation to an end. He didn't glean much more from the two other interviews that followed. They were all besotted with their boss. They probably would have jumped out of a window, or into the River Limmat, or off the top of the Eiffel Tower if Philipp Bettlach had asked them to. Whether it was because of his money, his laugh or his beautiful hands, they each adored him in their own way.

As far as his work was concerned – assuming that his activities could be described as such – Philipp Bettlach seemed to have had no small amount of success and had acquired all kinds of customers thanks to his charm, whether they were old money or jet-set types and nouveau riche show-offs. Philipp was everyone's favourite guy, a veritable Prince Charming, and every bank in Zurich had seemingly been more than happy to do business with him.

When Eschenbach walked back through the glass doors onto Rennweg, the heat almost knocked him off his feet. He looked at his watch. It was nearly four o'clock. He had completely lost track of time.

The sun burned his face and the tarmac beneath his feet felt like soft carpet. He thought about the ozone levels and the reports warning people against playing sports outside. For some reason unknown to him, this reminded Eschenbach of his cholesterol levels. Then he remembered Jagmetti and the dummy. He felt dizzy.

He crossed over to the shady side of the street. He marched past shops selling Swiss Army knives, digital weather stations, greetings cards, cuckoo clocks, cook's aprons, and other knick-knacks, and made for Paradeplatz.

He was sweating. It started at his temples. Then it crept over his hairline, onto his forehead, and then into his eyes. It burned. Failing to find his handkerchief, he tried to use the sleeve of his jacket to wipe it away. Wool wasn't very absorbent.

Why was he even wearing a woollen jacket and not one made of linen or cotton?

Now his forehead was itchy, as were his temples and his neck. He scratched them. His hand came away wet and his shirt looked as if it were formed of large puzzle pieces in different shades of blue.

At Paradeplatz, he got into a taxi and told the driver to head for the golf club.

Chapter 4

'This is the fifteenth hole here,' said the woman at reception, pointing a manicured finger at a mini map featuring a large number of small green spots. 'You're best off going to the back nine and then cutting across between holes twelve and thirteen.'

The inspector looked at her blankly. He took the piece of paper, which was printed with a map of the whole club site, and went outside. At that moment, he realised he had left his jacket on the back seat of the taxi, along with the Dictaphone and his notes on the interview with Johannes Bettlach. He swore quietly. He hastily checked his trouser pockets and was relieved to find that he still had his mobile phone at least.

'Mobile phones are not permitted anywhere on the premises,' hissed a middle-aged man, marching past Eschenbach briskly with his little golf cart.

'Yes, yes,' replied Eschenbach, searching through his contacts for Jagmetti's number. He took a couple of steps, then left the gravel path and strolled straight across the matting towards a huge cherry tree. In the shade, he found the number at last.

Beneath the dark-green canopy of leaves hung fat, blue-black cherries.

'Boss, where are you?'

'Under a cherry tree on the back nine.'

'On the golf course?'

'Yes.'

'I'll come and get you. Where are you, exactly?'

'I told you, I'm on the back nine!'

'Holes ten to eighteen are all called the back nine,' replied Jagmetti.

'In that case, just stop under the cherry tree . . .' Eschenbach looked around. 'By the sand traps.'

'There are sand bunkers all over the course. Is there a building nearby . . . or some kind of landmark?'

'It's about a hundred metres from the entrance. I can see the clubhouse terrace . . . just come here.'

'OK.'

The inspector saw Claudio Jagmetti from a distance and waved.

'Just drive over here,' he called and pointed directly in front of his feet. 'Those things drive on grass too.'

Jagmetti and the electric buggy left the path and jolted over the lawn towards the cherry tree, where the inspector was waiting to get in.

They drove back via the same route and Eschenbach enjoyed the breeze as it dried the hair plastered to his brow.

'So, any progress so far?' The inspector was forced to hang onto the roof of the buggy as Jagmetti left the gravel path at full speed and steered across the green. He seemed to be enjoying himself.

'We can drive straight to the fifteenth hole now. Everything's been set up.'

'Uh-huh,' mumbled Eschenbach. He ran his left hand through his hair, which was now almost dry. His other hand was still clinging to the roof.

'Did you manage to find a dummy?'

Jagmetti told him about his visit to the department store, how he had gone from pillar to post, and how, after providing a reason for his purchase and a deposit, he had finally managed to acquire a dummy from the sales director's assistant – to whom he had been nothing less than charming.

He also explained that the specimen was a female dummy, with pale, solid breasts, and that he had had to walk halfway across Zurich with the naked lady under his arm and his cheeks burning in order to reach Dr Salvisberg in time.

They jolted past a group of golfers who were prodding with their clubs at a slope covered in knee-high grass, looking for a ball that one of them had lost.

'So, is the lady with the firm breasts ready for us at the fifteenth hole?' Eschenbach has enjoyed the story, picturing Jagmetti's gangly figure hurrying along Bahnhofstrasse, packed with tourists and business people, the dummy under his arm.

'She's not naked any more,' said Jagmetti. 'Johnny, the golf pro, and I have dressed her. It's a matter of etiquette, the club says.'

Eschenbach thought he sensed a tinge of regret in Jagmetti's voice. 'So, there's even a dress code for dummies,' he said, clicking his tongue. 'They've certainly got style here.'

They drove over a small hill overgrown with shrubs and long grasses and could just make out the crime scene below.

It was hard to ignore as it materialised like dashes of colour against a green background. Like a host of ornamental fish in an aquarium, scrapping over feed among plants and pebbles covered in algae.

There were several different outfits on show: yellow and blue checked trousers, a red tank top, one light-blue and one sand-coloured polo shirt, white and brown shoes and a hat. There was also a white shirt worn with a dark-blue blazer.

But which was the dummy? Eschenbach made a show of trying to identify the different figures. The one in the dark blue and white with the stripy tie, now that one had to be Aebischer, the club manager. The red tank top with the hat had to be the golf pro.

They drew nearer. The two people in the yellow and blue checked trousers moved. Both were wearing dark-blue baseball caps.

Under one of the caps Eschenbach could see blond hair, tied back in a ponytail. The other cap was on the dummy.

They were still about ten metres away.

'Who's the blond woman?' asked Eschenbach.

'Doris Hottiger. Pretty, isn't she?'

'I can't really tell from here.'

Claudio Jagmetti blushed. He wished he could take back what he had just said. 'She works here at the club. She's Aebischer's assistant or something.'

'What do you mean by something? Is she his lover?'

'No, she's far too young. She's only twenty-ish.'

'Hmm, what does "ish" mean?' Eschenbach raised his eyebrows. Jagmetti brought the buggy to a stop. It was a quarter past five. The scorching heat had abated and a couple of clouds floated over from the Glarus Alps.

'Inspector! Where have you been?' Aebischer, a brisk man with his tie perfectly tied and the club emblem on his chest pocket, came over with his hand outstretched.

'I was held up,' replied Eschenbach sullenly.

The sun was no longer as high in the sky and from time to time Eschenbach could feel a light breeze stir the muggy air.

'That's a very capable assistant you've got there.' Aebischer pointed to Jagmetti, who was fiddling with the dummy's head.

'That's always good to hear.'

'He's had us run off our feet. Cordoning everything off. After all, we don't want anyone knowing that somebody was killed here . . .'

Too right, thought Eschenbach. He had taken a dislike to the highly bronzed manager. He was wearing a blazer and had black, bristly hair, thin lips, a trimmed moustache and air of pomposity. Eschenbach disliked him so much, in fact, that it took some effort to hide it.

'Who's that young woman over there?' Eschenbach gestured towards the girl with his chin.

'Doris Hottiger, my assistant. She's very efficient.'

'Has she been with you long?'

'Just a few weeks . . . Part time. She's studying at the university in Zurich. History . . . or German, I think. Something like that. She runs classes for our younger guests during the summer holidays.'

'I see. Does she play golf, then?'

'Yes, she's a golf instructor. She has a handicap of twelve.'

'Is that good?'

'It's very good. She takes after her father.'

'Does he play at the club too?'

'No, he doesn't play golf, as far as I know.'

Eschenbach frowned. 'So, how—'

'With her sporting spirit, I mean,' Aebischer interrupted him. 'And her ambition. She taught herself to play golf.'

'Does she have any siblings?' asked Eschenbach.

'No, just her father. Her mother died in childbirth ... it's tragic. Her father's lived alone ever since, as far as I know.'

'Did she know the victim well?'

This question made Aebischer hesitate.

'We all knew him.'

'I mean, was she close to him?'

'Am I being questioned?'

'No, I'm just interested ... do you know something?'

'Not directly.'

'What does that mean?'

'Just rumours. Nothing concrete. But why don't you ask Ms Hottiger yourself?' He pointed to the girl who was speaking to the golf pro.

They walked over to them.

Eschenbach greeted Johnny, the golf pro, and Doris Hottiger, who flashed him a sunny smile. She certainly is pretty, he thought.

'Did you know that a good golfer never turns his head when he tees off?' Claudio Jagmetti asked.

'No, of course I didn't. Why would I?'

'Don't you see, boss? That's it.'

'What? What are you doing with that?'

Jagmetti was standing behind the dummy, which was dressed in a blue baseball cap, beige polo shirt and turquoise shorts. He was trying to stop it falling over. It was slightly stooped and both its arms were pointing forward.

Johnny knelt in front of the dummy. He had removed his straw hat and was holding the dummy's arms. Doris stood nearby, directing them. She had a soft, pleasant voice. 'Yes, that's how he must have been standing if he was aiming for that hole over there.'

'And what does that mean?' asked Eschenbach.

'It means that he . . .' Jagmetti, who was still supporting the dummy with both hands, lowered his head and looked out over its cap. 'The murderer must have taken aim from up there.'

Now Eschenbach could see the forty-centimetre long pin that was sticking out of the dummy's head at a right angle above the temple, having first passed through the blue cap.

'The pin represents the angle of entry. Dr Salvisberg attached it,' said Jagmetti, pointing to the pathologist's construction.

'I see. And you're sure that this is how he was standing when the bullet struck?'

'Yes,' replied all three in unison.

'Why?'

'You explain it to him, Johnny,' said Jagmetti, who was frantically clinging on to the dummy to keep it in position.

'The thing is, Inspector . . .' The golf pro stood up; he was shorter than Jagmetti, tanned, with a snub nose. 'A golf ball is approached and struck the same way all over the world.'

'The *approach* is the position you adopt before you take a shot,' Jagmetti interjected.

'Exactly, like when hunting,' said Doris. 'I think that's called an approach too.' She realised at once how dark her comment sounded and looked down.

The golf pro proceeded with his explanation. He demonstrated the approach stance and how to take a shot. He did this with and without a golf club and the inspector quickly came to understand that there actually was such a thing as a universally correct position for standing and taking a shot. A position that varied very little among good golfers.

'Assuming the person was right-handed,' added Johnny. 'Otherwise it would be the other way around, of course.'

'Really? Was he right-handed, then?' asked the inspector, interested.

'Yes, he was. He took golf classes with me.'

'We also checked the clubs,' said Jagmetti. 'They show whether a player is right-handed or left-handed.'

'Very good,' said Eschenbach. 'Now we know how a good golfer stands, how he aims and how he strikes the ball. But none of that is any good to us. We need to know *when*. What I mean is, at what point during this sequence of movements was he hit?'

Eschenbach took a club out of the golf bag next to him and mimed a shot, the way Johnny had demonstrated. 'See, everything moves. Legs, arms, shoulders, head. Everything turns.' Eschenbach repeated the same shot again. 'We have to know – to the nearest tenth, perhaps even the nearest hundredth of a second – exactly when the bullet hit. And that's impossible.'

'Not necessarily, boss. You don't move your head, you see.'

'What? Of course you do.' Eschenbach went to take another shot.

'A good golfer never moves his head. At least, not until his club meets the ball. Johnny, show us again.'

Jagmetti set down another ball, as if he were performing an especially challenging circus act that required its own introduction. 'Even once the ball's been hit, for a fraction of a second the eyes remain fixed on the point where the ball was.'

Johnny had taken a club from the golf bag and positioned himself in front of the inspector.

'I'll show you a shot now. Any good golfer would take the shot this way if he were trying to make the fifteenth green. Watch my head. I'll repeat it a few times.'

It was just as they had said. Johnny's head remained still, hardly moving at all as he struck out in one big movement. His eyes were fixed on the point in front of his feet where the ball sat. Then his arms, hands and club swung.

'And Bettlach would have done the same thing?' The inspector still seemed uncertain.

'Exactly the same thing. He was an excellent golfer,' said Doris. Eschenbach looked at Johnny, who nodded in agreement.

'So we're on the right track then.'

'Yes, boss, you could say that . . .'

'But . . .?'

'But there's always the possibility that the bullet struck after Bettlach had moved his head.'

'That is a possibility, but it's less likely.' Eschenbach picked up the golf club from the bottom end and slowly lifted it until it was level with his shoulder. He pressed the club end to his right shoulder, as if he were holding a rifle, and aimed. The golf club had become the murder weapon.

'We've got a long distance. Four, maybe five hundred metres.' Eschenbach spoke quietly, as if he were talking to himself. 'The victim's head can't move, otherwise he'll never make the shot. The murderer has just one opportunity. The weapon has a rifle-scope. He waits. Watches. Takes his time. He knows his victim's movements just as a hunter knows a deer's. And then . . . Bang!' Eschenbach lowered the club and looked at Jagmetti, who was standing to his left with rapt attention. 'He waits. At the very last moment, he shoots. The people from forensics found the ball on the green, three metres from the flag. He must have hit it cleanly.' Eschenbach thought for a moment. 'A fraction of a second later – and he would have missed his chance.'

The three looked at the inspector, saying nothing. Nobody wanted to interrupt him.

'How tall was Bettlach?' asked Eschenbach, eyeing the dummy.

'About 5'11", I think. Wouldn't you say?' The golf pro looked at Doris for confirmation.

'Yeah, maybe. 5'11".'

Had Hottiger and Bettlach really been in the relationship, as Aebischer had implied? It wouldn't be difficult to find out, Eschenbach was sure. But it would take time.

Jagmetti and Johnny repositioned the dummy. This time they held it ten centimetres higher to take into account the height difference between the dummy and Bettlach.

When everything was in position and Johnny was satisfied, Eschenbach positioned himself to the right of the dummy and tried to gauge which direction the pin was facing.

It pointed towards the edge of a nearby wood, located on a patch of higher ground. The grass was tall, and numerous branches and saplings offered plenty of cover. It looked like the perfect place for someone to lie in wait for hours on end. Eschenbach estimated the distance to be half a kilometre or more.

Above him, on the right, half hidden by the wood, Eschenbach could see a farmhouse. Or was it an inn?

Chapter 5

Washington, DC – On 2 July at 3.33 p.m., a bullet shattered the window of a hair salon before tearing into Joan Cartridge's left forearm. At 4.02 p.m., George H. Franklin, 59, died in the car park of Howard University. On 3 July at 9.20 p.m., security agent James L. Buchanan was killed while cleaning his pool, at 12.10 p.m. . . .

Marianne Felber was thirty-two years old and originally from Germany. She had been working as a journalist at the *Zürcher Tagblatt* since the beginning of the year. She was looking at the police report on the Washington Sniper, emailed to her by a colleague at the *Washington Post.*

The sniper's criminal profile reminded her of films like *Seven.* In the film, the perpetrator had wanted to exert control over the police. The desire for power was also evident in the case of the Washington Sniper. The press had not long started calling him the 'OAP Killer' when he started targeting young people instead. He didn't want to be restricted to a certain pattern.

She knew of a colleague who had done research on the sniper case for *FOLIOS*, the weekly magazine. Marianne flicked through her diary and lit a cigarette. It was the tenth one she had had that Friday. The tenth from her second pack. She had wanted to stop smoking the day before, but that was before the press conference.

She left a message on the answering machine at *FOLIOS*, explaining why she was calling, and left her number.

She had never researched a murder case before. She had done a bit of lifestyle and fashion, six months at a foreign tabloid and two reports for a travel magazine. This was followed by an abandoned economics course, an abandoned relationship and a broken heart.

She wouldn't have got the murder case under normal circumstances, this she knew. But Randegger was on holiday and Oswald was in hospital with kidney stones. There was nothing they could do about it. Thank God, she thought.

Everyone gets their chance at some point, she told herself, when the Hamburg thing fell through and Ralph moved in with Andrea. Andrea! She had been the one who introduced them at the farewell party, before she moved to Hamburg. They could at least have waited until Christmas. It was a question of class, she felt. And that was something both of them were lacking. Ralph had no style, Andrea even less.

Marianne's article for tomorrow's paper was in the bag. Front page, domestic news. Bruhwyler had cut it a little, but no one could take the rest away from her. Ralph could go to hell.

She called *FOLIOS* again. This time she got through. Half an hour later, she left the editorial department and headed towards Limmatquai.

'So you were at the press conference today too?'

'Yes.' Marianne Felber tried to appear cool in spite of the heat and fingered the cellophane on her packet of cigarettes nervously.

She was at Avalon on the banks of the Limmat, sitting under a cheap parasol, waiting for a Prosecco and a water. Across from her lay the Ladies' Pool. Row upon row of half-naked bodies lay next to one another under the blazing sun, tightly packed like roast chickens on faded wooden boards. It was baking, and Marianne was wishing she could have a shower. She would have preferred to have this conversation over dinner, but Hannes had to leave at seven.

Hannes was the acting editor-in-chief of *FOLIOS* and was keen to meet her. He had something about the Washington Sniper case in the drawer, he said, and the murder on the golf course would make it highly topical again. This story was hot.

As a weekly paper, he said, *FOLIOS* was able to cooperate with the dailies, but it might not necessarily fit. He was more interested in the background to the story.

Marianne was pleased. Her experience was different. At home in Germany, her colleagues would have been less open or keen to help. Journalism was a real shark tank; everyone was always tearing into the same piece of meat. She thought about Andrea, about Ralph, how she would rather be writing for a weekly paper. Day-to-day journalism just didn't excite her.

She lit a cigarette as the waiter brought her Prosecco and Hannes's bottle of Evian and a glass.

'These sniper guys are total nutjobs.' Hannes took a hearty sip of water. 'I managed to speak to one of them. We met in this remote valley in the Grisons.'

'And?' Marianne sipped her wine and tried not to appear overly curious.

'They all give themselves pseudonyms. The guy I met called himself Snoopy – you know, the dog from *Peanuts*. He's thirty-two, lives in the Canton of Grisons and is a civil servant and sergeant in the Swiss Army. He does his mandatory training at the shooting range every year and he always gets the certificate – with a maximum of one, or very rarely two, points lost.'

'What kind of guns do they use?'

'They use standard-issue Swiss Army assault rifles,' said Hannes. He wasn't sure whether Marianne would know what he was talking about, as she was German. In Switzerland, almost everyone had a gun at home.

Marianne didn't know. Ralph was American, so he hadn't been liable for compulsory military service in Switzerland.

'Other than that, he's got a Blaser R93 Tactical, .308 calibre.'

'I see,' said Marianne. None of it meant anything to her. 'Why Snoopy?'

'They're afraid to disclose their true identities. In Germany, shooting with a riflescope is common practice, but in Switzerland it's frowned upon.'

'Why? Why here, where everyone has a gun at home?'

'I don't know. In Switzerland we've got people using combat rifles, air rifles, crossbows and muzzle-loaders that use gunpowder. But no other group has been ostracized and viewed with as much suspicion as snipers have.'

'And what kind of distance can one of these Blaser things shoot from, with a riflescope?'

'Well . . .' Hannes looked around, then pointed towards the Ladies' Pool. 'Point it at a gnat buzzing over there and you'd hit it right in the arsehole.'

Marianne swallowed, then coughed. 'Come on, don't talk crap.'

Hannes laughed, took off his sunglasses and wiped the perspiration from his brow with an old handkerchief.

She saw his eyes for the first time. Two thin slits, behind which sat two reptilian pupils, jammed between fleshy lids and tear ducts.

'Distance doesn't matter much on itself.' It had become clear to Hannes that Marianne knew nothing about firearms. 'What's important is distance combined with precision. Long-range rifles can hit their target from up to a thousand metres away. It's quite normal to aim for targets eight hundred metres away – vinyl discs that fall over when hit, for example. A real feat is hitting a five-franc piece from three hundred metres away.'

'So that's . . .' Marianne made a circle with her forefinger and thumb, about the size of a five-franc piece. 'Wow, so you weren't far off with the gnat after all.'

'Yep. And that's from three hundred metres away.' Hannes pointed to the swimming baths. 'It's not even a hundred metres to the pool from here.'

Marianne tightened her finger and thumb into a smaller circle. 'That's a half franc piece! That's incredible.'

'Perhaps. I can't be sure. Either way, they're extremely accurate.'

'The sniper in Washington, I read he shot from a distance of eighty metres,' said Marianne, who was having trouble with all the talk of distances and coins.

'Yep. That was child's play compared to what these guys can do,' replied Hannes. He called the waiter over and ordered the same again, then went on: 'Every shot is entered into a logbook. There are tables detailing the accuracy of each shot. Humidity, altitude, wind speed. It all plays a part.'

'It's crazy.'

'These guys are at the top of their game, physically. The wind can disrupt the trajectory of a shot, ammunition explodes differently depending on the temperature, and the type of ammunition is crucial. A Swiss-made cartridge costs between 2.5 and 11 Swiss francs, if it is manufactured by hand or at least quality-controlled by hand. For comparison, a standard shot for an assault rifle goes for 45 rappen.'

A glass-bottom boat laden with tourists floated past them almost silently, travelling upstream towards the lake.

'The average annual consumption of ammo is about a thousand shots.'

'But that's over ten thousand francs!' This was enough for a two month holiday for Marianne.

'And the guns cost almost as much again.'

Another two months' holiday, thought Marianne.

The terrace was filling up. There were people from the media or bank employees who had come straight from work; they had something to drink and then left. Marianne loved it here. If she sat for long enough, she would start to feel as if she was moving instead of the water. She enjoyed seeing people coming and going, letting her mind run wild. She observed Hannes, the way he spoke, and made a few notes.

He had a soft voice. She had imagined him differently when they spoke on the phone. Now that she saw him, the way he sat, his black T-shirt with sweat stains under the armpits, his pale neck, the extra five kilos he carried on his hips and on his chin, she was actually glad that he wasn't free tonight. She would call Jürgen. Jürgen was always free.

Chapter 6

It was almost 6.30 p.m. and the people from forensics had yet to arrive. Eschenbach had arranged for them to be there at 6 p.m.

Jean-Baptiste von Matt, head of the forensics unit for over twenty years, was a man of sterling quality. He was prim and as picky as the manager of a five star hotel. If von Matt was late, there must be a reason. But where was he, and where was Aebischer?

Eschenbach sensed that something wasn't right. He felt for his phone, checking his left trouser pocket, then his right. Then he went to the electric buggy and was relieved to see it sitting in the drinks holder.

Before he could decide whether to ring the club secretary first, or ring von Matt, he heard voices. Jagmetti, the girl and the golf pro stopped talking; they had heard them too.

It was Aebischer's staccato, followed by a broad, Bernese legato. The familiar voice of von Matt. Then silence.

They could now see the electric buggy, hitherto hidden by the nearby hills, coming towards them.

Aebischer was driving and von Matt was sitting next to him quietly. They approached the crime scene accompanied by the sound of whirring and jolting, which reminded Eschenbach of the old sewing machine he used to enjoy playing with as a boy.

Eschenbach waited for Aebischer to park up next to him. With great force, the club manager hit the break, which snapped into place and stopped the buggy with a rattling noise.

'This man,' cried Aebischer before he had even alighted, pointing his thumb at von Matt, 'wants to bring his *dog* along.'

He stressed the word 'dog', as if it were the most awful, repugnant and vile thing he could possibly imagine.

'So?' Eschenbach, knowing what von Matt was up to, raised his eyebrows in amusement.

'Dogs are not allowed!' exploded Aebischer.

'Even police dogs?'

'All dogs are prohibited.'

The club manager had no time for niceties and – as Eschenbach well knew – no sense of humour either.

The inspector would have liked to play along a little longer, but time was short. There were three hours at the most until nightfall, tops. That was assuming it didn't start raining. Eschenbach eyed the clouds anxiously; a wall of dark grey was forming in the north-east. They had to make progress.

Was the hill on his left, near the edge of the forest, hiding something? Might there be a patch of trampled grass, a snapped branch, or a discarded match that could provide some clue about the sniper? Was the hill even the right place to be looking?

Surely they would find something; Jean-Baptiste von Matt always found something, if you left him to it. And it was up to Eschenbach to make sure that happened.

The inspector didn't like to use coercion. So he wasn't proud of what he did next. He had an ambivalent relationship with authority and hierachy. He had a brief word with Aebischer.

Though he spoke quietly, almost in a whisper, he assumed the tone of an officer giving orders to a subordinate. He was an auditor instructing an accountant. And once Eschenbach had finished his short talk with the club manager at the fifteenth hole, everything changed.

Not only did Aebischer stop hindering the investigation, he helped wherever he was instructed to and wherever he could.

While von Matt searched the area around the hill with his team, taking in each blade of grass, each shrub, Aebischer brought out sandwiches from the clubhouse. He set up a trestle table, which he carefully laid with a white tablecloth. He set out beer, wine, apple juice, mineral water and iced tea, with help from his pretty assistant.

Even Tadaeus, von Matt's Bernese mountain dog, was treated to a bowl of chopped-up sausage in the shade of a tree. And he remembered a bowl of water too.

Von Matt's men made records of wheel tracks and footprints. They photographed and made notes on their finds on a laptop which they carried in a black leather case.

At certain points, they took samples of the lawn, which they would later view under a microscope, looking for individual fibres.

Eschenbach climbed the hill, keeping his distance from forensics. He would only get in the way, stepping on something clumsily or causing a hindrance in some other way.

Not far from the place where von Matt and his team were at work, he found a hiking trail partially overgrown with grass. Eschenbach followed it for three hundred metres or so and came to the farmhouse that he had noticed before.

He had been right. The farmstead, which comprised a main building and an annexe, was actually an inn.

The front of the main building was covered in wooden tiles all the way down to the ground. The original light brown of the wood had been darkened by the sun's rays, until it was almost black. There was a sign bearing words in a yellowing, brown script: 'This way to the Golden Egg'.

There was a large clearing in front of the annexe, where once hay had been unloaded or wheat threshed. It was now a car park. There were at least a dozen cars and a few motorbikes.

Eschenbach took the steps up to the entrance to the restaurant and went inside.

Inside, he found a hive of activity. Clouds of smoke hung beneath the low wooden ceiling; four regulars sat at a table playing cards. Most of the tables were occupied by people eating. Behind the counter stood a woman with imposing upper arms, pulling a beer. She had short, greasy blond hair.

Unlike the card players, who had taken no interest in Eschenbach, the woman noticed him at once. Her small, bright eyes seemed to survey the whole room. She eyed Eschenbach from head to toe, then turned around and pulled another beer. She didn't greet him. Not a nod, not a smile, nothing.

Eschenbach walked through the packed restaurant, past tables and benches, towards the woman.

'Evening, my name's Eschenbach . . .'

'To your good health, Inspector,' she replied, placing a glass of beer in front of him and walked off carrying a tray of several more.

'I'll be right back,' she shouted, without turning her head.

Eschenbach took a sip, then another, and then another. It occurred to him that he hadn't had anything to drink since midday. He set the empty glass down on the counter.

The woman with the greasy hair came back. Her tray was full, this time with empty glasses and plates. She set it down on the shelf to the left of the kitchen hatch.

There was a plate of *bratwurst* with *rösti* waiting to be taken out. The till receipt lay on the side, bearing grease stains; the sausage was dark, a little overcooked. Dirty dishes sat alongside untouched meals, glasses of beer next to empties.

The woman swore. She called through the hatch to the kitchen. Then she wiped her hands on her greasy apron.

'These foreigners, they just don't work quickly enough,' she said to Eschenbach, gesturing to the hatch with her head. Eschenbach cleared his throat. How should he respond? Despite his years working in the police, this sort of everyday racism still disgusted him. 'Why don't you employ Swiss staff, then?'

'They don't wash dishes,' was her prompt reply. 'At least not for the kind of wages I can afford to pay.'

'There you go, then. Poor work for poor pay.'

'I don't pay poorly.'

'I don't care, I'm not from the Labour Office. I'm here about another matter.'

'About the golfer who was shot.'

'Yes.' Eschenbach wasn't surprised, he knew how quickly news of this kind spread. He looked at the *bratwurst*, still waiting to be taken to its table.

'Could you spare half an hour tomorrow morning? I can see you've got a lot on at the moment.'

'Tomorrow's Saturday . . .'

'I just thought it would be easier than coming all the way to headquarters in Zurich. Say, nine – would that work?'

'All right.'

'See you tomorrow, then. And thanks for the beer.'

It was almost dark when Eschenbach left the smoky restaurant and stepped out into the evening air. There was a stiff wind. In the car park, two customers were fiddling with the roof of their sports car. There was no one to be seen on the hill.

Eschenbach followed the track back towards the golf course.

If it was true that the shooter had lain in wait here, he had to be on his guard. It's a hell of a long way to shoot, he thought, looking out at his people, down towards the fifteenth fairway.

He had thought the three hundred metres required by the military's mandatory programme was a long way. This must have been six hundred metres or more. It would have been an excellent shot.

As Eschenbach traipsed back down the slope through the knee-high grass, he noticed Aebischer trying to fold the white tablecloth. The cloth was being buffeted about by the wind and made it look as though the club manager was waving an enormous white flag.

Eschenbach smiled. He appreciated the symbolism.

It occurred to him that at the firing range a white flag was a sign that a shot had not hit its target. He had to laugh.

By the time he made it back to the crime scene, everything had been tidied away. Aebischer was sitting in the electric buggy and waved him over.

'Come on, Inspector, we have to get back. There's a storm coming.'

Eschenbach got into the buggy and sat down on the black leather seat next to a cheery Aebischer. The buggy set off with a jolt.

'Those are some hard-working people you've got,' said the club manager as he steered the vehicle between bushes and shrubs in the half-light.

'You think so?'

'Oh yes. They even had a computer with them.'

'And a police dog.' Eschenbach couldn't resist.

'Yes, Tadaeus found the site instantly.'

'Really?'

'Von Matt said he was in Avalanche Rescue.'

'Who, von Matt?'

'No. The dog, of course.'

'Of course. Silly me.' He tried to excuse his absent-mindedness with a smile. 'Von Matt is a terrible skier.'

'Well, it would surprise me if the dog was a good one,' replied Aebischer drily.

Eschenbach smirked, whilst trying to choke back a fit of laughter. He imagined von Matt's mountain dog in flamboyant yellow ski boots, gliding over the slopes with an avalanche transceiver device and a cask of rum around his neck.

Eschenbach's body juddered as he tried to bring the laughing fit under control.

Then he remembered the ski course that he'd attended in the Flumser Mountains, not long after his divorce from Milena. He remembered the ski instructor in his red ski jacket with the logo of the local ski school, the young lady in her tight, peach-coloured outfit and the elderly lawyer from Travemünde who refused to let even the most horrendous crashes put him off; in his mind, they were all transformed into Bernese mountain dogs.

Even Elsbeth, the art student from Berne with whom he had had a short but intense relationship during his skiing holiday was suddenly a dog with a wet nose and fluffy black-blond ears.

Eschenbach wiped the tears from his eyes with the back of his hand and managed to compose himself as the brightly lit clubhouse came into view.

'I thought you had no sense of humour, Aebischer.'

'And I thought you were one of those civil servant arseholes.'

'Well, appearances can be deceiving.'

'Apparently so.' Aebischer parked the golf buggy behind the club building. 'Now for something to eat,' he said, jumping out of the vehicle.

This was fine by Eschenbach. He looked at his watch. It was a quarter past ten. He had had nothing to eat all day and very little to drink. As he thought about food, he suddenly felt an aching heaviness in his legs.

Eschenbach piled his plate high with a second serving of roast veal.

They were sitting at a large round table. There was von Matt and his two accompanying officers – one of whom Eschenbach already knew – as well as Johnny, Doris, Jagmetti and Aebischer.

Von Matt gave a brief summary of the afternoon. He avoided making any rash statements or revealing any clues. Despite this, he spoke in such a fascinating way that Doris, Johnny and Aebischer were hanging on his every word. He made references to famous cases in criminology and was glad to have such an attentive audience.

'So, do you really think there's no such thing as the perfect murder?' This question came from Doris.

'No. There are unexplained murders. But no perfect murders.'

'But if a murder is never explained, if the killer's never caught, then surely it is a perfect murder?' Johnny suggested.

'Not necessarily. The killer could have made a mistake that hasn't been discovered – at least, not yet,' countered von Matt, stuffing his pipe.

'But surely that's impossible,' said Aebischer. 'How can you know that a mistake has been made in an unexplained murder? You have to find the mistake to prove that it exists at all.'

'So you're saying that when the mistake is found, the case can be solved,' mumbled Eschenbach with his mouth full.

'Exactly, Aebischer beamed and Eschenbach took a third helping of mashed potato and veal.

'Not quite. Even if a mistake is found, the killer might never be sentenced.' Von Matt was not giving up.

'Oh right, does that happen?' asked Aebischer, trying to square this with his own notions of law and order.

'It happens more often than you think,' replied Jagmetti, raising his eyebrows suggestively.

'Oh yeah, and the murderer is always the gardener,' said Eschenbach, putting his cutlery to one side at last and wiping his mouth with his napkin. He flashed a smile at the others around the table. 'Anyone for dessert?'

Everyone laughed.

'Then Gregor must be the murderer,' said Johnny.

'Why Gregor?' asked one of the police officers and Doris Hottiger in unison.

'He's the gardener ... or, to be more precise, he's our green-keeper,' said Aebischer, who was the only one who had understood the joke.

They all laughed again; Johnny guffawed and slapped his thighs, and made sure to repeat the joke another three times within the hour.

In spite of the cheery mood that gradually took hold, despite the mashed potato and roast veal, the crème caramel, the glasses of Barbaresco and three rounds of grappa, Eschenbach couldn't quite bring himself to relax.

He had a murder case to solve and no leads to speak of. Checking the members list given to him by Aebischer would descend into a sheer mindless slog, he knew. But perhaps it would dredge something up. There might be some office drama or something similarly awkward that could give them a clue as to the motive.

When he had had a chance to speak to von Matt in the Gents, he had sounded confident. But that was just his way. He was a professional optimist.

What would the tyre prints and the other clues throw up? Could it be a woodsman? Or perhaps some campers, a couple or – as Johnny had said – the gardener? They had taken a wrong turning a hundred times before. And waiting tormented him all the more as he got older.

'A detective has less luck than a eunuch that guards a harem' was one of von Matt's favourite sayings. The eunuch can't join in, but at least he's around for the action. As for us, he'd say, we only get there once the fun's over.

Eschenbach had never found it funny, but that didn't mean it wasn't true. He felt alone, despite the party going on around him.

He thought about Corina, about visiting her and Kathrin in the Engadine over the weekend. What were they doing right now? It was half eleven. Were they already asleep? He thought about his notes from his conversation with Dr Bettlach, left in his jacket in the taxi. He hoped he would get them back. He had no murder weapon, no motive, and no suspects.

Everything was spinning. He knew he shouldn't have drunk that schnapps. Now it was too late. He had another and washed it down with a beer.

Chapter 7

Linus Breitenmoser was a headhunter, specialising in executive recruitment. He worked on behalf of corporations, scouting for people for management positions. The annual salaries he dealt with would be upwards of 250,000 Swiss francs: he had no time for small fry. He poached employees from other companies. If a certain individual agreed to move from company A to company B, he would receive the equivalent of 30 to 35 per cent of their annual salary. Plus expenses, of course.

Marianne Felber had known Linus from his time as head of business at the second largest bank in the country. Eight years had passed since their brief relationship had ended.

When she arrived at the lounge of Hotel Storchen, Linus was already sitting at a small table, reading the paper. His hair was light brown, turning white towards the temples, and he wore gold-rimmed glasses and a dark, pinstriped suit. He was in his mid-fifties.

'Thanks for taking the time to meet me,' she said, kissing him lightly on the cheek and plonking herself in the chair opposite.

'I thought you'd fallen off the face of the earth.' He looked at her and smiled. Then they spoke about the past as well as what they were doing now.

'I read your article – it sounds exciting.'

'Murderously exciting.' She pulled a face. 'I was given the story completely by chance . . . luck probably had something to do with it too.'

He nodded.

'Did you get the CV?' she asked, lighting a cigarette hurriedly.

'Yes, it's here.' He waved the piece of paper in front of her. 'I've just taken another look at it. It's interesting. He placed the document on the table, next to his glass of white wine. 'Is Chardonnay OK?'

'Yeah, great.'

He waved the waitress over.

'So, when you say interesting, what do you mean?' She was playing with a small, orange plastic cigarette lighter, looking at him expectantly.

'Philipp Bettlach was an interesting guy.'

'Did you have anything to do with him?'

'Yeah, a couple of years ago. He asked me to get someone for him. A supervisor for a high-end private customer.'

'Really? Go on.'

'We met for lunch at the Kronenhalle. He wanted to know how I worked – my contacts and my methods for approaching candidates and selecting them. Bettlach didn't say much about himself, but he listened intently and asked the right questions.'

'So, a likeable guy, then . . .' Marianne pulled a few folded sheets of A4 out of her folder and laid them out in front of her: 'Matura Type A with distinction. Graduated with distinction in economics from Stanford University, MBA at INSEAD in Fontainebleau . . . sorry, but he sounds like an arrogant arsehole.'

'Is that how you view education?'

'Not necessarily. But if you're about to tell me that he was well-dressed and could play the recorder, I might have to laugh.'

'You would have liked him,' countered Linus.

'That's where you're wrong.' Marianne stopped. 'There's not a single black mark anywhere on these three pages.' She slapped her hand down on the paper. 'No failures, no slip-ups. It's just not normal.'

'Of course, there are always exceptions.'

'But not at fifty-six years of age. There must be something missing.' She stubbed out her cigarette in the ashtray with some force.

'It's probably jealousy.'

'I'm not jealous, just sceptical.'

'The motive for the murder, I mean. It could be jealousy, couldn't it?'

'Perhaps.' Marianne thought for a moment. Then she shook her head. 'But I don't think so.'

'Either way, I managed to seal a deal with him,' Linus explained, with no small measure of pride. 'I presented him with five candidates, all with several languages under their belts and the best references. He invited each of them for several hours of interviews and then chose the best.'

'The most expensive, I assume?'

'Either way, he really knew how to deal with people; he had an incredible eye for talent. He was open, intelligent . . .' Linus searched for the right adjective. 'Two weeks later, I had my fee.'

The young waitress brought a second glass of Chardonnay to the table.

He raised his glass to Marianne.

She took a sip and set the glass down on the table. 'Be serious for a moment, Linus. Imagine this wasn't a client's CV, imagine it was a candidate's CV. Wouldn't it make you think twice?'

Linus held his wine glass up to the light. 'Too clean, I'd say.'

'The wine or Bettlach?' asked Marianne impatiently.

'Both.' He laughed. 'But when someone has something to hide, it's not likely to be on their CV.'

'Then where?' asked Marianne.

'Hidden. Between the lines . . . or at home in the cellar. I don't know.'

'Where would you look?'

'His private life, perhaps. There's not much here.'

'Divorced, no kids, golf.' Marianne read aloud from her notes. 'Yep.'

'You mean, maybe he wasn't such a fluffy bunny after all?'

'I didn't say that . . . I just think, when a person lays out all their skills like this, their top qualifications, they might be leaving something out.'

'Is that just prejudice speaking, or what?'

'Let's call it a working hypothesis.'

'You know something. Come on, out with it . . . the guy's dead.'

'That banker that I found for Bettlach . . .' Linus hesitated.

'Yes?' Marianne took another cigarette out of the pack. 'What about him? Don't make me wheedle it out of you.'

'Six months later, he had left again.'

'You mean he was sacked?'

'No. He went of his own accord.'

'Do you know why?'

'The chemistry wasn't right, he said. He didn't want to elaborate.'

'Where is he now?'

'Back at Credit Suisse.'

'Can you give me his name . . . can I call him?'

Linus shook his head.

Marianne would not give up that easily. They sat talking about it for another forty-five minutes, enjoying a second, and then a third glass of wine. And then she finally got what she wanted.

The editorial office at the *Zürcher Tagblatt* was understaffed. The world seemed to know it, too, because there was nothing spectacular to report that day. Old stories were brought out of drawers and people went to press conferences which they would otherwise have ignored.

The Bettlach murder case was an exception, and since Marianne's article had appeared her colleagues had come to know her and greet her around the office.

Dario Hollenweger from sports editorial stuck his head over her shoulder inquisitively. 'Any news?' he asked.

'Maybe.' She smiled knowingly.

When Dario realised that he wasn't going to get anything out of Marianne, he took to grumbling about Zurich FC's shocking performance in a recent game against their city rivals, the Grasshoppers.

'The last home victory was in August 1984,' he said mournfully.

'If two Zurich clubs play each other in their home city, then there's bound to be a home victory,' Marianne pointed out. 'Unless it's a tie.'

'I only know about Hamburger SV,' she said. 'I used to go to see them with my dad when I was ten or eleven.'

Dario dismissed the idea and said he had something else to do.

Marianne dialled the number for Credit Suisse in Zurich. After being transferred twice, she was put through to Konrad Affolter, head of the foreign client desk on Paradeplatz.

'Hi, I found your name through Linus Breitenmoser,' she said before getting straight to the issue at hand.

'I don't want to talk about it,' said the banker.

Marianne sensed the unease in his voice. 'I assure you that we treat our sources with utmost confidentiality.'

'It was a mutual decision, that's all I can say.'

'After just six months?' asked Marianne, digging deeper.

'I really can't say anything more on the matter.'

'Linus thinks that the chemistry wasn't right between the two of you. Was that it?'

'Yes, you could say that.'

'Have the police already been to see you?' Marianne asked.

'Why? I mean, why should they?' The banker sounded on edge.

'I mean, assuming the two of you had a disagreement . . . I don't know. Either way, this all sounds very confusing. Some might get the impression that you wanted revenge.'

'But I didn't . . .' Affolter breathed in. 'I was the one who terminated the contract.'

'Then you must have had a good reason for doing so. Philipp Bettlach was an extremely honourable, conscientious man.'

'Maybe from the outside. I don't know how well you knew him.'

'I didn't know him,' replied Marianne. 'But I've only heard good things.'

'Well, I don't mean to say that he was a bad person.'

'No?'

'No, just ... difficult.' Affolter cleared his throat. 'In some ways, he was very accommodating and charismatic, exactly how he came across in public. But in others, he could be very hurtful, even malicious. Believe me, Philipp Bettlach was not the person that everyone thinks he was.'

'Could you be more specific?'

'I really can't say any more. After I terminated my contract with Zurich Commercial Bank, I signed a confidentiality agreement.'

'Did they offer you money?'

'Like I said, I can't help you. I'm sorry.'

'Did you speak to his brother, Johannes Bettlach, about it? After all, the bank is—'

Konrad Affolter had hung up.

Chapter 8

'Here, the Viamala starts,' announced the woman sitting across from Eschenbach in the dining car of the Rhaetian Railway train. She was well groomed and wore a blouse which was pulled much too tightly over her large bosom. 'It's also known as the Bad Path.'

The train was standing at the platform in Thusis and was about to set off. It would take him through Tiefencastel, Filisur, Bergün, Preda, Samedan and Celerina into the Upper Engadine, and was scheduled to arrive in St Moritz Bad at 1.55 p.m.

Eschenbach looked out of the window. He had heard of the story of the Viamala before. What Swiss child hadn't? The old road between Thusis and Zillis, flanked by steep rocks, which led over the Splügen Pass into Italian Chiavenna.

He had told his daughter countless stories about it when she was little, most of them made up. Stories of highwaymen and rich merchants. Stories of shady characters who smuggled goods on mules from Italy to Switzerland at twilight.

At some point Kathrin had stopped being interested in stories, and sometime later her sole interest became boys.

Eschenbach had also lost interest in his neighbour's stories, though this didn't seem to bother her. She had been a middle school teacher in Graubünden for over thirty years and was immune to uninterested and bored listeners.

'. . . and just over there, about five kilometres south of here is one of Switzerland's most impressive ravines. Walls of rock three hundred metres high form an enormous gorge,' she continued cheerfully. Her bosom shook and her dark eyes, magnified by her thick, horn-rimmed glasses, gleamed like ripe cherries.

Eschenbach had got up early that morning. He loved the early hours of Saturday morning, when Zurich was still quiet.

He walked along Storchengasse to Münsterplatz, turned into Bahnhofstrasse and headed down towards the lake.

The much-needed storm that had been due the night before had failed to materialise. The sky was clear and cloudless once again. He could make out two motorboats coming into port. Were they early risers or night owls on their way home? He guessed the latter.

The seagulls were screeching and performing their morning flight training. Soon the motorboats and steamers would be there, docking or taking off. They would load their cargoes of people into their fat bellies and onto their sweeping decks. The seagulls would accompany the ships as far as Rapperswil and back to Bürkliplatz. Some would hurry ahead, others flying behind. Harbingers and stragglers. With daring manoeuvres, they would catch breadcrumbs thrown into the air and screech.

Eschenbach took a drag on his Brissago and slowly made his way home. Sometimes he stayed there, watching the greengrocers setting up their stalls or offering a friendly greeting to anyone who seemed to know him. From time to time he would hear the screech of a half-empty tram. It was a different sound to the seagulls' hoarse cries.

After packing a few things in his travel bag at home, he had driven to the Golden Egg.

Greasy Locks had washed her hair and breakfast was served. There was bacon *rösti* and fried eggs, fresh bread, huge portions of cold cuts, dried meats and salami. There was also hot coffee, fresh milk and butter from a farm nearby.

Greasy Locks's real name was Hildy Gaffner. She had been running the business by herself since her husband had run off with a Russian waitress two years ago.

Her main customers were regulars. Forestry workers, motorcyclists, bikers, people from the land surveying office, farmers from the area and pensioners with their dogs, she told Eschenbach. A large number of them were retired people, killing time with a game of cards and a glass of wine. Simple people. They were just happy to be out of the house and enjoying a good meal at a reasonable price.

From time to time, she also had customers from the army. She needed them, she said. You had to be tolerant of people. Except foreigners, of course – especially Russians.

When Eschenbach asked if Philipp Bettlach had ever been to her restaurant, she said no. The golf club was a different world, she said. But she had noticed a beige car in the car park. A VW or an Opel. She couldn't be sure. She had noticed it because it had the typical black army number plate, but there had been no army chaps at the restaurant at the time.

The lads from the army always checked in with her, officers included. Even if they were just popping in for a beer, a coffee or an Ovaltine. You had to be tolerant, she said again, otherwise there'd be no one to look out for them when the Russians came.

'The car was there, Inspector,' she had said. 'I'm absolutely sure of it. It was there on Thursday . . . and yesterday too, when I took the scraps out to the pigs.'

Eschenbach felt uneasy when he remembered them all standing in plain view on the golf course. Like antelopes grazing just feet away from a watchful lion.

She couldn't remember anything about the military symbol. Eschenbach would have been surprised if she had, but it pointed to a theory that the inspector had already considered.

Anyone who could shoot someone in the head from over six hundred metres away must be a damned good shot. There were maybe only two dozen people in the country who could pull off such a shot and they were bound to be involved with the police or the army.

After a generous breakfast more fitting for a hungry lumberjack, and some homemade kirsch – the landlady's main source of sustenance – Eschenbach left the Golden Egg.

He had eaten too much and his stomach burned all the way up his gorge. He felt exhausted again. He still had Salvisberg's report in his pocket and wanted to read it, so he decided to leave the car and take the train to Engadine.

He had been looking forward to reading the paper in peace and spending some time with his thoughts. It was just a stroke of bad luck that an old, chubby woman with a huge bosom and remarkably thick glasses had arrived in his compartment just after the train reached Chur and, later, sat down at his table in the dining car.

'. . . and I went down for the first time when I was training to be a teacher in 1974. Into the Viamala Gorge. It was over three hundred steps, imagine that. It wasn't as safe back then. And I did it all with thirty-two ten-year-old children in tow . . . it'd be unthinkable today.'

Eschenbach lit a new Brissago and looked out of the window. The greenery was sparser here than in the valley. Nature had adapted to ensure that the summers were shorter, and the winters longer.

He yawned, but it didn't help.

He was treated to descriptions of the bridges in the eighteenth, nineteenth and twentieth centuries. This was followed by the usual stories about robbers, and after they passed Tiefencastel his neighbour slipped seamlessly into recounting the history of Graubünden.

Eschenbach ordered another bottle of red Veltliner, which led inevitably to a lecture about the Veltliner Massacre of 1620, a brief illumination in the dusty chapter of Graubünden's reign of terror.

The inspector topped up his glass, not forgetting his neighbour's, and was rewarded with an extensive and spirited discourse on the Thirty Years War.

Next to Eschenbach lay Salvisberg's report and the *Zürcher Tagblatt*. 'TEE TIME EXECUTION!' by Marianne Felber stood out on the front page, and the twelve-page report from the Institute of Forensics detailed the medical facts of the case.

Neither told him anything that he didn't already know or think he knew. The projectile, a .308 calibre, had been found by von Matt's people on the day of the shooting. It was a common calibre for long-distance rifles.

No matter how hard he tried to make sense of it, Salvisberg's findings on the body, including stomach contents, blood type and similar, gave him nothing to work with.

He kept coming back to one word: *execution*. It suggested a motive: revenge, retribution. But revenge for what?

The most common motives for murder were jealousy and greed. The order of priority varied according to country and the period of history. Money or love: whichever mattered more to the killer.

Greed seemed an unlikely motive to Eschenbach. Philipp Bettlach hadn't been robbed. His ex-wife was, as Dr Bettlach had said, financially independent and hadn't been in his life for a long time. And his older brother was one of the richest men in Switzerland. He had had no children.

'It's terrible, isn't it?' said the woman, interrupting his thoughts. She was midway through recounting a romantic adventure undertaken by two of her students, whom she had caught together in a hayloft at the ski camp she had supervised twenty-two years before.

She pointed to the article with a pudgy hand. 'What sort of madman could do such a thing?'

'What do you mean?' asked Eschenbach. 'Imagine it was your husband you'd caught gallivanting in the hayloft.'

'I would have killed him!'

'Well, there you go.'

'My poor Duri, God bless him. I would have killed them both. On the spot.' She slapped her hand down on the table and it rattled. She meant business.

Two concerned American tourists at the next table turned around and the old man behind them adjusted his hearing aid angrily. The dining car was silent for a moment.

Eschenbach laughed quietly.

A little embarrassed at first, then pleased with her hidden strength, the woman leant over the table slowly. 'Do you think it was his wife?' she asked almost in a whisper, her face deadly serious. Her eyes seemed blurred through her glasses.

Eschenbach, who was now familiar with her love of drama, pressed his lips together and took a deep breath through his nose. He raised his shoulders, then shook his head briefly before collapsing back into his seat and breathing out deeply. 'I don't think so.'

'That's a shame.' She sighed and said nothing.

Eschenbach's mobile phone beeped, forcing the woman to keep quiet.

He glanced at the number and could see it was Jagmetti calling.

'Jagmetti, what's is it?'

'Er, it's me boss,' said Jagmetti, surprised Eschenbach had used his name.

'I know, so what's the latest?'

'Hottiger and Bettlach had a relationship.'

'Of course they did.'

'What? Did you already know?'

'No, not exactly. I had a feeling. Aebischer mentioned something. Pure conjecture, of course. But there was something in the air. Did she tell you?'

'Yes.'

This was a surprisingly brief answer from a usually talkative Jagmetti. Eschenbach had a bad feeling about it.

'When exactly did she tell you this?'

'Last night. We went to Kaufleuten after we dropped you off.

Kaufleuten was a club. Eschenbach had heard of it from Kathrin. You went there to have fun, not conduct interviews. He didn't like the sound of Jagmetti's story at all.

'And that's where she told you?' he persisted.

'Yeah, er . . . no, later on.'

'When later on? Come on, Jagmetti, don't dick around.'

'I think I already have, boss.'

'Ms Hottiger is a suspect, Jagmetti. Are you mad?'

The two Americans turned to look. Eschenbach realised that he was shouting and had banged his fist on the table.

'Are you still there, boss?' said Jagmetti, hesitantly.

'Yes.' Eschenbach was counting to ten silently.

'Am I suspended?'

'No.'

'Did you really mean that?' he replied.

'What?'

'I mean, is Doris Hottiger really a suspect?'

'No.'

'Good. I definitely don't think she is.'

'I don't give a toss what you think,' Eschenbach retorted.

'She could be one . . . and any sensible judge would agree.'

'Yes, I know.'

'Well, that's something.'

'Now what?'

'Now you go enjoy your weekend, Jagmetti.'

'Thanks, boss.'

'And without Ms Hottiger, if possible. Understood?'

'Yes, boss.'

Eschenbach had held the rest of the conversation out of earshot of the dining car and swore quietly to himself. He switched his phone off and returned to the table, grim-faced.

Bug Eyes cleared her throat. 'So, I was right after all,' she said, with a meaningful look. 'It's just like I said.'

'Like you said?' Eschenbach raised his eyebrows and saw her eyes twinkling.

'It was the woman that did it.'

'No.'

'It's always the women, Inspector.'

Chapter 9

The briefing which Eschenbach held every Monday at eight – traditionally with coffee and croissants – yielded nothing new. A few break-ins, one boating accident, a mass brawl on Langstrasse. It was normal for that time of year.

After some encouragement from Eschenbach, Jagmetti gave his report on how the murder case was progressing. He looked tired and his eyes bore dark, shadowy circles. Had they recently witnessed wild nights of love, or was his guilty conscience getting to him?

Over the weekend, Information Services had tried to locate Eveline Bettlach – without success. It was the holiday period and Max Kubly from Info Services complained that he didn't have enough people in the department. 'Most of them have children and they have to comply with the school holidays . . .' Eschenbach's hair stood on end; he simply couldn't understand why a bunch of people as intelligent as Info Services could do everything except plan their own holidays. At least Kubly had succeeded in finding out that Eveline Bettlach's maiden name had been Eveline Marchand. It was something that Johannes Bettlach could have told him, if only he had been able to reach him. He had tried in vain to call him on Sunday. He tried his house in Herrliberg and the bank, but no one had answered the phone.

'I have Salvisberg on the line,' Rosa Mazzonleni's voice stuttered through the intercom.

'Put him through,' said Eschenbach, taking the last croissant from the meeting that morning.

'Am I disturbing you?' This was Salvisberg's standard greeting.

'No, never,' was the standard reply. It was a ritual that they maintained like an old couple.

'The dead man . . . Philipp Bettlach – do you know anything about him?'

'He was a banker, charismatic, reasonably successful, as far as I'm told. Why, is there something off?' Eschenbach took a sip of water to wash down his last bite of croissant.

'We found traces of stimulants.'

'What does that mean?'

'There are amphetamines and cocaine residue in his blood. It wasn't picked up in the provisional report I sent you on Saturday.'

'Hmm . . . drugs, then,' murmured the inspector.

'Was he undergoing psychiatric treatment?' asked Salvisberg.

'No idea. We've only been on the case three days.'

'These stimulants – if that's what we're calling them – they're not uncommon. Especially among high-flying types.' Salvisberg stopped for moment. 'What alarms me is his age.'

'What's so worrying about it?' Eschenbach was only six years younger than Bettlach.

'You don't start these things at the age of fifty-six. It's usually much earlier . . . and there's often an underlying unstable personality type at play.'

'So, where would this type of thing . . . I mean, are there specific reasons why someone might get into them?' Eschenbach asked.

'It often goes back to childhood. Traumatic experiences, for example . . . There's a whole host of different theories.'

'Bettlach grew up without a father – he was "illegitimate", so to speak. Could that have played a role, do you think?'

'Perhaps, but not necessarily. I'd be sure to pursue the matter either way. You never know.'

'I'll make sure we do. Thanks for the tip.' Jagmetti poked his head through the door a second time and Eschenbach waved him in.

'Feel free to give me a call if you need anything else,' said Salvisberg. Then he said his goodbyes and left.

'Shall I close the door, boss?'

Without waiting for an answer, the young police officer shut the door and pulled up a seat with the enthusiasm of a condemned man faced with the electric chair.

'Cheer up, Jagmetti, life goes on.' The inspector was in a good mood.

He had enjoyed his weekend in the Engadine. Corina had encouraged him to join her on a hike through the Roseg Valley while Kathrin went biking with her friends. In the evening, they had gone out for dinner. Afterwards, Kathrin had dragged them to a disco, which they left some time later without Kathrin. At home, they had enjoyed another glass of wine and made love. Twice.

They hadn't heard Kathrin when she got back early that morning and they didn't wake her when they had their breakfast at half nine.

Now, sitting in his office chair, Eschenbach felt his legs aching; the muscles in his lower back were painful and tense. Even so, he felt at least ten years younger.

Jagmetti looked the exact opposite.

'Boss, I screwed up.'

'Yes, I'm aware of that.' Eschenbach wasn't letting anything ruin his good mood. 'It's always the women,' he said, thinking back to the podgy lady with her thick glasses.

Jagmetti didn't know what Eschenbach was talking about. He was confused, and when the inspector laughed he tried to laugh too. It went very wrong. Clumsily, he ran his hand through his already dishevelled hair, bit his bottom lip, then looked past Eschenbach, first right, then left.

He looked at the white bookcase, which was overflowing, stacked with important criminology textbooks interspersed with literary and philosophical works. There was a pile of manuscripts of Eschenbach's lectures and speeches. 'The Influence of Freudian Psychoanalysis on Modern Criminology'. There were books by Freud, Carl Jung and psychologists Jagmetti had never even heard of.

He had attended Eschenbach's course and was fascinated, captivated by this great, ponderous man's mind, so sharp despite his apparent clumsiness. If he was going to be any kind of police officer, he told himself, he wanted to be like Eschenbach. Sometimes he dreamt of taking up a position in the Federal Foreign Office. But it was a dream, nothing more.

The previous autumn, when he had applied for the training position in Eschenbach's department, he had been given preference. There had been twenty-two applicants. And he, Jagmetti, was selected. Based on his grades, apparently.

And now there was this murder. This high profile case, and he was on the front line.

His fellow students were doing their training at the Central Archive, organising mouldy files, grappling with drug dealers and prostitutes on Langstrasse or distributing parking tickets in the city centre, all in the mid-summer forty-degree heat.

But not Jagmetti. He was working on the murder case that the papers were screaming about.

If only Doris Hottiger hadn't appeared.

If only they hadn't gone to that dreadful club after leaving Eschenbach.

If only he had just drunk water instead of gin and tonic and called Doris a taxi instead of driving her home.

If only he hadn't gone inside for an espresso.

If only he hadn't been such a frigging arsehole and tried thinking with his brain and not his dick.

What now? Was he going to screw up his first traineeship, his path to a career in the civil service before it had even properly begun? Why was Eschenbach so happy? Couldn't he see that he was finished? Was he trying to torment him? Was this bullshit cheeriness one of the inspector's psychological tricks to get rid of him?

'Good God, Jagmetti! Get a grip on yourself!' The inspector felt sorry for the young man.

'You can talk, boss. It's not you who's slept with a possible murderer.'

'She's not the murderer, believe me . . . and for God's sake, stop calling me "boss".' Eschenbach thought back to his night with Corina and wondered how he would feel in Jagmetti's position, if he had been trying to prove that she wasn't a killer.

'I'm not so sure any more . . .'

'Oh, what a load of tosh.' Eschenbach was tired of speculating. 'She's got no alibi.'

'What? Have you checked?'

'She told me. She had taken the afternoon off when it happened.'

The morning sun streamed through the blinds and projected a striped pattern of light and shade onto Jagmetti's unhappy face.

'She was at home, then she went to the lakeside promenade. She read a book. No witnesses.'

Eschenbach lit a Brissago and watched the rising smoke revealing the strips of light shining through the window, illuminating the young police officer.

'And now you think that the lovely Ms Hottiger, with a mere . . . wait, how old is she?'

'Twenty-two,' replied Jagmetti.

'So you think that Ms Hottiger, with a mere twenty-two summers behind her, the same Ms Hottiger who is, if you'll allow me, still a little wet behind the ears, you think that she spent Thursday afternoon lying in wait, preparing to kill Philipp Bettlach? That she used a long-range rifle with a riflescope and shot her former lover in the head, killing him stone dead? It's a bit far-fetched, don't you think?'

'Maybe. But it's possible, isn't it?'

'Yes, yes, it is possible.' Eschenbach was growing a little impatient. 'Lots of things are possible. But not probable.' Eschenbach took a drag on his cigarillo and Jagmetti's eyes, briefly illuminated, slipped back into the shadows.

'There are maybe two dozen people in Switzerland who could have pulled off that kind of feat from over six hundred metres away,' rumbled Eschenbach. 'Of course, it's a little crass to refer to it as a feat at all.'

'I know.'

'And Ms Hottiger is hardly likely to be one of them.'

'She's a former shooting champion,' said Jagmetti timidly, almost in a whisper.

'The Swiss Shooting Federation has over half a million members. That includes thousands of former shooting champions. They can be found in almost four thousand different sectors of society. Shooting is a national sport in this country, Jagmetti. We've got military service. It's mandatory. Just like learning French ... and English, more recently. First, we pick up our dummies, then we pick up our guns.'

'But girls don't,' retorted Jagmetti.

'We're back to girls, then, are we?' Eschenbach thought of Kathrin, who was more interested in his service weapon than he was.

'Doris ... I mean, Ms Hottiger was a big-time shooting champion.' This time, Jagmetti's voice was solid, confident. He seemed to be trying to shake off his misery and despair. 'Doris is the first and the only girl to have won the Zurich Young Champion's Shooting Competition. Her winning streak was the best the competition's ever seen.'

'What do you mean?' Eschenbach knew of the Zurich Young Champion's Shooting Competition, which took place on the second weekend in September; he didn't like it much.

Jagmetti pulled a couple of crumpled sheets of paper out of his jacket pocket before smoothing them out hastily and spreading them over his knees. 'These are Doris Hottiger's results from the shooting competition six years ago.'

'She was just sixteen then,' said Eschenbach, raising his eyebrows.

'Fifteen.' Jagmetti corrected him. 'She's a Sagittarius – you know, the Archer.'

'So, you could say it was written in the stars,' joked Eschenbach, gesturing to the sheets of paper with his half-smoked cigarillo.

Jagmetti was in no mood for jokes. 'She was born on the tenth of December.'

'So, tell me more about this archer of ours.'

'Look, here.' Jagmetti pointed to the papers. 'Out of 1200 participants, she managed to shoot a 35 twice.'

'Is that good?' Eschenbach had no idea.

'You shoot A-targets with an SG 550 assault rifle. The distance is 300 metres.'

'I see. So, the usual distance.' Eschenbach thought back to his desperate attempts during his time in the army.

'Each marksman . . . and every markswoman has one turn to shoot. You take five shots.'

'That makes a maximum of thirty points,' said Eschenbach; he knew that each A-target was worth six points.

'Exactly. And for every strike – that's when you hit a target – you get an extra point.'

'So that's how you get 35,' Eschenbach was catching up. 'Hot-tiger shot a 35? That's not half bad.'

'Well, there you go. Out of 1200 participants, only a couple manage it.'

Eschenbach frowned and thought back to his own scores. 'What happens after that, then? Who's crowned king . . . or queen?'

'The participants with the same number of points shoot again. Each one shoots the same number of targets in a play-off until someone wins. Usually, a participant will win the play-off with thirty or thirty-one points. It gets to them, you see – the nerves, the pressure. You know how it is.'

Eschenbach knew only too well.

'The press are there. People from the local TV station. Everyone's watching you. No one shoots a thirty-five.'

'And Doris?' Eschenbach asked.

'Doris Hottiger shot another thirty-five.'

'Really?' The inspector took a drag on his Brissago, lost in thought, and blew out the smoke in little puffs that rose through the sunlight streaming through the window; he was starting to understand why Jagmetti was so uneasy.

'I spoke to the people in charge. The adjudicator, a Mr Balz Oberhänsli, still remembers her. She'd been something of a phenomenon. She wasn't part of a shooting association or a society that trained marksmen. And she made no use of the practice shoots that took place before the actual event.'

'So she came, took her shot and left. Then it must have been a fluke,' said Eschenbach.

Jagmetti looked at his superior. He saw his absent look through the wisps of smoke and knew that he didn't mean what he'd said. The inspector didn't believe in flukes, and certainly not this one.

'A fluke. That's what they thought too, Oberhänsli told me. All of them, the army types and the gunpowder enthusiasts. They simply couldn't believe it. So they asked her – their newly crowned queen – if she could do it again. Five more shots. Just a bit of fun, playing to the gallery. For the local TV station. For the sceptics who didn't believe what they'd witnessed. Who couldn't believe it, even though they'd counted the shots themselves.'

'And did she do it?'

'Yep. But only four shots.'

'And?'

'Four sixes.'

'And the fifth shot?'

'After the fourth shot she stood up, adjusted her crown – which she had been wearing the whole time – and said: "This last shot is for Gessler."'

'For who?' asked the inspector, unsure whether he had understood.'

'For Gessler. You know, the story of William Tell? Gessler made him shoot an apple off his son's head, so in the end he shot him with his second arrow . . .'

'Yeah, I know. I know the story.' He had understood, then. William Tell. And his second shot on the Hohle Gasse road, the shot that killed Gessler.

'She's an incredible girl.' Eschenbach had been sitting as if petrified and now spoke slowly, taking the cold Brissago from his lips and placing it carefully on the rim of the ashtray.

'Indeed. And it was a juicy story for the press. "Fräulein Tell", they called her in *Switzerland Illustrated* and the Society for Women's Equality hailed her as a new Joan of Arc. She was showered with offers of sponsorship and invited onto every talk show in the country. She refused it all and disappeared back into obscurity.' Jagmetti was calmer now. He had regained his composure; he was sitting upright and there was no sign of the nerves that made him keep running a hand through his hair. It was as if the story had been weighing on him like several tonnes of ballast; at last, he was free.

'So, did she keep at it? I mean, did she ever shoot again?' asked Eschenbach.

'No. From that age onwards, she would have been eligible to compete in the main shooting competition. But she never showed her face there again. She didn't attend any of the other events she was invited to. That's all I could find out, anyway.'

Chapter 10

'I didn't shoot him, if that's what you mean.'

'That is what I mean,' replied Eschenbach.

He was sitting at the round conference table in his office, smoking. His light-grey linen trousers were clinging to his legs and his backside. They were too tight for him. He wished he could undo the button on his fly and breathe out.

Across from him sat Doris Hottiger. She was wearing a pale-blue dress and a necklace of small, shimmering pearls. No other jewellery. Her skin was bronzed and gleamed beneath the pearls. And she was sweating.

That morning, just after his conversation with Jagmetti, Eschenbach had summoned Doris Hottiger to headquarters. In the afternoon, at half four on the dot, she appeared. He had been questioning her for over an hour now. A little family history, the matter of the shooting competition and her affair with Jagmetti. Little else came up.

Yes, she knew how to shoot, she said, even as a little girl.

Her biological mother had died in childbirth and her father, a colonel in the army, had been on the Olympic shooting team. He had been one of the best of his generation. He would have preferred a son. Doris had suffered as a result. She had had to wear trousers and had short hair until she was in Year 3. A crew cut, to be precise.

'He would give me a bath every other Sunday. Never lovingly or with any hint of tenderness. No, for him, it was like shining your shoes or cleaning a pipe. After my bath, he would dry me. First my feet, so that the floor wouldn't get wet, then my body and my hair. And then, last of all, he would cut my hair. He did it quickly, without much care. I'd get lice if he didn't, he said. You'd have a hard job getting rid of them, he said. I would cry all night long and, at school, everyone would laugh at me. Because of my short hair and my red eyes. If only he had treated me with the same love and attention he showed his guns. If only he had wiped my face with the flannel as tenderly as he ran the polishing cloth over the barrel of his pistol . . .'

Doris Hottiger spoke quietly, without a trace of bitterness or scorn.

'On my ninth birthday, I decided to learn to shoot. I began to take an interest in my father's guns. His shotguns and pistols, his double-barrelled rifles, his repeating rifles and his air rifles. His Winchester, his revolver, and all the others. I wanted to learn how to hold a gun and how to aim. Rear, front, aim. Breathe in. Breathe out. Instead of crying night after night, I practised handling the guns. I made quick progress and soon learnt how to take them apart and put them back together, clean them, oil them and reassemble them. I got really good.'

A shy smile flickered across her lips.

'I accompanied my father to competitions, observed the shooters, how they prepared, took aim and shot. I listened to their tips and stood nearby when they analysed their hits and cleaned and greased their guns. I took it all in like a little sponge and, with time, my talents were recognised. At first, by my father's sporting colleagues. Then by him.'

Doris hesitated for a moment, then she went on.

'It wasn't what other girls got from their parents; it wasn't love that he gave me. My father had no love to give. But at least it was some kind of recognition. He wasn't capable of more than that.'

Eschenbach listened quietly. He caught himself thinking about Kathrin. He wondered whether he would have loved his biological daughter – if he'd had one – more than he loved her.

Had he been a good father? When he first met Corina, Kathrin had been five or so. She was often tetchy and had preferred playing with dolls to trains. Would he have preferred a son back then? Eschenbach couldn't think of an answer. He just didn't know.

Doris Hottiger looked at the inspector as if she had guessed what he was thinking. Then she continued with her story, calmly, thoughtfully – as if it wasn't her life she was describing but another person's, one she had read about or heard of somehow.

'By the time I was twelve, I was shooting so well that my father had a job keeping up with me, and by the time I was fourteen, I was regularly shooting better than him. There had been recognition, but now there was pride too. And it stayed that way. On my sixteenth birthday, I gave up. It wasn't about the crowns and the sports badges for me. It was about something else. Now I could grow my hair as long as I wanted and wear high heels and skirts. I could go to the disco in the evenings. In short, I could do everything that other girls my age could do. That's what mattered to me.'

Eschenbach had been listening attentively for some time; he rubbed his eyes with both hands.

'So that's what you meant by the Gessler reference.'

'Maybe, yes.' She smiled briefly and ran the back of her hand over her high cheekbones, soothing herself. 'The media got totally the wrong idea. They wanted a heroine. But that's not me.'

'A smart girl who can shoot well and who's . . .' Eschenbach hesitated for a moment. 'Who's as pretty as you? That's a heroine in my book.'

'That rubbish with the fifth shot, it was just nonsense . . . it just happened. Just like it would for any other marksman. He takes aim, focuses, breathes out slowly, and shoots. That's how it happened. Suddenly I felt free of the past. After the fourth shot, I got up and left.'

They had been sitting talking for two hours at this point and Eschenbach felt stuck to his seat. It was as if he were at a dead end.

Intelligent and strong-willed, Doris Hottiger was an extraordinary woman in every respect. And somehow he got the feeling that she was hiding something. Something important that he knew nothing about.

What was the key to it all? Where should he start? The parental love she'd never received, her father's coldness? How did she relate to men? To Bettlach?

Life had left its scars. Scars from wounds so deep it was a surprise she hadn't bled to death. But Doris Hottiger hadn't died, she had grown stronger.

The information she provided on Bettlach was inconsequential. It was just an affair, like any other. A search for love and security. A father substitute, perhaps, and nothing more. Was that what it was?

It was up to Eschenbach to guess and he decided to call her bluff. 'Were you depressed when Bettlach left you?' It was a shot in the dark. But it was worth it.

'Bettlach didn't leave me. I left him.'

'Why?'

For the first time she hesitated. For a brief moment she looked at the inspector, asking him to answer for her. A shadow of sadness lay behind those searching blue eyes.

Should he speak up? Or wait until she offered him the key to it all? Should he try a follow-up question? Should he try to provoke her, risk her clamming up? At last, like an experienced marksman firing a sudden, unexpected shot – breathing out – he spoke again.

'Did you sense your father's coldness in Bettlach too?'

'No.' Her eyes narrowed, and the shadow disappeared. 'Bettlach was a bastard!'

Eschenbach said nothing. He sat there without moving and watched her eyes drop.

Her hands had been resting on the armrests but now moved to her lap, as if she wanted to protect them.

Through the gap in the window he could hear the sound of traffic getting louder and then quieter, like waves crashing on the shore. A tram echoed like the screeching of the seagulls and muffled steps could be heard in the hallway.

'And when you realised that, you left him,' he said quietly, nodding.

'Yes.' She looked up. She glared defiantly at Eschenbach, as if to say: 'Do you really not know?'

Eschenbach said nothing.

'I wasn't bothered by his affairs. I knew he was lying to me and using me, that was nothing new. I already knew all that before I started sleeping with him. But I had no idea about what he did to other people.'

Hottiger was still talking in riddles and Eschenbach hadn't the faintest idea what she meant, but he knew that the key to it all was close at hand.

'How did you find out?'

'I had only found the photos at first. It was an accident. I was using his computer one morning, trying to save a letter. The recent files seemed strange to me.'

'Then what?'

'I sat in front of the screen, just thunderstruck. Young girls . . . and boys. They were just children, Inspector!' Her voice shook. 'I saw these cruel men violating their bodies and their minds. Bodies and minds that weren't mature enough to understand what was happening to them. There were hundreds of images, neatly filed in folders. I slapped myself in the face and bit the back of my hand until it bled. I didn't want to believe what I'd seen; I wanted to wake up and run away.'

'What happened next?' Eschenbach's throat felt dry. He didn't want to think about Kathrin, but he couldn't stop himself.

'I ran home. I ran the whole way. I ran across the road without waiting for the lights to change, I ran over rail tracks and embankments and I was almost hit by a tram several times. I wanted to run so fast that the pictures wouldn't be able to catch up with me. At home, I threw up several times. I took a shower, washed myself . . . and then came the crying fits. I hadn't wailed like that for ten years. My eyes swelled up until I could hardly see anything. Just the blurry outlines of my flat. And when I shut my eyes, I saw the faces of those girls and boys again, saw them whimpering, saw the hopelessness in their eyes.'

Eschenbach cleared his throat. It was getting to him more than he let on.

'Why didn't you go to the police?'

'I wanted to . . . the next day. But then I started having doubts and . . . I was curious.'

'Curious?' asked Eschenbach, astounded.

'I wanted to know if there were more. More that I didn't know about.'

'And? Were there?'

'Yes, there were.' She took her hand from her lap and brushed a strand of hair out of her face. Her voice was hoarse.

'I still had a key and I knew roughly when he would be away and when the cleaning lady would be there. I didn't have to look for long before I found the videos. Half a dozen of them. Child porn . . . I couldn't really watch them. Just short clips.'

'And what was on them?' Eschenbach was still sitting paralysed in his chair and was alarmed by the curiosity he felt.

'Can I have a glass of water, please, Inspector?'

Eschenbach pressed the button on his intercom system and asked for two glasses of water.

Mazzoleni's reply rattled through the loudspeaker. 'Still? Or sparkling?'

Rosa Mazzoleni's distorted voice lent the situation a bizarre quality and cut through the uneasiness that weighed down on both of them.

Doris Hottiger smiled, shook her head gently and Eschenbach assumed from the way she moved her lips that she wanted still water.

'Still, please.'

They waited in silence until the water came. Then she went on.

'It was . . .' Doris Hottiger was lost for words. 'The videos are much, much worse, you see. The cries . . . the whimpering. One of the girls can't have been six years old. It was appalling.'

'And Bettlach?'

'He must have recorded two of the films himself. I heard his voice, and in one clip I saw his arm and his watch.'

'Were they filmed at his house?'

'Two or three of them must have been, yes. I didn't recognise the other location.'

'Was anyone else there?'

'There was another man . . . they worked as a pair. I didn't see their faces. But like I said, I could only watch small clips. I was also worried that someone would arrive at the house all of a sudden. I didn't know who else might have a key.'

'Wouldn't that have been the right time to go to the police?'

'Yes.'

'So, why didn't you?'

'He was shot two days later.'

'And those two days weren't enough time?'

'In retrospect, yes, of course. But how was I to know that it would all be over so quickly?'

'Where are the videos now?'

'I don't know. I assume they're still in his house.'

'You didn't take them with you?'

'No. How could I? I thought he would have noticed.'

'Do you still have the key to the house?'

'Yes.' She felt around in her handbag, which was sitting on the chair nearby, and took out a dark-brown key case. She opened it and pulled out a standard security key. Her hands were steady and Eschenbach couldn't make out the slightest tremor when she offered the key to him with her hand outstretched.

'Here. I don't need it any more.'

Eschenbach took the key and placed it on the table in front of him.

'When did you last see Bettlach?'

'In the morning, before I saw the pictures,' she replied without hesitation.

'When was that?'

'About two weeks ago. If you want me to be more precise, I'll have to check.'

Eschenbach declined. 'Maybe later.' He thought for a moment. 'And he didn't call you or see you at the golf course?'

'He did call me. Several times. But I managed to avoid him.'

'Anything else?' asked the inspector. 'I mean, can you think of anything else – something that might have happened between your discovery and the murder?'

She thought for a moment.

'Did you speak to anyone about it? Does anyone else know about your discovery?'

Doris Hottiger hesitated, then nodded. 'Yes, my father ... I had to talk to someone about it. I couldn't keep it in any longer.'

'How did he react?' asked Eschenbach.

'He was cautious ...' she said with a bashful smile. 'He's always cautious. I think it's something to do with his job.' She plucked at a strand of hair. 'He just listened.'

'Nothing else?'

'Well, yes.' She bit her bottom lip. 'He said I should go to the police.'

Eschenbach said nothing.

'And he asked if he should come back.' She chewed her lip again and avoided Eschenbach's gaze. Then she added, hastily: 'I know I shouldn't have waited.'

'You mean, your father isn't in Zurich?' Eschenbach raised his eyebrows in surprise.

'No, he's in America. Penn State University. He's a guest professor there for the summer. He's teaching military strategy . . . or something like that. I called him during the night, when I couldn't sleep.'

'Do you have a number I can reach him on?' asked Eschenbach.

Doris Hottiger rummaged through her handbag again, took out a notebook and pen and wrote the number on a slip of paper. 'Here, this is his mobile number.'

'Thanks. I think that's all for today.' Eschenbach took a look at the clock and was startled. It was ten to seven. Kobler had wanted to see him at six. He'd have to rearrange it; he couldn't face it now.

Doris Hottiger fingered a charm in the shape of the sun that was hanging from her bag.

'Has what happened between me and Claudio – I mean, Mr Jagmetti – caused problems for him? Is he in trouble because of me?'

Eschenbach stood up, holding his lower back. Doris Hottiger rose as well and looked at the inspector expectantly.

'You've both cocked up a bit there. Just stay in the city and forget about it.' He cut the sentence short and held out his hand with a smile.

'For God's sake, Eschenbach!' Kobler yelled down the line. 'You could have at least called.'

'I know,' he replied once his boss had finished her lengthy reproach. Despite saying so little, the inspector still struggled to conceal the sullenness in his voice. She was right, of course, and he felt terrible about it. It wasn't his style to miss meetings, especially without calling to apologise.

His conversation with Doris Hottiger was preying on his mind. He left headquarters shortly after she did and walked through the quiet side streets along the Sihl and down to the lake. He felt as if he were wading through ankle-deep mud, all of the world's filth sticking to his shoes. What kind of world lets grown men abuse helpless little children?

Feelings of contempt rose inside him as his steps grew louder and his breathing heavier. Was this hate enough to drive one to commit murder? Did anyone have the right to end the existence of someone who had robbed innocent children of theirs? Wasn't it a kind of murder to extinguish the light in a child's eyes forever?

Eschenbach wondered how many answers there could be to such questions. How would a judge answer? What about someone seeking revenge? What guiding principle would be referenced in an abuser's psychological report, what answers were there to be found in the words of a victim's therapist? And what about him: how would he answer these questions? As a police officer? As a man? Or as the father of a sixteen-year-old daughter? Could objective truth exist in this labyrinth, beset with subjective, psychological chasms? The more Eschenbach thought about it all, the more the line between right and wrong, between cause and effect, seemed to blur.

When he finally sat down on a wooden bench next to the water, forcing down bites of *bratwurst*, watching the black water despondently, he felt glad that the final judgement didn't lie with him.

Chapter 11

It was pouring with rain. The droplets beat down on the newly restored cobblestones. The water ran along grooves in the street, criss-crossing the ground like the lines of a complex circuit diagram.

The square that surrounded Basle Minster was empty when the taxi turned into Münstergasse and later stopped in front of an old half-timbered house on Münsterberg. The taxi driver left the engine running and got out of the car, opened an old umbrella – cursing – and heaved a large, leather suitcase out of the boot. He gave the suitcase to the passenger who had got out of the car in the meantime – without an umbrella. He thanked him for the generous tip and said goodbye.

'Your customer card will be charged, Mr DeLaprey,' he added, before getting back into the vehicle and swearing one last time. Loudly, this time: 'Bloody weather, horrible business.' He tossed the sodden umbrella onto the passenger seat and steered the old Mercedes off the pavement, back onto the flooded road.

DeLaprey stood in the corridor, feeling around for the keys he had assumed were in the outer pocket of his leather bag. Nothing. He vowed to pay more attention when packing next time. Raincoat – outer pockets. Raincoat – inner pockets. Nothing. He pulled off the coat and held it in front of him like a wet dog. It was dripping. With his other hand, he kept looking. Jacket – outer pockets. Jacket – inner pockets. Still nothing. He set the coat down on the wooden floor, next to the puddle. At last, he found them. In his jeans, which were lying folded at the bottom of his bag. He turned the key, opened the door and stepped inside.

The lights were on throughout the flat. There was a pair of women's shoes next to the coat rack and he could hear the quiet hum of the extractor fan in the kitchen. Through the half-open door, DeLaprey made out his sister's chestnut-brown mop of hair. She had tied it back with a hairband and was just about to slide a casserole dish into the oven. Typical Hera, thought DeLaprey. He knocked on the door and stepped in with a quiet 'Hello'.

'Leandro!' she cried happily. She wiped her hands on her apron and came over to hug him.

'I've moved out of Pierre's,' she said. 'He's an arsehole,' she muttered, before breaking down in tears, interrupted occasionally by a single, short sob.

They stood there for what seemed like an eternity. He stroked her hair. Over and over, like a parent soothing a child after a bad dream.

DeLaprey looked outside. It was still raining. The rain had slowly found its way through the thick canopy of leaves that sheltered the snug seating area on the terrace outside. Single drops fell silently to the ground at odd intervals.

Rain clears the air, just as tears cleanse the soul, thought DeLaprey, and before long it was time to take the casserole out of the oven.

He was wrong. It was bland and dry. DeLaprey wondered whether it was true what they said about cooks in love spoiling their food. It seemed to be the exact opposite for Hera. If the taste of the fish was anything to go by, her heart must have been broken pretty badly.

The story that she recounted over dinner didn't make the casserole any better, but more meaningful. She had wanted to surprise Pierre, she said; she came home too early, with too little warning, and surprised the girl that was lying in bed next to him.

Then there was the usual row. Insults were thrown as well as punches. Then there was the bag, which she packed with her things, and the door, and the echo as she slammed it behind her.

DeLaprey had always wondered whether the ups and downs of his sister's love life would make good TV. Now, looking at Hera's sore red eyes, he wasn't so sure.

He had never liked Pierre. He was a pretentious 'artiste'. A conceited musician, pompous and boring, with his stupid flute. Poncing about in tails and a white cashmere scarf that he insisted on wearing even in summer.

But Hera liked his playing and his romantic streak, as she called it. She could listen to him for hours and accompanied him on the piano.

She had sat in the front row countless times when he had played at the City Casino with the Basle Symphony Orchestra. And every year she took at least one unpaid holiday so that she could be by his side on one of his numerous tours.

At Christmas, traditionally a time for celebrating with family, she was often missing. She preferred to spend it sitting alone in a church in some backwater dump, simply because Pierre would be giving his best Ave Maria for the five-hundredth time and could never say no to a moderately well-paid gig.

In Hera's eyes, Pierre Oliver was akin to James Galway, a wonderful artist and musician. He had the kind of talent that appeared once a century. In Leandro's eyes, he was the Pied Piper of Hamelin.

But now that the disaster he had foreseen had become a reality, he had no interest in gloating. He felt sorry for his sister. One man's comedy was another man's tragedy, he thought. And though he felt in some way relieved, tonight tragedy had the upper hand.

He sat there in silence, topping up Hera's glass of wine from time to time, listening to her patiently. Always the same story with the same sad ending. *Da capo al fine.*

At half two in the morning, he guided her to the guest bedroom. At half four the last sobs subsided and he finally dropped off, with Hera drifting into a fitful sleep in the room next door.

The telephone rang just before nine. It was the second time it had rung that morning and it was some time before Leandro, still woozy from too much wine and too little sleep, picked up the receiver.

'Is this Mr DeLaprey?' asked the voice of a man he didn't recognise.

'Yes,' his voice sounded hoarse.

'Do you know a Ms Hera DeLaprey?'

'Yes. She's my sister. Who am I speaking to, please?'

'Adrian Melzer. I'm a police officer.'

DeLaprey swallowed drily. He was standing in the kitchen with the cordless phone to his ear and wanted to get himself a glass of water from the tap. He scratched his neck.

'Do you know where your sister is at the moment?' The officer was very friendly.

DeLaprey hesitated briefly. But why should he lie? He had no reason to. 'She's here, at my house. She's still asleep.'

'Do you know what her relationship was to . . .' The police officer seemed uncertain. 'Maybe I had better ask your sister. Could she come to the phone for a moment?'

'Of course. One moment.' DeLaprey went to the guest room lost in thought and knocked on the door. He didn't wait for a reply and stepped inside. No amount of knocking would wake Hera after the brief night's sleep she had had. He could just make out a couple of strands of her hair peeping out like dark feathers from between the white pillows and the thin duvet.

'Could we call you back?' asked DeLaprey. 'In a few minutes?'

'I'm happy to wait,' said the police officer.

He was reluctant to wake her up. When she opened her eyes, she would be struck by the sad reality that she had struggled so desperately to escape just hours before.

Her eyes were swollen and unhappy. He gave her a glass of water and a chance to compose herself.

'Just a moment,' he said, trying to stall the police officer. DeLaprey wondered whether he should broach the subject of her separation from Pierre. He decided not to, because it seemed wrong to claim mitigating circumstances without knowing the issue at hand.

Hera took the receiver and told the officer her name. She spoke very quietly. So quietly that the officer evidently hadn't understood her. She repeated herself. Loudly and more clearly this time.

She looked pale and fragile in her red plaid pyjamas; they were too big for her. She was sitting half upright with pillows at her back, pressing the receiver to her left ear. She didn't speak, other than to say 'yes' or 'no' a few times. The officer at the other end of the line seemed to do most of the talking. DeLaprey could hear the noise coming out of the earpiece but couldn't understand a word.

And suddenly, as if the conversation had ended, she handed him the receiver. Her nostrils alone revealed that she was still breathing. Then her features twisted into a grimace.

DeLaprey was startled. It was unexpected and sudden, a response he had only seen in babies. That abrupt shift from a contented gurgle to a horrifying scream. Her almond-shaped eyes, which could laugh with such mischief, were now little more than two dark slits in her skin. She pressed the duvet to her face, as though trying to stem the flow of blood from a wound. She screamed and sobbed. She rocked back and forth. Back and forth.

DeLaprey didn't know what to do. He grabbed her by the shoulders. She pushed him away, sobbing and rocking all the while.

He took the receiver and checked that the officer was still on the line.

'What's happened?' he asked. 'My sister can't talk any more. Please tell me what's happened.' DeLaprey was agitated.

He tried again to hold his sister still as she swayed back and forth like a rocking horse.

'Pierre Oliver is dead,' said the voice at the end of the line. 'We're at his flat right now.'

'Why did you contact me?' DeLaprey asked simply. It wasn't what he wanted to ask. He didn't care. He was worried about Hera.

'The name Hera DeLaprey is on the door . . . she's registered here. There are four DeLapreys in Basle and you were the first one we called. Sometimes you get lucky.' The voice sounded friendly, even a little relieved. 'We wanted to let your sister know. That's all.'

'Why did he . . . I mean, how did he die?'

'Sleeping tablets. We suspect an overdose of sleeping tablets. We'll clarify that later, though.'

'What, because Hera left him? But he—'

'We can't assume the reason, Mr DeLaprey. His cleaning lady called us when she found Mr Oliver dead in his bed this morning.'

'What about the woman?'

'What woman?' The officer sounded surprised.

'The woman who was in bed with him?' He regretted this as soon as he'd said it.

'There was no woman in his bed, Mr DeLaprey.' The friendly tone was gone.

'Well, er . . . we all die alone in the end, don't we?' DeLaprey wished he could slam the receiver against the wall.

'Tell your sister that she has to report to us. Today, if possible. We have a couple of questions, just a formality . . . and then she will need to identify the body. It's unavoidable, I'm afraid.'

'I know.' DeLaprey nodded and made a note of the address the officer gave him. Then he switched the phone off and placed it on the nightstand.

Hera had stopped swaying. The bedcovers, which she was still holding over her face, stifled the sound of her sobs.

'They're saying it was an overdose of sleeping tablets . . .' he said, more to himself than anything. 'It doesn't make sense. I could imagine him killing someone else . . . but not himself.'

Hera said something that he didn't understand. He couldn't make it out amid the whimpers and sobs. He tried to take the duvet off her face.

'Pierre never took sleeping tablets,' she said, sniffing.

'Are you sure?'

Hera pressed the bedcovers between her knees and looked at him in astonishment. 'What are you asking me? What do you mean by that? I slapped him one. And that bimbo of his. Then I packed what I needed and left.'

'And?'

'And nothing!' She sniffed again. 'He laughed, like it was all some crappy stage play. . . he didn't give a shit.' She stopped and gasped for breath. 'You've got to believe me, Leandro, he didn't kill himself. Not Pierre.' Hera was sitting bolt upright in bed now. She had a nervous look in her eyes, almost of fear. 'Something's not right about this, Leandro, I can feel it. Pierre would never have killed himself.'

Chapter 12

Files lay piled left and right on the desk. The in-tray was overflowing, and the out-tray was empty.

Five days had passed since the murder and, for the first time, Eschenbach felt stuck. The search for a psychiatric clinic that might have treated Philipp Bettlach had been unsuccessful so far. The same could be said for the search for Eveline Marchand, and Johannes Bettlach – who might have been able to help – was ignoring his calls. He was on a business trip, the bank said, only agreeing to divulge his mobile number after Eschenbach insisted. When he tried the number, he was met with the sound of Bettlach's cheery voicemail message. None of his calls were returned.

Eschenbach crossed his arms behind his head. The tubular steel frame of his swivel chair bent alarmingly beneath his body and the black leather creaked. In front of him on the desk lay a half-smoked Brissago on a saucer that served as an ashtray. Two empty espresso cups stood nearby.

The man sitting opposite him in a grey business suit was at least ten years younger than Eschenbach. He had short blond hair and wore rimless glasses framing his intelligent eyes. He wore a white shirt with a button-down collar and no tie. With his smart get-up, he could easily have been mistaken for a business student.

Marcel Bucher was head of special tasks at the Federal Office of Police, or FOP for short. He was the head of the special commission dealing with investigations of cybercrime.

When he called to speak to Eschenbach just after half nine on Tuesday morning, it was with an air of utmost secrecy. He wanted to speak to him about a top-secret matter, something of an especially delicate nature. He would be bringing a confidentiality agreement with him for Eschenbach to sign. It was imperative to keep the number of persons involved as low as possible, despite this being a difficult undertaking for a project of such magnitude. Eschenbach was number 412 on the list.

Though he hated secrecy and loathed the federal police and all its administrative machinery, he kept an hour free in the afternoon to meet with Bucher. It couldn't hurt to listen, he thought, and secretly he had to admit that he was a little curious. He was interested to know what top-secret projects his colleagues in Berne were messing about with.

As the young officer sat opposite him, briefing him – no pretension, just facts – Eschenbach thought he might have to revise his preconceptions of the FOP. Or at least have a good think about them. There was no sign of the pomposity that had struck him on previous cases. Were things changing down in Berne? Perhaps Bucher was just an exception to the rule.

'It all started with this website, Landslide.' Bucher spoke quietly; his Bernese accent seemed to have stuck with him through his studies at the Institute of Technology in Zurich and the time he spent living in the US. The US Postal Inspection Service had investigated this website and arrested the people operating it – an American couple – two months ago. Landslide allowed its users to make credit card payments in return for access to over

300 child porn sites. Customers from 61 countries obtained material from it, for which Landslide registered over 150,000 payments.'

'And there were Swiss citizens among them, of course.' Eschenbach sensed what was coming.

'Yes. The American authorities passed the raw data – primarily credit card data – on to Interpol. It came to us via them.'

'So, how many are Swiss?'

'Over 3,600 sets of raw data were linked to Switzerland. These included the usual repetitions and errors that you always expect with data of this kind.'

Eschenbach felt clueless. He knew nothing about data and even less about raw data. He puzzled over what the difference might be between raw data and other kinds of data. He could barely tell the difference between raw and cooked eggs. Suddenly, Bucher was talking about replications and overlaps. Eschenbach strived to listen and give the impression that he knew as much about data as he did about eggs.

Bucher's glasses had slid down the bridge of his nose and sat askew and too far forward. Bucher pushed them back up. He spoke in a nasal, even tone which in any other dialect would have sounded arrogant. In Bernese German, it sounded pleasant.

'Once we checked the data and filtered everything out, we were left with 1300 units of clean data.'

'So by clean . . . you mean dirty?'

Bucher paused, then grinned. He liked wordplay. 'Yes. The filth, as it were. Landslide's 1300 Swiss customers.'

'But what if some of them hadn't meant to click on it? Say they'd done it accidentally, or out of curiosity?'

'Then we'd have a real job of it, Mr Eschenbach.' He smiled. 'No, this list is just the big guns. All of them are people who have repeatedly downloaded pornographic material featuring children from the internet to the tune of thousands of francs. Images. Videos. The whole disgusting hog.'

Eschenbach swallowed. He thought about the videos that Doris Hottiger had mentioned, which had been delivered to headquarters at his request. He still hadn't got around to watching them. And it wasn't for want of time.

'The raw data was extensively filtered. As far as we were concerned, once is as good as never, and we also excluded those paying a few hundred francs. Mercy before justice, you could say. These 1300 people, they're the big fish.'

'So what now? I mean, what happens next?'

Bucher pulled a file out of an old, dark-brown leather folder and placed it on the table in front of Eschenbach.

On the front of the file were the words 'Project Genesis' and, underneath, 'Canton of Zurich'.

'Now we catch the bastards.'

'Time to do the dirty work.' Eschenbach flicked through the documents without really reading them.

'Yep. Time to muck out the pigs.'

'Left to the cantons, as usual.' Eschenbach shrugged his shoulders. 'So what am I expected to do with all this stuff?'

'This stuff, as you call it, is a result of the largest concerted police campaign against child pornography that Switzerland has ever seen.' Bucher smiled. 'On federal orders, we're informing the commanders of the cantonal police corps and their representatives. Then it will be a matter for the cantonal authorities. 'You're on my list as the deputy . . .' – Bucher flicked through his papers – '. . . to Commander Elisabeth Kobler. I've already spoken to Ms Kobler. I assume my information is correct.'

Eschenbach nodded. Now he knew what he was in for. Hundreds of house searches. Crates of PCs and hard drives which would have to be taken from houses and apartments and carted all the way to headquarters. Hundreds of videos and images. All the stuff that would need to be seized and viewed. 'How many are there?' he asked blandly.

'About four hundred.' The officer from Berne fingered his glasses; he didn't seem comfortable in his skin. 'You can find the exact number in the file. There's also a list with names and addresses.'

'Four hundred! That's almost a third!'

'It's also available digitally. On a CD. That's in the back. We thought it would be helpful.' The officer watched Eschenbach as he drew listlessly on his Brissago, his eyes half closed. He felt sorry for this tall man who seemed so strong, as if nothing could get to him; a man before whom lay a grey federal folder with four hundred cases of the most hardcore filth. He knew the CD wouldn't be of much help.

'A third,' murmured Eschenbach. 'Why isn't the scum more evenly spread? There are twenty-six cantons. It doesn't add up. Why isn't it one twenty-sixth? Or one thirteenth . . . it's all the same to me. Or an eighth? Haven't we got enough on our plates with the Russian mafia? And the Czech mafia? And the Serbian, Croatian, Azerbaijani and Kosovo Albanian mafias? We're already a Mecca for drug addicts, not to mention the biggest brothel in Europe. And now we're home to a bunch of paedophiles too.' Eschenbach took the file and went to stand up. 'Why don't they live in Aargau? Or Thurgau? Or Appenzell, for all I care?' He stood up, slapped the file back down on the table and walked towards the window.

He looked down at the street below. The tarmac had absorbed the rain from the night before. Or, perhaps, the rain had evaporated in the sun. Either way, it was dry once again. So dry it was as if it had never rained. New dust was beginning to settle. You couldn't see it, but Eschenbach knew it was there – that fine, grey dirt. It lay perfectly camouflaged on the streets and the pavements. It hid quietly in crannies and grooves until it was swept away by a new storm or a road sweeper during the next campaign to tidy up the city. New dust and dirt would come. A perpetual mobile of microscopic grime. What looked quaint and clean to the naked eye was, in reality, a filthy pigsty.

And yet, he loved this city. He loved the dusty courtyards in the Fourth District, where as a child he had played football between the metal frames used for beating carpets, where these days his job as a police officer saw him stopping drug dealers from selling heroin to minors. He liked the elegant streets and the smartened-up old houses, selling legions of tourists a piece of Swiss idyll every summer. He loved the smell of the lake and the view of the snow-capped Alps, which seemed so close they could have been standing in the water.

He loved Zurich in the winter too. When the cold and damp increased, creating mist, and the city regained its gravity and melancholy, that it had lost in the summer. Then he loved it even more.

He turned, went back to his desk and sat down.

Bucher was still sitting there; he had stretched out his legs and sat up again as Eschenbach returned. He adjusted his glasses and tried to smile.

'This is a fine bag of tricks you're trying to fob me off with,' Eschenbach pointed to the file. 'This is massive, I'm telling you . . . and it'll blow up in our faces.' He sounded tired and weary.

'It won't be that bad,' said Bucher. This time he managed a smile. 'It's in good hands with you. We'd be happier if there were more people like you—'

'Well, even hypocrites have to die someday.' Eschenbach interrupted him. 'If you're trying to flatter me, I'll happily hand this back to you right now.'

They both laughed.

'If you need help, my number's on the report.'

Eschenbach dismissed the idea. Then he thought about the videos from Bettlach's house which he had asked be moved to headquarters.

'One small request, though.'

'What's that?' Bucher had been in the process of getting up to leave but he sat back down again.

'I've got a handful of videos. Child porn, horrible stuff. Evidence for a murder case that we're working on here.'

'The murder at the golf course?'

'Yes. I still haven't managed to take a closer look at them.' He hesitated for a moment and looked at Bucher as if hoping that he might grant him absolution in return for his dubious plea.

Bucher was silent. He scratched his chin and waited.

Eschenbach wondered whether he should leave it at this little white lie. He was too embarrassed to admit that he hadn't watched the tapes at all.

Bucher looked at the inspector, whose vacant gaze fell on the floor in front of him.

'I've never watched a child porn video. I've seen plenty of other stuff, of course. Charred remains, drowned corpses, bodies shot to pieces, stab wounds, but this . . .' He pointed to the cupboard where he was keeping the videos. 'I always thought I'd be able to escape it somehow.' Eschenbach looked up.

'There's no way around it, I'm afraid,' said Bucher matter-of-factly. 'So, what can I do to help?'

'I'd like photos. Prints, if you see what I mean. Whole body shots and also more detailed close-ups, if possible. Anything that could help us identify people. Faces, hands, feet, shoes, belt loops, God knows – whatever's on there.'

Bucher thought for a moment. 'But you've got specialists who could do that.'

Eschenbach wouldn't relent.

'OK,' said Bucher, after a moment's hesitation. 'I'll do it. But only because it's you.'

'Thanks.'

'So, all participants?'

Eschenbach stopped for a moment.

'I mean, just the adults, or the children too?'

Eschenbach swallowed; the question brought back the horror of what they were dealing with. 'All of them.'

'Anything else?'

'No, that's it.'

Eschenbach thanked Bucher again and gave him the videos he had been keeping locked away. They said their goodbyes.

The inspector was relieved to be rid of the videos, if only for a short time. A few days, perhaps. Though he knew that he hadn't been spared the task of watching them all himself, he was pleased to have it postponed. Perhaps photos were easier to bear. At least to begin with.

Chapter 13

The Old Shepherd was full to bursting. A group of bankers were celebrating the sale of some company which provided some service or other. They had already reached the stage where no one knew or cared any more. Champagne flowed into glasses, over rims and onto the brightly polished counter. The floor was a little sticky.

An oversized, three-pronged fan made of mahogany and rattan, a relic from the fifties, was spinning on the ceiling, slowly mixing the cigarette smoke with the smell of dried-on alcohol and perfumed sweat. Joe Cocker was singing something about friendship and the feeble sound system made his voice sound hoarser than usual. One of the barmen was shaking a cocktail shaker. His long dark eyelashes seemed artificial. So did his laugh.

Doris Hottiger was sitting at a small table at the back of the bar, wearing jeans and a white T-shirt. The jeans were too low, the T-shirt too short. Her belly-button piercing was just right. A good-looking man tried to sit at her table, flashing her a winning smile with Colgate-white teeth. She turned him away, apologising with a smile that was really anything but. She turned the next one down too, as she had done for the five – or was it six? – before him. The chair next to her was empty – the only empty chair in the room.

Would he come? She had left a message on his answering machine giving the time and place. She looked at the clock. It was half eleven. She had said to be there – no, she said *she* would be there – at eleven.

She began to doubt whether he was coming or not. She felt silly sitting at the table alone and wondered if she should get up and get a drink at the bar. She was tired of waiting.

The empty seat next to her attracted the revellers. It drew them in – go-getters and men about town, the shy ones and the cocky ones – like moths to a flame. And like moths, they would bash their soft, dusty heads against the hard glass of a lamp and fly away clumsily, giddy with heat and light, only to return and be drawn in again. Butterflies of the night. The seat stayed empty.

She didn't want to smile any more, nor did she want to keep turning them away. She felt tired. Worn out. The smoke that hung in the air irritated her. She rubbed her eyes. First, just with the backs of her hand and then with both hands, as the irritation worsened. She liked the irritation, somehow. She saw dark-red waves breaking in yellow foam, saw the sun rising and setting, rising and setting again. She concentrated on a pale cloud that hopped up and down as she moved her eyes.

'Hi, what are you having?'

She recognised the voice, opened her eyes and, through a thick veil of tears, saw two legs dressed in dark trousers. Pearls of light danced against matte blackness and then the veil seemed to lift and she saw Claudio Jagmetti looking at her with concern.

'Are you crying?' He took the seat that she had been saving for him, pulled it up next to her and sat down. He kissed her tenderly at the corners of her eyes and ran his lips over her eyelids and her nose. He could taste the salt of her tears on his tongue, breathed in the scent of her neck and her temples, and suddenly remembered why he had thrown caution to the wind and driven straight there.

'Do you know how many good-looking guys I've had to fend off? I was scared you weren't coming.'

'I just had to see you.'

'Me too.' She took his hand and rubbed her damp cheek against it, licked it tenderly, kissed it, poked her little nose between his fingers and looked at him for a long time without saying a word.

'Should I come to yours? I mean, we could . . .' Jagmetti didn't know what he wanted to say.

'I don't know if that's wise, Claudio.' She ran her fingers slowly through his and held his hand still as if it were threatening to slip away. 'I just wanted to see you again before I go.'

'What is it that you want?' Jagmetti faltered. He squeezed her hand and saw her tanned fingers go white. 'It's not a good idea to just vanish.'

'Perhaps.' She hesitated for a moment. 'But I have to get away, Claudio. Things are coming to a head. As far as I can tell, I'm a suspect.'

'If you take off now it'll seem like a confession of guilt. They'll find you.'

'I haven't killed anyone. I know it and you do too. You're the sort of person who can sense these things.'

'Eschenbach thinks the same.'

'Really? It's only been a few days since Philipp was murdered and the pressure on Eschenbach is growing . . .'

'He'll manage it.'

'Maybe he will. I hope so anyway. But what if he doesn't? In a few weeks' time, you might be the only one who still believes me. You're not neutral any more, Claudio. You're—'

'Just an trainee?' he interrupted her. 'Is that what you're try-ing to say?'

'No, it's got nothing to do with that. Even if you were an inspector . . . . As far as a jury's concerned, you've been compro-mised. You're a nice, honest police officer. A police officer who's in love and therefore completely unreliable.'

'And what about you?' He ran his fingers along the small scar on her wrist, looked at her and smiled. 'What am I to you?'

'You're . . .' She smoothed down the strands of hair that had fallen in curls over her chin. 'I don't know. I feel like we've known each other for ages, Claudio.' She looked at him silently for a long time. 'When time's short, suddenly you're lost for words. I just wanted to see you again.'

He wanted to say something and opened his mouth, then shut it again. He couldn't think of anything.

'I'm not a murderer, Claudio. Look at me.'

Jagmetti looked at her. Her freckles were hidden beneath her smeared mascara and the fine lines in the corners of her eyes were barely visible. We call them laughter lines, even when we're sad, he thought.

'I've done some things that you don't know about. They might come to light at some point, then you'll have to decide for yourself. I don't want to talk about it. It's nothing illegal. At least not to me.'

Jagmetti nodded. He thought about the night they had spent together. Pictured the way her small breasts rose and fell, the way she straddled him, felt her moving, the way she pressed up against him and took him tenderly into her. He saw her laugh and her bright blue eyes. 'Will I see you again?' He couldn't stop himself. 'I mean, someday, when all of this is over?'

'Maybe.' She stood up and kissed him on the tip of the nose. 'Take care, Claudio . . . I think it's better this way.' She smiled briefly again, then she turned her back on him and edged through the crowd, towards the exit.

It dawned on Jagmetti that he couldn't just let Doris go, and he jumped up. He hurried after her white T-shirt, bumping into a young woman with white-blond hair. She'd appeared out of nowhere, wearing high-heeled cowboy boots and a knowing smile. The drink she was holding splashed upwards and spilt over her, him and several bystanders.

Tomato juice, thought Jagmetti, that's odd. He was on the floor, running his tongue over his split lip.

'You've broken his nose,' the blonde was shouting at a great hulk of a man standing next to her, rubbing his knuckles. Her thin, beige top was flecked with ugly dark-red stains.

That can't possibly all be blood, thought Jagmetti. Maybe it's a Bloody Mary . . . He groped at his face. Touched his nose, chin and upper lip. A light-red substance clung to his fingers. He ran his tongue around his mouth again. At least his teeth were intact. He stood up.

'Damn it,' grunted the guy standing next to the girl. 'You've wrecked her dress.'

'All right, all right,' stammered Jagmetti. 'I didn't do it on purpose. Sorry.' He was in no mood for a fight. The only thought running through his mind was of Doris. He mumbled a few words of apology and looked to the exit. His eyes wandered over the heads of the other guests. Then he looked to his left, through the open window out onto the pavement.

Doris Hottiger had disappeared.

Chapter 14

The rain fell like spools of grey thread. Eschenbach had no umbrella; he wasn't sure he even owned one any more. He didn't know where he had left the last one. At the very least, he had got his jacket back and – more importantly – his notes from his conversation with Dr Bettlach.

Rosa Mazzoleni had checked all the taxi companies. Eventually she struck gold and made arrangements to have the jacket picked up. It stank terribly. Like bacon fat and one of those green tree air fresheners: notes of woodland calm. A shot of stale smoke rounded off the unique bouquet. Eschenbach held the jacket over his head as he crossed Löwenstrasse in great strides and found shelter under the awning of a department store on the other side of the road. Men in pinstriped suits stood between women wearing headscarves – these days they wore them in accordance with their beliefs and not to keep the rain off.

The men and women were waiting for the rain to subside. It was bucketing down in torrents from the awning. Eschenbach felt like he was up to his ankles in water. It doesn't matter if they're quality English-made shoes, he thought, they're not meant to be waders. Why hadn't he got them resoled? Giuseppe, whom he had been going to for years, was always hassling him to get it done. Zurich was not Milan and it made no difference that the shoes were from England. Leather was leather and it could only tolerate moisture in certain quantities. Be it in Zurich, London or Milan. Rubber soles were a must, especially in winter. It was summer now, at least on paper. Or perhaps it was over already?

In the department store, the 'End of Summer' sale was under way and colourful signs boasted of slashed prices, inviting customers to splash out.

There's enough splashing out here, thought Eschenbach. First the heat, then this apocalyptic rain. He decided to wait and have an espresso at the juice bar. He didn't want juice. It gave him heartburn and he didn't think the vitamins were worth it. Pinstriped suits stood at the bar and housewives sat at the tables. They were waiting for the rain to stop and the prices to drop.

The meeting had gone just as he had hoped. Elisabeth Kobler had expressly asked to come with him. He rarely attended the meetings that Kobler held with the commanders of the city police. The cantonal and city police were two different things and had a unique relationship to one another. Like a mother and daughter, when the daughter has been going through puberty for several years. That was Kobler's view, in any case.

Eschenbach had no trouble with it; he had been with the city police for a long time and knew most of them, except for the newbies. He got on well with almost everyone, and when it came to serious crimes the canton would now take on the case, and his boss would pick up the baton. In the end, the most sensitive cases would end up on his desk. Murder and cross border crime were his area; that was how things had worked out over the years, and he wasn't unhappy about it.

Eschenbach was happy that he was no longer in charge of checking prostitutes' work permits and detaining pissheads. He had seen and processed it all. To his mind, he'd seen enough to last for a lifetime. Nights on patrol, crippling tiredness, nothing to report and a thermos full of bad coffee that was no help at all.

Not that he liked murder and homicide any better, or preferred dealing with the international mafia, the FBI or the Federal Office of Police – far from it. From time to time, he wished he could go back to the days before the Berlin wall fell and Zurich, before the internet and Interpol, was still a criminal backwater.

Sometimes he missed it, the rascals and rogues, the gamblers and dealers bustling around the dark alleyways and streets of Zurich. He missed them, just as he missed Aunt Emma's on the corner between Badenerstrasse and Langstrasse, or the candles on his birthday cake, baked by his grandmother. If they were still around today, they would be in a museum of local history. They were like Winnetou and Old Shatterhand in the old Westerns he had read as a child.

And yet, murder was murder. Regardless of the circumstances, which varied, and the times, which had changed. Had times really changed? Or was it just people? Eschenbach didn't know the answer.

The file he had brought with him in his scuffed leather folder seemed to be connected to the murder of Philipp Bettlach. But how? He had gone through the list carefully. Some of the names were relevant. That reassured him in a way. There were also names he knew, names he wouldn't have dreamt of seeing. That alarmed him. Members of the governing council of Zurich and public officials. Teachers and people who worked in the Church, in the community, in major institutions. Eschenbach had to reread the names several times before he believed it. He was relieved to see no one he knew personally among them. Perhaps there were errors. Perhaps they were just lucky.

The one name he had been expecting to see – the name he was certain would be on the list – was missing: Philipp Bettlach. There was nothing under B or under P. Nothing at all.

Was the list just the tip of the iceberg? He couldn't find a satisfactory explanation for it.

At the very least, he had the videos, the computer with the hard drive and the images. It was more than he needed. The fact that he hadn't found the name on the list was just a minor anomaly he would have to live with.

About half of the four hundred suspects lived in or close to the city. The Zurich squad would have to deal with them now. They had enough people. At the meeting, Kobler had been preaching to the converted. The case had been snatched from her hands, and Eschenbach was happy to be rid of some of the work. There were still two hundred suspects for him and his people to look at. It was a lot, but it was doable. Competition is a boon, he thought.

The rain had subsided a little when he got back outside and his feet had gotten used to the wet socks. But he still couldn't bring himself to put his jacket on. As well as the smell of must and air freshener, it also gave off a sour stink of wet wool. The cheap red plastic umbrella that he had purchased for nine francs and ninety rappen was blown away by the wind. The struts stood up at a right angle. He decided he was better off leaving it somewhere next time the sun came out.

He walked quickly up Löwenstrasse, crossed the Sihl and made for the tram junction at Stauffacher. He suddenly felt happy as the trusty revolving doors catapulted him into the heart of head-quarters, where he found dry, dark-grey linoleum beneath his feet once again.

Rosa Mazzoleni was in a bad mood, which was rare for her.

She greeted him without a word and without the usual smile that he was so used to. She didn't even look up from her screen and clearly had no intention of asking him how the meeting had gone and whether he wanted an espresso. Was it the weather, or had their years of domestic bliss finally come to an end? He would have preferred to scurry past her silently, but his shoes prevented it. He had no chance. They slipped, slapped and creaked like he was in a Roman galley. Behind him, he imagined her turning her head, raising her eyebrows and watching him stomp past and disappear into his office.

He had just removed his sodden socks and hung them over one of the interview chairs when Elisabeth Kobler called.

'It didn't go too badly this morning,' he joked, pulling a Brissago out of the cardboard packet.

'Hmm . . .' was all his boss said.

Eschenbach slid the Brissago back into the packet and waited. With Kobler, silence was never a good sign.

'Why have you been bothering Hottiger?' She said, her voice brimming with venom.

'I interviewed her the day before yesterday. She was friends with the victim. Anyway—'

'I mean her father,' Kobler interrupted him gruffly.

'Her father . . .' Eschenbach thought for a moment. 'Jesus, we haven't interviewed him yet. He's not even in the country!'

'Oh really!'

'He's in America . . . at some university, as far as I know. So please tell me—'

'So please tell you what?' He heard her drumming her fingers on the desk.

'How could we be bothering him . . . when he's in America?'

'Councillor Sacher called me just now. She wanted to know why we're harassing Ernst Hottiger.'

'Harassing him?' Eschenbach burst out laughing. 'We checked a few details, that's it.'

'Did you speak to him in person?' asked Kobler.

'No. Someone from the information service called the deacon of the university.' Eschenbach tried in vain to recall the name of the institution. 'And they also spoke to the secretary's office. Hottiger is there, so he's not a suspect. That's it.'

'Perhaps it would be a good idea for you to call him and apologise. You know he advises the government on security matters . . . we have a good relationship with him.'

'Apologise? What the hell for?' Eschenbach raised his voice. 'For doing our job? I can't just exclude people from the investigation. I don't care whether he works for the government, whether his name's Hottiger or whether he's the Almighty himself. It's procedure for God's sake!'

'I know,' said Kobler calmly. 'I don't want to criticise your work. It'd just make me happier . . . oh, you know what I mean.'

Eschenbach took a deep breath.

'And next time, please inform me before you embark on any more risky ventures.'

'Risky ventures?' grumbled Eschenbach.

'And remember to call him, OK?'

The inspector was silent for a moment, then they said goodbye.

Eschenbach had gone through his in-tray, as well as two cigarillos. He had read the two dozen emails and replied to some. He found nothing of particular interest to the case. A confidential dossier about trained snipers, two confessions from a couple of lunatics and a press summary with all reports hitherto published about the murder. That was everything on the Bettlach case; the rest was the usual bureaucracy. Reports sent back and forth, picked up and rewritten. Papers on revisions to the law and their consequences in implementation. New contracts, resignations and transfers. A reminder that the canteen was being renovated. Various receipts. He threw them in the waste paper bin, but then fished them out and placed them right at the top of the heap of papers for Rosa Mazzoleni to deal with. She dealt with everything that the civil servants around him worried about. The whole shebang of organising paper and files and more paper. Ordering and filing. Especially the latter. She did it all with the smile of a muse and the precision of a Swiss watch. The smile might occasionally slip, but she never missed a beat.

Given the many piles of papers she had to attend to, Eschenbach wondered whether the smile would still be intact. He wanted to give her more time, so he took the smaller stack of files and looked through the sniper dossier. Hottiger could go hang.

As he had suspected, most of them were involved in the military or the police. Names, jobs and ranks were all listed. Another column displayed education and training. Courses on weapons, shooting and explosives. A bunch of specialist terms and abbre-viations. Eschenbach knew the most common ones. He marked those he didn't with a pencil. The last column was titled 'Special remarks'. Some were empty, but others provided information on special talents, possible additional training and similar.

The second list was organised less clearly and with fewer details. There was information about civilians who used weapons in their free time, about whom it was assumed that they could handle a long-distance rifle. The intel came from a mixture of official and unofficial sources. Most of them were from the Swiss Shooting Association.

Eschenbach was primarily interested in the first list. He looked at it for a long time; taking a pencil, he underlined and circled certain sections. He noted down question and exclama-tion marks, wiggly lines and small right angles. He didn't know what criteria he should be looking for. Their military division? The proximity of the military training area to the golf course? Age, marital status, children? What linked the murderer and the victim? What was the motive? Was it revenge, as Marianne Fel-ber from the *Zürcher Tagblatt* had insinuated?

'TEE TIME EXECUTION!' Felber's article was included in the press summary. Two dozen others followed, one referenc-ing the other. There was very little original content. They dis-cussed the police's ineptitude – including personal criticism of Eschenbach himself – the link to the killer in Washington, a detailed explanation of the Firearms Act in Switzerland, security on golf courses, tennis courts, football pitches. It was everything you might expect.

His favourite was the background report on the Swiss sniper scene by Hannes Kollwitz from *FOLIOS*. He seemed to know what he was talking about and it was very readable. Perhaps he would have to meet him.

Rosa Mazzoleni pre-empted him. Eschenbach had just been about to call her when he heard her voice rattling through the intercom. The inspector couldn't tell from her voice whether her smile had returned. He pressed the button. 'Claudio Jagmetti is here.'

Eschenbach stood up – and when Jagmetti walked in, he sat back down. 'Bloody hell, what happened to you? You look like you've been hit by a train!'

Jagmetti cracked a smile. His right eye was still just a slit, the skin beneath it dark red and swollen. There was a white strip of gauze stuck over his nose and a second on his bottom lip.

'It's not as bad as it looks,' he mumbled. 'My nose isn't broken, thankfully, and I only needed two stitches in my bottom lip.' He sounded plucky.

'Jesus Christ,' Eschenbach gestured to the empty chair opposite. 'Sit down and tell me what the hell happened.'

Claudio Jagmetti recounted the events of the night before at the Old Shepherd. When Eschenbach had got a handle on the situation, he ran both his hands through his hair and closed his eyes. He could smell the rain through the open window. He breathed deeply.

Rosa Mazzoleni's voice brought an end to the silence: 'Mr Bucher from FOP is on the line. Shall I put him through?'

The inspector mumbled something incomprehensible into the intercom, then picked up the receiver.

Marcel Bucher sounded unusually subdued. Was it raining in Berne too? Was the world about to end? It certainly sounded like it. If so, Eschenbach had a feeling he'd have to do some-thing to save it, so he pulled himself together. 'We were with the city squad today. Matters are well in hand. They've got things totally under control in the city . . .' Eschenbach didn't feel like his usual self. He didn't know what had got into him. Then he thought of the videos that he had given Bucher the day before. 'And how about you? Have you had the opportunity to take a look at the material?'

'Yes, that's why I'm calling.'

'And?' Eschenbach was embarrassed that he hadn't asked at the outset, when it had first occurred to him.

'Are you pulling my leg?' It sounded like an accusation.

'No, not at all. What do you mean? I hope you haven't gone to any trouble on my account . . .'

'Trouble? I haven't had any trouble. I'd have liked to have had some trouble, to be honest. There was nothing on the tapes!'

Eschenbach said nothing. He couldn't believe what he was hearing. Optical illusions existed, so why not auditory ones? Perhaps he had misunderstood or expressed himself clumsily. Or perhaps it was the line. A defect in the digital transmission of their voices. With the echo of Bucher's muffled voice still in his ear, he tried remembering exactly what he'd said.

'Are you still there?'

'Yes. Sorry, I don't quite understand what you're telling me. There's nothing on the tapes?'

'Zilch. No child porn, no normal porn, nothing. No news, no sitcoms, not even bloody *Sesame Street*. The tapes are blank.' Bucher sounded relieved to learn that he hadn't been tricked.

'Are you sure?'

'Mr Eschenbach! You don't need a degree from the Institute of Technology to see that there's nothing on the damn tapes. You could have discovered that for yourself, without my help. Anyone could have.'

'But I did—' the inspector faltered.

'You didn't watch them at all . . . is that what you're trying to tell me?'

'Yes . . . I mean, no. I couldn't bring myself to do it somehow. I'm sorry.' Eschenbach bit his bottom lip.

'You gave me tapes that you assumed had something on them, when in fact you had no idea. You couldn't have. Did no one check the tapes? None of your people?'

'I don't know.' He thought of Doris Hottiger. But she wasn't one of his people. Then he thought about the people from forensics. They must have taken a look – a random sample at least.

'But that can't be right . . . now we don't even know if there was ever anything on them. I simply don't believe it!'

Eschenbach said nothing.

'Do you have other material?'

'Yes. A computer.'

'Thank God for that. Take a look at it. Right now.'

Eschenbach hesitated.

'You can't avoid it. Believe me. In the next few months, you'll see so much of this stuff, you'll lose the will to live . . .'

'Is it that bad?'

'It depends on the kind of person you are. Sometimes I see the images in my dreams, wake up soaked in sweat. My wife says she can't take much more of it . . . she's moved into the guest bedroom. Do you have someone to help you with the PC?'

'Yes. I'll find someone.'

'Make sure you do. Give me a call if not.'

'OK.'

'And make sure you're there when it's checked. You can't trust anyone. Not even on Operation Genesis. Especially not them. You've seen the sort of people on that list. Some of them have a lot of money and influence. A great deal of money . . . and power. Keep an eye out.'

'Will do.'

'Sorry if I was a little fired up, but . . .'

'It's all right. Reckon I deserved it.'

Eschenbach hung up and looked at Jagmetti, who was sitting opposite him prodding the stitches on his lip. 'No tapes, no Hottiger . . . nothing. What a shitshow!'

Chapter 15

'That's the second time we've lost for no good reason. Didn't you see Gabriel gave away all his hearts?' Christian Pollack lit a Marlboro irritably. He was forty-eight with sparse hair and a successful law firm. But tonight he had had the extraordinary bad luck of being Eschenbach's partner. 'You haven't played this badly in ages. It's going to cost me a fortune if you carry on like this.'

Eschenbach gave up defending himself and counted his cards. He was pleased that he could manage that, at least. Sod Gabriel's hearts. He had forgotten about the three of spades too, but obviously no one had noticed. 'One hundred and three . . . and that last trick makes one hundred and eight,' he counted. 'Could have been worse.'

'Yeah, we could have been forced to play! And with those cards too . . .' said Christian, drawing nervously on his Marlboro. It wasn't the game that was making him nervous. Christian was always like this, always blowing his top. Company takeovers, mergers and all that jazz – it wasn't healthy in the long run. He was separated, his wife lived in his villa and their two children were at boarding school. Money couldn't buy you happiness, but Christian would have been even unhappier without it.

Eschenbach shuffled the cards, handed the pile to Gregor, who dealt them, and they started again.

Gregor Allensbach was the exact opposite of Christian Pollack. He was small, almost stocky. His full beard was a hangover from '68 and he smoked a pipe because tendonitis had left him incapable of rolling roll-ups. He was the epitome of warmth.

The three of them knew each other from their time at Gottfried Keller Grammar in Zurich. The Three Musketeers – all for one and one for all. Whatever the subject, be it maths, geography or Latin, one of them had been good at it. The others had copied from him or muddled through.

Gregor was still at the grammar school. Now, it was his students who muddled through and he was supposed to punish them for it – something he rarely did. Cheating was a matter of character, he felt, and those who didn't learn had themselves to blame. When it came to cards, Christian had a watchful eye and Gregor stuck mostly to his principles where cheating was concerned.

Twice a month they would play cards at the Sheep's Head, where Gabriel worked. Christian knew him from the army; he had been the chef in his company.

Ten years ago, when they had started meeting and playing cards, the Sheep's Head in the Seefeld district of Zurich had been a pub. It had wooden tables and wooden floors. The food fit the setting: plain and simple fare. It had the best *rösti* and the best veal stew in Zurich. Delicious tripe and a legendary dish of sheep's head – which was actually a calf's head – which you had to pre-order.

Over the years, both food and customers had improved. There were white tablecloths and cloth napkins; silverware and crystal carafes. The best wines found their way into the cellar and the restaurant was showered with awards and praise. It scored seventeen out of twenty in *Gault-Millau* and won a Michelin star.

It would have scored even higher if someone had thought to get rid of the rough wooden table inlayed with a large piece of slate, which stood in a cosy corner in the back of the restaurant, together with the four illustrious men who played cards at this very table at least twice a month.

Gabriel didn't give a toss, he said. Points or no points. Who knew what tomorrow would bring? And if it all came crashing down, the Michelin stars and the awards, then at least he'd still have his friends. Friends were a constant. Just like the table with its slate top, where they would note down the score in chalk.

Eschenbach went on playing as badly as he had begun. Christian smoked his Marlboros and tried to save something that was past saving. These carefree evenings did them all good. They chatted freely and could talk about anything.

Gabriel sliced up dried meats and Salsiz sausage and, at around eleven when most of the diners had left, he made a *rösti* with fried eggs – just like he used to, back when all the tables had looked like their rough wooden one.

Eschenbach had politely declined Christian's offer to drive him home. It wasn't raining any more, and the short walk would do him good. After Bellevue, he followed the Limmatquai as far as Muenster Bridge. He resisted the urge to make a detour to Niederdorf. It was half one and would not end well. Plus, he had completely forgotten to call Corina.

He listened to the message on his phone. She sounded tetchy; she said something about storms and blue skies, that her muscles ached from riding her bike and that Kathrin was in the grip of disco fever.

As he pulled the heavy front door closed behind him and climbed the wooden steps up to their flat, he accepted the fact that all of the clues that might have pointed to Bettlach's paedophilic tendencies or activities had been completely wiped out.

After the call from Bucher, he had phoned the head of forensics. They had checked the videos, he assured him. But they hadn't found anything. They had also checked the PC and found nothing suspicious. Eschenbach hadn't wanted to believe it and had deployed one of the specialists from IT to carry out an inspection of Philipp Bettlach's PC with him. It was as empty as an ice hockey arena in summertime. Someone must have switched the hard drive.

The specialist from IT said that data was never fully erased. 'We can usually find deleted data,' he had said. 'But someone has replaced the hard drive.' The man put on his specialist's smile.

Eschenbach fell into a fitful sleep. He dreamt of huge computer processors crushing one of the towers of Zurich Cathedral to dust, as if by magic, and filling the lake with cured meat. Hundreds of PCs were lined up in front of the orphanage, demanding their data back. Rain washed videotapes along the gutters, down the drains into a dark abyss.

At half five he woke up bathed in sweat and, after trying and failing to get back to sleep, he took the newspaper out of the letterbox and ran himself a bath.

Chapter 16

The Grossmünster church was packed out. The organ droned through the nave and echoed off the walls and high windows. The chords blasting from the organ's great pipes came together in a melancholy chorus.

The people sat reverently in the pews dressed mostly in black. They lowered their heads and clasped their hands. Some seemed to be sleeping and others weren't far off it.

The funeral was due to begin at ten o'clock.

Eschenbach was sitting in one of the back rows. This allowed him an undisturbed view of what was happening, while enabling him to observe the people who had known Philipp Bettlach.

Dr Bettlach's silver mane gleamed from the first row, and his secretary sat next to him. Eschenbach recognised her by her profile: sharp features with high cheekbones. Aside from the two of them there was no one in the first row, typically reserved for family members. It occurred to Eschenbach that he knew nothing about the family: either there weren't any, or they were absent for some reason.

A woman with a face like a barrel sat next to the inspector. Everything was black apart from her pale, almost translucent skin – she was dressed all in black – hair, mascara, lip gloss and nail polish included. Her pudgy hands lay one on top of the other on her legs, which were clad in black corduroy.

The president of the local Lions Club delivered a pompous speech.

Eschenbach gave his neighbour a smile, which she promptly returned, chin rolls trembling.

'Were you a friend of Philipp's?' The woman's flawless white teeth irritated Eschenbach. It occurred to him that if a person had pale skin, their teeth often looked yellowish. Hers sparkled like porcelain.

'I'm a police officer. I'm investigating the case . . . so I'm here in an official capacity, really.'

'Ah.' She rolled her eyes in acknowledgement.

'How about you? How did you know Philipp?'

'I'm a childhood friend,' she said smiling. 'I've known him since we were at boarding school together.'

'At Zuoz?' asked Eschenbach. Christian had told him about it. It was the only boarding school he knew by name.

'No, Raschnitz. Were you at Zuoz?'

'No. I went to school in Zurich.'

'Oh, it's a lovely city. I would have liked to go to school there. My parents died young and my uncle, who I grew up with, only wanted the best for me. I would have liked a home to call my own. But you can't choose these things.'

'Do you know anything about Philipp's family?' asked Eschenbach.

'He never mentioned his father, and his mother died a few years ago, as far as I know.'

'Anything else? Siblings, spouses, relatives?'

She pulled a smirk that rippled down her face, stopping at her surprisingly tight cleavage. 'Look,' she whispered, inclining her head forward. 'The one with the silver hair over there . . . that's his elder brother.'

He nodded. 'And his wife, I mean, his ex-wife . . . is she here?'

'I haven't seen her . . . I would be surprised if she were.'

'Why?' asked Eschenbach.

'It's not a happy story.' She raised her eyebrows. 'Most partners eventually make their peace. They meet up, talk about this and that and realise that they didn't speak to one another enough. And they often find that they understand one another better . . . than when they were living together.'

Eschenbach nodded. He knew what his companion was talking about. 'But that wasn't true of Bettlach and his wife?'

'No. It was a very sudden split – completely out of the blue. She moved out – and on – overnight. They never spoke to one another again afterwards, never met up. When it came to the matter of dividing their assets, her solicitor stood in for her. I think she lives in Paris now.'

'Do you know what name she goes by these days?'

'Marchand. Eveline Marchand. She went back to using her maiden name.'

Info Services had already told Eschenbach that her maiden name was Marchand; it was easy to assume she had started a new life somewhere under this name. But where? If it was Paris, that explained why the search had been unsuccessful thus far. It would take a while to find someone with a common French name in a huge metropolis like Paris. 'You seem to know a lot about his family relationships for someone who claims to be a childhood friend,' he said with a wink.

'Oh well, you see . . .' She didn't wink, but rolled her eyes again. 'Philipp would often ring me. Whenever he needed something or wanted to vent. I was a bit like a refuse bin for him. Maybe it's something about me.' She pointed her chin resignedly. It wobbled ominously. 'We all have our cross to bear.'

For a moment, Eschenbach wasn't sure he had understood. 'What was Philipp Bettlach's cross?'

At that moment, a woman turned to him from the pew in front. She shot him a contemptuous look, twinkling in her diamanté necklace and hissed an angry *Shhh* through false teeth, shaking her head unsympathetically.

'I have to leave as soon as the funeral's over,' the woman next to him whispered, leaning towards him at an alarming angle. Eschenbach felt her breath on his ear and smelt the musk of her heavy perfume. 'But do call me.' She held out a business card, which was jammed between her fingers. It read: 'Dr Rania Oberholzer, Lecturer in Periodontics & Bridge Restoration, Institute of Dentistry, University of Berne'.

He thanked her and assured her that he would call.

The tennis club was followed by the yacht club and, later, the golf club. Eschenbach couldn't shake the suspicion that the clubs had pre-written speeches for occasions such as these, which they embellished with personal details about the deceased.

A striking number of pretty young women were sitting in the middle and back pews. He couldn't see Doris Hottiger anywhere.

When Eschenbach left Grossmünster church and walked outside, a woman was suddenly standing in front of him, an old brown leather file under her arm.

Not the bloody press, he thought fleetingly. He had no desire to talk to a hack.

'Marianne Felber,' she said pleasantly, brushing a strand of chestnut-brown hair behind her ear. 'I write for the *Zürcher Tagblatt.*'

'I know,' growled Eschenbach. 'Tee time execution.' He raised his eyebrows. 'Are you new?'

'Why do you ask?' replied the journalist, irritated.

'Just because . . . The press conference was the first time I'd seen you.'

'Oh, right. I thought—'

'I don't have time now,' he interrupted her sullenly.

A young man in faded jeans and a black T-shirt was taking photos.

'Just for one minute.' The journalist was smiling keenly.

Eschenbach felt inside his jacket for a business card. 'Come to headquarters in the morning.'

'OK, but only if I get two minutes.'

'Fine by me.'

Marianne Felber eyed the small, greyish piece of paper bearing the Zurich crest and Eschenbach's address. 'You're a doctor?' she asked, surprised.

'I studied law,' he said casually. 'It comes in handy sometimes.'

'Then why are you a police officer and not a judge?'

The inspector paused for a moment, then said politely, 'I really must go now . . . see you tomorrow.'

'Promise?' The journalist winked at him.

'Promise. And give me a call before you come. You've got my number.'

'OK, will do.'

Chapter 17

The wake was held in the great hall of the Rüden guild house, just a stone's throw from the Grossmünster.

The brief conversation Eschenbach managed to snatch with Johannes Bettlach on the way to the guild house yielded nothing. The questions as to whether his brother had been undergoing psychiatric treatment, and whether anything had occurred to him since their previous meeting, were met with an apathetic shake of the head. He wasn't interested in where Eveline Marchand was living. It was the arrogance of a powerful old man, on whom the questions broke like soap bubbles against a wall.

It was no use – not now, he thought, as he took his leave before they reached the entrance on Limmatquai.

Lost in thought, Eschenbach strolled the few steps to Münsterbrücke and crossed the Limmat. Then he walked up Storchengasse on the shady side, towards Paradeplatz, through Waaggasse to the Zeughauskeller. He loved this restaurant, its traditional home cooking and its rustic décor. Most of the guests were sitting outside in the street at wooden tables in the shade of huge umbrellas. Inside, it was pleasantly cool and Eschenbach managed to find himself a table.

He ordered a large beer and the special for lunch. While he waited for the food to arrive, he doodled a stick man on a beer mat and thought about the case. The shadows in the dead man's past had dwindled to nothing and any traces of wrongdoing had been washed away. So why did he still believe the story? Why was he so certain that Doris Hottiger wasn't just pulling his leg? Why was he so sure, when she remained the only person to have seen the tapes and the images?

The tapes he had given to Bucher were all brand new. This had been made thoroughly clear to him, until he felt like a trainee himself. So why hadn't he noticed when he received the tapes? It was simple: they hadn't looked new at all; they came in cardboard cases, without the usual cellophane wrapper.

Six unwrapped, blank video cassettes – it just didn't make sense. It was obvious that someone had switched them.

The PC told the same story. It had a brand new hard drive. Programs, data – all gone. It was impossible not to see how staged it all was. It could have been done so much more successfully. Why hadn't they simply switched the child porn tapes for bog-standard sex videos? Since Beate Uhse had opened her first sex shop, they had been part of every Swiss household, like tinned ravioli or bottle openers. They would barely have noticed.

Why hadn't they simply wiped the sensitive data from the PC and left the rest behind? These days, even new PCs came pre-installed with operating systems and a plethora of programs, images and data. A blank hard drive screamed that it had been tampered with.

The longer he thought about it, the clearer it seemed to him that this was more than just a shoddy attempt to cover up the evidence. It was a message left for him, and whoever had left it wanted Philipp Bettlach to go to his grave without a scandal, to rest in peace with his honour intact.

The landlord, Heinz, a small man with little, lively eyes and a moustache like a walrus, came to Eschenbach's table with two cups of espresso and a bottle of grappa.

'Crap day, eh?'

'Not too bad. It'll be much better after your ham hock.'

'My brother-in-law's taken up golf, you know. At a Migros golf course. Did you know that they do golf courses now?'

'No, but it doesn't surprise me. Corina did a yoga course with them once, and t'ai chi – and a computer course, come to think of it.'

'They do everything. They've got restaurants and wellness centres too. Not too bad for a supermarket. I told him I don't mind if he plays golf at Migros, as long as he eats here.'

'Better than the other way around.'

The small man laughed and blew through his nose, which was about two sizes too big for his face.

There was another round of grappa.

'I've been thinking about whether I should take it up.'

Eschenbach wondered whether he meant grappa or golf.

'But if people are getting shot on the courses, then it's probably too dangerous for me.' His nose hair rustled again. 'I think I'd be happier down here in my bunker.'

'Have people been talking about the murder? You get a lot of bankers in here.'

'It's the usual rumours, nothing more. Most of them head for the beer gardens at the moment. It's crap weather for summer.' He waved the waitress over and ordered another two cups of espresso.

'What do you mean, rumours?'

'Just that he wasn't a nice guy. A phoney. His brother owned the bank and pulled the strings. He got piles of money but no real say in running it. He was abroad a lot, and when he was here he would just hang around, playing golf or screwing girls.'

'Young or old?'

'How should I know? I wasn't there.'

The espresso arrived and Eschenbach went to pay.

'Leave it. The police are my friends.'

'It's out of the question.' Eschenbach insisted, and they agreed that he could pay for the meal.

'Then at least have another grappa.'

'Another time, thanks.' He held his hand over his glass, warning him off. Disappointed, the landlord pushed the cork back into the bottle.

'This thing about the girls ... Do you know someone who ... was there?' Eschenbach rounded the total up and placed the money on the small tin plate that held the bill.

'Just rumours.' The landlord shook his head and sucked a couple of drops of grappa from his moustache. 'But I can keep an ear out, if you like.'

'Only if something comes up. Don't go playing the detective.'

'I've got it. Delicate situation, eh?'

Eschenbach raised his eyebrows meaningfully and said nothing more. They said goodbye with a hearty handshake. It had just occurred to him that the restaurant was half empty.

The sun blinded him as he walked out. Summer was back, and people were sitting out on the overgrown terrace of the Mexican restaurant at the end of the street.

He noticed straight away that Rosa Mazzoleni was smiling again. It's rare, he thought, to be so struck by something you usually take for granted.

'You'll have an espresso, I expect?'

He wanted to say no, but he realised that it wasn't a question. It was a command.

'What makes you think that?' Something seemed to have changed. What, he didn't know.

'We've got a new machine!'

'Why did we need a new machine?' he asked, surprised.

'A coffee machine! I mean, it's actually an espresso machine.'

'What's wrong with the old one?'

'They took it away. Someone spent half of yesterday poking about with it. He was at a complete loss. Stood there with his phone in one hand and a screwdriver in the other. Can you imagine?'

Eschenbach shook his head and laughed.

'But he spent more time on the phone than fixing anything. All in Italian. In the end, he just took it away. There was nothing else he could do. *Completamente distrutto*, he said. Now we've got a new one.'

'How much did it cost?'

'Have a guess.'

Eschenbach was not keen on guessing. The radio and TV channels were filled with these kinds of quizzes. He had no time for these games, which had made a comeback recently. He found it ridiculous that people were once again playing the lottery under the guise of 'education'. Corina thought it had something to do with his job. Perhaps she was right.

'I'll give you a choice.' Ms Mazzoleni was sticking to her guns. 'A: 100 francs. B: 200 francs. C: 500 francs, or D: nothing.'

'Was the coffee included?'

She thought for a moment and then said, 'No.'

'Can I phone a friend?'

'No,' came her swift reply. 'No lifelines either.'

'What brand?'

'Come on, it's just a game. A, B, C or D?'

'Tell me the brand and then I'll give you my answer.'

'Lavazza,' she said reluctantly.

'Then it's D. And if the coffee was included, C. At least,' said Eschenbach.

'D is correct, C is wrong.' Rosa Mazzoleni had taken off her glasses which were now dangling over her bosom from a gold chain. She was playing the presenter of a well-known game show, gesticulating, concentration settling on her round face, as if there were half a million euros to play for. 'How did you get C?' She seemed disappointed by his answer.

'Because coffee's bloody expensive,' said Eschenbach, grinning widely.

'But I clearly said it didn't include the coffee.'

'And I clearly said D. What do I win?'

'A cup of espresso, of course.' She giggled at her own joke.

'Is that it?'

'It's a decent prize. You said it yourself, coffee's bloody expensive.' With a last bat of her lashes, she disappeared in the direction of the kitchenette and the new machine.

Eschenbach went into his office and listened to the distant rattle of crockery, followed by a clicking noise and a long, sonorous hum.

On the desk sat at least a dozen phone messages. Ms Mazzoleni had organised the pre-printed slips – provided by the administration in ugly exhaust-fume grey blocks – in rows of four on his desk, at right angles. It reminded him of the game 'Memory' that he and Kathrin would play together when she was a child. For now, *Big Brother* and pre-prime time series held all the cards, as far as Kathrin was concerned. And Eschenbach's experience with cards was limited to the evenings he spent with his friends at the Sheep's Head.

Ms Mazzoleni brought the coffee in a cone-shaped cup with a matching saucer, sugar bowl and cream jug. A small bowl of amaretti sat on the chrome tray that she placed on the table. The flawless white porcelain reminded him of Dr Oberholzer's teeth.

'It's all new,' said Ms Mazzoleni and, before he could say anything, added: 'I'll take the cream and the sugar bowl back. I know you drink it black . . . but it looks so much prettier this way.' She beamed as brightly as the crockery itself.

'Can we even afford these kinds of things at headquarters?'

'Have a guess . . .'

'Not again!'

She insisted.

'Well, since you're so keen to ask, then D . . . I assume this didn't cost anything either.'

'Correct.' She was back in the role of presenter.

'And of course, you've also won free entry into a prize draw for a washing machine.'

She had to laugh.

'Let's hope the Lavazza fairy buys all our coffee in the future, then.'

'Italians are just very generous . . . that's all.'

Mazzoleni's honest, airy tone embodied everything that made Italy so wonderful and everything that made the espresso in front of him so irresistible. They left it at that.

Thanks to Rosa Mazzoleni's obsession with order, Eschenbach had an immediate overview of who had called in his absence. He was quite convinced that his secretary had very consciously organised the messages in a particular way. The first message – top left – was from Elisabeth Kobler, then his wife, followed by two colleagues. He piled up the messages in the bottom row and chucked them in the bin. Rosa Mazzoleni's order of priorities seemed largely identical to his, though he would have swapped Kobler for Corina. But here, understandably, their opinions differed.

In the middle row, he found Marianne Felber from the *Zürcher Tagblatt* and a few names which were either new or unfamiliar to Mazzoleni. One name stood out to him: Eveline Marchand and, beneath it, a Paris number.

Chapter 18

He very nearly missed the 18.30 train from Basle to Paris.

Leaving the hustle and bustle of Basle station behind him, he walked towards the platforms serving trains bound for France. The mix of hellos and adieus that reigned on the Swiss side seemed suddenly washed away.

His footsteps echoed emptily off the unadorned walls as he approached the customs officers who were talking to a dark-haired girl and gesticulating wildly. Eschenbach waited. He looked at the clock on the wall next to the customs office. He had three minutes.

He didn't understand why two customs officers were required for just one girl. There was clearly a language issue. She was speaking broken English, the customs officers broken French. If neither of them can speak English, then it's no help there being two of them, thought Eschenbach. The girl was anxiously finger-ing her braids, which stood out from her head in all directions like a Christmas wreath. If he understood correctly, the conver-sation had something to do with an address in Mulhouse where her sister lived, or worked, or both.

Eschenbach would have liked to help, but he doubted his rusty high school French would do much to improve the girl's situation. The inspector didn't know how far he had to walk to his platform, where the train stood waiting to depart. It was over ten years since he had last taken the train to Paris.

Trains don't wait, not even French ones, he thought. When he realised that the customs officers had no intention of splitting up and dealing with the task at hand, he strode purposefully past them. His pace quickened and he began to run. If he missed his train, he would have to take the night train and he wouldn't arrive in Paris Gare de L'Est until the following morning. He had no desire to spend the whole night in a French railway carriage. As he ran, he prepared himself to have to stop and turn around. It was an unusual feeling, having customs officers on his tail. He wondered whether to look behind him, but decided against it; he concentrated on what he could hear. A call perhaps, or a whistle. The thought of a warning shot crossed his mind.

Even once he had turned left at the end of the corridor and disappeared out of sight. It was just the echo of his pounding footsteps, nothing more. His travel bag, into which he had packed the essentials for a night's stay, was jammed under his right arm to keep it from banging against his hip as he ran.

The shrill sound of a whistle split the quiet evening air and Eschenbach was rooted to the spot. It took a moment for him to realise that the station master had blown the whistle. He was a small man with a red hat and a red shoulder strap with a red bag. Just what he had imagined a stationmaster would look like when he was a child. He winked at him energetically and shouted, 'Venez, venez!' Then he waved his arms to indicate that he should keep running and board the train.

Once Eschenbach had pulled himself up the two steps into the carriage in a single movement, the guard shut the door, gave two short blasts on his whistle and waved the train on. Shortly afterwards, the train moved off with a powerful jerk.

He managed to find his compartment. They were all empty except for two. Eschenbach chose a smoker-friendly compartment, sat next to the window, took off his shoes and stretched his legs out on the turquoise seat with a sigh of relief.

The inspector was soaked through. His escape from the French customs post, which hadn't really been anything of the sort, the muggy summer evening, the railway guard's whistle – it had all worn him out. Perhaps it was his age, he thought. Maybe a younger police officer would have simply shrugged it off.

His eyebrow twitched. Just a glitch in the autonomic nervous system, he thought. Like a chicken that flies a few metres once its head has been cut off. He had seen it happen once, on a farm as a child. It had stayed with him for a long time, the image of the chicken, flying away without its head. It was unreal somehow, that life could be composed of mere mechanics. He wondered how long he had left, whether he might have a heart attack right now. Would he make it to Paris? His temples were throbbing.

Out of his luggage, he took the white T-shirt he had brought to wear in bed and mopped his face and neck. It smelt of the fabric conditioner that Corina had started using recently. Kathrin had insisted that the old one was too floral. It smelt like old ladies, she said. She wanted something subtle, not too sweet, or maybe a mixture of the two. Eschenbach sniffed the material and found the scent neither subtle nor lacking in sweetness: it smelt like violets – or was it roses? Now that it had absorbed his sweat mixed with traces of his cologne, it was something else altogether. Not subtle, but certainly not sweet.

Realising how much he was missing the two women in his life, he took his phone out of his pocket and brought up the number for the house in Engadine. Eschenbach was caught out by an automated message in French. He hadn't added the code for Switzerland and it occurred to him how infrequently he had to travel abroad for work. He had actually needed written permission from Kobler to make this trip to Paris.

Transnational investigations were a different beast. But since he was only accepting an invitation, he could hardly call his trip to Paris an investigation. He didn't have his badge with him or much in the way of identification. Not to mention his gun. It was still with Büchsenmacher and because he never carried it with him, it usually stayed there until the next mandatory shooting test.

When he dialled the Engadine number again – this time with the code for Switzerland – it was engaged. Was it Corina or Kathrin? Whoever it was, she would be some time. He put his phone to one side and rifled through a pile of papers and magazines from his bag. He had stocked up in Zurich and enjoyed rummaging lazily through the day's press, puffing away on his bent cigarillos.

He thought about the telephone call he had made to Eveline Marchand that afternoon. She had a light, clear voice often found in classically trained singers, typically sopranos. He didn't know what her job was, but from her voice he found it easy to imagine that she sang. Either professionally, or privately in a choir. Bach cantatas or Handel's Requiem cried out for those kinds of voices. He told her that he had been at her husband's funeral that morning. She corrected him politely: 'ex-husband'. She had heard from her brother-in-law that he was leading the investigation and had been told he was 'a very nice man'. Eschenbach wondered why she said brother-in-law and not ex-brother-in-law. Perhaps husbands and brothers-in-law didn't follow the same rules.

She would be happy to talk to him about a few matters concerning her ex-husband, she said. The time had come, now that he was dead. Not on the phone, she said, but in person. And since she was loath to leave Paris, she was grateful that he would be visiting.

Although she spoke Swiss German with no accent, there was something alluring about her voice. Perhaps it was something in her tone, her intonation, the way she modulated her sentences, or in the subtlety of her words. Perhaps he was missing the city on the Seine which he had long wanted to return to.

His phone chirped. He saw the number on the display, the number which had been engaged forty-five minutes before.

'You must have tried a few times.' It was Corina, and Eschenbach noticed that there was something alluring about her voice too.

'You'll never believe where I am.'

'Where?'

'Have a guess.'

'It's eight o'clock . . .' She thought for a moment. 'Then you're either still at the office or with Gabriel at the Sheep's Head.'

'I was with Gabriel yesterday. Shall I give you some clues?'

'Please tell me you're not into these stupid quizzes too. Not after you got all worked up about people "playing the lottery"—'

'Under the guise of education, yes. I thought you liked those quizzes.'

'Not really.'

'But?'

'But nothing. I watch them sometimes. That's it. And why not? Kathrin likes them. I'd rather she watched that rubbish than crap like *Big Brother*. So, tell me. There's something rattling in the background. Are you on a train?'

The guard had pulled the door of the compartment open with a jerk and almost lost his balance as the train took a bend.

'I've just got to . . .' Eschenbach felt for his travel bag. 'I'll call you back.'

Corina's protestations echoed unheard on the line and Eschenbach fished out the tickets that he had stowed in the outer pocket.

'New York, Paris, Hong Kong or Tokyo,' he said when they resumed their conversation.

'Oh, don't tell me you're going to Paris! I thought we were going to go back together . . .'

'And we will, I promise. How did you guess?' He could tell she was disappointed.

They had spent their honeymoon getting to know Paris together. Hanging out in bistros and bars until the small hours, living off baguettes, *vin rouge* and love. Instead of queuing out-side the Louvre with thousands of tourists, they browsed little antique shops and visited the galleries around the museum. The old Breuer chair that they bought at the flea market by Porte de Clignancourt for the impressive sum of 150 francs now stood in their kitchen, next to the wine rack. The wicker seat began to sag as the years passed, and when both of them were concerned that it would break, they decided to use the chair to store news-papers. They were both superstitious and viewed the continued existence of the wicker seat as a symbol of the strength of their relationship and made sure that the chair was spared heavier burdens.

Chapter 19

'You have to look at people very carefully, Jagmetti, especially their alibis,' his boss had said, pressing the list of snipers into his hands.

The young police officer had been counting on having two hours to check each military base, as well as people being available when he arrived. He was woefully mistaken on both counts.

The military training area in Näfels was number four. He had spent the two previous days in Landquart, Arth Goldau and Mollis.

The barracks were deserted and it took more than half an hour for him to find the sergeant, who was playing cards with three NCOs in the Lion.

'Bad luck, they're all out on an exercise. They won't be back until tomorrow evening.'

The NCOs confirmed this with a nod and seemed pleased not to be taking part in the exercise.

'Could you at least call Captain . . .' – Jagmetti had to check the list – '. . . Meierhofer?'

'That'll be a challenge.' The sergeant sucked air through his teeth and made a grim face. 'They're shooting somewhere in the mountains. It'll be hard to get hold of them.'

'Is there a mobile number I could have? There must be some way of reaching them.'

'Mobiles aren't allowed.' It was a swift reply and the NCOs nodded in agreement. 'At least in theory,' added the sergeant, taking a sip from his beer glass.

Jagmetti looked down at the table in disbelief where, alongside a slate tablet, a piece of chalk and several bottles of beer, there were four mobile phones.

Noticing Jagmetti's surprise, the sergeant added, 'You're only allowed to use them during leisure time. Then you can do what you like.' This seemed in large part to include drinking beer and gambling.

'And what about in the mountains . . . I mean, during exercises. Do you have leisure time then?'

'No idea. I'm only responsible for internal procedure. Up to and including barracks. When they're away, it's up to the commanding officer. And that remains the case until tomorrow evening at eight.'

'And what the hell is the procedure if something happens?' Jagmetti was growing impatient. 'If you need to get hold of someone urgently . . .' He hesitated for a moment. Then he continued loudly and clearly in the same tone. 'A death in the family, for example?'

The NCO who was in the process of dealing the cards paused and the sergeant looked at him.

'That would be classed as an emergency. You could have said so straight away.'

'But I didn't know if there were special regulations in place . . . what happens now?'

'The emergency number's in my office.' The sergeant wiped the foam from his top lip using his field-grey sleeve and went to stand up; then he changed his mind. He shouted across the restaurant to a soldier who was sitting alone at a corner table on the telephone. 'That's Koni, the office orderly. He'll run and get the number for you.' When the man in question showed no sign of moving, the sergeant stood up, pulled his tongue and his lips into a vulgar grimace and let loose a piercing whistle. 'Oi, Koni! Over here!'

The office orderly, a lanky chap in his mid-thirties with blond hair held together by a hairnet like a ball of pressed straw, looked alarmed and ended his phone call without another word. If he hadn't been caught between the wooden bench and the table, he would have shot up, clicked his heels and stood to attention. He squeezed himself out of his corner, hurried to take the felted top part of his uniform and his belt off the bench and made his way to the table where his superior was playing cards.

'Run and get the emergency number from the CO's room,' grumbled the sergeant, who had sat back down and was arranging by colour the cards which he had fanned out in his left hand.

'I'll go with him,' said Jagmetti, and took his leave of the soldiers, remembering his own time in military service. He didn't want to spend a minute more than was necessary in such miserable surroundings.

Without a word, the office orderly and Jagmetti crossed the barracks and made for the main building. It was a factory-like, flat-roofed construction which looked as if someone had thrown down a concrete shoebox and simply left it there. The wide steps that led to the entrance had been renovated in places. Specks of render shimmered in different shades of grey, looking like over-sized pieces of chewing gum rolled flat.

The glass double doors separated the complex into two equal halves. On the left and on the right, tiny windows ran in two parallel rows to the end of the front façade.

The CO's office was situated on the left side of the building. It was smaller than Jagmetti would have imagined. Four wooden desks, which had seen better days as school desks, stood pushed together in the middle of the room. A few chairs stood around. In the corner were stacks of military boxes with office materials, and on a folding table by the wall stood a fax machine and a photocopier.

A map of the region and various operational plans were attached to the wall with drawing pins. Next to this was a magnetic whiteboard bearing colourful magnets and sheets of white A4.

The emergency number was in the left-hand corner and read 'Instructions for Emergencies'. Next to and underneath this were additional notes: 'Daily Instructions', 'ABC Protection Instructions', 'Uniform Instructions', 'Discharge Instructions'. One slip simply read 'Menu'. Jagmetti wondered whether it should have read 'Menu Instructions'. He noted down the number to contact the commander 'in case of emergency' and stuck the slip of paper back on the wall.

'I brought these from home.' The office orderly, who had hitherto not spoken, pointed to the left at the magnetic buttons which looked out of the white wall like huge, round eyes in bright red, yellow, blue and purple. 'Brings a bit of colour to this gloomy den,' he said. His shy smile revealed a golden canine which stood out clearly against his brown teeth. 'I'm always breaking my nails on the drawing pins.'

'Do you play guitar?' asked Jagmetti, who had noticed the long fingernails on his right hand when he closed the office door.

'Finally, someone's noticed!' The office orderly clicked his tongue in appreciation. 'The guys here have no idea ... You wouldn't believe what a fuss it causes every time someone sees them. Just because I won't cut them.'

'What's it like these days?' asked Jagmetti, surprised to be learning about military discipline and nail care.

'When I refused, they told me I should make a fist when the colonel comes.' He made a fist with his right hand and shook his head. 'I've nothing against the colonel.'

'Why are you here anyway?' asked Jagmetti. 'You could play in the military band ... they need guitarists. Big bands are all the rage now.'

'I won't play military stuff.'

'Oh.' Jagmetti smirked. 'Are you a pacifist?'

'No, I'm a musician!'

'What do you play, then, if you don't mind me asking?' This time, Jagmetti was unable to stop himself laughing.

'I like jazz best. But you can't make a living from it. At least, not a good one. So I do whatever comes my way. Mostly studio recordings. Touring's too stressful.'

'Studio recordings?' asked Jagmetti, who couldn't imagine that Gold Tooth had ever seen the inside of the seediest recording studio, let alone been on tour.

'Before I was enlisted, we recorded the new Phil Collins CD in London.'

'You mean, *the* Phil Collins?' Jagmetti looked at him, disbelieving.

'Do you think I'd make such a fuss about my fingernails just to strum out a bit of Dylan for some mates? That's what you thought, wasn't it?' The office orderly looked visibly disappointed.

'To be honest . . . yes, I did.'

'I thought so.' He bit his bottom lip. 'That's the problem. That's what everyone here thinks.'

'Does it surprise you?' asked Jagmetti who didn't really know what to make of it all.

Chapter 20

Eschenbach slept like a log.

When he awoke that morning at half six to the sound of car engines, he couldn't remember where he was at first. Traffic sounds the same everywhere, he thought.

The little hotel that Rosa Mazzoleni had found for him lay on the Rue de Lille, a few blocks from the Seine. She had found it in *Charming Parisian Hotels*. She owned similar guides on London, Brussels, Munich, Venice and a dozen other cities. Ms Mazzoleni had printed off for him a review of the hotel, a site plan and a price list that she found online. And she didn't forget to point out that Eschenbach absolutely must visit the Louvre or the Musée d'Orsay – only if he found the time, of course – both were just a stone's throw from the hotel.

When it came to foreign cities and foreign lands, monuments, museums and churches, Rosa Mazzoleni was unstoppable. She was at home abroad. She travelled whenever she found the time, and were he less selfish, Eschenbach would have told her to open her own travel agency long ago. Rosa would have found plenty of business at headquarters, and plenty more in the city administration once word got about, certainly enough to run a successful agency. But he needed her. And because he knew that she only stayed for his sake, he accepted that people would call almost every day asking for her advice. She knew who was going on holiday and where, which hotels the mayor had stayed in, if he was spending time in Brussels, Paris or London on business or for pleasure. She knew the inns where her inspectors ate when they spent the weekend abroad. They were, after all, her recommendations; and it was increasingly the case that she organised the trips herself. It was a part of her job that she rarely talked about. She did so discreetly, without a fuss, without it affecting her regular work. She would not accept money, Eschenbach knew this, just a bunch of flowers now and then – and postcards, of course! They were everywhere: on the fridge in the kitchen, on the doors and cupboards. She had even stuck some on her computer. It was a mosaic of colourful landmarks. And sometimes, when grey mountains of files threatened to engulf her, Rosa Mazzoleni would escape somewhere; she would go to listen to the sound of the sea or the bells of Notre Dame.

Eschenbach decided to take a short morning walk. He showered, pulled on the fresh white shirt that he had brought in his travel bag and left the hotel shortly after seven. The morning sunlight covered the sandstone façades opposite in a radiant ochre yellow. It was very quiet at this time of day. Just a few cars sounding their horns when a wide waste collection lorry got in their way. The men, dressed in dark-blue trousers and sleeveless white tops, would not be kept from their work. With a mighty noise they docked a metal container onto a hoisting crane and tipped its contents into the jaws of the lorry. A steel rake squashed the rubbish down until it disappeared inside the vehicle. A couple of bags that lay on the side of the road were picked up and swung into the moving vehicle in a high arc with the ease of a child tugging at a balloon.

Eschenbach turned into Rue des Saints-Pères and took the few short steps down to the Seine. It flowed past him in a stream of velveteen purple. On Quai Voltaire, he stood for a moment enjoying the view of the Pont Royal, before striding across to the other side of the Seine with his short but powerful legs. He had read somewhere that there had once been a wooden bridge which allowed the aristocracy the shortest possible path to the opposite bank. He decided the revolutionaries must have had a point. On the bridge, he paused again and took in the light-soaked beauty of the city around him. He dismissed the idea of perhaps lingering a day longer before he had even finished thinking it.

On the way back to the hotel, he stopped off in a small bistro. The wicker chairs reminded him of the Breuer chair that he and Corina had bought at the *marché aux puces*. He flicked through a French newspaper and washed down his three croissants with a pot of *café au lait*.

The woman in her late forties who opened the door to Eschenbach was completely different from what he had expected. She was small and dainty, with a well-proportioned, almost doll-like face and dark, fashionably dishevelled shoulder-length hair.

'So glad you were able to come, Inspector.' Her happiness seemed natural and the charm that her voice had hinted at on the telephone was confirmed in her eyes and the way that she smiled.

'The pleasure's all mine,' said Eschenbach, trying to reflect the warmth that radiated from her.

It was a large, spacious apartment on the first floor of a grand building on Rue Gay-Lussac. The wooden flooring creaked under the inspector's heavy steps. He was fascinated by the artwork beneath his feet. The wood panelling and inlays meshed together to create a unique, magnificent mosaic.

'Wonderful,' he said. 'You don't get floors like these nowadays.'

'It's a shame.' She smiled bashfully.

He nodded and wondered whether he should take off his shoes. Then he saw that she wasn't wearing slippers either.

She led him into the living room. Long curtains of beige brocade silk hung down to the floor, giving the space an aristocratic air. The furniture in no way detracted from the grandness of the space and provided a fresh take on the past three centuries: Louis IV to VI, Chippendale, rococo, an art nouveau lamp, a bureau from the turn of the century and a few classic modern pieces.

The armchair she offered him was much more comfortable than it looked. Surprising, he thought; usually, the opposite was true.

'It's a prototype by Philippe Starck,' she said. 'Unfortunately it turned out to be a faulty design. Wrong angles, wrong material. All wrong.'

'Perhaps that's why it's so comfortable,' said Eschenbach, and they both laughed.

'But I'm sure you didn't come all this way to talk about my furniture.'

'No, not just that . . .' He took a sip of *café au lait* which the maid – a young woman in her early twenties, introduced to him as Astrid – had set down on the table.

Eveline Marchand sat down opposite him. She took off her left shoe and pulled her leg up onto the sofa. Though she didn't hide her age – she didn't seem to want to – she looked youthful. She was wearing washed-out jeans and a white T-shirt. 'I left Philipp when I realised that he had a thing for young girls.' She paused and smiled shyly.

When Eschenbach didn't respond, she went on.

'It happens to many women of my age . . . One day, they simply find their husbands have found a younger model. Perhaps it's biological, I don't know.' She stroked her hand over her bent knee and looked Eschenbach in the eye. 'But that wasn't the problem with us. I think you already know.'

Eschenbach nodded.

'Now you're bound to be wondering why I didn't go to the police. That's what you're thinking, isn't it?' Without waiting for a reaction, she continued. 'I've also wondered about it. Over and over again. Every night I prayed that nothing else would happen. That he wouldn't want to do it to anyone else . . . I put myself in God's hands. It was possible, I thought. God provides all and judges all. That's what it says in the Bible, isn't it?'

Eschenbach stayed quiet. How should he respond? He had no idea when he'd last read the Bible.

'Do you know the Lord's Prayer?'

He nodded. He knew it, but would he be able to recite it? When was the last time he had prayed? He had no clue about that either.

She began quietly to recite the first lines. At some point, she paused. 'You see, it says, "Thy will be done, on Earth as it is in Heaven. *Thy will* . . ."' She repeated it again. 'How can it be God's will for tiny, innocent children to be raped? Do you understand it . . .? I mean, can you possibly understand it?' Her voice had become loud and harsh. She ran a delicate hand through her hair and closed her eyes for a moment. 'It's our fault, Inspector. Our eyes look away, they don't want to see what's right in front of them. We stay silent.' She took her foot off the sofa and made to stand up. 'I kept quiet . . . always. Because I was too much of a coward to put an end to it all. It's my fault that it didn't stop. I'm the only one who knows . . . I don't know why . . . why I couldn't do it.' She let herself drop back onto the sofa and began to sob quietly. 'You can't put all the blame on God . . . you can't just cross yourself and go on believing you're absolved.' She looked at him sadly.

Eschenbach thought carefully about whether he should say something, whether there was anything he could say, and suddenly he had the urge to take Eveline Marchand into his arms. He stood up and sat next to her on the sofa. A picture of misery, she sat there with her elbows propped on her thighs, hiding her face in her hands. Hesitating, he took her wrist in one hand and with the other he handed her a folded tissue. He couldn't manage anything more and, somehow, it made him feel ashamed.

Chapter 21

When the maid came in with an empty tray to clear away the crockery, she noticed that the jug was still half full and that the croissants in the bowl lay untouched. She hesitated for a moment. Then she wondered whether she should brew another jug of coffee.

Eveline Marchand had composed herself. She kneaded the crumpled tissue between her fingers like a rosary and tried to smile. Then she asked for a fresh jug of coffee.

'Your late husband, *n'est-ce pas?*' said the maid sympathetically before disappearing again with the tray; somehow, she seemed relieved to see there was a good reason for her mistress's tears.

'The girl saw the obituary that Johannes sent to me.'

'You mean Johannes Bettlach, Philipp's brother?'

'Yes.' Eveline Marchand nodded. 'Actually, he was only his half-brother, but you'll know that already.'

'No.' Eschenbach was surprised. He wondered why Johannes Bettlach hadn't mentioned it. 'I don't know much about the family at all. I thought you might be able to help me on that matter . . .' He attempted a smile.

'It was Johannes I came to know first.' She thought for a moment and it seemed as though she was going back through the years. 'That must have been in spring 1979. In London. I had just decided to take a break from my studies and was working in a gallery. My father wanted me to either continue studying or return home to Zurich. Otherwise he would stop sending my monthly allowance, he said. I stayed and he stopped the payments.'

Eschenbach listened carefully and bit into a croissant. He would have liked to dunk it in his coffee first.

Eveline Marchand mustered a smile and went on.

'I found my first job with Lievercoed & Westingfield. At the time, it was still very much a newcomer. We had good contacts on the American Pop Art scene: Roy Lichtenstein, Andy Warhol, Keith Haring. They were some guys, let me tell you . . .'

Eschenbach nodded. He had heard their names before and liked their work, even if he found the sums people were willing to pay for their pieces a little excessive.

'Though these artists were already being lauded in America, things hadn't taken off in Europe. The second oil price shock, the economic crisis . . . like I said, the gallery just couldn't get going. Things were going so badly that Westingfield paid me for my first month's work with pictures from their own collection. Looking back, I'm grateful . . .' She smiled. 'But back then . . . I couldn't pay for anything with the pictures. So I moved into a smaller apartment, down by the docks. It was a hole, really. There was no hot water and the stove only worked when it felt like it. Most of the time, it didn't work at all.'

Eveline Marchand was a masterful storyteller. She imitated the whoosh of the gas stove, gesturing with her slender hands, shyly brushing her hair back into place when she realised she had got carried away.

Eschenbach felt the pain she had felt when nobody wanted to buy anything; he felt the chill when the stove broke down and rejoiced when everything finally worked out for the best. He let her talk, straying from the topic at hand, and listened quietly.

'Johannes was one of my first customers. He was really good looking, and charming in a gentle way. He had a phenomenal nose for trends in art . . . and he had something else that mattered, from a purely professional point of view: money. He invited me to dinner a few times. I think he did it more out of politeness and because of the art than because he had any interest in me. I wasn't kidding myself, even if I found it easy to imagine him as my lover.' She smiled and indicated the fresh coffee that the maid had brought. 'This time we'll drink it while it's hot. Do serve yourself, Inspector.'

Eschenbach drank some coffee and tore another croissant in two with his teeth. 'What about Johannes? Isn't he married? I only saw him with his secretary at the funeral.'

Eveline had also picked up a croissant and her mouth was full. It took a moment for her to wash it down with a sip of coffee before she replied. 'No, he never married.'

'No women at all?' interrupted Eschenbach, raising an eyebrow pointedly.

'Of course, of course.' She laughed. 'He's not gay, if that's what you mean.'

'That's not what I meant.' Eschenbach laughed too. 'I just thought . . . . He's an unusually charismatic person.'

'He's very compelling, yes.' She paused briefly, as if wondering whether to leave it at that. 'Attractive . . . and yet, in a certain way, not. He can be very distant, even cynical sometimes.'

'Bitter?' suggested Eschenbach, who thought cynical sounded a little odd.

'Bitter might not be the right word. What do I know . . .? Sometimes I think you can never really know him.'

'What about the women?' Eschenbach stuck to the topic.

'Oh, there's not much to speak of there. He was always very private about it.' She seemed to be dodging his questions again.

As if she had read his thoughts, she continued:

'There was a woman that he was with for a while.'

'Oh yes? Did you know her?'

'She was from western Switzerland, from Lausanne. From a Jewish banking family, if I remember correctly.' She thought for a moment. 'I can't remember her name.'

Eschenbach didn't know why, but he was sure that she was lying. Perhaps he had developed a sixth sense for it over the years. Eveline Marchand had barely taken a moment to consider. She knew the name. Why wouldn't she tell him it?

'Johannes brought her to one of our openings. That's where he introduced me to her, and to his brother Philipp.'

'Was there a spark? Between you and Philipp, I mean?'

She laughed. 'I wouldn't go that far. He tried really hard. Philipp could be very charming . . . and generous. He downright showered me with gifts and . . .' – she hesitated for a moment – 'and eventually he got what he wanted. That's how I'd explain it.' Eveline Marchand leant back and smirked. 'Would you like another cup of coffee?'

Eschenbach accepted and helped himself as she slid the bowl of croissants across to him. 'Tell me a bit about the Bettlach family. It doesn't sound like a Swiss name. Were they from Germany?'

'Yes. When the war broke out, the Bettlachs had a little guest house in Meersburg on Lake Constance. The father, an ordinary soldier in the armed forces, was conscripted, fought and died late in the summer of 1943. Somewhere on the Eastern front, between Vitebsk and Orsha, I was later told. But who can know for sure? Either way, he never came back.' Eveline Marchand shrugged her shoulders. 'Johannes was just a child at the time. Too young to fight and too old to be spared an understanding of what was going on in Germany. Adele, his mother, ran the guest house on her own, and he helped. As best he could at his age.'

Eschenbach nodded.

'There was something else, aside from the everyday work at the guest house . . . I've always wondered about it, to be honest.' Eveline Marchand paused and thought for a moment.

Eschenbach waited.

'Adele Bettlach helped people escape . . .'

'Oh really? What do you mean?'

'She helped German Jews escape to Switzerland.'

She paused again. 'We never really knew why she did it. She wasn't Jewish herself . . . and she wasn't part of the resistance. She had no link to Judaism at all. She was German. German through and through, if you see what I mean.'

Eschenbach wasn't sure he did.

'But she did it anyway. Later, we often asked her why she had. She never made it clear. Once, she said: "If you can help, then you must. It's as simple as that." That always really impressed me.'

'How did she manage it?' asked Eschenbach, who had heard similar stories before.

'She must have had a good relationship with the Swiss border guards. And the police stationed on the lake. She never revealed anything more specific. But, as I say, it must have been a good relationship because three years after the war ended, she was pregnant.'

'With Philipp Bettlach?'

'You've guessed it,' she said, smiling.

'Did you know Adele Bettlach?'

'Yes, she was a gentle and clever woman. And though she was over seventy by the time I came to know her, you could tell that she must have been incredibly beautiful once. I can still remember when Philipp introduced me to her. It was a warm evening in August. The first of August, to be precise. They had long since moved to Switzerland. It was the Swiss National Day and the two brothers had planned a big firework display for that evening. She was sitting in a shady corner of the villa's garden, under a great plane tree. Despite the heat, she had a crocheted woollen blanket over her legs. When I asked if she was too warm, she simply smiled. "When you get old," she said, "the cold gobbles you up; warmth is a distant memory." The blanket would help her to keep hold of that memory for longer, she said. Later, when Philipp told her that we wanted to get married, she tried to dissuade me. "Child," she said, pulling at my sleeve. "You won't be

happy with him. I'm an old woman and I know these things."
She said it lovingly, and even though I was approaching thirty, it
didn't strike me as belittling in any way. She was serious. I must
have looked at her strangely, because she said, "I know, I know,
you're a young woman after all and young women do as they
choose." Then we both laughed.'

'Astounding,' said Eschenbach, taking the last croissant.

'I thought so too. She never talked much about the past. I think
she took most of it to her grave.'

'When did she die?'

'About twelve years ago. One morning, she was found dead
under the gazebo in the garden of her villa.'

'What was her relationship like with her sons?'

'Very good. She loved them, in different ways.'

'What do you mean?'

'Johannes was strong and dominant. She relied on him, went
to him for advice and to discuss her problems and worries. He
had a solution for everything.'

'A replacement for her fallen husband, perhaps?'

'Maybe, yes. In a way.'

'And Philipp?'

'She loved him ... oh, I don't know. Mothers love their
children, don't they? He was obviously the weaker of the two
brothers. And yet, he was her favourite. Always cheerful, fun
and witty.' Eveline Marchand talked without the slightest hint
of emotion, as if she were giving a rundown of stock market
values on the news. As if she had opened the phone book and
was reading out names at random, names that meant nothing
to her. 'If only he hadn't had that dark side, that emptiness, that
incredible coldness.' She wrapped her hands around her bare

foot, which she had pulled back onto the sofa, and stared at the empty coffee jug.

'When did you find out?'

'Do you know, Inspector, if Philipp was a book, you could say I judged that book entirely by its cover. The stuff inside, the stuff that mattered, that would come later, I thought.' She smiled. 'Naive, isn't it? Perhaps what's inside doesn't matter so much when you're young. He was rich and good looking. There were fast cars and a pearl necklace on the stands at Ascot.' She was back to reading from the phone book. 'Not a bad package, from the outside, I thought.'

Eschenbach nodded.

'After the first few weeks, I realised that it wasn't love with a capital L. Perhaps it wasn't love at all. But there was dancing, sex and candlelight. For a long time, I was living for the moment, day and night. Things were going well at the gallery, people were buying paintings and the money was rolling in.'

'And the marriage?' asked Eschenbach.

'Ah yes, the marriage. It happened the way it does all over the world, only faster. Getting to know the family first, adjusting to each other's idiosyncrasies, romantic evenings together and then a proposal that can't be refused.'

'Why not?'

'Because it had always been clear where we were heading. Sometimes in life, the answer comes before the question.'

Eschenbach said nothing. It had certainly been that way with Milena, his first wife.

'After the wedding, everything changed. Instead of flowers, there was conflict, instead of candlelight, regular slaps in the face. He would stay away for nights on end. He made no attempt to hide the fact that he was sleeping with other women. He bragged about it and enjoyed humiliating me.' She placed her foot back on the floor, raised her shoulders and – as if reading Eschenbach's thoughts – added: 'I still don't know why I didn't just pack my things and leave.'

'And Johannes, I mean, his brother – did he not do anything about it?'

'Of course. But it was no use, and somehow we all knew it was hopeless. He comforted me, listened to me. He was my rock throughout all the chaos . . .' She thought for a moment. 'He just stood there and listened . . . but it didn't change anything. And yet . . .' She faltered, stood up and went to the window.

'And yet you didn't tell him what was really going on?'

Eveline nodded at first, then shook her head. She had turned her back to him and was looking out onto the street in silence.

Eschenbach stood up and went over to her. The sound-proofed windows made the hustle and bustle of the street outside seem like a silent film. Lunchtime comings and goings. Sandwiches eaten on the go or carried back to workplaces in little bags. Groups of men and women rushing past ambling tourists in their dark business suits. Two women in elegant two-pieces picking their way along the pavement in high heels, chatting away.

The silence inside the apartment gave the chaos outside a pantomime-like melancholy. Somehow the action seemed slower without sound, Eschenbach thought.

'What was the real reason that you left?' Eschenbach interrupted the silence with his question. 'The trigger . . . the thing that made it all easier?'

She thought for a moment.

'There are some women who stick by their men, regardless of...' Eschenbach didn't know how he should end the sentence.

'Simply shut their eyes and stick a Cartier necklace around their necks, is that it?'

'Not necessarily. I'm just asking if there was something that gave you the courage to make that final decision.'

'You know what he was capable of.' She gave him a tired smile.

'You knew it too. Long before you decided to leave him.' Eschenbach was surprised; he hadn't realised how harsh he sounded. 'What happened before you left, Ms Marchand?'

'I can't remember.'

'You're lying!' Eschenbach felt his stomach cramping. Eveline avoided his question again. 'It doesn't make any sense! First you live with a man who you don't love – who you've never loved. A man who belittles you and who you *know* screws kids!'

Eveline Marchand winced.

'You knew what kind of man he was ...' Eschenbach tried to calm down and took a deep breath. 'But you stayed, you did nothing ... You could have prevented so much misery, for crying out loud!' Eschenbach noticed he was shouting again. 'Now he's dead, the horse has bolted, and you think you can offer up a few measly lines of the Lord's Prayer and say, well, that's that!'

Eveline looked at him for a long time and the inspector knew that his outburst had broken the delicate bond of trust that had developed between them. He thought about Kathrin: the way she had taken a shine to anyone when she was a little girl, embracing them with open arms. The innocence of children and idiots.

Eschenbach was furious with himself for having lost control. What was it that had made Eveline leave? Why so suddenly, like a scalded cat? No argument, nothing. She had gone quietly, left him forever. What had provoked such an abrupt break in this woman's life? He had been so close and now he'd bungled it, just when the oyster had been poised to reveal its treasure of its own accord. And without looking at her, his shoulders drooping, he whispered: 'The truth, Ms Marchand. Why did you leave?'

She looked at him fleetingly, side-on. 'It was like my life had no meaning any more. Like the life had been sucked out of me. I knew I had two options: kill myself or start again.' She looked at him again and both of them knew that this was only half the truth. The rest lay buried beneath the surface.

Chapter 22

'Hottiger runs sniper courses for the army.' It was Claudio Jagmetti, calling to tell him the news. He sounded tired and irritable, but there was also a hint of victory in his voice.

Eschenbach had made himself comfortable in an empty compartment. The last few hours with Eveline hung in his mind like a spider's web. There was nothing concrete, nothing he could use. As Kobler – with her love of Americanisms – would say, there were *no hard facts*. And she would have hit the nail on the head. And yet, there was something there. Something about Eveline irritated him. Why was she keeping secrets from him?

He bit into the sandwich he had bought at Gare de L'Est. A baguette filled with sheep's cheese. Why did they only have these in France? He wondered why he was enjoying it with a Coke and not a bottle of red wine. What in God's name was wrong with him? He dialled Jagmetti's number. The young police office answered at once.

'Father or daughter?' asked Eschenbach, without bothering to name them. If his theory was right, it must be the father, but Jagmetti's message was vague enough to require clarification.

'The father,' Jagmetti replied quickly.

Eschenbach grunted.

'Sorry if that wasn't clear. Colonel Ernst Hottiger. Successful sports marksman, member of the 1960 Swiss Olympic team in Rome.'

'And he's still training recruits?' interrupted Eschenbach.

'No. Not recruits. Elite troops. He's got to be one of the best in his field.'

'And what field is that?' Eschenbach noticed that he sounded sardonic and he suddenly realised that his understanding of the workings of the Swiss Army was a little rusty. In the early nineties – when he had been a lieutenant in the signal corps – he had decided to leave the army for good. At the time, he was head of criminal analysis for the city of Zurich and in the process of divorcing Milena. Old Franz Locher had offered him the opportunity to stand in for and, later, replace him at the CID. He had accepted and the new job had helped to grow a thick, lush carpet of moss over the ruins of his first marriage.

'Psychological warfare in hostage situations, security planning, the fight against terrorism and all that stuff. He must be pretty good,' said Jagmetti. 'Boss, even the army have relaxed the rules for him. They're now taking on more and more civil specialists.' He must have noticed Eschenbach's disdain because he added, 'It was news to me too, boss.'

'I know,' he replied, grumbling. Eschenbach lit a Brissago and coughed. Was he scornful because he felt it was his area? Was it the smouldering jealousy of a self-proclaimed 'top dog'? He drank the rest of the Coke and threw the empty can at the bin on the other side of the compartment. He missed, of course, but only just.

'Hottiger has his own security company. He's quite a big deal.'

'I know,' murmured Eschenbach. He said this more to himself than to Jagmetti, for whom everything was new territory. 'Ernst Hottiger is the *éminence grise* when it comes to matters of security. A guardian angel for the rich and powerful across the country.' The cynicism had disappeared from Eschenbach's voice. Now it sounded like a mixture of recognition and resignation. 'In the last three decades, there have been several highly explosive cases that Hottiger is rumoured to have had a hand in. He's kept a low profile, but he's always been successful. His reputation reaches far beyond the Swiss borders and he's got an international network seeking out other people like him.'

There was silence at the other end of the line.

The Coke can rolled back towards Eschenbach, who picked it up, threw it, and missed the bin a second time. 'Are you still there, Jagmetti?'

'Yes, boss,' Jagmetti replied. 'What you're saying is certainly interesting . . .'

'When the head of the CIA is visiting Switzerland, he speaks to Hottiger first,' continued Eschenbach. 'His official residence is a suite in the Schweizerhof Grand Hotel . . . watched twenty-four hours a day, when he's there. But he only uses it occasionally. We've always assumed that he stays with Hottiger. At his villa on Lake Sihl, which few people even know exists.'

'I didn't know either . . . I mean, that he lives there,' replied Jagmetti, who really just wanted to show that he was still on the line.

'There's no way you could . . . Like I said, it's all pretty secretive. It's never reported in the media.' Eschenbach paused; the only pictures of Hottiger he could remember were from his successful international shooting competitions. And they were over forty years old. After that, it all went quiet. Very quiet. Eschenbach tried to imagine how he looked today. 'How do you know this about Hottiger? I mean, about the sniper courses?'

'Documents. Some kind of instruction guide or something,' said Jagmetti. 'It was lying around at one of the barracks that I visited. I can't be more precise. I'll have to take another look.'

'What?' Eschenbach noticed how loudly he was talking. There was silence at the other end of the line. He tried to control himself. 'You just swiped it?'

'No, of course not, I just . . .'

'Stole it?'

'No.'

'What, was it a gift? Complete with a field-grey ribbon and a trumpeter blaring out a tattoo?' Eschenbach realised he was shouting again.

'No, of course not, but—'

'But what? Jagmetti, you're doing my head in!'

'I copied it.'

'So you did steal it.' Eschenbach took his feet off the seat opposite and stood up, pacing the compartment like an ocelot in a cage. 'We can't afford to make any mistakes, Jagmetti!'

'I know, boss.'

'You know nothing, Jagmetti. And stop calling me boss!'

'OK, boss. I mean . . . OK.'

'If Hottiger has even the slightest thing to do with this, then we can't afford to put a toe out of line.' Eschenbach thought about Kobler and remembered that he still hadn't apologised to Hottiger.

'The original is still in its place,' said the young police office, trying to placate him.

'Who let you . . . I mean, how did you get into the office in the first place?'

'With the office orderly.'

'What? Just like that?'

'The sergeant . . . he was playing cards in the restaurant.' Jagmetti told him the whole story.

'Oh, for Christ's . . .' Eschenbach sat back down in his seat. 'And you're sure that the original is back where you found it?'

'Yes, boss. A hundred per cent.'

'You're calling me boss again!'

'What else am I supposed to call you?' Jagmetti sounded annoyed. 'Non-boss, perhaps? Would you prefer that?'

'Yeah, maybe!' Eschenbach grunted. 'Did you put it somewhere safe?'

'No. It was lying on the table . . . What do you mean, safe?'

'You put it back on the table?'

'Yes, obviously.' Jagmetti clearly didn't understand why Eschenbach was making such a fuss.

'Do you have it on you, Jagmetti?'

'Yes.'

'I mean the copy.'

'Yes, the copy, obviously, boss.'

'Non-boss,' grumbled Eschenbach.

'Obviously, Non-boss,' Jagmetti sniggered.

'Then look after it. Lock it away. Sit on it, sleep on it . . .'

'I will.'

'I want to see it as soon as I get back. Is that clear?'

'Yes.'

'Just me, no one else. Is that clear?'

'That's clear too . . . yes. I think I've understood.'

'And now what? Is there anything else?'

'No – except that, I mean . . .' Jagmetti hesitated for a moment.

'Except what?' the inspector asked.

'There's still no trace of Doris Hottiger . . . as far as I know.'

'Yes, yes, the girl,' muttered Eschenbach. 'We'll find her, don't you worry.'

'Do you think so?' Jagmetti sounded less confident.

'There is a huge manhunt under way looking for her – she won't get far, believe me!'

'OK, then, if you say so.'

'Jesus Christ, don't be so pessimistic! We'll find her all right. It's ridiculous to think otherwise.' Then Eschenbach thought about how easily he had managed to slip past customs in Basle. 'Is that everything, or have you got something else?'

'No. Nothing else . . .' This was followed by a short 'OK' and then the line went dead.

Eschenbach rolled the knobbly cigarillo between his finger and thumb. He took a drag and exhaled. Ugly spotlights shone into the compartment and the grey-blue smoke played in the light. Despite the pungeant smoke, he remembered the subtle scent that he had noticed when Doris Hottiger sat opposite him on that muggy afternoon in his office. It wasn't overpowering. It wasn't that strong, heavy musk that he associated with many expensive ladies' perfumes. It was a light, lively sensuality concealed, purring playfully, behind a thousand pastel-coloured scent molecules. Light, almost transparent yellow and orange. Lemon, orange blossom and cinnabar. Eschenbach had no idea what cinnabar smelt like. But he imagined it smelt the way it looked. Pale, cinnabar red. Shimmering transparently, like the cloak of the setting sun.

Suddenly he knew what had been irritating him in Eveline Marchand's apartment. It was those light, dancing molecules of perfume, the same ones that had surrounded Doris Hottiger and which he had spent the whole time trying to remember. She was there – perhaps not physically, but in some figurative sense she was present. Something linked the two women and he was sure that it was something more than their perfume.

A pale and sickly-looking guard asked to inspect his tickets. His white, knotty fingers flicked lethargically through them, and it was some time before he managed to punch the right hole in the ticket with his shabby hole-punch. His lank hair kept dropping into his face, obscuring his view; his glum, grey-blue eyes seemed to look inwards. The whites of his eyes were yellow. It wasn't the pastel shade, but a sad, dirty yellow, littered with small red veins. Alcohol and drugs, thought Eschenbach. And most likely some kind of hepatitis that had long needed treatment. A few years ago, Eschenbach might have arranged to have the guard taken in at Swiss customs and strip-searched. He would bet anything that the guy had a packet of heroin, crack or something similar on him. Often, they would pack the stuff inside a condom and shove it up their rectums. On this occasion, it just made Eschenbach sad and he decided to let it slide.

A while later, a little old woman in an old-fashioned dress opened the door to the compartment, carrying her hand luggage. She looked disapprovingly at Eschenbach's feet, which lay on the seat opposite. With a shy smile, the inspector took his legs off the seat, sat upright and began looking for his shoes.

All he could find was the Coke can. He pushed it into the bin under the window, grumbled an '*Excusez-moi*' and offered the woman a seat. She coughed, and Eschenbach heard her mutter, '*Incroyable*' before shutting the door from the outside with a big shove.

'She's not wrong,' he said, standing up and pulling the window down as far as it would go.

A mild night-time breeze flooded into the compartment. He propped his arms on the window ledge and looked out. Strings of black hills and trees rattled past him. Here and there, he could make out the lights of houses, or a lonely car making its way along an unlit country road. He stood there – motionless – for some time.

Chapter 23

Eschenbach slept badly after the long train journey, much of which he had spent dozing. He got up several times in the night, poured himself a glass of water and sat in the reclining chair on the small, open-air veranda. Above him, the night sky was clear and it seemed as though he was looking at a sea of lights beaming from a distant city. He discovered more and more tiny, winking sparks. Lights from a single solar system. It made him giddy to think that his solar system was just one of many.

He brooded over the Bettlach case and somehow he couldn't escape the idea that his was just a tiny drop in an ocean of similar cases.

He missed Corina and Kathrin and he suddenly remembered that he had forgotten to water the plants for days. He stood up, feeling the warmth of the stone slabs beneath his bare feet and examined the wilting basil that stood in a small pot next to the wooden table. He brought the garden hose out of the kitchen and watered the clay pots, the seedlings and the trugs of flowers which had claimed a large part of the terrace as their own. He couldn't resist holding his head under the cool stream of water once he had finished. The water flowed over him and his T-shirt clung to his stomach like a wet sail.

The inspector was the first one in the office that next morning: a rare occurrence. It was going to be a very hot day and he could only think sensibly when it was cool. The *Zürcher Tagblatt* lay open on the table in front of him. Several dried-on coffee rings decorated the front page of the domestic news section bearing the headline 'IS GOLF COURSE KILLER A SWISS ARMY OFFICER?' in fat black letters. Eschenbach was chewing a half-smoked Brissago, swearing incessantly. That bloody cow. Who was she getting her information from?

He knew that he had got himself into this mess, that he had underestimated Marianne. He had wanted to call her before he left for Paris, but he had forgotten; he had broken his promise. Now she had got her own back: a whole sodding page of it, with a photo of the inspector grinning stupidly in front of Zurich Grossmünster.

It was just after seven and it wouldn't be long before the calls started coming in: the Ministry of Defence, the Swiss Federal Officers Association, the head of department for the canton of Zurich, and God knows who else. He flicked through his box of business cards and found the number for the dentist he had sat next to at Bettlach's funeral.

'Can I bring you an espresso?' a voice warbled through the loudspeaker. On this particular morning, the metallic droning and whistling of Eschenbach's poorly adjusted intercom system could do nothing to mar the cheery voice of Rosa Mazzoleni. Her voice was music to his ears.

'How about this weather, then!' Rosa Mazzoleni beamed. 'On the radio they said it would be the hottest month since records began.'

'I see. And when did they begin?' Eschenbach was thinking about the fact that he was on to his last clean shirt.

'In 1540,' she replied, quick as a flash.

'Ah. What about the Ancient Greeks? Didn't they keep records?'

'Yes. But it's been cooler since 1540 . . . on average, apparently.'

'Who's been coming out with this nonsense?'

'Someone on the radio . . . a famous climate researcher.'

The phone rang.

'I'm not here,' said Eschenbach, waving dismissively.

'No, he's not here . . . no idea. He's in meetings all day. Yes, I'll pass it on.' She hung up. 'How impolite!' Rosa Mazzoleni rolled her eyes.

'And why have we only been recording temperatures since . . .' asked Eschenbach, ignoring the phone call altogether.

'Because that's when the thermometer was invented.' She smiled knowingly. 'Do you know who invented it, by the way?'

'Not another quiz, Ms Mazzoleni.' Eschenbach slurped his espresso.

'Do you know, or don't you, boss?'

Now she's calling me boss too, thought Eschenbach, and sighed. 'Leonardo da Vinci!' he said stubbornly.

He knew he didn't know the answer, he knew was wrong. But he didn't want to spoil her game.

The phone rang again.

Rosa hurried out of the office, pressed a button and the automatic message played.

'Leonardo da Vinci is incorrect,' she called, mincing back into the office, smiling like a sphinx. 'You have one more guess.'

'Christ, I really don't know. Don't be so strict, let me have da Vinci!'

'Why?' Rosa Mazzoleni looked at him indignantly. 'You want to catch the right culprit, don't you?'

'But Leonardo da Vinci definitely would have invented it, if it hadn't already been invented.'

'Oh really? Our boy Leonardo can't have invented everything.' Rosa Mazzoleni smiled.

'Why "our" Leonardo?' Eschenbach knew what she was getting at and winked. 'You're the Italian one, not me.'

'I know. I don't mean you and me, I mean us Italians.'

The phone rang again and the automatic message played.

'So tell me, who did invent the thermometer? It can't have been an Italian, can it?'

'Yes, actually!' she replied, triumphantly. 'Who else?' She laughed and Eschenbach feigned amazement. 'It was Galileo Galilei, of course!' She cleared away the empty espresso cup on the tray, took the pile of post out of the outgoing basket and danced away towards the door. 'What about Paris anyway? Did you like my hotel?' The question wasn't snarky or petty. She said it more to herself; quietly, but loudly enough that he couldn't help but hear. It was a way that intelligent women had of showing men like Eschenbach where their limits lay. The inspector called out to her, but the door had already closed behind her.

Eschenbach watched her go, annoyed with himself. He could never just say thank you! Corina always said that a small thank you now and then was as good as a bunch of roses. Now he thought about the withered basil on the veranda and made a note to replace it, as well as the dried-out rosemary bush and the freshly planted trug of flowers next to the door to the veranda, their green leaves now resembling the grass of some arid steppe. The rest had survived, if only just.

He pressed the button on the intercom and waited for a moment. There was no reply and he knew that he would have to get up, leave his office and go over to Rosa's desk.

'You really liked the hotel, then?' she asked as he appeared. She was carefully sorting through a stack of files and didn't look up.

'It was wonderful. Small, charming, close to the Louvre. Just the way you described it. Have you been there before?'

'No, not yet, I'm afraid. Friends of mine are always raving about it. I might go in the autumn.' She smiled forgivingly. 'Only if I get a few days off, of course . . .' Eschenbach was reluctant to comment. Rosa Mazzoleni knew that her boss would never stand in the way of her attempts to quell her wanderlust; after all, she was only ever away for a couple of days at a time.

'Can you get me the number for Ewald Lenz? I think we'd better take a closer look at old Hottiger.'

'Is that the father of the young lady who was here last week?' She glanced up from her desk and threw him an intrigued look over her glasses. 'Isn't he—'

'Yes, the famous "guardian angel for the rich and powerful",' he interrupted, adding, with a smile, 'Councillor Sacher will be thrilled.'

Rosa raised her eyebrows and fanned her face with a couple of sheets of A4. 'Looks like this chap could have done with a guardian angel of his own.' She handed him a three-page fax which included a man's photograph. 'From Basle CID. Came in just before you went to Paris. They've got their own murder to solve. Well, murder or suicide. I don't think they're quite sure themselves . . .'

Eschenbach took the fax, read the title page briefly and walked towards his office, lost in his own thoughts. 'Oh yeah, is Jagmetti in yet?' he called without turning around.

'I haven't seen him. Shall I send him in when he arrives?'

'Please.' He shut his office door, sat down and read through the rest of the fax that Mazzoleni had given him.

On the whole, he found suicides suspicious. Not just because most of them could also have been murders but because they *were* murders. They had it all: a killer, a murder weapon and a motive. Unhappy love affairs were a common motive, one that even the simplest minds could understand, all the way back to the tale of Romeo and Juliet. But this didn't look like a case of unrequited love. It was the man, after all, who had been having his fun with someone else, or so his girlfriend had claimed. And only in the very rarest of cases did men kill themselves because of a guilty conscience.

Eschenbach read the case a second and third time. It was the statement provided by the girlfriend – a certain Hera DeLaprey – that niggled at him and raised a serious question mark over the prospect of a suicide. 'Pierre would never have killed himself; he would be more likely to kill someone else,' she had said on record. Eschenbach thought this was a curious statement. And yet, women usually knew their men – the opposite was rarely true.

The inspector realised that he accepted the woman's claim and strongly doubted the suicide. It made no sense to him: why would a successful and exceedingly egocentric musician like Pierre Oliver kill himself? Especially after spending the night with a lover?

If it really was murder, then it looked a lot like a professional hit. No signs of force, no witnesses – except for the lover, who was suddenly impossible to trace. It looked like he'd been executed. Eschenbach stopped. He recalled the title of the article that Marianne Felber had written about Bettlach's murder in the *Zürcher Tagblatt*: 'TEE TIME EXECUTION!' Could it be possible that the deaths were connected? Had someone taken it upon themselves to execute paedophiles? The idea seemed absurd to him at first. He found it difficult to imagine that a man who played the flute so beautifully could be a child molester. Then he thought about the names on the list. Canton councillors, teachers, ministers and judges – so why not musicians?

The longer he thought about it, the less ridiculous it seemed. He decided to inform his Basle colleagues about the story behind the Bettlach murder. But what would he say? He had *no hard facts*. The child sex story was pure hearsay at this stage. Bettlach was not on the Genesis list and he had no other concrete evidence to back up his convictions. After everything that Eveline Marchand and Doris Hottiger had said, it seemed clear as day that Bettlach had been a child molester – and yet he had no proof. Not a scrap of it. Should he expose himself to the ridicule of his colleagues in Basle?

Eschenbach stood up, stretched his lower back, and walked over to the file cupboard. He took out the Genesis folder and leafed through it. The list of names only covered the canton of Zurich; Pierre Oliver lived in Basle. With the file open in his hands, he went back to his desk and found the number for Marcel Bucher at the Federal Office of Police in Berne.

The chief picked up.

'I hope I'm not disturbing you,' said Eschenbach, clearing his throat. 'I wondered if I might be able to take a look at the Genesis files for the canton of Basle, it might be useful . . . in connection with the murder I'm investigating.'

'You mean the names?'

'Yes, just the names.'

'You can find them at the back, on the CD-ROM; it's got all the data for the whole of Switzerland.'

'I see.' Eschenbach flicked to the back and found the case with the disc.

'What name are you looking for?' asked Bucher.

'Oliver – Pierre Oliver.'

'The musician?' asked the chief matter-of-factly.

'Yes, is he on the list?'

'Just a minute . . .'

Eschenbach felt for his packet of cigarillos and realised he didn't have his lighter.

'Basle city or Basle state?'

'Basle city,' said Eschenbach, picking at random. 'Maybe both . . . I don't know.'

There was another pause and Eschenbach searched for his lighter amid the mountains of files, clear plastic folders and newspapers.

'Nothing, sorry.' Bucher's voice sounded friendly. 'The musician's clean.'

'Damn ...' Eschenbach took a breath. 'Would have been good. Thanks anyway.'

'That's all right, happy to do it. Good luck, *buddy.*'

They said goodbye and Eschenbach wondered how long it would be before American English became the fifth official Swiss language.

It would have been the perfect hook. A vigilante, doling out justice to child sex abusers.

It would have all fitted together so well. But if it wasn't a vigilante, what was it? Death by misadventure, or a genuine suicide? Eschenbach didn't believe in coincidences – and he didn't believe in mistakes either.

He would have liked to share his suspicions with his colleagues at the Basle police. *Police work should be devoid of vanity.* It was one of the maxims that he liked to trot out in lectures. But as things were, there wasn't the slightest indication that his theory was correct. Secretly, though, he hoped he was right.

Chapter 24

It was high time that he called Lenz to talk to him about Ernst Hottiger. Eschenbach dialled the number for the Central Archive. The line was engaged.

As far as Lenz was concerned, his intelligence and his education should have afforded him a well-paid position as a teacher or a researcher long ago. His problem was that he didn't particularly like people and he didn't care one jot for all that was good and beautiful in the world. Ewald Lenz had also been known to drink on occasion. Not the way that one might imagine an occasional drinker drinks. Lenz would get drunk. He did this three or four times a year, deliberately, and usually until he passed out.

Before the inspector learnt how to deal with the phenomenon that was Lenz, he had had a long chat with him. It was when Eschenbach had just taken up his role as detective chief superintendent at the CID and Lenz had been working in the intelligence archives for over ten years. His quarterly breakdowns, occasionally followed by short stays at mental health clinics, had troubled Eschenbach and he wondered why nobody had taken exception to his behaviour before. Had it really not occurred to anyone, or did they just not want to see it?

When Lenz sat across from him, alert, exhibiting none of the classic signs of alcoholism, and told him that alcohol wasn't his real problem, he had taken him at his word. Eschenbach was very familiar with the excuses of classic alcohol dependents. But Lenz was different, and therein lay his problem. Due to some vagary of nature, he lacked the normal human ability to forget.

He forgot nothing, he admitted quietly, his grey-blue gaze fixed on his hands. It wasn't nice to not be able to forget anything. In fact, it was terrible. Even the smallest, most insignificant detail, something he might have read once in some report or other – it all clung to his brain like flour on wet dough. This is what forced him to 'wash it all away' from time to time, as he put it. Afterwards, it wouldn't be gone – but it would be easier to endure.

Eschenbach had pursued the matter for some time. He talked to several neurologists and went to the clinic where Lenz sometimes received treatment. Eventually, he found a doctor who attended to Lenz and made it possible for him to continue his work in the archive. It was the beginning of a long and occasionally quirky relationship between two very different people.

Just as he was about to try the number for the archive again, Jagmetti came into the office with a small briefcase under his arm.

'Not disturbing you, am I?' he asked politely.

'Take a seat . . . and show me that.'

Eschenbach looked at the photocopy that Jagmetti placed on the table before him. It was a complete training plan for prospective general staff officers, addressed to a Captain Steiger. The level of classification marked on the document was, as Eschenbach had guessed, 'confidential'.

'And the original is back where you found it?' mumbled Eschenbach without looking up.

'Yes.' The young police office refrained from pointing out that this was the third time Eschenbach had asked him the same question.

The training plan comprised a good dozen subjects, split into learning modules and spread across the year. Evidently the commander, in whose office the plan lay, was also taking part in the training course. A few topics were underlined and notes had been made in the margins in a scribbled hand. Hottiger was teaching the modules on 'Secret Service', 'Strategic Warfare' and 'Kidnapping Negotiation Practices'. Two of the courses were taking place that coming autumn. One had already finished. It had begun in early July at the Kulm Hotel on Lake Aegeri in the canton of Zug.

'Then Hottiger wasn't in America when the murder happened.' Eschenbach pointed to the training plan and took a deep breath. 'Well, isn't that something?'

'Yep,' said Jagmetti, crossing his legs. 'That's what I thought.'

It was just twenty minutes' drive from Lake Aegeri to the golf club. Eschenbach thought for a moment. So, it would have been possible for Hottiger to cover the short distance with a military service vehicle and shoot Bettlach dead and then drive back. It would have taken an hour, he reckoned. It wouldn't have drawn much attention during seminars on negotiation practice. He looked for a more detailed plan with seminar times but couldn't find one. There was just a note to say that the details for the courses would be sent to participants separately, two weeks before the course began.

'Talk about a stroke of luck,' said Jagmetti, crossing his arms and bracing himself for Eschenbach's bad mood.

'Luck? We've not had much of it ...' grumbled the inspector, flicking back to the last page of the document. 'It's just a clue, nothing else. And actually we should have ...' – he paused briefly – 'been able to get here without it.' He waved the bound pages and began fanning his face. 'Tell me, Jagmetti,' he paused again and leant back against the steel backrest. The black leather creaked menacingly and the young police office wondered what would happen if the whole thing collapsed.

'Tell you what?' Jagmetti replied. He wanted to stop the backrest from bending further and keep Eschenbach from forgetting his question.

'What exactly did Doris Hottiger say when she told ... I mean, when she hinted that she was going to disappear?'

Jagmetti thought for a moment and ran through that night at the Old Shepherd in his mind again. He saw her sitting there, confident yet fragile. He saw the strands of blond hair that she kept brushing out of her face – and her mouth, the way it moved.

'"I'm not a murderer ..."' Jagmetti heard her soft voice, and wondered where she was right now. 'Yes, those were her exact words.'

'That can't be all she said,' joked Eschenbach. But despite his smile, the young police officer couldn't help but notice that Eschenbach's gaze was stern, his voice calm. 'What else? Did she mention her father?'

'No. If I'd known, I would have thought to ask. She hinted at something else ...' He seemed unable to find the right words, hesitated and went on. 'She said she had done some things that weren't entirely within the law, things that would soon come to light. I can't remember her exact words; I didn't pursue it. I didn't want to ruin that special moment.'

'Don't get sentimental, Jagmetti,' snapped Eschenbach. He didn't like sentimental police officers. In fact, he hated them. 'Vanity and sentimentality are the devil's playthings, believe you me. That and the inability to think things through to their conclusion . . .' he blustered.

'I know,' said Jagmetti, running his hand through his hair. The right side of his face gleamed black and blue and the dark stitches that held his bottom lip together were clearly visible. Then he looked at Eschenbach stubbornly: 'What about you, boss? Do you always keep your feelings in check?'

'Yes,' grumbled the inspector. 'Which means no. Of course not . . . but there are certain principles, Jagmetti: business and pleasure are like oil and schnapps – they don't mix.'

'I don't drink schnapps,' said the young police office drily.

'It's a metaphor!' Eschenbach mopped the sweat from his brow. He didn't really have anything against sentimental people. He was one himself – but not at work. At least in theory. 'No booze and no soppy stuff, Jagmetti! You can do all the boozing and bonking you like afterwards . . . or before, just not when we're right in the middle of a case.'

Jagmetti said nothing. He didn't want to fight with Eschenbach. The inspector was in a bad mood and it was no good insisting that he hadn't slept with Doris Hottiger since the day they met for the first time. Why should he justify himself? Why should he say he rarely drank, that he hardly ever got drunk? Never, to be precise. Drunk on love, perhaps. That had been his problem that night. That was the truth of it. And perhaps he had been a little tipsy. But he couldn't put it down to a couple of drinks.

The truth was, he was crazy about her. Crazy about her laugh and the light in her eyes. Crazy about the delicate little dimples in her cheeks when she laughed. When he had felt the bass thumping through her stomach on the dance floor in Kaufleuten, when she had looked fleetingly into his eyes in the bouncing strobe light, everything else had shrunk into insignificance. It was more than boozing and bonking. Much more. But what was the point in explaining that to Eschenbach, the old cynic? He would never understand anyway, certainly not enough to really care. Some old wounds never healed. Some things could never be undone. Some things you just had to swallow. To the last bitter drop.

'You're hopeless, Jagmetti!' Eschenbach was puffing and panting. Then he started to grin: 'When I hear you spouting this romantic nonsense, I . . .' The inspector hesitated for a moment before going on. 'I feel like I'm listening to myself, when I was your age.'

The inspector's sudden openness took Jagmetti by surprise, and yet, at the same time, it felt liberating. He laughed, feeling relieved.

'Laugh all you want,' said Eschenbach. 'It might make it easier for you, but it won't for me. I'm well on my way to being a grumpy old man. So keep your nonsense to yourself.' Then he picked up the telephone receiver and tried the number for the Central Archive again.

It seemed like an eternity before anyone answered. It was the unfamiliar voice of a young woman. 'Please could you put Lenz on the phone?' he growled impatiently. There was a click and a pause in which decades seemed to fly by.

During the summer holidays, the Central Archive was a playground for students, glad of a summer job. The temps were looked upon fondly by the archive's employees because they brought life to the place, at least for a few weeks. Eschenbach dreaded it. He thought about all the information down there, freely accessible to clueless students.

Eventually, he heard the voice of Ewald Lenz.

'What's going on? Are you having a party down there or has everyone gone to sleep?' Eschenbach felt the sweat rise on his brow and thought about the cool basement rooms. He knew, of course, that the archive was inundated with work and that his little remark would provoke a classic Lenz-grade tantrum.

'Getting a bit hot for you up there in your sauna, is it?' he replied sweetly. 'It's a pleasant twenty degrees down here and we're cracking open a couple of cold beers.' Instead of the usual cursing, he laughed hoarsely. 'The temps are doing a wonderful job, so I've been having a little catnap,' he chuckled, sniggering to himself.

'Are you mad? With all the classified information you've got hidden away down there? Keep an eye on them, please!' Eschenbach realised too late that he had fallen for Lenz's trick. Lenz sniggered and was quiet for a moment.

'All joking aside, we've obviously got everything under control. I'm just pressing ahead with "Eagle Eyes".'

Eschenbach stifled a grin. The fact that someone had thought to name a project that revolved entirely around scanning dusty old files 'Eagle Eyes' said it all.

Ewald Lenz had a penchant for the bizarre. But perhaps you had to when you spent your whole life grubbing through archives, rooting around in databases and surfing websites. Lenz liked it that way. He was a walking hard drive; his sole mission was to store and replay information.

'Then you'll have time to put together a little file for me . . .' joked Eschenbach.

'Anything for you,' came his friendly reply. 'Who've you got in your sights?'

'Ernst Hottiger.'

'The security specialist?'

'The very same. Do you know him?'

'He's a quiet one, old Hottiger, you know what they say . . . intriguing,' said Lenz. 'In this case, the system won't yield much. I'll have to dig deeper and rekindle my relationships with a couple of informants. Tell me, what's the main focus? Business or private life?'

'Private life. Specifically, his family . . . perhaps his close friends. He has a daughter, Doris Hottiger, twenty-two. She's quite a special girl. I spoke to her a few days ago. Now she's disappeared . . . make sure Interpol's on the case. Perhaps you'll find out where she might be.' Eschenbach wondered for a moment whether he should mention the business with Jagmetti, but he let it slide.

'Let's see what we can do,' said Lenz. He sounded confident.

'Her mother is supposed to have died in childbirth. Check that for me, please. I want to know her maiden name, where they met, where they married and the name of the hospital where Doris was born. Look out for certificates, photos, if you can find any . . .'

'You don't sound too confident?'

'I don't know, it's just a hunch. Oh, and the name of the midwife, and the priest . . . anything you can get your hands on.'

'Will do.'

'I'll send someone by, you could use some help.' Eschenbach looked at Jagmetti, who looked down at his hands and sighed.

'I'd rather you didn't. I can manage on my own,' replied Lenz evasively.

Eschenbach had expected nothing less. 'No, you can't, Lenz. His name's Claudio Jagmetti . . . he's never been to the archive before. He'll come straight down and give you a hand.'

'If you insist . . .' Lenz sounded anything but enthused. 'Have you told him about me?'

'Don't need to. I trust him and he knows the case.'

'All right, then,' he said tersely. 'And by the way, I'd like it if I could have a few days off. I mean, once we've dug all this stuff up . . .'

'I know, no problem. And it sounds like "Eagle Eyes" is under control.' The inspector couldn't resist mentioning it one last time. He grinned and put the phone down.

'So . . . ?' Jagmetti raised his eyebrows. 'Is it sorted?'

'He's looking forward to it,' Eschenbach lied, and then laughed. 'Basement, third floor.'

Jagmetti stood up.

'Take the stairs, Jagmetti. You need a key to take the lift to -3. Lenz will send someone to open the door for you.' Eschenbach thought for a moment. Should he mention the 'Lenz phenomenon' to Jagmetti? And was it right to put the young police officer on the Hottiger case, working on Doris's father? The inspector pushed his doubts to the back of his mind and felt for his packet of cigarillos, which were in the top drawer of his desk. 'By the way, Lenz isn't just an archivist, Jagmetti,' he shouted after him, before he pulled the office door closed. 'He's the most brilliant mind I've ever worked with . . .' He felt that he owed Lenz that much.

'Got it, boss. Might be good to learn something for once,' groaned Jagmetti, before shutting the door.

Chapter 25

The inspector drew up the summons for Ernst Hottiger himself and addressed it to Penn State University, Texas. The tone was matter-of-fact, almost friendly, he thought. It would reach him in the evening, via fax, and in the original no more than two days later, via FedEx. Assuming, of course, that Hottiger was actually there.

Max Kubly from Info Services was very sure of himself. 'He'll be there . . . a hundred per cent,' he had assured him, and Eschenbach believed him. Ultimately, there was no way that Hottiger could know that the inspector knew about his little trip to Switzerland. Jagmetti's discovery of the training plan for general staff officers had broken the rules and perhaps that was why Eschenbach was so nervous.

The inspector sent one copy of the summons to Kobler and a second to Councillor Sacher. He had included a short explanation and a note on the state of the investigation. Then he made his way to the railway station.

The journey to Berne took it out of Eschenbach. The air conditioning wasn't working. It had broken down, the guard said, appearing in his sweaty shirt and giving Eschenbach's ticket a fleeting glance. Eschenbach didn't believe him; either the carriage had been recently retrofitted with air conditioning and all the technological frills, or it had never had air conditioning to begin with. The inspector guessed the latter. He had opened the window as soon as he arrived in the carriage – another sign that the guard was wrong, or that he was lying. Air-conditioned carriages had sealed windows. He sat in the compartment reading a discarded copy of the *New Zurich Journal*, smoking and sweating.

When he arrived in Berne, he would have liked to jump into the River Aare and spend the rest of the day dozing in the shade. Instead, he bought three shirts – light blue – in the 'End of Summer' sale at Loeb. It was 'three for two'. He would have preferred two for one, or, ideally, one for nothing. But you couldn't compete with special offers, much less with the rule of three.

At the taxi rank, he looked for the latest Mercedes model with air-conditioning and tinted windows.

'It'll cool down in no time,' the old man at the steering wheel assured him in a pleasant Bernese accent. 'We can't run our engines. It's to do with the law and the hole in the ozone layer.' Eschenbach wondered what had greater influence: the law or the hole in the ozone layer? He doubted that the ozone layer would have received much attention at all if it hadn't been for the law.

It took him ages to take the shirt out of the cardboard box and remove the tissue paper and pins. He shivered, sitting there topless, pulling on a fresh shirt.

The Institute of Dentistry at the University of Berne was located at 7 Freiburgstrasse. The taxi driver stopped in front of the steps to the main entrance. It was an ugly, five-storey building from the eighties. If it had been a tooth, it would have been pulled years ago. Eschenbach wondered whether he would make it from the steps to the entrance without having to change his shirt again. Should he sprint or walk slowly – which was the best tactic? He paid, wrenched open the door and the heat took his breath away. He decided to walk. He took several leisurely strides up towards the entrance, and when he reached the door he was glad that he hadn't run.

'Dr Oberholzer will send someone straight away . . . you can wait up there. This is the patients' lounge.' The woman behind the Perspex screen was cold, positively frosty compared to the beautiful weather outside. She was wearing a loose-cut sleeve-less dress. Her face, neck, cleavage and arms were as tanned as the old cherry wood wardrobe on Corina's side of their bed-room. It made her seem hard, Eschenbach thought. Especially when she was skinny and wiry to begin with.

He walked through the lobby over to the lounge that Mrs Pinocchio had indicated. It was a game that Corina liked play-ing. She has a knack for nicknames and their conversations about other people would be littered with references to 'Mousetrap', 'Squabbles', 'Jägerbomb' or 'Tomtit'. Most people had no idea they even had a nickname, apart from a few exceptions. These were the fault of Kathrin, who had unwittingly revealed them when she was little. 'Rat-tails', for example, had been a rather cruel name for Corina's sister, Aunt Gabi. When she found out, Eschenbach had hoped the ground would swallow him up. But when Gabi put on a brave face and transformed her lank 'tails' with a stylish perm, everything changed: she found new love, new clothes and moved to Geneva. But 'Rat-tails' stuck, followed soon after by 'Napoleon' for her husband, a Frenchman called Frédéric.

Corina was quite relaxed about it and it wasn't uncommon for a nickname to suit a person better than their real name. Children had an instinct for it, she thought. She was very laid back on such matters, and Eschenbach loved her for it.

The young man who came to get him was evidently another member of the Pinocchio family. The inspector thought his tan looked more natural on him. Perhaps it was because he was a man, or because he was younger. It made him look more masculine. Despite his leathery tan, he seemed shy, with soft, dark eyes and bright white teeth.

'Hi. Tobias Eigenmann, I'm Professor Oberholzer's assistant,' he said proudly. 'Pleased to meet you.'

'Is she a professor or a doctor?' asked Eschenbach, recalling that Mrs Pinocchio had said 'Dr Oberholzer' at reception.

'She's almost a professor, Inspector,' said Tobias Eigenmann importantly. 'She's a private lecturer, to be precise. That's the role you assume before you become a professor. She'll become one next semester. She's already given her inaugural speech . . . she's an expert in her field, you know.' His perfect teeth were testament to the department's area of expertise.

'So that's how it works.' Eschenbach nodded as if the boy had explained a complex surgical procedure. Naturally, he knew about the conventions for acquiring academic titles from his time at university. But the young assistant beamed with such enthusiasm that his student – Eschenbach – gave him a grateful nod.

In the lift, they stood next to one another in silence. Eschenbach tried desperately to think of something else to ask. He hated the quiet anxiety of lifts. It reminded him of a scene from a film where

Peter Sellers, playing Inspector Clouseau, takes the lift in silence with a gang of crooks. Doors opening – doors closing. The young assistant flashed his pearly white smile.

As they walked side by side along the long corridor to Professor Oberholzer's office they were greeted time and again by smiles. People in white coats, white trousers and white shoes. Their gleaming teeth held their own against their spotless clothing; they were clearly an important part of the uniform. Eschenbach thought about his own teeth and kept his mouth closed.

'Here we are.' Tobias Eigenmann gestured to the open office door, bowed in a manner more befitting the reign of Kaiser Wilhelm and waited until the inspector had stepped past him into the room. Then he shut the door carefully from the outside.

'I see you've met my darling Eigenmann. Gay as a maypole!' Rania Oberholzer guffawed. 'But a gifted dentist.' She greeted Eschenbach like an old friend. 'Gay or not, if I were straight, I'd gobble him up, bones and all!' She laughed again and Eschenbach took her at her word.

With her barrel-like figure and round face that descended into three chins, she was bigger than he had remembered. At thirteen stone, he was only slightly larger than her.

'We've got the perfect set-up for a good working relationship. Did you know that most cases of sexual assault occur in the workplace? If you exclude assault within families, of course,' she added.

'Speaking of which . . .' replied Eschenbach, making the most of her openness. She was dressed all in black, which he found refreshing in a place dominated by white. 'You're still wearing black?'

'I always wear black, Inspector. White coats make me sick. Too much white is like too much good weather. Take a look outside.' She pointed to the window. 'We've had positively tropical weather for over six weeks now. Are people happy? Are they heck! They're tetchy and desperate for rain. Too much sun, too much white, too much stress . . . you name it. Variety is the spice of life, don't you think, Inspector? Not to mention that black is slimming!' She laughed again. It was an earthquake of a laugh that gripped her entire body. Despite her unshapely figure, there was something endearing about her. Something captivating that made you feel that nothing on earth could harm you.

'Come, let's sit down. I've got flat feet and I can't bear standing for long.'

Perhaps it was her laugh, her directness, her lack of inhibition that endeared Eschenbach to her. She stated the reality that others preferred to ignore; she practically shouted it. And she devoured every budding embarrassment with a laugh as deep as the ocean. Eschenbach could well imagine that there were people who would entrust Rania Oberholzer with their life story within minutes of meeting her.

'I assume you know everything about Philipp Bettlach,' he said suddenly, before collapsing into the chair that she had offered him.

'Ah, you think?' She poured two glasses of water and emptied one of them in a single gulp. 'And what makes you think that, may I ask?' She refilled her glass and drank it down.

'I'd tell you everything if it were me,' lied Eschenbach.

'I have to drink a lot of water, my doctor says. Four litres a day! Imagine that! Kidney stones . . . it's miserable, let me tell you.' There were four large bottles of Evian on the round table where they were sitting. She refilled her glass again. 'Help me get through this stuff. I hate still water.' Eschenbach drank and said nothing.

'Philipp Bettlach ... poor sod,' she said after the fifth glass. 'He spent his life pining for a father and his brother outdid him in every way.'

Eschenbach listened intently. He knew this much already.

'Do you know what it's like? Growing up without a father?'

Eschenbach thought about his own father, who had died four years previously. He opened the second bottle of Evian and refilled the glasses.

She hadn't expected an answer and went on. 'I grew up without parents. They died in a car accident when I was a child. But at least I had pictures of them. My aunt and my uncle who I lived with told me about my mother and my father and, in time, they brought them to life again. At least at night, when I was supposed to be going to sleep ... and in my dreams.'

He understood what she meant and nodded.

'His mother hardly spoke about his father. He was a Swiss border guard, she said. Helped Jewish refugees to make it to Switzerland illegally. Their relationship survived the war but not the years following it. Somehow, he suddenly disappeared off the scene. Went to work in Nigeria with the Red Cross and died there tragically. That's all Philipp could get out of her. No photos, no one who knew him. He remained a ghost throughout Philipp's life. I think it tormented him. At first he lived with his mother and brother, and then she put him in boarding school.'

'Where you came to know each other,' interrupted Eschenbach. He remembered that she had mentioned it at the church.

'Yes . . . Raschnitz.' She was silent for a moment and it seemed to Eschenbach as if she were disappearing into the past. Then she looked up with a jerk and was back. 'You were paying attention, Inspector. Horrible funeral, wasn't it?'

'I find funerals to be little else,' said Eschenbach.

'Oh really? I'd like to go to one where people dance. With a gospel choir and the congregation tapping their feet . . . can you imagine it?' Rania Oberholzer stretched out her arms and her body shook.

Eschenbach hadn't given his own funeral much thought. 'Of course, there are different ways to mourn.'

'I don't think singing and dancing's a bad one.' She laughed.

'Perhaps,' mumbled Eschenbach, who was hopeless at both. 'Tell me about Raschnitz.'

'It was about five in the morning. It was a grey Tuesday, after Easter. I can't be sure now. I know it was a Tuesday, though.' She opened a new bottle of water, the third. Eschenbach took it from her and refilled the glasses. 'Our class had a free period when his brother's huge, dark-blue car drove up. I thought Johannes was his chauffeur at first. It was just the two of them. Normally both parents come, or just the mother and a driver. At the time, we didn't know that Johannes was his brother. He simply wasn't old enough to be his father, though they did look very similar. The fathers of boarders are older and the mothers are younger. Much, much younger.' She laughed. 'And sometimes it's the other way round.'

'Were you the same age?' asked Eschenbach, whose limited knowledge of boarding schools came from things he'd overheard.

'Yes, almost to the day. He was born on the twenty-seventh of October, I was born on the twenty-eighth. We were both

Scorpios!' She rolled her eyes. 'There were eight girls and four boys in our year. Philipp was the fifth and the prettiest of the lot. He was lanky and had long, dark-blond locks that fell to his shoulders.' She looked out of the window thoughtfully.

'And?' Eschenbach could think of nothing else to say and hoped it would be enough to keep the story going.

'I think it was his eyes. Sometimes the sun beamed out of them.' She paused. Then she ran the palm of her hand over a couple of drops of water that were shimmering like pearls on the smooth wooden surface. 'But mostly they glowed pale, like moonlight.' She thought again. 'Do you ever feel the effects of the moon, Inspector?'

'My wife thinks so.'

'And? Is she right?'

'Perhaps. I can't be sure. But I use it as an excuse for my bad moods.'

'The moon has a greater influence on us than we think: on the tides, on menstruation, on growth and death.'

Perhaps Corina would have granted Rania Oberholzer the nickname 'Mrs Doom'. The way she spoke about Bettlach and the moon, and sat there in her black T-shirt that hung over her shoulders like a poncho, with her black fingernails and dark lip gloss. Eschenbach might have objected. In reality, she was much too lively, open and playful. What next, a werewolf story? The tale of the Bogeyman who came out at night to gobble up little girls?

'We were all crazy about him. We flocked to him like little moths to a light bulb.' She dabbed the sweat from her brow with her right sleeve. 'Years later, I met a gypsy. Cats and dogs followed

him around the way we ran after Philipp. Pets would simply abandon their masters and trail after him. Can you imagine?'

'So, did you two have a thing?'

Rania Oberholzer burst out laughing. 'Me? We all had a thing
with him! He screwed everyone . . . including most of the boys.'
She opened the last bottle of water and Eschenbach poured
them a glass each. 'We were his little slaves, Inspector. The whole
school was in his thrall. And I don't just mean the students.' She
laughed and seemed to grind her words between her teeth. 'Are
you familiar with your submissive side, Inspector?'

Eschenbach grinned shyly. 'I'm not sure I have one.'

'That's what I thought too. And then along came this lanky
boy with his angel face and his deep-blue eyes, and suddenly it
all changed.'

Eschenbach wanted to disagree, but said nothing,

'Yes. I don't know if he really was what you would term a pae-
dophile. I spent a long time thinking about it afterwards, while I
was studying medicine.'

'Was he a sadist, do you think?' Eschenbach had read a little
on the topic.

'Perhaps. Whatever that means. He was cold, and ruthless.
And the tragic thing was that he knew it. There were times
when he would shut himself away. He was unapproachable and
wouldn't say a word to anyone. Once, he burned a hole in his
own arm with a cigarette. He screamed as he did it and it stank
of burnt flesh.'

'Was he in treatment?'

'Later, yes. I think at some point his brother noticed what was
wrong with him.'

'Do you know where?'

'Burghölzli, the psychiatric hospital' she replied quickly. 'And Basle, as far as I know.'

'Did you see his files?' asked Eschenbach, watching her drinking and looking out of the window.

'What makes you think that, Inspector? I'm not a family member and Philipp isn't . . . I mean, *wasn't* my patient.'

Eschenbach didn't know why he was sure that Rania Oberholzer had Philipp Bettlach's files. 'So you do have them. Can I see them?'

She turned from the window and looked at him for a long time without speaking. Then the defiant laughter returned. 'I can tell you're not daft, Inspector. And I don't want to lead you on. I'll give you them.' She looked at him seriously. 'They're copies, but as far as anyone else is concerned they've been destroyed . . . I assume we understand each other?'

Eschenbach nodded.

She stood up, took a couple of steps towards the wall and opened the drawer of a filing cabinet. It took her a moment to find it. It was a grey, unlabelled file.

'Here. Just make sure you find Philipp's murderer.' She placed the file on the table and stood there.

'You seem to care a lot about it. I mean, does it really matter to you that we find the murderer?' asked Eschenbach, leafing through the documents.

She looked at him and it seemed as if she were asking the same question. 'Yes. When it comes to dentistry, it's important not to pull out the wrong tooth.' She hesitated for a moment, then went on: 'Philipp was sick . . . but he was also my friend.

My sick friend. But I think murder is an exceptionally bad cure for the sickness he had, and not just from a medical perspective.'

'These files are over thirty years old,' said the inspector, surprised. 'Did he not receive treatment more recently?'

'Yes, as far as I know, in foreign clinics, mostly in the US. He didn't talk about it much. Switzerland is a small country and Philipp Bettlach was a prominent name in local circles. I assume he wanted to do it as anonymously as possible.'

Eschenbach nodded. It explained the regular trips abroad, and now he knew why his inquiries at Swiss clinics had yielded nothing.

She held out a large, fleshy hand.

'One last question,' he said as they shook hands. 'Do you know why Eveline Marchand left him so suddenly?'

'Yes, she had a child.'

Eschenbach stumbled. 'By him?' he asked.

'No.'

'Are you sure?' Eschenbach would not let go of her hand. He clung to it, as if it were the key to the information that he so badly needed.

'Yes. Back when he found out about the child, there was a dispute over custody. It was only brief because the paternity test proved he wasn't the father.' She looked at his hand clutching hers. She did not go on until he had let go. 'At first, he was furious, he wanted to know who had cuckolded him. But not long after, he lost interest.'

'And do you know who—' Eschenbach continued to dig as they walked to the door.

'No idea, Inspector. But I'm sure you'll find out.'

When they were standing out in the hallway, she held out her hand again, without a word, as if they were old friends. Then Eschenbach walked past the long white wall towards the lift, his mind racing. Somehow, he thought she was right. Too much white made you sick.

Chapter 26

A storm was brewing but refusing to break. One of Mother Nature's threats, Eschenbach thought. Dark clouds had gathered and the wind flattened the shrubs along the train platform.

When he arrived in Zurich, it was a beautiful summer's day once more. The first evening commuters flocked onto the trains, taking them home safely to be reunited with their families in the suburbs. Eschenbach was reminded of cattle trucks and was glad that he was able to walk to work.

He loved the train, as long as he was able to travel in the opposite direction to the crowds, in a half-empty compartment. It excited him: the rhythmic rattle of the carriage wheels, steel grinding on steel and tonnes of iron sliding over delicate tracks. It often helped him think – and sometimes it helped him sleep. Both were good.

He had read the reports that Rania Oberholzer had given him. The first report came from a professor, Dr Eberhard Meierhans, the then acting head of psychiatry at the University of Basle. The second came from a Professor Dr Max Zogg, former head physician for psychiatry at the University Hospital of Zurich. Both agreed on the fundamentals, though the Zurich report was significantly shorter and more concise. Perhaps that was a privilege granted to head physicians. Perhaps it was all in the names, thought Eschenbach. With a name like Zogg, you couldn't afford to be long-winded.

If the doctors were to be believed, Philipp Bettlach was an 'emotionally unstable personality with narcissistic tendencies and masked bipolar disorder, caused by asocial development, coupled with sexual disorders with their roots in a discordant psychosexual development'.

Somehow this climed with the image Eschenbach had formed of Philipp Bettlach following his conversations with those who knew him. The absence of a true identity. The pursuit of extreme experiences – mostly sexual. A sort of moral blindness. Was that it?

On Saturday, when Corina and Kathrin returned from Engadine around midday, the terrace boasted a brand-new basil plant, a new rosemary bush and a new trug of flowers. Eschenbach had just finished watering the stone slabs, as well as his own feet. The last particles of fresh earth, evidence of his repotting campaign that morning, were whisked away by the water spray.

They sat under the two broad umbrellas eating cake and drinking coffee. There was no talk of the new herbs or the freshly planted flowers. Nor did they touch on the old ones, which he had allowed to wither and die, and which were now tied up in a sack in the bin outside.

Kathrin told him about Engadine. The permanent white peaks had turned brown in the heat, with huge piles of rocks threatening to come crashing down from the mountains.

Corina said the thing she was worried about crashing was Kathrin.

'Out at the disco until half three – and she's just a teenager,' she said.

'I'm already taller than you, Mum,' she replied with her mouth full.

'Bigger, perhaps. Height has nothing to do with it,' Corina countered, snatching a piece of cake off Kathrin's plate.

'Oi! You've got your own!' Kathrin complained, pulling her plate closer. 'You know how much I hate that.'

Eschenbach tried to muster a stern look, feeling happy that they were back.

He told them about the events of the past few days, about his trip to Berne and the new Lavazza machine at the office. Later on, Kathrin spent an hour on the phone to a friend, before heading off with her rollerblades under her arm.

Eschenbach thought she looked like a gladiator, black skating pads covering her bare knees and elbows, wearing gloves and wrist supports. She was pretty; she had Corina's long legs and sensuous mouth. Her scruffy denim hot pants sat on hips that were more boyish than womanly and she was wearing a thong that matched her black outfit.

Later that day, as Corina lay naked on top of him, perspiring and breathing hard, they wondered aloud how long it would continue like this. Was she already seeing a boy? Corina's smile assured him he was the last to know.

'Do you think I should join a choir again?' Corina asked casually when they were back out on the terrace. She was lying on an old reclining chair, stretching her feet in the evening sun.

'A choir?' Eschenbach was thumbing through the *Swiss Journal* weekend magazine and was only half listening.

'Yes, a choir.' She said it loudly and clearly. 'Are you even listening to me?'

'Of course I am.' Eschenbach put the magazine to one side and turned to Corina. 'So, singing, you say?' 'You've got a lovely voice . . . so why not?'

'You think so?' She smiled.

'What kind of choir were you thinking of?'

'I don't know,' she said, pulling her legs towards her and resting her chin on her knee. 'Not a church one anyway.'

'No Bach cantatas, then?' Eschenbach grinned.

'Why, do you like them?'

'You know I like Bach.'

'Yes . . . but I'd rather sing something else, something with a bit more swing to it. Like at that concert before Christmas.'

'The Cats' Choir, you mean? The women's one?'

'It's the Bo Katzmann Choir.' Corina stifled a laugh.

'The one with the good-looking conductor, I know . . .' He raised his eyebrows and grinned.

'You're not taking me seriously,' she said, pouting. 'Bo Katzmann teaches in Basle. I'd like to find something here in Zurich.'

'Well, that's a relief,' he teased. 'He was quite the stud. Is his name really Bo?'

'No, his real name's Reto Borer.' A hint of embarrassment passed over her face. 'And if you're about to ask me how I know that—'

'I'm an idiot,' said Eschenbach, who had already stood up and disappeared into the apartment through the veranda doors.

He sat at Kathrin's computer for half an hour, browsing the web until he found what he was looking for: Pierre Oliver's real name was Peter Oliver Deck.

It took him two hours to find what he needed. Once he arrived at the office, he loaded the Project Genesis disc and found Peter O. Deck, just as he had anticipated. Then he called the CID in Basle and got the number for Dirk Meidinger. He managed to reach his colleague at a barbecue and was pleased to hear that they had already cottoned on to this information in Basle.

'We still haven't found anything suspicious on Deck,' said Meidinger. 'But as soon as we do, we'll let you know.'

Eschenbach thanked him and left headquarters shortly after half eight. His stomach rumbled, and when he arrived home Corina greeted him in a summery evening dress.

Once Eschenbach had freshened up, they went out to eat. Kathrin brought along one of her girlfriends, which was fine by them. 'I prefer it if she brings her friends home, then at least we know what's going on,' said Corina, and Eschenbach resigned himself to the fact that their home would now be open to any and all of Kathrin's friends. Sometimes, he wished things could be a little calmer and more orderly. At least at home.

The Alvarez was a little open-air restaurant on the lake, well known for its freshly prepared paella. Eschenbach ate like a horse and Corina asked at least three times whether they thought she had gained weight. She lifted her T-shirt up to her navel and everyone could see that her stomach was beautifully tanned and slim. The girls whispered amongst themselves, stopping ever more frequently to send flurries of text messages into the warm summer night.

Monday morning dragged by uneventfully. Half of the staff were on holiday, the other half had nothing to report – nothing exciting at least. It simply wasn't normal for an investigation to stall at this stage. Even Kobler's Monday morning call, which usually came around half eleven, failed to materialise. It dawned on Eschenbach that she had taken a few days' holiday. South of France, did she say? Or the French Atlantic coast? He couldn't remember, nor did he care. He was sure Rosa Mazzoleni would know, if only for emergencies. Perhaps she had even organised it herself.

He wondered whether he should call Lenz and ask how his research was going. He knew Lenz would hate him for it. I'll be ready when I'm ready, he would say. And if he were to page Jagmetti and ask for an interim report, Lenz might end their friendship there and then. He decided to let them be.

The inspector got up and left his office. 'Anything from Hottiger?' he asked Rosa Mazzoleni. He looked at a couple of the postcards on the partition wall in the secretary's office. 'Has anything come in this morning?'

'That's the third time you've asked me that.' Rosa looked at the clock. 'In the space of two hours.'

'What about customs . . . have they called?'

'No, nothing from customs either.' Rosa Mazzoleni snapped shut the folder on her table, irritated. 'No faxes, no calls, nothing! Just the usual office stuff.'

'Nothing, then,' muttered Eschenbach.

'Good God! It's Monday morning and it's the summer holidays . . . it's not that unusual, is it?'

The inspector grunted and picked up a postcard that had fallen onto the floor by his feet.

The manhunt for Doris Hottiger had been under way for several days; the border police had intensified their checks. As far as the girl's father was concerned, Eschenbach had arranged to inspect the passenger lists for all transatlantic flights. If Ernst Hottiger returned to Switzerland, he would be the first to know. And if he didn't manage to track the flight, Hottiger's house on Lake Sihl had also been fitted with surveillance cameras.

The inspector had prepared for every eventuality: for an arrest followed by hours of interrogations, for the lawyers that might be called in to defend either of the Hottigers – or for a rebuke from Councillor Sacher. He was ready for anything.

What he hadn't counted on, however, was the mind-numbing, dawdling pace of that Monday morning.

He had no interest in the mountain of post piled in the in-tray. He had glanced over it briefly and found nothing that would have helped him in the slightest.

Eschenbach was making for the door when Rosa Mazzoleni's voice warbled through the intercom.

'Basle on the line. Are you still there?'

'I was just about to . . .' Eschenbach took the receiver and sat down.

A quarter of an hour later, after his call with Inspector Dirk Meidinger from Basle CID, Eschenbach was a new man. His prey was in his sights once more. The temptation to pack it in and head out for lunch was long gone.

Pornographic material involving children had been found in the dead man's home in Basle. In a hidden compartment, behind the wine bottles in the cellar. There were photos, an address book and several videos. Eschenbach felt like rejoicing. Yes, it might have been nicer to stumble upon Troy or a hitherto undiscovered burial chamber in the Valley of the Kings, or even a bunch of keys that you thought you had lost. But Eschenbach was delighted all the same.

How many times had his hunches been proven right in his twenty years in the force? He'd sensed it as soon he first heard about the murder in Basle, with the fax in his hands: the two murders were linked. He didn't know why he thought this, nor did he really want to think about it. What made it so convincing was that he didn't need to think about it. Now he had proof that he was on the right track. Something connected the two murders; a cause – however bittersweet it might be – for celebration.

He caught himself wondering whether he should drive over there himself. Was he paranoid, or just anxious that he would be proven wrong? And what difference would it make anyway? The police in Basle had kindly prepared copies of the material for him and assured him they would be ready for collection in two hours' time.

He called the patrol car control centre and gave his name, rank and identification number. 'Are Lohmeier and Wullschleger on duty at the moment?' he asked. It took a moment for the friendly woman's voice to reply.

'Yes, till eight o'clock. Shall I put you through, Inspector?'

'Thanks, I'll wait.' Another two minutes passed, which Eschenbach spent searching for his open packet of cigarillos; he later realised he had been holding it the entire time.

'Patrol car seven,' announced a familiar voice. It was Steffen Lohmeier. There followed the usual banter that had developed into a kind of standard greeting over the years.

'Do you know what I'm getting the wife for Christmas?' asked Lohmeier, not expecting an answer. 'A chair . . . I've already bought it. All I need to do now is to connect the electricity!' He laughed hoarsely. The misogynist jokes – Lohmeier delivered another two of his best – were all part of it. It didn't really suit Lohmeier, who was actually quite a sensitive person. It was as unbecoming as his goatee and the roughneck image he cultivated.

Eschenbach explained where and who they needed to visit. He stressed that the package would need to be brought straight to him at headquarters. 'No one else is to touch it,' he said. Steffen Lohmeier laughed as if he had spotted some kind of double-entendre.

Eschenbach made another three calls. He informed Lohmeier's superior about his special mission, called the lab and arranged for two technicians and a room. He couldn't reach Corina. He left a voicemail, apologising, and explaining that he wouldn't be home for dinner.

When Eschenbach crossed the Sihl Bridge, making for Bahnhofstrasse, it occurred to him that he had forgotten to call Dr Mallner. Joachim Mallner was a police psychologist and he wanted to show him the two reports on Philipp Bettlach. He switched his phone on and waited for the irritating beeps – heralding an incoming message – to stop. He called Rosa Mazzoleni's number, crossed the street and found a patch of shade by the entrance to a children's clothing shop. It was Jagmetti who answered.

'Ah, back from the catacombs, are we? How was it?'

'It was . . . the whole weekend, boss!' Jagmetti sounded tired.

Eschenbach tried and failed to hold back a laugh. 'Did you find anything?'

'You know Lenz!' he replied. 'When he's got his teeth into something . . .' Jagmetti tried to think of a suitable way to finish the sentence

'Then he won't let go,' said Eschenbach. 'I can imagine.'

'It was pretty intense. Almost forty-eight hours of nonstop searching. Boss, Lenz, he's . . . I mean . . . you know, don't you, he's a pretty special guy.'

Eschenbach leant against a colourful elephant standing on a bright red base, a coin-operated ride for children. 'Yeah, Lenz is a special guy, you're not wrong. Get some sleep.' Eschenbach's body shook with laughter once more and the elephant began to rock, despite no one having deposited a coin inside it. 'Oh, one more thing. Put me onto Ms Mazzoleni before I forget.'

'She's away at the moment. I'm covering the phones.' He sounded harassed.

Eschenbach noticed the way the shopkeeper kept throwing him dirty looks through the window. He got a hold of himself, took his phone in the other hand and moved away from the see-sawing elephant, which was smiling sweetly, quite unaffected by the altercation. 'Then have a quick look at her address book. I need the number for Dr Mallner, and you can give me Lenz's number too.'

It didn't take long. Eschenbach realised he had nothing to write with. He went into the shop and gestured for a pen. The shopkeeper handed him a ballpoint pen and a pad with a look of disdain and he wrote down the number. He nodded his thanks. 'Now go get some sleep, I don't expect to see you until tomorrow morning,' he said, ending the call. The shopkeeper shook her head uncomprehendingly, without disturbing her perfectly coiffed hairstyle. Eschenbach could see that she would never approve of a profession where staff went to sleep at four in the afternoon. He smiled politely, dropped a two-franc piece in the UNICEF box, said goodbye and left the shop.

Eschenbach wondered whether he should go to the Zeughauskeller, then he looked at the time. It wouldn't be sensible, he thought. Heinz was never there at this time. He strolled along and found a shady spot in one of the countless cafés along the street. The tables were littered with open street maps and tourist guides. People from all over the world were bent over them, tracing streets with their index fingers and searching for churches and monuments.

He ordered a large beer and the sausage salad special. He would have preferred to order a ham hock but, like everything on the main menu, it was only available from 6 p.m. The sausage salad special was the largest dish on the daytime menu. He typed Lenz's number into his phone and waited; no one picked up. When his beer arrived, he tried again. This time, he succeeded; there was a click on the line and Lenz picked up.

'Still clearing up?' Eschenbach wiped the foam from his upper lip.

'Oh, it's you.'

Eschenbach couldn't tell whether Lenz was pleased or disappointed. 'I heard you were finished. Did you find anything?'

'That boy of yours ran himself ragged. He dozed off on me twice in the night. I let him sleep. He's a good chap though. We've compiled a great pile of stuff for you. Mazzoleni has it all under lock and key. Take a look at the CD. We didn't print much out. But I think you'll find what you're looking for.'

'Really? Tell me something. Got any suspects? Any bad eggs?' The young Tamil man, dressed in a white apron, went to place his sausage salad on the table in front of him and frowned: 'They're not eggs ... they're sausages.' Eschenbach gestured to show he was on the phone.

'You'll find out soon enough. Jagmetti should be able to help, he knows the material. Let him get some shut-eye first though. He looks like a body you'd find in the basement.'

'After spending the weekend with you? Sounds like he got off lightly.'

Instead of answering, he grunted out a laugh. 'I'm clearing off for a couple of days. If you need me I'll be on cloud nine. "Eagle Eyes" can fly without me.'

'All the best, then,' said Eschenbach, wondering what he meant by cloud nine. 'And let me know when you're back on your feet.'

But Lenz had already hung up.

Chapter 27

In the technical room, the projector hummed. On the screen, two men were raping an eight-year-old girl. They took turns – one holding the girl, the other holding the camera. No faces were visible except that of the little one screaming and whimpering, looking intermittently into the camera with great, hollow eyes.

Once he had vomited the beer and the sausage salad special into the nearest toilet bowl, Eschenbach felt better. At least physically. The technicians had turned the sound off; despite the smoking ban, one of them was smoking a cigarette.

'Was that the last one?' asked the inspector when the image on the screen went black. He felt his stomach acid rising and his mouth was dry, even though he had just rinsed it out with water.

'Yes, five tapes. That was the last,' said the technician, throwing his cigarette into a white plastic cup half filled with water. It hissed.

'We need to print off close-ups of the men's bodies. Hands, feet, watches, rings, birthmarks, anything and everything.' Eschenbach looked first at one technician, then at the other.

'Of course, no problem. When do you need them for?'

'Now. We'll need to make them now. Is that all right?'

'Sure. We just thought, you might perhaps, I mean, it might take a while . . .'

'That's not a problem. Tomorrow morning at the latest.'

The technicians looked at Eschenbach as if he were from another planet.

'It'll count as double overtime, of course.' Nobody did this for free.

'It's not about that,' said one of the young men, who hadn't spoken before. 'I mean, we've half a basement full of this filth and no one's been interested in it until now. There's material seized from house searches and raids on sex shops. They haul the stuff down to us in crates. You're the first one from upstairs to come down, take a look and tell us what we're supposed to do with it.'

Eschenbach didn't know how he should answer. He thought about Operation Genesis, which hadn't really begun in earnest; this was a small first step. Suddenly, he felt sorry for the men. Without knowing it, they would soon become the gatekeepers of the largest hoard of child porn in Switzerland.

'Let's get to it, lads!' said the inspector, slapping his hand down on the light-grey table. 'Let me know how I can help you. Let's get going!'

The two technicians looked at one another briefly and stood up. Eschenbach thought he noticed a certain glimmer of relief in their pale faces. Somehow, they were happy to have a job to do at last, and a common goal.

When Eschenbach arrived home at half four, Corina was sitting on the terrace in the dark, wearing a light nightdress. When he turned on the kitchen light to get himself a glass of water, she turned her head and looked at him, saying nothing. He switched the light off, went out and sat next to her.

'Tell me something, are you crazy? Do you realise that I've been calling all over for you? I called Christian, Gabriel – at the Sheep's Head and at home, headquarters, the Zeughauskeller ... God knows where else.' The words gushed out of her and Eschenbach was struck by how long she was able to speak without drawing breath. 'Nobody bloody knew where you were! And your phone was off...'

He sensed what was coming and said nothing. His glass of water tasted stale. Tap water, he thought. He had recently read a report detailing the excellent quality of Zurich's water. You could confidently do away with expensive mineral water, the authors concluded unanimously, and one of them was a city chemist. As far as mineral content was concerned, Zurich's water clearly contained a greater number of minerals than most mineral waters, it said. He wondered if restaurants would now offer cold tap water – at the same price as Perrier or Valser. Or whether those who were already doing it would now do so with a clearer conscience. Eschenbach didn't know why all of this ran through his head and why he didn't like the taste of the water.

Corina hadn't finished. She looked at Eschenbach and saw that he was not in the mood for an argument. She no longer needed to ask whether he was having an affair. No lover in the world would send a man home so miserable. It was just a pretext anyway, a cover for her worry. Suddenly, she became very childlike.

'We found the child porn tapes.' He spoke quietly, almost mechanically in the half-light. 'We're taking close-ups. We might be onto something.'

'Do you want to talk about it?' asked Corina, who had got up and straddled his legs.

'Perhaps in the morning,' he murmured, exhausted. Then he poured the rest of his water into the pot of basil.

'It's morning already,' she whispered into his neck, and they held each other a while longer.

The Brissago's pungeant smoke stopped him from closing his eyes completely. He was reading Lenz's report. From time to time, his mind ran away from him and he didn't know whether he had already read the page in front of him or not.

He looked terrible, that was Rosa Mazzoleni's verdict. She hadn't said it directly, which was worse. She asked whether he had worked late the night before, looking at him concernedly over the rim of her glasses. Eschenbach wasn't fooled: what she meant was that he looked pale, exhausted, sullen and, if he were being honest, sick as a dog. Almost nothing helped. Not a Lavazza espresso in a pearly white coffee cup with a sugar bowl on the side, nor yet a few amaretti and a smile that promised to grin and bear it. Keeping his door shut was the only thing that helped.

Eschenbach assumed that Jagmetti was still sleeping and decided not to call him.

Lenz had divided the folder into four chapters: Military, Sport, Family, Career. How easy it was to split a life into chapters, Eschenbach thought.

Where had Lenz found his information? There were confidential documents covering significant periods of Hottiger's military career. How in God's name had he got hold of such material? He would have liked to call him, but he knew it was no use. Certainly not in the condition that Lenz was likely to be in now.

One photo showed Hottiger as a young captain of general staff, another showed him as an instructor in a colonel's uniform. In this one, he was much older and had a short, greying beard. Beards were uncommon among high-ranking officers, thought Eschenbach. For some reason, soldiers liked to be clean-shaven – ideally behind the ears too. Eschenbach thought Hottiger looked better with a beard. There was a touch of Ernest Hemingway about him, something daring and romantic. Eschenbach read some of the testimonies written by people who knew Hottiger. They were all exceptional. Intelligent, strong-willed and assertive were the most common attributes. Reading one of the testimonies, he stopped. He read it a second time. It wasn't the words that struck him, it was the person who had written them:

Captain Hottiger led the Aurora exercise with typical strategic brilliance. Despite extensive disruptive action from those managing the exercise, he never lost sight of the goal. He possesses a high degree of intelligence and the ability to understand the enemy's position. Though this is an individualistic trait, he is able to subordinate his aims for the greater good.

I wholeheartedly recommend Captain Hottiger for the next training course for general staff officers.

General Staff Colonel J. Bettlach

Johannes Bettlach and Hottiger knew each other from the army! Towards the back of the folder, Eschenbach found the same name again. This time, it was as chief witness at Hottiger's wedding. Bettlach and Hottiger were friends.

Eva Matter and Ernst Hottiger had married on 23 May 1981 in a civil ceremony in Horgen in the canton of Zurich. He could find no record of a church wedding. Hottiger had been forty years of age at the time, his wife sixteen years younger. She must have already been pregnant, because seven months later, on 10 December 1981, she had given birth in Lachen Hospital in the canton of Schwyz. There was a copy of Doris Hottiger's birth certificate. And Eva Hottiger-Matter's death certificate. Issued on 18 December 1981 by a Dr Beat Leibundgut from Feusisberg in the canton of Schwyz. Eschenbach stopped when he read the dates. It must have occurred to Lenz too, because he had circled them in black pen.

Eschenbach had assumed that Eva Hottiger had died in labour the same day that her daughter was born. The paper he held in his hands proved that she hadn't died until a week later. The cause of death was 'sudden cardiac arrest'. Could it be a delayed consequence of the birth? Eschenbach knew about sudden infant death syndrome. He knew about the anxieties entertained by new mothers, the fear that their newborns would stop breathing and die. But a mother's sudden death?

Lenz had scribbled two words on the copies of both certificates, birth and death. The word 'CHECK' stood out in capitals, and underneath was something illegible which he deciphered as 'Originals?' Did Lenz doubt the authenticity of the certificates? And if he did, why? How had he managed to track down the documents in such a short space of time? They were all questions that he would have liked to ask him – questions that Jagmetti might well be able to answer, too, when he finally made an appearance.

He wrote a couple of names, addresses and telephone numbers in his notebook; then he dialled the number for Johannes Bettlach. To his surprise, he got through to the banker on his first attempt.

'I'd like to talk to you about Eva Matter.'

The line crackled; Bettlach's voice was very faint: 'I'm ... at the moment ... bad ... abroad until ... hello?' Scraps of sentences stuttered in a noisy abyss.

'Are you still there?' Eschenbach shouted.

The line went dead.

The inspector swore and called Rosa Mazzoleni to ask for the number for Zurich Commercial Bank.

'He's abroad all week,' Bettlach's secretary piped up. 'He'll be back in the office around three on Friday. Can I take a message?'

'Tell him to call me,' Bettlach grumbled. 'Immediately.' The inspector made an appointment for Friday and ended the call. He flung the report into his drawer bad-temperedly. As he went to lock it, he realised that the key was missing. He didn't know whether he had ever had one.

He left his office and asked Rosa to make sure that no one went in while he was away.

'I never let anyone into your office.'

'What about when you're not here?' Eschenbach asked hurriedly.

'Then I lock it. I've been doing it for ten years. Did it never occur to you?'

'Why would it when I'm not here?' Eschenbach raised his eyebrows; it was a lame argument. Of course, he knew that she locked it before she went home in the evening. But he hadn't known that she also did it when she went for a chinwag on the first floor.

'Imagine someone just turned up. Anyone could get in,' she said, shaking her head. She was organising a mountain of files and had paper clips between her lips. 'And how would that end?' she continued, without looking up. 'To think that I'd just let someone slip into the detective superintendent's office . . .'

At that moment, Jagmetti came plodding along the corridor. He looked like he had slept well. Nevertheless, the inspector could tell that his weekend down in the basement had wreaked havoc with his blood pressure and his self-confidence.

'Hello, at your service.' He winked shyly. Neither Mazzoleni nor Eschenbach responded to his greeting. 'Things not going well?' he added cheekily.

'No, they're going splendidly,' said Mazzoleni through gritted teeth. She looked up briefly over the rim of her glasses and buried herself back in the mountain of files that lay before her on the desk like sheets of badly bound waste paper.

'It's all right,' murmured Eschenbach. 'We've got plenty to do, you can come along. We're driving over to the upper shores of Lake Zurich, to Lachen.' He stressed the first syllable of the last word so that it was clear it could only be the place, bearing no similarity to the German verb *lachen*, to laugh.

'Then haaaaave fun!' Mazzoleni hissed from behind the mountain of files. 'And by the way, there's a wonderful designer hotel in Laaaach-en.' She took the paper clip out of her mouth and twirled it in her fingers. 'Fantastic Mediterranean food. I'll give them a call now and reserve you a table.' She checked her address book. 'Al Porto, here we go. It's right on the lake.

You'll be sure to find it.' She had already picked up the receiver when she thought better of it and wrote the number on a notepad. 'Here, call them yourself.' Without waiting for a reaction, she fished a key out of her desk, stood up and walked over to Eschenbach's office door. Then she put the key in the lock, turned it twice and smiled: 'I'll be taking my break now, gentlemen!'

They drove Eschenbach's old Volvo on the motorway, which ran along the northern bank of Lake Zurich, making towards Chur.

Jagmetti looked pale

'Are you all right?' asked Eschenbach.

The young police officer grimaced.

'Quite a stunt. No breakfast, I'd be feeling rough too.' He rolled down his window and the summer breeze whistled into the car. 'We'll drive straight over and get something to eat, then you'll be back, guns blazing.'

After leaving the car at a car park in front of the entrance to a petrol station shop, they bought sandwiches and cola and sat quietly on a bench to eat.

'Better?' asked Eschenbach after a while. Jagmetti nodded, chewing, and washed the rest down with cola. Then they drove on.

'How did you come across those documents in the end?' the inspector asked.

Jagmetti simply shrugged. 'He didn't tell me. I wasn't brave enough to ask him, to be honest. Somehow, he managed to get into the right databases. The old guy's pretty savvy, I wouldn't have expected it. And certain documents were faxed to us.' Jagmetti thought for a moment, before going on.

'I mean, obviously, we are authorised to do so and should be able to retrieve the documents in the course of investigations.'

'I know that, for goodness' sake.' Eschenbach rolled his eyes. 'It's all legal, Jagmetti. Don't you worry. I just wonder how he managed to get it all together so quickly. But speed isn't a crime.'

'Except on the roads,' said Jagmetti.

Eschenbach grinned and took his foot off the accelerator.

Chapter 28

'We'll take the country roads the rest of the way,' said Eschenbach, steering the car down a curving slip road. 'Pfäffikon, canton of Schwyz. It used to be a bit of a backwater. Now it's a tax haven for the super-rich.' He pointed to the hills on the right, a luscious, inviting green, offering a wonderful view over the lake. The bottom third was replete with split-level houses, which glimmered in light, subtle colours. Now and then a crane rose up before them. Above these were a few newly built villas which sat enthroned on their own generous plots. 'Once upon a time cows pastured here, now it's capital,' Eschenbach murmured. 'Sometimes I wonder whether tax policy is the only policy that works in this country.'

Here and there they could see older houses, old-fashioned, built in the poor provincial style. They looked like poor relations next to the white façades of the new millionaires' homes; the last traces of forgotten poverty.

They drove over a bridge above a small road and saw Lachen church. The twin spires stood out between the houses like four-cornered posts, sturdy, somewhat severe, and its curved, domed roofs looked like dollops of cream topping. Eschenbach was inevitably reminded of the towel turbans that women wrapped over their wet hair when they came out of the sauna.

The road led through the crooked heart of the town in narrow bends, and when they thought they had gone too far, they discovered the white and blue signpost that pointed to the hospital.

Like the rest of the town, the hospital was composed of a new building and an old building. The maternity department was in the new building. Stairs led up to the entrance. On the wall to the left there was a quote by Albert Schweitzer:

The most profound and noble cause that binds humanity together is the will to work together for the greater good.

Eschenbach stood there. He read it a second time and then a third time before he was able to grasp it. He began to doubt his mind. Perhaps it was the heat, or the four hours' sleep he was missing.

Opposite the wall was a cafeteria. People, mainly elderly, were sitting on modern aluminium chairs under electric-blue umbrellas advertising mineral water. Most of them were quiet, staring at the coffee cups in front of them or at the Albert Schweitzer quote.

They waited for just fifteen minutes on the coloured upholstered seats. There was little in the way of bustle in the maternity department. Eschenbach looked at the photos of babies on the birth charts, which hung on the wall like a colourful mosaic. They tried to guess from the photos which ones were girls and which were boys; one would cover the name and the other would have to guess. Jagmetti won 7 to 4. When it came to Andrea, they weren't sure whether it was an Italian boy or a Swiss girl, and they agreed that a baby with a Turkish name must be a girl, though neither of them had heard the name before.

Sister Claudia was a sturdy woman in her mid-fifties with a red face and bright, cheerful eyes. She had wanted to freshen up beforehand, she said, because she rarely received official visits from such esteemed individuals. Eschenbach smirked. In Lachen, a village police officer was still a person to be respected. As were postmen and teachers, he thought. He wished he could say the same for Zurich.

Yes, she said, she remembered the Hottiger couple well. They were an unusual pair, she thought.

'You know, Inspector, if I hadn't seen the papers proving they were a married couple, I would have thought they were father and daughter.'

Eschenbach could have sworn that the redness in her cheeks deepened a little.

'Not because of the age difference, if that's what you're thinking. I've no problem with a young girl going off with a man of such . . . maturity.'

He liked the way she expressed herself.

'That wasn't it. That sort of thing wouldn't bother me.' She looked at Eschenbach and smiled. 'No, it was more the way that they interacted with one another.' Without waiting for questions, she continued: 'You see, I've brought whole villages of children into the world over the last thirty years. And do you know something?'

Sister Claudio allowed them a moment to shake their heads briefly. 'It doesn't matter how shy or snappy a couple are with each other – they can fight like cat and dog – but when their child comes into the world, they're united in love.' She paused briefly.

'But not the Hottigers. Even though they had only married six months before.'

'What about the birth? I mean, how did it go? You may have heard about . . .' Eschenbach didn't go on.

'That's the thing. There were no complications at all. It was a caesarean section . . . at the mother's request. It was textbook, I'm telling you. Then, barely a week later, I saw the obituary. Such a pretty young woman. Tragic. We were all shocked.'

'How long did she stay in hospital?' asked Eschenbach.

'Four days.'

'What?' Jagmetti piped up, surprised. 'My sister had a caesarean because the baby was breech. She stayed in hospital for over a week.'

'That's completely normal too. At least a week, we always say.' Jagmetti nodded.

'But the Hottigers wanted to go home after four days. She would be in good hands, they said, and they had a maid, so Dr Bamatter, our head of gynaecology, allowed it in the end.' Sister Claudio shrugged and all at once her powerful arms looked weak and helpless. 'If only she had stayed, perhaps the little one would still have her mother.'

'And what about Dr Bamatter? Is he still alive? I couldn't find him anywhere.' Eschenbach dabbed at the perspiration on his brow with his handkerchief.

'Oh, old Willy. He's been dead a long time. It was one of his last operations. He retired a year later. At seventy, you know. It tormented him, hearing about the girl, I can tell you. But Mrs Hottiger had recovered quickly from the operation and had a strong constitution . . . it's not nice to experience something like that, especially so close to retirement.'

Eschenbach nodded. 'Did he pursue the matter? I mean, it must have seemed quite unusual to an experienced doctor like himself, for a young girl – with a strong constitution like you say – to just drop dead.'

'Yes, he talked of nothing else for days on end. He talked to the doctor who issued the death certificate. What was his name?'

'Dr Leibundgut?' offered Eschenbach. The name had stood out to him.

'Yes, Dr Leibundgut. But it was too late. The body had already been cremated when the obituary appeared in the paper. A small family funeral, you know.'

She shrugged helplessly again. 'It's not easy to start your retirement that way.'

Eschenbach nodded and thought uneasily about the number of unsolved cases he would leave behind.

The two police officers thanked the nurse and walked to the lift, before deciding to take the stairs. A short walk would do them good, Eschenbach thought, fishing a cigarillo out of the packet.

'A strange story, don't you think, boss?'

Eschenbach said nothing. He trudged silently down the stairs, thinking.

'Lenz and I tried to find something on this Eva Matter,' said Jagmetti. 'Former residences, parents . . . anything.' The young police officer shook his head. 'You won't believe it, boss. We found nothing. A total blank! Despite what the certificates might try to prove. Matter doesn't exist.'

Eschenbach said nothing again. The only sound was the echo of his leather soles on the stairs. Silence, clack, silence, clack. All the way to the ground floor.

'Did Lenz say that?'

'What?'

'The thing about Matter, that she doesn't exist?' Eschenbach stood still. They had arrived. Stairwells are lonely, sterile and ugly, especially in hospitals, he thought.

Jagmetti opened the door to the entrance hall. 'No. It's just my opinion – Lenz never says anything like that. Just facts, data. It seems that nothing else interests him. I think he takes the easiest route, to be honest.'

Eschenbach laughed. He thought about how Lenz would be feeling now and how damned hard it was for him. 'If you can't forget anything, then you're better off focusing on what's true and what's false.'

'But these things are never just black and white,' protested Jagmetti.

'Yeah, that's why.'

'We should check the originals, he said. The birth certificate, marriage certificate, death certificate.'

'Can you imagine a life without certificates, Jagmetti?'

'Not really.'

'And what about certificates without a life?'

Jagmetti didn't know what he meant by this, but he could tell that Eschenbach was onto something.

At Al Porto, they enjoyed the view over the small harbour and the lake. A couple and their two children were tying up their motorboat. They were all helping, but it didn't seem to be working. The boat was lopsided, the waves threatening to come over the jetty. The father was blaming the mother, while the boy, a particularly awkward teenager, blamed poor manoeuvring. The daughter pulled at her bikini and pouted. Just like in real life, thought Eschenbach, as he took another bite; the grilled sole was delicious. Then he wiped his mouth with his napkin and hurried over – still chewing – to help.

When the boat was tied down and anchored, there were smiles all round and the father hissed at the mother that there had been no need to panic. This earned him several poisonous looks.

Eschenbach sack back down at the table, ordered a large bowl of ice cream and declared it to be the most beautiful spot on Lake Zurich. Jagmetti opted for strawberries and whipped cream.

'If something's worth doing, it's worth doing right,' said the inspector, sticking his spoon into his ice cream. 'For what we've forked out for this dessert, you could get a week's meals at the police canteen.'

'If you say so . . .' murmured Jagmetti, sticking a cream-covered strawberry into his mouth.

On the way back, Jagmetti drove while Eschenbach made back-to-back phone calls.

Salvisberg's secretary at Pathology assured him that her boss would call him back immediately. He was currently otherwise engaged. Eschenbach imagined Salvisberg stuck in the refrigeration chamber with his corpses. He had delivered the close-ups from the child porn videos to him and asked him to 'compare' them to Bettlach's body.

The second person he was unable to reach was the registrar who had married the Bettlachs. Eschenbach asked him to call him back and left the number for headquarters.

Sister Claudia was the only person he managed to reach, after being connected internally three times. Pathologists and registrars were proving unreliable, but nurses you could depend on.

Eschenbach thanked her for her help and readiness to provide information. He said something about how precisely she had been able to recall details and how much it had pleased him. She listened attentively. When he eventually asked her to come to see him at headquarters in Zurich in the evening for a brief discussion, she agreed at once.

When they were sitting in traffic just outside Zurich, Eschenbach got through to the corporal who had led the search of Bettlach's home. He asked him to bring him all the dead man's photos and family albums to headquarters.

The inspector leant back, stretched his legs and meditated on the case. Perhaps he had been lucky and his plan was coming together. Then he could forget the issue of the original documents and the search for Ms Matter, which threatened to go on forever.

The breeze blowing through the open window grew muggier and his exhaustion, which had previously disappeared, crept up on him again. He shoved his phone in his trouser pocket, lit a Brissago and turned the radio on. 'What a Wonderful World' came warbling out of the old loudspeakers in Louis Armstrong's famous baritone, and Eschenbach wished that it was a wonderful world.

Chapter 29

They were sitting at the round conference table in Eschenbach's office. Jagmetti brought in a tray with espresso, biscuits and mineral water.

'So this is what a detective superintendent's office looks like,' said Sister Claudia, her eyes scanning the room. 'It's very different to how it looks on TV.'

'Life is very different to how it looks on TV.' The registrar, who was wearing a colourful bow tie, seemed to know what he was talking about. He had introduced himself as Elmar Gabathuler. He seemed to Eschenbach to be one of those people who always wants to appear bright and cheerful despite – or perhaps because of – their serious and melancholy nature.

Eschenbach gave his guests some time. He thanked them for coming and waited until the nerves on their faces had settled. He wondered whether he should show them the photos separately.

He didn't know what was holding him back. He was hoping they would inspire one another, but what if one remembered something and the other just went along with it? Did he think that they would feel surer of themselves as a pair? How suggestive was police work anyway?

Eschenbach wondered how a person would be able to remember a face that he or she had seen once twenty years before. A single face among thousands. One marriage and one birth per week would mean two thousand and eighty faces each, over twenty years. And there were more than that, he thought, imagining how many new faces he came across, in a week, in a month, or in ten, twenty, thirty years. The number would increase tenfold. How was anyone supposed to remember one face in ten thousand? He thought inevitably of Lenz and decided to visit him the next day.

Eschenbach placed the three photos that he had chosen on the table between Sister Claudia and Gabathuler. 'Is this the woman?' he asked. 'Do you recognise her?'

'Yes, that's her!' cried Sister Claudia without a moment's hesitation. 'Ms Matter, the woman we talked about this morning. Is she still alive, then? She looks older in the photo and her hair's shorter.'

Eschenbach didn't react. He looked at Gabathuler quietly, who was fastening his tie nervously.

'Do you really think so?' The registrar was uncertain and looked over at Sister Claudia, like a schoolboy who wasn't sure that what his neighbour was whispering in his ear was the right answer. He picked up the three pictures and looked at them carefully, one after the other. He nodded. 'It could be . . . though . . .' He fingered his bow tie again, as if it gave him a sense of security. 'But the young woman had—'

'Long, blond hair,' interrupted Sister Claudia. 'And here she's got dark hair and it's shorter. I noticed that too. But look.' The midwife pointed at the second picture. 'Look at the dimples on her cheeks, the striking chin and here . . .' She seemed

to have discovered something she had seen before. 'Her eyes
... And the creases on her forehead, when she laughed, like
these in the photo.'

She picked up the photos one by one and looked at them in
silence, before saying: 'She's got sad, vulnerable eyes.' And, after
a brief pause: 'But it's Eva Matter, there's no doubt about it!' She
looked at Eschenbach defiantly, as if she were ready to fight for
her convictions. 'And do you know what, Inspector?' she added.
'Her eyes look the same in every picture.'

'I can't be sure.' Gabathuler, who was sitting bolt upright on
his chair with his fingers pressed together, did not seem comfortable in his own skin. 'I wouldn't want someone to be prosecuted
because of my statement.'

'You don't have to worry about that,' said Eschenbach. His fear
had been realised. An idea flashed through his mind. Something
that he hadn't considered before and which now appeared before
him like the colours of a rainbow caught between the sun and a
wall of cloud. He stood up and went to his desk, where the rest
of the photos from Bettlach's house lay in a pile. The inspector
flicked through them carefully, hesitated for a moment and then
picked out a photograph. He placed in on the table in front of
Gabathuler and made sure that Sister Claudia couldn't see it.

'Yes, that's it! That's her.' The registrar spoke without hesitation, in a loud, clear voice, as if he were performing a marriage
ceremony. Then he gave it to Sister Claudia. She looked at the
photo for a long time. It showed Doris Hottiger laughing, her hair
falling across her cheeks and shoulders in thick, blond tresses.
Sister Claudia looked up at Eschenbach, who was still standing.
Their eyes met for no longer than a second and Eschenbach was
pleased when she said nothing.

They said their goodbyes and Eschenbach accompanied his guests down to the foyer. Gabathuler let himself be borne out into the open by the revolving doors, while Eschenbach shook the nurse's hand once again.

'Women see things differently,' he said, and before she disappeared through the revolving doors, he shouted, 'I'll be in touch.'

When Eschenbach returned to his office, he saw that Jagmetti was still looking at the photos, which he had neatly arranged in a line.

'The similarity is astonishing. Why didn't it occur to us earlier, boss?'

'Because we're men,' said Eschenbach. He took the photo of Doris Hottiger and gave it to Jagmetti. 'This is for you.'

'Are you allowed to do that?' he asked, receiving it as you might a precious gem.

'Take it.' Eschenbach thought about the archives in the basement, all the material that no poor sod took any interest in. Then he scooped up the three pictures that lay on the table and placed them on his desk, one on top of the other. They showed the same woman in a number of different poses: Eveline Marchand.

Salvisberg called him the next morning at half six. Eschenbach was sitting with Jagmetti in a crowded waiting room in Zurich airport.

'Ever the early bird,' grumbled the inspector.

'Life doesn't look kindly on night owls,' said Salvisberg hoarsely at the other end of the line. 'Everyone at mine's still asleep,' he added, laughing.

Eschenbach had no desire to come up with a counter-quip; not at this hour, anyway.

'I've got two pieces of good news.' Salvisberg had noticed that Eschenbach was in no mood for jokes. 'The bodies in the close-ups are matches for Bettlach and Pierre Oliver in Basle. I called my colleague in Basle yesterday evening. He agrees with me. Scars, body hair, wrinkles etc. I'll spare you the details . . . it's all in the report that I still need to send to you. But I thought you'd like to know straight away.'

'Yes, thank you.' Eschenbach thought for a moment. His suspicions had been right: it looked like someone had executed two child molesters. But who was this someone, who had appointed himself judge, jury and executioner? They didn't seem to be wasting much time in separating the innocent from the guilty. 'What do they think in Basle: suicide or murder?'

'Suicide's not very probable. The dose of sleeping tablets was too low, they think. I don't want to pre-empt my colleagues though. The investigation is still ongoing.'

'I know,' murmured Eschenbach. 'So, it was murder, then.'

'On the contrary,' countered Salvisberg. 'They're proceeding on the basis of it being natural causes . . . just a mishap.'

'What?' Eschenbach was dumbfounded. 'You don't agree with them, do you?'

'Why not? It's the most common cause of death, don't forget. People die at the drop of a hat, sometimes in accidents. Being murdered is a privilege granted to very few people.'

'Oh, stop it, Salvisberg. The two men knew each other. Someone's had a hand in it, I'm dead certain!'

Salvisberg laughed again. 'Have you been to see the Salzburg Festival? Next weekend, *Everyman* is playing. Veronica Ferres is playing Buhlschaft. I find the story fascinating, from a purely pathological perspective. Do you know it?'

'Of course I know it.' Eschenbach was obviously annoyed. 'It was murder, Salvisberg! Sounds to me like they're making things a bit too easy for themselves over in Basle.'

The woman at the counter put out a call over the loudspeakers for passengers travelling to Paris to prepare their passports and boarding passes and present them at the desk.

'And where on earth are you getting the idea that it was just a mishap? Can you at least explain that to me?' Eschenbach stood up and took his place in the queue next to Jagmetti, who already had his ticket and his boarding pass in his hand.

'Oliver had a weak heart. He was taking digoxin. There's evidence to support this. Perhaps he muddled up the sleeping tablets and the tablets for his heart, maybe his heart couldn't tolerate the sleeping tablets, maybe both.'

'That's nonsense, Salvisberg,' the inspector blustered, searching for his tickets.

'If someone with a weak heart suddenly drops dead one day, natural causes are obviously a more likely cause of death. Is that so hard to understand? It could be a self-inflicted mishap, contraindications with other medicines etc., fine. But you must have a damn strong hand to be claiming murder à la Agatha Christie.'

Eschenbach realised he was next in line for the boarding desk. He went to let the people behind him pass and noticed that he was the last in the queue.

'But it is possible that someone killed him. They could have given him the sleeping tablets first, then killed him in his sleep. That would be possible, and it could look like heart failure, couldn't it?'

The woman behind the desk took his boarding pass and passport and looked at him, eyes wide. She was about to call a colleague for help when Eschenbach held up his police ID. She nodded, stamped his passport and tried to smile.

'Of course it's possible. Anything's possible,' said Salvisberg impatiently. 'If your rusty old wheelbarrow suddenly falls to bits, then sabotage is a possibility. But it's not very likely. Prove it, if you like. Perhaps you're right and it's foul play. I just wanted to let you know how things stand at the moment and what I've been told, that's all.'

'All right,' mumbled Eschenbach.

'Oh yeah, he had also had sexual intercourse before he died,' Salvisberg added. 'With a woman. Perhaps she was the one who broke his heart.'

Eschenbach thanked him, switched off his phone and walked across the boarding bridge and onto the aeroplane.

Chapter 30

Travelling to Paris by air wasn't without its risks, Rosa Mazzoleni had warned him. It had nothing to do with the plane. The real hazard was the taxi ride from the airport into the city. Eschenbach wondered whether she knew how much he hated taxis. It didn't matter whether they were in Paris, Zurich or anywhere else. 'Pick an older driver in a jacket and tie,' she advised him.

The only driver wearing a jacket and tie in the forty-degree heat was an old Chinese man from Hong Kong. This, as it later transpired, was the wrong decision.

They found themselves speeding along in the clapped-out Renault at 160km/h, though this was just the first in a list of woes. The Chinese man employed the horn and the headlights with great enthusiasm, as well as the entire breadth of the six-lane motorway.

You shouldn't judge people by what they're wearing, thought Eschenbach. As an articulated lorry loomed ever larger before them, he stretched out his right leg and pressed down – a reflex – on the floor, before realising that passenger seats did not come equipped with brake pedals. The old Chinese man changed lanes at the last moment and spent the whole time talking frantically into the wire that led from his left ear to the mobile phone lying on the passenger seat.

As well as the fear that he had to endure, it depressed Eschenbach to see Jagmetti sitting calmly next to him, flicking through the pages of *Paris Match*. He might as well be lying in a hammock. Did youth not see danger or did it simply not appreciate it? Or was it his maturity that overestimated the danger, conscious of the finite nature of life? Eschenbach hated himself; for his cold sweats and the way he clung to life, like an addict to a needle.

He peered over at what Jagmetti was reading. It was a double-page spread with Princess Stephanie camping in Switzerland with her deluxe caravan. 'Gypsy Princess' ran the sneering headlines. She had had an affair with a circus ringmaster and now she had moved on to an artist. A step down, by all accounts. You could see her bodyguard bringing her a pizza. A cardboard box in place of a silver tray. The magazine was appalled; it was quite unbecoming for a princess.

The prince kept quiet, the press were loud and disparaging as ever. Princesses did not belong on campsites, nor did pizzas belong in blue-blooded stomachs. The world's turned upside-down, thought Eschenbach.

Complex ideas circled his mind. What's in our genes and who are they beholden to? What laws do we follow? Maybe the princess came from a very different world. Maybe Princess Grace had also had an affair with a circus artist or a gypsy and no one had ever heard about it? Would that explain the young princess's wild life, or was life itself just an illusion?

'I don't know about you, but I definitely feel freer when the speedometer's reading 160 and the driver is short-sighted,' he said to Jagmetti, who looked at him with annoyance. Eschenbach closed his eyes and did not open them again until the taxi driver had stopped and requested his fare.

'Our paths cross again, Mr Eschenbach.'

Eveline Marchand opened the door of her Parisian apartment to the two officers; she was smiling. She was wearing a light summer dress with a pattern in pink and pale blue.

'Not for the last time, I hope,' said Eschenbach, pleased to be free of the awkwardness that had lingered after their last conversation.

Eveline led her guests into the living room. The old wooden floorboards creaked and Eschenbach noticed that Eveline had no shoes on. Her small, delicate feet flitted over the century-old oak. Three drinks stood on a low coffee table finished in black Chinese lacquer.

'Watermelon, kiwi juice and a little shot of Cointreau. My summer cocktail,' she said, gesturing at them to sit down. 'Your secretary told me you were coming . . . I thought a little refreshment couldn't hurt.'

She had the same charm, the same bright eyes and the same dimples underneath her high cheekbones that had bewitched Eschenbach on his first visit.

The two policemen sat down on the leather couch and waited for Eveline to join them. She sat across from them to one side, on an expansive armchair covered in brocade silk.

Without much ado, Eschenbach broached the topic at hand.

'You were pregnant with Doris when you left Bettlach so suddenly. That was the real reason, wasn't it, Ms Marchand?' His question exploded like a bomb, without an echo. He looked into her light eyes and she was quiet for a moment.

The inspector cleared his throat. 'I don't want to waste your time, believe me. So, let's talk plainly.'

She nodded.

'You married again under another name and had a child. Doris Hottiger. Is that correct?'

She nodded again.

Claudio Jagmetti, displeased by his boss's abruptness, leant forward on the couch and picked up one of the drinks. His hands left two damp marks on the dark-brown leather.

'Can you tell us a little about your marriage to Ernst Hottiger?' the inspector continued. 'It isn't valid, because you were still married to Philipp Bettlach at the time . . . but that's not important for now.' He paused briefly and looked at Eveline Marchand: 'Is he the father of your child?'

Eveline hesitated. She looked at Jagmetti, who had swallowed and was coughing.

'We know, because of the paternity test, that Philipp doesn't come into it,' continued Eschenbach, refusing to be put off by Jagmetti's coughing and spluttering.

'Yes, Doris is our child,' she murmured, hunching her shoulders, as if to apologise. Then she looked at the young police officer, distracted: 'Are you quite all right?'

'Yes, yes,' gasped Jagmetti, his face bright red. He held his hand over his mouth and another coughing fit followed. He didn't improve until Eschenbach gave him a couple of powerful thumps on the back.

Eveline looked relieved. She took one of the bulbous glasses and said, 'Then, here's to you!'

'Cheers!' said Eschenbach.

'Santé,' said Jagmetti, gasping a little.

They were quiet for a while.

'I always wanted a child, you know.' Eveline had put down her glass and pulled her legs up onto the armchair. 'Right from the beginning, when I was still in love. I always thought it was my fault.'

'What about Doris?' asked Jagmetti. 'Did she grow up with you? In Paris?'

Eveline smiled, 'Yes, she spent the first years with me, and later on she spent more time with Ernst in Switzerland. The schools here are nothing special, you see . . . and we didn't want her to grow up in a big city.'

Eschenbach didn't know much about the French education system, but he knew enough to know that the schools weren't the real reason why Doris had returned to Switzerland.

Eveline seemed to read his thoughts and added: 'It's what Ernst wanted . . . he's very attached to her. It's because of his own childhood. A child needs a father . . . he was firm about that. In the end, Doris started going to school in Switzerland.'

'In Zurich?' asked Eschenbach.

'No, in Einsiedeln, at the convent school. We didn't lock her away.'

'Have you always lived separately?' asked Jagmetti.

'Yes, actually. I kept my apartment here.' She hesitated, then went on. 'When I was in Switzerland, I would stay with Ernst at his house on Lake Sihl. And in the school holidays, Doris would usually come and stay with me. Ernst was very busy with his job in Switzerland and my secret had to remain undiscovered. I had to disappear out of Philipp's life once and for all. For the child's sake, see?'

The officers nodded. It was a very normal explanation of a relationship that was really nothing of the sort.

Eschenbach looked at the artwork hanging on the walls, dominating the space in vibrant colours: two stick men in red and blue, hugging. They had no faces – no eyes, ears, noses or mouths. And yet there was a sensuality about them, something that lived, laughed, even smelt. The inspector liked the pictures by Keith Haring; they were simple in form – and yet so unambiguously clear in what they expressed. 'Do you love your husband?' he asked, as if the red and blue couple had inspired him to do so.

'You ask a lot of personal questions, Inspector.' Eveline smiled, but there was no shyness this time. 'I'm happy to answer them . . . but I doubt you'll be able to do much with them. Isn't it ultimately a matter of opinion, how we define love?'

Eschenbach looked at the clock. He wanted answers, not questions.

'Yes, I love Ernst. He's a wonderful man, a strong man.'

Eschenbach nodded, pulled a cotton handkerchief out of his trousers and dabbed his brow and temples.

'When did you find out that Doris and your ex-husband had been in a relationship?' Jagmetti asked.

'Sometime in May . . . a couple of days after Pentecost,' she said calmly. 'Ernst called up and told me. We had a huge fight about it. I said he should have stopped it . . .' She paused for a moment. 'As if it's easy to prevent these things. I made a real scene, believe me. To think that he and Doris were playing golf at the same club . . . sheer carelessness, in my view. The sort of carelessness that I would never have expected from Ernst.' She stopped and looked at the inspector for a long time.

'But do you know what made the whole thing so absurd?'

The police officers shook their heads.

'They didn't even know each other from the golf course. They met in Ticino. Doris was there with a friend. They met in a grotto somewhere on Lake Maggiore. Strange, isn't it? The golf club had nothing to do with it.'

Eschenbach wondered if she was trying to convince herself. If Philipp had returned to Zurich and Doris to Paris after their first meeting, would it have ended the same way? Did geographic proximity and the golf club have some role to play? Doris had taken a job there at least. It's possible to challenge fate, he thought. And yet, was it really predetermined? Where did fatalism start, where did it end? It was a topic that Eschenbach gave more thought to than he liked, something he only spoke of occasionally. Too many questions and too few answers – it was better to say nothing.

'What about Ernst Hottiger, what did he have to say?' Eschenbach suppressed a yawn.

'He blamed himself of course. He's a very conscientious person and he hates coincidences. It's because of his job, naturally.' She ran a hand through her hair and smiled. 'But at some point, children grow up. At some point, trees grow towards the sun, not the way the gardener wants them to grow.'

'Whose view is that, yours or Hottiger's?'

'Both.' She smiled again.

'When Doris discovered the truth about Philipp Bettlach . . . I mean, did she blame you?'

'Yes and no. We haven't spoken about it much. There are some things that have to settle before you can talk about them.'

'Is she here now, with you?'

Eveline Marchand hesitated. 'Yes. She has registered for the next semester at the Sorbonne. Philosophy.' She laughed. 'As if there aren't enough questions in life already . . .'

Jagmetti slid forward on the couch. 'Can I see her?' he asked, his hands folded on his knees.

Nothing remained of the morning's freshness. The July sun fell through the large window and threw its harsh light into the space.

'She didn't want to be here when we talked. I think it's better this way,' said Eveline, looking at Jagmetti, as if it only concerned him. 'She's told me a lot about you . . . I think she misses you.'

Jagmetti didn't know what to say. It wasn't quite an answer. He was glad when Eschenbach spoke again.

'I assume that Doris is staying with you and that both of you can be reached here if necessary.'

'Yes, she's staying here with me for a while. You can call any time.'

'And Johannes Bettlach . . . do you still see him? Now that it's all over . . .' The inspector ran his fingertip over the rim of the empty glass.

'Johannes is a friend, a very good friend. He always was . . . and always had been.' She looked at the clock. 'It's after midday, shall I get you some lunch?'

Eschenbach was shocked to see that it was nearly one o'clock. He would need a good hour to reach the airport, given the traffic at this time of day. It was time to leave. 'That's very kind of you, thanks, but we have to get back.'

The three of them stood up and Eveline Marchand accompanied them to the door.

'Do you still love him?'

She looked at him quizzically.

'Your good friend, I mean?' Eschenbach looked into her pale eyes and raised his eyebrows.

'Isn't friendship the most noble form of love?' She laughed. It was a happy, spirited laugh and the two of them left it at that. 'I'll call for a taxi right away, it'll take a couple of minutes.'

Eschenbach nodded and told Jagmetti to go ahead. There was something else that he wanted to clarify with Eveline Marchand in private.

The taxi had already arrived and the motor was running when Eschenbach stepped out of the cool hallway into the street. Jagmetti, sitting in the back seat of the car, was surprised when his boss pulled the door open.

'Get out, Jagmetti,' yelled the inspector cheerfully. He had a broad grin on his face. 'You're staying here.'

Jagmetti stayed put.

'You've done plenty of overtime . . . and a few days in Paris never hurt anyone.' He laughed. 'It's Friday tomorrow, I expect you to be back on Monday.'

His assistant slid awkwardly over the seat towards the open door and got out, without saying a word.

'Eveline knows. Call headquarters, Ms Mazzoleni will book you off,' Eschenbach called to him once he had taken a seat in the back of the car and told the driver his destination. 'And by the way . . . there are these chairs at the flea market at Porte de Clignancourt . . . they last a lifetime.'

Jagmetti stood on the pavement and watched the taxi go. What could Eschenbach mean about the chairs? He couldn't make head or tail of it, and as he walked thoughtfully back to the door, he noticed his stomach growling and realised he was hungry.

Chapter 31

Eschenbach had mused on the case at length. Flying was particularly good for this, he felt. You were completely unreachable, soaring in solitude above the clouds; it seemed eternal, out of time.

When he had called headquarters on the way to the airport to call off the manhunt for Doris, they already knew. Not only that, but Ernst Hottiger had landed in Switzerland – two hours before, flying with Air France via Paris. The message had just come in from the Zurich-Kloten airport police, they said.

Eschenbach's plane was half empty. The inspector had two seats to himself. The real luxury on a flight is not the champagne, he thought, but the space.

Things were not going well for the Swiss airline that he was flying with; in fact they were worse than people thought. Or so the experts were saying. Two years before, the situation had been so dire that the airline had eventually run out of money for fuel. No one had believed it until the planes were stuck on the tarmac. Thankfully, it had happened on the ground and not in the air. No one's going to take you for a beggar when you've a Swiss flag on your chest, Corina had said at the time; Swiss companies had no business claiming poverty with all their banks and chocolate back home.

Swiss self-confidence has never been the same since, thought Eschenbach. It had become transparent, fragile somehow. You could see it in the faces of the air stewards and the pilots. Behind the macho pilots' glasses and pasted-on smiles, shame lingered where once had been pride. Even the aeroplanes didn't have the same shine to them. Vulnerability was hard to come by in this country. Perhaps it lay on the tops of the high mountains, in the deep lakes or in the self-imposed pressure to always be neutral in everything. Perhaps it was its size, its language, which no one understood, or the fear of slowly becoming isolated in an ever-growing Europe.

Eschenbach read the editorial in the *New Zurich Post* on the situation in the Middle East and the report on the imminent Swiss National Day in the domestic news section. Two worlds, one large, one small.

They touched down.

As was always the case at this time of year, the airport was bustling. Hosts of flip-flops and half-unbuttoned shirts mixing with finely stitched leather and cotton thread. Half-naked torsos clad in sleeveless T-shirts competed with high-necked business attire. The world of holidays and the world of business shook hands and it occurred to Eschenbach that things were far less hectic in the business world. He thought about Kobler and called her in the south of France as he took a taxi to headquarters.

She seemed relieved at the news that they had found Doris Hottiger. Missed clues and disappearing evidence were a sensitive issue, especially in a murder case, she said. And, of course, she was right.

He said that he hoped she enjoyed the rest of her holiday and she thanked him; not without pointing out that she had taken plenty of work with her, and still had four days left. She would be back next week, she said, and he knew where to reach her if anything serious came up. It sounded like an apology and smacked of a guilty conscience.

Eschenbach imagined Kobler lying under a palm tree in the south of France, reading files in her bikini and flip-flops.

He had almost mentioned that he was expecting to be able to close the Bettlach case that same week – and that he was toying with the idea of taking a few days' holiday next week. Swimming and fishing off Gabriel's boat or sleeping on the shore of the lake. Under Swiss plane trees, without a file in sight. That was crucial.

He didn't know what drew him towards the idea. Perhaps it was the exhaustion, or the heat that bothered him more and more as the days went by. It was just a feeling. He always got it when he spent a long time working intensely on a case and the threads inside his mind began stitching themselves into a solution.

On the shelf next to Rosa Mazzoleni's desk there was usually a bowl of small, colourfully wrapped chocolate bars. In its place now stood an electric fan; it was an ugly grey colour like an old computer. It turned its head from left to right, humming, as if it were watching a game of tennis.

'Don't look so horrified. I know it's not exactly a beauty . . . but it was all I could get.' Ms Mazzoleni looked over the rim of her glasses and wiped her brow with a handkerchief, though she wasn't sweating. 'Completely sold out, they were . . . This was one the cashier was using herself; she was so friendly she let me buy it.'

'At an inflated price, I assume,' said Eschenbach, grinning. 'Now you'll have to buy a discounted heater to even things out.'

Eschenbach worked late into the night. He set to work on Lenz's report again. This time he paid no attention to the separate sections, as Lenz had intended it, instead reading it chronologically. It was impossible to split a life into such arbitrary categories; it was a single, cohesive piece of art. If you wanted to understand a picture, it was no good organising it by colour. It would lose not just its integrity, but also its meaning.

He read each of the three hundred pages carefully. He took them out of the folder and looked for their true place in Ernst Hottiger's life, before rearranging them. Memory is an indelible factor in how we make judgements and how we act. Today's mysteries are often explained by what happened yesterday, he thought.

The secret to Ernst Hottiger's story lay in his childhood. It was one of those tragic events that defined a life the way switches determine a train's course.

Ernst was an unremarkable boy until his parents separated. Ilse Hottiger had become a mother at a very young age and emigrated to Canada with a young artist three years after the end of the war. The father, who was assigned custody of the boy, had little luck afterwards. He suffered because his wife had left him and he drowned his shame in drink. This was soon followed by financial ruin for his saddlery and his son was ultimately taken away by social services.

Ernst Hottiger was ten years old when he was placed in an orphanage. Life's a vicious old dog, thought Eschenbach.

Barely a year later, his father killed himself. Tied a sack of stones to his neck using the laces from his old army boots and jumped into the Limmat. No one told the boy about it. He thought he was missing. It wasn't until fifteen years later, when

Hottiger began making his own enquiries, that he discovered the truth.

Weapons had held a particular fascination for young Hottiger from an early age. He would spend hours on target practice, aiming a slingshot he made himself at jars he had stolen from the kitchens. Using hazel switches and a couple of old pieces of wood, he could fashion a bow and arrow or a crossbow. He had always been intrigued by shooting – and making sure his shot found its mark.

In an attempt to find controlled channels for his interests, the head of the orphanage allowed him to participate in youth shooting courses and, later, in the traditional Knabenschiessen shooting competition. He would come second and third, but never won first place. For his fourteenth birthday, he received a second-hand air rifle. A foundation that supported talented orphans covered the cost. It was his passion. Two years later, he was accepted onto a Swiss talent promotion programme, and at eighteen he became a member of the Swiss national air rifle team. Years later, he proved that they had been right to show confidence in him, winning bronze and gold in the 1960 Olympic Games in Rome. Small-calibre military rifles and large rifles. Prone.

Thereafter followed a long career in the army. Fortress squads, command of a forward company, sniper courses and ultimately training as an officer of general staff. This was where he met Johannes Bettlach, and their friendship grew slowly from there. In the late seventies Bettlach helped him set up his own security company.

The network of relationships that he built during his time in the military reached as far as the upper echelons of the worlds of politics and finance. This was followed by successes in business, and wealth. And yet there was little trace of him anywhere. Not in the media, not in public – not to mention the parties thrown by Switzerland's rich and almost famous. Eschenbach couldn't find the faintest hint of a scandal, and what was even stranger was the total absence of any women.

Nineteen eighty-one saw the emergence of Eva Matter who, as they had discovered, was actually Eveline Marchand, Bettlach by marriage. Then came his marriage to her, followed soon after by the birth of Doris and then Eva Matter's staged departure.

This section read like a piece of theatre. And the longer Eschenbach brooded over it, the plainer it became that it *was* one. How else to explain the doubts the midwife cast over the newly married couple's love? As well-staged and consistent as the story was, they hadn't played their roles well enough. They had bungled the love scenes, good and proper. It stood out because the midwife who attended to them hadn't just wanted to observe, she had wanted to empathise.

Eveline simply didn't fit into Hottiger's life. She was a foreign body. Hottiger didn't seem to have had any relationships with women and, if he did, they were abnormal. Eschenbach was sure of it. He had had a mother who crept away from her responsibilities, abandoning her husband and child. It was hardly a surprise. And the fact that there had been no hint of a woman in this successful man's life – save for his mother, a few secretaries and housekeepers, and Eva Matter – was more than enough of a clue.

Why, then, have a liaison that was actually nothing of the sort? Why the sudden marriage? Was it because of the child?

Yes, Hottiger was loyal and had an almost exaggerated sense of responsibility. That much was clear from his background story. Of course, he would have stuck with his wife and child. Even it had just been a 'faux pas'. But Eschenbach couldn't bring himself to believe in an *amour fou*, a brief, intense romance. The midwife's recollections had been too clear, too believable. Doris Hottiger was not his daughter and he had not been her mother's lover. The whole thing was just a pantomime, a contract or, in some sense, a favour. But who had commissioned it?

Eschenbach read through the report again, feverishly. This time he hit on reconstructing the network of Ernst Hottiger's relationships. Childhood friends and sporting acquaintants. His sponsors, the whole army gang, the administrative boards at his companies and the clients that Lenz had discovered and drawn a question mark over. He wrote the names down on a blank sheet of paper, linking them with lines and arrows, highlighting them: red for friends, green – of course – for the army. Blue stood for finance and black for political ties. It made quite a pretty picture, he thought. And at the heart of this network of interrelationships stood the two names on which everything hung: Ernst Hottiger and Johannes Bettlach.

Night-time noises drifted up from the street and through the open window into his office, penetrating the cloud of smoke and lamplight and, in the distance, he could hear the church clock marking the next quarter past the hour. His tiredness had turned to exhaustion. He recognised the feeling, when the heaviness in his body threatened to overwhelm him. It was the moment when, after a long, hard period of interrogation, the truth would come loose, like a diamond prised from the walls of a neglected mine. But who had he been interrogating?

Himself? And where did the truth lie? He looked at the diagram before him. The names and the lines flowed into each other like the shapes in a kaleidoscope.

He blinked, rubbed his red eyes and lit a last cigarillo. Then he took a black pen out of the drawer and drew two circles around the names swimming before him. Two thick, black circles.

Chapter 32

The lake reflected the morning light into a cloudless sky. Ernst Hottiger shut the door to his boathouse, took a few leisurely steps along the shore and sat on a stone bench next to the water. He loved the early morning, when the lake was still and calm, gleaming like quicksilver. The inspector had said he would be there for nine. He had two hours left. It was more than he needed, he thought.

There was no wind that morning. The Swiss flag hung motionless on the mast, the white cross hidden from view. It stuck to the whitewashed wood like a bloody rag.

It was the Swiss National Day. Soon the fireworks would be crackling again, Hottiger thought to himself, wondering if he was a patriot. He remembered standing on the podium in Rome with the national anthem blaring and the flags waving above him. He knew every word of the national anthem, every note. The way it started, slowly, rhythmically. A noble pace, befitting of kings – kings and the Swiss mountains, perhaps. If the Finsteraarhorn or the Eiger were to disappear one day, they would surely go marching off to that same rhythm. Nobly, proudly, skating past the peaks of Jungfrau and Mönch.

Was he a patriot? Because he loved the mountains, trained soldiers and had won an Olympic gold for Switzerland? Would he not have much preferred to have been a caring father? No heroic deeds and gun smoke, just a normal father? The kind you might find in Italy, Portugal, Croatia or elsewhere. Did nationality really play a role in the most important things in life? There was still no wind and he wondered whether he had time for a swim in the lake.

He had been told not to underestimate this inspector from Zurich. He was nothing sensational, but he was persistent. Eccentric, intelligent – and unpredictable. He ran his hands over his face, over his grey beard, and heard a sound, like a fish coming up for air. The ripples grew larger, fading, then disappearing altogether. Could it have been a pike, or was it just a zander?

He stood up and took the gravel path back to the house.

He didn't know why he was choosing the Beretta. He could have taken the SIG out of the firearm locker, or his old, much-loved 7.65 Parabellum. He had carried both during his time in the service. Perhaps that was what disturbed him, and why he chose the Beretta.

He checked the magazine and made a few adjustments. Once upon a time, he had taken great care in cleaning and oiling them. But now there were too many. Magdalena Rüdisühli, his housekeeper, stubbornly refused to take on the task herself. She had little interest in anything beyond the dust that settled over the showcases and racks.

A few retired friends from his time in the service looked after his collection. These were men of mettle, who couldn't stand being stuck at home and who knew more about pistols and rifles than they did about their wives. Hottiger smiled.

*

Eschenbach was running late. He had a meeting with Bernhard Rytz, the director of investigations, at seven, and wanted to know how it was going with the Genesis file. Kobler had insisted that he pass the file on to Rytz so that he could concentrate fully on the Bettlach case. He did not have a good feeling about it.

The meeting did not go well. It all seemed to be going much too slowly, Eschenbach thundered. All they needed now was for the press to find out and then they'd lose everything: the suspects, the evidence and Rytz, too, if he didn't get his head down and bloody well take care of the case.

Eschenbach took the exit towards Einsiedeln, meandering along the country road which led up towards Lake Sihl in a broad curve. In the opposite direction, the traffic was at a standstill. A farmer was juddering casually down into the valley with a huge cargo of hay.

It was just before nine when he turned right and, after a few more turns, reached the peninsula where Ernst Hottiger's estate lay. A large sign announced that it was private land and he noticed surveillance cameras installed in two places. Apart from that, there were no barriers or fences. Nor could he see any barbed wire.

Access to the house was by means of a narrow path, lined with trees. There was no entrance way in the usual sense, as was common for houses of that size. No steps leading up and no sheltered doorway. All that Eschenbach could make out was a white wall. Tall and wide. Nothing else. It protected the estate, which he assumed ran down behind the wall as far as the lake.

He parked his Volvo, got out and walked slowly up to the wall. A surveillance camera panned towards him and buzzed a quiet greeting. Eschenbach stood looking politely into the steel guardian's glass eye. Nothing happened. He waited a moment longer, then he looked at his watch; it was just after nine. Then he noticed the recessed door. He pulled the metal ring out of its place, turned it and pushed. The door wouldn't open. He paused; it didn't budge. Then he walked to the left, along the wall, and noticed that the door was part of a large gate. The inspector assumed it was a gate to the garage and walked along to the end of the wall. He saw that he was right. A huge garage, open on both sides, was concealed underneath. He counted four cars, with space for ten, and behind it he saw the main house – a white cube. The shape of the building reminded him of the Bauhaus style from the 1920s. The entrance was plain, almost forbidding. When Eschenbach arrived at the building, he pressed the button of the intercom system and waited. He pressed it a second time, waiting a few minutes before pressing a third time, knocking at the door and calling out.

Ten minutes had passed and still nothing happened. The inspector wondered whether he should call for backup. His phone was in the car, his gun was still with Büchsenmacher. He didn't know which of these facts annoyed him more. He pushed the handle and realised that the door was not locked. Without a moment's hesitation, he stepped inside. Dark stone floors greeted him. In the centre of the space was a sweeping staircase that led upstairs. He found a huge living room with an impressive glass façade that revealed a view of the lake.

'At last, you're here!' A harsh voice tore through the silence. 'I'm upstairs, on the right, in the library.'

Eschenbach walked up the steps and into a darkened room. He recognised Hottiger, who was sitting in a dark-green leather armchair, with his feet on a stool.

'I'm here, for God's sake! You're too late.' His thin lips barely moved beneath his grey beard.

'You didn't make it very easy for me. I was here at nine. Why the game of hide and seek?'

'You're too late, Inspector . . . We're both too late, believe me. Life has no mercy for latecomers.'

Eschenbach noticed for the first time that Hottiger was holding a pistol.

'Give up, Hottiger. My people know where I am.' Eschenbach stayed calm and waited.

Hottiger laughed. It was a hoarse, mirthless laugh. 'Surely you don't think I would shoot you? The one police officer that I could trust to clean up this scum once and for all?' Hottiger took his feet off the stool and pushed it towards the inspector. 'Here, sit.'

Eschenbach preferred to stand.

Hottiger moved the pistol from his right hand into his left. Then back into his right. He looked as if he were testing to see which was better. 'I've been shooting my whole life. Clay pigeons, cans, bottles – in the army – people. I've used practice ammo . . . for practice. I always hit my targets – always, see? Right in the middle, where the big points are . . .'

He paused.

'And? Now what?' Eschenbach looked at the pistol, which had switched hands again.

'I did wonder for a moment whether it wouldn't be better to just shoot myself . . .' He laughed. 'But I don't think I can do it.

It's hard for a marksman not to have his target in front of him.' He looked at Eschenbach. 'Could you do it? I mean, could you shoot yourself?'

'I haven't ever given it much thought . . . I don't think so, no,' said Eschenbach.

'I always thought it would be easy. At least, for me.'

Eschenbach could hear him breathing heavily.

'It's more . . .' Hottiger was quiet for a moment; he looked at his hand, at the black metal that shone between his fingers. 'It's all the damn questions that stop me sleeping at night. They're like black shadows. Question marks, huge question-ing faces. Shadow monsters . . . they follow me. Do you ever get that?'

Eschenbach just stood there, waiting.

'Why did my mother run off like a hen ready for laying? And what sort of father drowns himself? First with the booze and then like a helpless creature in the Limmat? Why in God's name would a father just leave like that?'

To Eschenbach, hours seemed to pass before he went on. 'What's heartache and financial ruin when compared . . . when compared to the loneliness of the homeless? We could have emi-grated and started again. You can always start again.' Hottiger stood up, uncocked the gun and slid it into the leather holster under his arm. Then he took a few steps and sat on the edge of the large oak table at the back of the room.

In the half-light, Eschenbach could only see the whites of his eyes. He sensed that Hottiger was looking at him.

'Do you know what it's like to grow up in an orphanage, Inspector?' He spoke quietly, almost whispering. Eschenbach had to strain to understand him. 'In the old days, I mean, when no one gave a toss about children's homes, or what happened behind closed doors? Do you know what I had to do to get an air rifle? To get ammunition and targets? How much "fatherly love" I had to suffer from men who were nothing of the sort? Then, for once in my life, I had a chance. A child who needed me, needed my love and my protection. And I realised that I couldn't do it . . .'

Eschenbach strained to see in the gloom. And suddenly, it flew at him out of the darkness – the answer that he had sought so desperately: how much it must have tormented Hottiger when Doris turned from him and sought protection and warmth in the arms of another man. A man of the same age, who might as well have been her father.

'It's strange thing,' Hottiger went on. 'It's like you reach out your hand and you realise that it's not there. It's just a stump at the wrist. You want to jump and realise you've got no feet, no knees. And when you've got nothing of value, even the easiest things become impossible. Do you understand? You can never be a father.' He stroked a hand over his beard, which looked almost white in the half-light. 'Do you have children?'

Eschenbach nodded. 'A daughter.'

'Is she yours . . . I mean, are you the father?'

'No.'

'Does that matter to you?'

'I don't know. Sometimes I wonder how it would be . . . I mean, whether I would behave differently towards my own child. I really don't know.'

'When Doris was little, she would splash about in the bath and reach out her arms to me . . . I couldn't even touch her without feeling like I was doing her wrong. The same wrong that was done to me . . . it sounds ridiculous, I know. But that's what it was like!'

Eschenbach nodded, though he wasn't sure he understood.

'I would wrap her in towels – clean, white towels, because I felt ashamed to look at her and to touch her.' Hottiger was quiet for a time. He perched on the heavy desk and ran a hand along the wooden edge. Then he stood up. 'I am not Doris's father, Mr Eschenbach . . . but I assume you already knew that.'

'I didn't know, but I guessed as much,' said the inspector. He was sitting on the stool that Hottiger had pushed towards him. He felt uneasy. He stood up again. 'Johannes Bettlach, right? He's Doris's father?'

'You see, Inspector, I don't really know – but I assume so, yes.'

'You never asked?'

'No, not directly. Does that surprise you?'

'Yes, to be honest. You were friends.'

'We still are. I don't have many friends.' He smiled. 'Eva and Johannes are my only friends, in fact. Friendship is a very particular thing.'

'You said Eva?'

'Yes, Eveline Marchand. I don't know why, but I've only ever called her Eva, since the beginning. She finds you fascinating . . .'

'Oh really?' Eschenbach coughed slightly.

'. . . and Matter is a common name. She was known as Eva Matter for a short while. We didn't want to take any risks. Because of Philipp, I mean.'

'What about Eva Matter's funeral? The body?'

'What? There never was a body.' Hottiger seemed to be growing excited. 'Today, millions of dollars are exchanged without a single coin changing hands. You can acquire and sell a pork belly with the stroke of a pen without ever having it in your hands. Why would it be any different for a body?'

'But the business with Philipp, that didn't happen by the stroke of a pen, did it?'

'No. Things like that prepare you. It wasn't a pen, no . . .'

He took a deep breath, like a swimmer before he dives and turns underwater. Then he went on. 'When Eva and Johannes came to me and asked me to take on this strange form of god-parenting, none of us knew that it would end this way.' He furrowed his bushy brows until they met in the middle. 'You can't keep two people apart . . . not for an entire lifetime.'

'A poor excuse for someone like you,' said Eschenbach.

'I'm not God, Inspector. I think you're a little confused there.' He smiled tiredly. 'I'm just the plumber . . . the one who lays the pipes and mends them when they leak.'

'Is that why you shot Philipp? Because of a leak in your security system? Because you let something happen that shouldn't have?'

'Philipp deserved to be put away for a long time. Somewhere with maximum security, if you ask me. But Johannes wouldn't give up. He ran him from clinic to clinic and in the end we all believed that he was cured and that it was all over . . .'

'Is that why you didn't intervene, because you thought he was cured?' Eschenbach looked at Hottiger, puzzled.

'I never could have stopped Doris and Philipp from meeting. I was in America when it happened. Suddenly they were a couple, what was I supposed to do? Then Doris rang me . . . hysterical, at the end of her tether. It was a perfect mess. I flew back to Switzerland and watched the videos. Then I knew that Philipp had never truly been cured.'

'Why didn't you go to the police? You had proof. It would have been easy to stop Bettlach.'

'Oh really, and then what? Clinics, reports and the whole charade all over again? The determination to see the good in people allows misery to go on forever. You should have realised that by now. Being a policeman, after all.' He smiled bitterly. 'But who cares? OK, I was too late, I cocked up . . . there's no doubt about it. It was my mistake. I was supposed to protect Doris . . . I know, there are some things you can't undo.'

'And yet you shot Bettlach?' Eschenbach knew what his answer would be.

'I can't take back what has happened . . . but it was happening again and again, see? Again and again and again . . .' Hottiger repeated it at least ten times. 'I had to stop it. I had to bring an end to it! If a record keeps skipping, you take it off the turntable.'

The two men looked at each other for a while without saying anything. Then Hottiger spoke again.

'It's not exactly a tragedy that he's gone, is it? The man ripped little children's futures apart . . . screwed up their lives. How long are you willing to wait before you bring that kind of scum in? How long?'

'There are laws, Mr Hottiger. Even for scum, as you call him.'

'That's a lame excuse, Inspector. You've got a whole file of names. All kiddie fuckers and people who get off on that sort of thing. And what do you do? You let it continue. And where's the file now? With some bureaucrat. Nothing will come of it, believe me.'

'How do you know that?' asked Eschenbach, astounded.

'Haven't you ever wondered how *you* know it?' He raised his eyebrows. 'From the Federal Office of Police, the FOP. And where does FOP get their information from?'

'From the US Postal Inspection Service,' said Eschenbach.

'Correct. And they got that information from the FBI.' He paused briefly. 'They kept chipping away until they could bring this stuff to light. And then you come along and forget about it, stick it on the shelf, where any unsavoury character could get hold of it. Do you know how much time and effort it took us to get Landslide going?' He looked at Eschenbach furiously.

'Why us? What have you got to do with Landslide?' Eschenbach asked.

'Landslide's my baby,' Hottiger smiled tiredly.

Eschenbach frowned.

'It's silly, I know. But it is. God knows how many of these bastards there are – running these portals distributing child porn. Usually you can't get anywhere near them; they're always rebuilding themselves. They're the real professionals, the ones distributing online. But with Landslide, I managed it.' He said this not without a degree of pride. 'Thanks to my links to the US, to the CIA.'

Eschenbach nodded thoughtfully.

'And when I was in the States, Bettlach made his move on Doris. I should have stayed here ... then none of this would have happened.' He closed his eyes for a moment and breathed deeply, before continuing. 'Now you've got the whole bunch of them practically on a plate. All you have to do now is catch them ... but you can't even do that, for Christ's sake!' He was half-standing, half-sitting, leaning against the table. 'There are studies that claim that over 50 per cent of perpetrators were abused themselves as children. Can't you see? It never stops . . . it's never-ending!'

Eschenbach said nothing. He thought about the names on the list. Over four hundred in the canton of Zurich alone. It was the tip of the iceberg. 'And now what? You want to kill them all?' he asked Hottiger. 'And risk killing the wrong men?' It was a tired argument, he knew. But he couldn't think of anything better.

'Bettlach and that . . . oh, what's his name, that egocentric musician from Basle . . .'

'Pierre Oliver . . . or Peter Deck,' said Eschenbach.

'That's it, Deck! They weren't the wrong men, Inspector. There are videos. I'd be happy to show you them . . .'

'There's no need for that,' said Eschenbach. 'I've seen the videos.'

'Well, there you go. Why the fuss? Though . . . Oliver was already dead when I got there.'

Eschenbach stopped.

'Heart problems, I found out later . . . Hard to believe, I know.'

'What's hard to believe?' asked Eschenbach.

'That someone like that has a heart to begin with.' Hottiger tried to laugh. It sounded like a hoarse cough. 'The girl and the sleeping tablets . . . it was all clearly too much for him. A pleasant way to go, if undeserved.'

'Was it you . . . I mean, the woman and the sleeping tablets?'

'It was fate, Inspector. We should go now.'

He stood up, felt for his glasses on the desk and put them on. Then he walked a few steps towards Eschenbach and stood there. 'If it's fate that a red car will drive you to your death, Inspector, then it happens. Believe me, one of these days an old red banger will transport you into the beyond.'

'Oh really? Who says so?'

'Does it really matter *who*? Isn't it enough to know that it's true?'

They walked down the stairs in silence.

'I've left my things in the boathouse. I'll be right back.' He opened the glass door to the garden.

'Just a moment . . .' Eschenbach took the gun out of Hottiger's shoulder holster. 'I know you can't do it . . . but it's better this way.'

Hottiger laughed behind his dark glasses.

Watching through the huge glass façade that reached to the floor, Eschenbach saw him walk down the gravel path to the lake and disappear into the boathouse. A sailing boat was cruising out on the water. The wind had picked up a little. The Swiss flag next to the boathouse was flying. Eschenbach was surprised to notice that it was at half-mast.

The inspector saw the explosion before he heard it. The window burst and glass flew at him like an enormous mosaic. Eschenbach threw himself to the ground. Splinters of glass showered down on him. He covered his head and neck with his hands and lay there for some time. When he stood up, he noticed that his arms and hands were bleeding. He pulled out the shards and walked to the entrance where he took off his shirt and trousers. Then he ran to his car and called for a patrol car and an ambulance.

Chapter 33

Hottiger did not survive. Forensics surmised that he had been right next to the explosive charge when it detonated. It would have been difficult to find any trace of him at all, they said.

Eschenbach was sitting at his favourite café on the Limmat, eating yoghurt – something he only did when he was ill or felt like he might be. His hands and arms were covered in plasters and he had a white bandage on his left forearm where a shard had penetrated deeply.

He was reading through the papers.

Although he had sent an extensive press release to the media, they had written little more than a few lines. Even the tabloids reported it in brief, factual terms, as if they were low on ink. He had almost overlooked it, between the multi-page spread on the ongoing heatwave and the photos of the princess camping. Even the holiday greetings from the Swiss B-listers and the article on the ban on fireworks for the Swiss National Day were larger, more colourful and prominent.

Despite the powerful explosion, it seemed that Hottiger died quietly and unnoticed in a *tragic accident*. Eschenbach envied him his connections, even *post mortem*.

Kobler, who he had called several times in the meantime, was jolly glad that the matter was still 'on the DL' and that the case could now be filed as 'solved'. She was more concerned about the forest fires on the Cote d'Azur. In St Tropez, the sky was raven black, she said. It sounded serious. Eschenbach assured her that all remnants of Hottiger's burning boathouse had been cleared away and the sky in Zurich was blue once more. He was now taking a couple of days' holiday, he added, knowing that she would be hard pushed to argue.

Johannes Bettlach appeared at four on the dot. Eschenbach had arrived early and was sitting in the shade of the plane trees in the Zurichhorn gardens with a glass of red wine. The boats sent little bobbing waves around the buoys on the lake. The ships swayed like drunkards, and here and there the bright metal fittings sparkled in the sun.

He only noticed the large, gaunt man once he had sat down opposite him, smiling. His wavy white hair, his dark complexion and large, slightly bent nose gave him the air of a Roman emperor, Eschenbach thought.

He sought out Bettlach's pale eyes, hidden behind dark glasses. Like a blind man. He suddenly had the feeling that the smile was not for him. He was looking past him, out towards the lake and frowning. Some slip of his facial muscles. Both of them were quiet for a while.

'So, are you happy now, Inspector?' He took the glasses off and looked at Eschenbach. 'You've solved the case. Bravo.' He spoke quietly and clapped a few times, suggestively. He did it so slowly that Eschenbach was able to count the age spots on his great hands. 'One less murderer for you . . . and one more body. It makes it easier, I suppose.'

Eschenbach was quiet for a moment. Bettlach sounded cynical but when he looked at him, he knew that it wasn't cynicism at all – it was grief. 'You were friends, I know. I'm sorry for your loss.'

'You don't need to be sorry, Inspector. You're the hunter . . . you were just doing your job, that's all.'

'What about you?' Eschenbach felt his stomach churn. Suddenly, Bettlach's distant air of calm irritated him. The way he stood above it all and pinned the blame on him, the 'hunter'. 'Where were you when this disaster began? Doris is your daughter, after all. Why didn't you ship your brother off to the loony bin before it was too late?'

It was a while before Bettlach answered.

'Have you ever been to a "loony bin", Inspector?' He spoke slowly, almost in a monotone. 'Drugged up to your eyeballs? Electroshock therapy and . . .' he paused for a moment. Then he went on: 'Philipp had visited more mental hospitals than you have hotels, Mr Eschenbach. There's hardly a leading psychiatrist, neurologist or therapist in the world that hasn't treated him. His trips abroad, holidays, time studying . . . he spent them all in secure institutions, in "loony bins", as you call them. So much therapy, and it never did what it promised to do. The entire pharmaceutical industry got rich off his back. And still, he was sick. And I could never give up hope. He was so healthy despite it all, so robust – on the outside, I mean. Cheerful, charming, witty . . .' Bettlach stopped. He ran both of his hands over his face, rubbed his eyes and picked up his sunglasses. He went to put them on, then placed them back on the table. 'It's hard to fight an illness that no one can see. One without ugly pustules or a raging fever. You can't operate on it, nor will it kill you.' He looked down and stared in front of him for a long time. Then he went to speak, hesitated and looked up at the sky, where the seagulls were screeching and circling.

Eschenbach swallowed and noticed that he hadn't drunk any of the wine that stood in front of him. Should he order something for Bettlach? He seemed to have aged years since the last time he had seen him. Somehow, he looked more fragile and more transparent than a Roman emperor. Eschenbach's feelings of resentment disappeared.

A slim girl with a tan and a piercing in her left nostril came to the table and brought a second glass of wine. Her sun-bleached, blond locks were tied back in a ponytail with a red hairband and reminded Eschenbach of Doris Hottiger. He wondered whether Bettlach was thinking about her too.

They sat for almost a quarter of an hour without speaking, drinking the wine that was now too warm. The staff were busy hanging colourful lanterns and garlands on the lines that they had strung between the branches of the trees. The tables were cleared then covered with red wrapping paper from one continuous roll. Then came white crockery, white napkins, candlesticks and little flags. It was the first of August, the Swiss National day.

When the young woman with the nose piercing pre-empted them by bringing the bill, it was Bettlach who took it and paid.

'We're just going,' he said in a friendly tone. Then he turned to Eschenbach: 'Doris called me, she's met someone. A young police officer … Jagmetti, his name was. He works here in Zurich too; do you know him?'

Eschenbach cleared his throat. 'Vaguely …'

'From the way she sounded …' He smiled. 'I think she might be in love.'

They stood up quietly and left.

'Dad, take these.' Kathrin was balancing on a garden chair, holding out a hammer and nails to Eschenbach. 'I can't reach … can you?' She pointed to the wooden beams under the eaves.

'What do I do?'

'Hammer in a nail . . . then we'll hang the lantern from it. Pretty, isn't it?' She was half a head taller than him as she stood on the chair. She got her long legs from her mother.

Eschenbach put his arms around her waist, lifted her off the chair, kissed her on the forehead and set her down on the warm stone floor.

'You don't like it when I'm taller than you, do you?' She laughed.

'No, but I also don't like it when you balance on wobbly chairs.'

'You might think red lanterns with Swiss crosses on are lame. But they're cool, take my word for it.' She held out the hammer and nail. 'Come on, Dad, be nice. Just one, honest . . . or two, max. Mum thinks they're cool too.'

'Did she say so?'

'No. She said pretty . . . or nice.'

'Or romantic? Didn't she say they were romantic?'

'Perhaps. But she meant cool.'

'If you say so . . .' Eschenbach laughed quietly. 'Then let's string a line from the balcony to the parasol, tie a clove hitch, then pull it up and fix it in place with a nail.'

'Wow!'

'And then we can hang all the lanterns we've got on it.'

'Fab!' She clicked her tongue. 'I'll get the string.'

'Or a strong piece of cord. In the second drawer from the top, in the kitchen . . .' he shouted after her, but she was already gone.

When Corina appeared at the door to the apartment, weighed down with bags, the cord had been strung up and all the lanterns had been hung. It looked like a Chinese market, Eschenbach thought. Corina thought it was pretty. 'Really lovely,' she said.

'And when it gets dark, we'll light the candles,' said Kathrin, sitting on the wooden bench by the wall, flicking through a fashion magazine. 'Then it'll be really romantic.'

'Cool,' said Eschenbach, casually, playfully. He grinned and helped Corina unpack the shopping. She looked at him, surprised: 'Not you too.' They kissed.

The weather report that afternoon forecast 'local storms with some heavy squalls'. Eschenbach could see the yellow warning lights blinking on the shore as if it were a matter of life and death. It would take him another five minutes to reach the Meilenbach restaurant. In his mind's eye, he trawled through the menu and chose the baked perch. A huge portion, with a beer on the side. Then he heard his boat's tiny motor gurgling in the waves before giving out altogether.

He was glad that he was alone. Corina didn't like waves and she certainly didn't like blinding yellow lights heralding an incoming storm. She felt sick if the boat rocked too violently.

Kathrin, who was still in the middle of her summer holidays, was out with her pals, 'hunting for bargains'. 'It's cool to be cheap, Dad,' she had said. He didn't question the deeper meaning of this proclamation, or who it really benefited. It wasn't her fault that five-franc T-shirts always made him think of child labour and exploitation in the Third World. Perhaps a monthly wage of one dollar was 'cooler' for eight-year-olds than prostitution and drugs. What did Kathrin know, and how would it help if she did?

*

'Come in, for God's sake!' shouted a voice from the shore. A man in a yellow waterproof and green thigh waders was waving frantically.

Eschenbach steered as best he could towards the wooden jetty where the man was standing. The waves slapped against the boat and he struggled to stay on course.

'Here, throw the rope over!' shouted the man as Eschenbach approached.

The rain lashed at his face as he left the cabin and threw the rope to the man in the waterproof. His thigh waders struggled against their bands. Once the front and back of the boat were lashed to the jetty, it creaked contentedly and swayed with the waves like an old-fashioned cradle.

The man in the yellow waterproof was a woman. Maggie Wullschleger, a professional fisherwoman from Horgen. 'You're a piece of work,' she said when they were sitting in the pub with two large glasses of pale ale in front of them.

Eschenbach, whose hair was flattened over his forehead with rain and sweat, raised his glass: 'To my salvation, and thanks again. Good catch!' He was wet through to his underwear.

'I should say!' she replied, and they drank.

The landlord, a stocky man in his late fifties with a receding hairline, brought a kitchen towel for the inspector to dry his hair and neck; and fifteen minutes later, there was a plate of beautiful baked perch on the table.

He pulled his mobile phone out of his wet trouser pocket; thankfully, it still worked. He dialled the number for headquarters.

'You're still on holiday . . .' said Rosa Mazzoleni reproachfully. 'Enjoying the rain?' she added. 'Where are you?' The concern in her voice had gained the upper hand.

'Stranded.'

'Stranded? Good God!'

'And saved.' Eschenbach grinned and looked at Maggie, who was fishing the last piece of perch from her plate with her fork.

'What are you like!' said Rosa Mazzoleni, relieved. 'You're a piece of—'

'So I've been told.' He cleared his throat. Then, more seriously, he said, 'Salvisberg wanted to give me something else. A grey envelope: test results. Could you just, I mean . . .'

'I'll have a look.' There was rustling in the background. 'Here we are. Shall I open it?'

'Please. Read it to me.'

'Dear Mr Eschenbach,

According to tests undertaken in our laboratory, the two hair samples you submitted, Sample A: Case C, Basle, and Sample B: D.H., Zurich, are not identical, with a probability of 99.99 per cent. Our results are based on the following analytical processes: DNA testing . . .

'Now it's just a lot of technical mumbo jumbo, should I carry on?'

'No, that's enough. Thanks, and . . . Mazzoleni?'

'Yes?'

'Can you destroy the report . . . in the proper manner, I mean.'

'I'll stick it in the shredder myself, don't worry. And you enjoy your time off, got it?'

'Got it,' he said. Then the line went dead.

Eschenbach felt a little embarrassed. He had never really believed that Doris Hottiger was in league with her foster father. But how could he have been sure? There had been the matter of the mysterious blonde in Pierre Oliver's bed – she could have put the sleeping tablets in his wine, in the champagne, or done something else before Ernst Hottiger did the rest. He had found the sample of Doris's hair at Philipp Bettlach's house and it had bothered him. Now, at least, he knew.

'Not all blondes are created equal,' he murmured to himself, nodding over to Maggie who was poking between her teeth with a toothpick. Eschenbach raised his eyebrows questioningly. She nodded. Then he ordered another two glasses of beer.

Chapter 34

Marianne Felder was sitting at her desk in the editorial office of the *Zürcher Tagblatt,* cursing.

'Shit,' she hissed repeatedly into the half-empty coffee cup pressed to her lips: 'Shit.'

'Give it a rest,' moaned Xeno Schluep. 'I can't listen to you any more!' Xeno had just shut down his computer and picked up the Freitag bag that hung on the back of the chair. 'Come to Avalon for a Prosecco. My treat.' He tried to wink.

'I just can't believe it,' Marianne spat. 'I can't believe it.'

'Saying that over and over again won't make it any better.'

'Yes, it will.' She waved the white sheet of paper around.

'Are you coming or what?'

'They're just ignoring it!' Marianne let her shoulders drop and sighed. 'I don't write my articles just for them to be chucked in the bin!' she wanted to shout. Instead, she was quiet, restrained, each vowel a cannonball. Shots fired with a silencer. She threw the three stapled sheets of A4 onto the desk. There was another sound. Why are men allowed to throw televisions out of the window when their football team loses? She could at least try throwing her mouse at the wall, she thought. Wireless by Logitech, 110 francs. She would replace it later. 'This article . . .'

She stood up. 'They don't want anything more to do with it. It's all done and dusted.'

'Yup,' mumbled Xeno. 'And if Randegger says so, that's it. Don't get yourself worked up.'

'Randegger is a bloody . . .' Marianne couldn't hold it in any longer and threw a poisonous look at her colleague. The way he stood there with his plastic folder and his unkempt blond hair, he looked more like a nine-year old boy than a man of forty-three.

'So, I'm going to go . . . are you coming?'

'No . . . I don't know. The man killed himself, blew himself to smithereens and the papers have only printed five lines about it. It's just not right, is it?'

'Seven,' Xeno corrected her.

'What do you mean, seven?' Marianne pulled at the dark-blue T-shirt that only just covered her flat stomach.

'There are seven lines, I counted them: seven in *Bund*, seven in the *New Zurich Journal* and seven by us. The same sentences, same wording.'

'So you think there's something off about it too?'

'No!' Xeno laughed. 'It all looks perfectly normal.'

Marianne frowned.

'It looks like there was some order from high up; but I wouldn't worry about it.'

'So there is something fishy going on?'

'No, but it looks like someone was keen to make the matter go away . . . quietly.'

'But there was an explosion!' shouted Marianne.

'Someone in the press, I mean. No fuss.'

'Oh! And that's normal in Switzerland, I take it . . .' Marianne rolled her eyes. 'In Germany—'

'I know,' Xeno interrupted. 'In Germany everyone does their business in public.'

'At least we have freedom of the press.' Marianne dropped back into her chair and crossed her arms. 'We've got that at least.'

'I know, I know. And the Stasi . . .'

'That was East Germany and it was over fifteen years ago . . . what do you know about it?'

'I read the papers.'

'Exactly!' cried Marianne triumphantly. 'And if there are only seven biased lines in there, you might as well stuff your shoes with them.' Xeno had once told her that during his time as an office orderly in the army he had had to stuff his superior's boots with newspaper.

Xeno laughed. 'How's it biased? It was the truth – just brief and concise.'

'And now no one's interested! Bit suspicious, don't you think?'

'How? The German press spent a year filling the papers with the political party donation scandal. And nothing came of it!'

She said nothing, pushing her sunglasses up onto her head and switching the screen off. She walked to the exit without a word.

It had been a peaceful evening and Marianne didn't know why she wanted to go back to the editorial office. Her article would not be printed: not tonight and at no time in the future. What was she looking for? The murder story was dead in the water. All thanks to a shit-scared editor-in-chief, or shot down by a system governed by unknown forces. Xeno thought she should accept

Randegger's suggestion and write an article for the magazine on Hollister. 'That brand's a real cult,' he had said excitedly.

After four glasses of Prosecco, she had to agree with him. They would give her three weeks for the research, including a few days in Los Angeles, all on expenses. Not a bad offer. She strolled over the Rathaus Bridge and watched the lights twinkling on the opposite bank of the Limmat.

Between the trees she could see colourful light bulbs, their reflections dancing on the water like bright sparks. Marianne took a deep breath and sat down for a moment on the huge bridge railing, pulling one of her legs up towards her. It was half ten in the evening, a cool breeze tickled the nape of her neck and made her shiver. Her hands felt the rough surface beneath her. The stone was pleasantly warm; it emanated a sensual warmth that made up for everything the day had not given her.

The thin leather straps of her flip-flops had made the skin between her toes sore. She pulled them off and looked at her feet for a long while. Then she jumped down onto the pavement and walked the few steps up to Limmatquai barefoot, sitting down on a bench to put her shoes back on.

When she slid her card through the machine at the entrance to the *Zürcher Tagblatt* building, it was almost time to go to press. Sentences would be undergoing a final polish, people would be sprinting to and fro in case there was something they had forgotten. No one noticed her amidst the chaos, except for Dario Hollenweger, sports editor, who offered a hello. It didn't really count as a hello. It wasn't for her, it could just as easily have been for a member of the cleaning staff or the errand boy. It was a reflex that came from the depths of a mental absence.

Marianne sat down at her desk and switched on her screen. It was a reflex action because she didn't really want to write or read anything. She just wanted to be alone, that was all.

The screen flickered.

She took the *Daily* and leafed through to find the piece on Hottiger; she wanted to read those seven lines again. Was it really seven? She came across the double-page spread of obituaries. 'It's like he died five times,' she grumbled to herself, turning the page to see if there would be a sixth on the next page. There were no others. Just the Swiss Technical University, the Swiss Officer's Union, the Rifleman's Association, the Swiss Olympic team from Rome and his daughter. They all mentioned their *sad duty*, their *sorrow* or the *unhappy honour*. Nothing about murder or manslaughter, no hint of revenge or retribution.

Marianne opened the bottom drawer and fished out a pack of Marlboro Gold that she kept there for emergencies – behind a dark-blue make-up bag. She had managed to go two weeks without one, drunk litres of water and stuck little patches on her back and stomach. She accepted the redness and the itching and, of course, the urge to pee and ever-present craving for one last drag. She thought for a moment, then she ripped the cellophane off the pack, stood up, took the matches from Xeno's desk and lit the cigarette.

The smoke swirled up over the obituaries, rising in small wisps beneath the glare of the halogen lamp, and dissipated. At first she just took a puff, then inhaled deeply and enjoyed it. She thought about how, after the last time the dentist had cleaned her teeth, she had sworn to keep them free of the ugly plaque that regularly formed on the inside of her canines. She wanted to laugh again and throw her head back, feel her polished teeth with her tongue.

It was like something out of a toothpaste advert. Visualise and hold. It was her first thought in the morning and her last before she went to sleep.

She wondered, as she compared the text of the obituaries, how Doris Hottiger would deal with her father's death and how it would feel to inherit Hottiger's fortune.

And then she saw the sentence: short, but long enough that it was impossible to overlook. At the bottom, just above the thick, black borderline. The same in every one:

> At the family's request, in place of flowers we ask you to consider making a donation to Fluntern Children's Home and the University of the Canton of Zurich.

The numbers for the bank accounts were included in brackets in bold letters. No flowers for a murderer, then, she thought; that seems right.

Marianne slept fitfully. A tornado swept over Los Angeles and the plane she was in crashed into the sea before landing. The fat American man next to her was wearing a Von Dutch baseball cap and took up half of her seat as well as his own. He claimed that the tornado was the work of al-Qaeda. When she woke up, she found herself lying on the edge of her wide bed, soaked in sweat.

Yesterday's *Daily*, featuring the obituaries, lay open on the bistro table in the kitchen. What linked Hottiger to a children's home and the University of Zurich? She dragged herself into the kitchen, ate half a watermelon and drank two glasses of multivitamin juice. She felt awful. It must have been because she was smoking again.

Perhaps it was stubbornness, perhaps it was her journalistic instinct pushing her to sit down at the computer, find the numbers and call.

Some people can reel off twenty-figure numbers at the drop of a hat, know thousands of prime numbers by heart. Iris Hegibach, secretary at Fluntern Children's Home, had no such talent. Her talent was for formulating each sentence as if it were an accusation: 'We're a private foundation, didn't you know? We do not divulge information to anyone.'

Marianne put on a pleasant voice and explained that – as a friend of Mr Hottiger – she wished to make a large donation, but would like to know more about his involvement in the Fluntern Foundation.

'If you're a friend of the family, surely you already know?' came the prompt reply.

Marianne smirked. Ms Hegibach was like an overprotective mother hen, guarding an institution of do-gooders against the riffraff. But she was not immune to a little flattery. It didn't take long before Marianne had what she needed. Ernst Hottiger was the president of the foundation and had spent part of his childhood in the care of the institution.

The second call she made was to the University of Zurich, and Marianne gradually came to find that she was quite enjoying winkling the truth out of people.

'Ernst supported a large number of charitable institutions – I certainly couldn't remember all of them off the top of my head,' she said, before repeating the number for the bank account from the obituary. Then she was connected.

'Professor Madulan,' announced a hesitant voice, and once again Marianne presented herself as a friend of Ernst Hottiger.

'What was your name, did you say?'

'Winkler,' lied Marianne, grabbing the packet of Marlboros off the small chest of drawers next to the table. 'Eleonor Winkler.'

'So, Ms Winkler . . . did you say Eleonora?'

'No, just Eleonor – without an "a" at the end. And Winkler with a "w", like winkle.' Marianne suppressed a laugh. She pulled a cigarette out of the pack and tried to light it. Either this old dragon's checking my name online, she thought, or struggling with her conscience.

'We're not able to give out information, I'm afraid,' replied the voice hesitantly.

'You don't need to give me any information . . .' Marianne whispered understandingly. 'But it would be good to know how Mr Hottiger was involved with your institution. I'd like to support you – financially, I mean.'

The woman sighed.

'So, it would help me to at least know a little context.'

'Yes, I understand that,' she replied irritably.

Marianne stayed stubbornly silent and waited.

'Mr Hottiger is a member of the patrons' association of our research institute.'

'Was a member, you mean?'

'Yes, of course. He provided us with a lot of financial support . . . even when it was no longer of any use to him.'

'What do you mean, it wasn't of any use to him?' Marianne's ears pricked up.

'As a patient . . .' said the woman, hesitantly. 'Mr Hottiger was a patient at our institution. But actually, I shouldn't . . . we don't give out information of this nature.'

'I know, of course.' Marianne noticed that her hands were clammy. Now she had to employ all her journalistic nous to find out what illness Hottiger had suffered from. 'Ernst was really pleased with the work your institute does and even read to me from a report on your research. He was convinced that you would be able to help him.'

The woman at the other end of the line said nothing.

'It's true,' Marianne persisted. 'He had good reason to be hopeful, don't you think?'

'You didn't know Ernst Hottiger very well, did you?' The woman's voice had turned cold.

'Can we ever really know anyone?' replied Marianne, lightning fast. 'Of course, he didn't tell me everything . . . and what do we really know about the people around us? Even the ones we're supposed to be close to?'

'But he read to you from the reports?' asked the woman pointedly.

'Of course,' replied Marianne. 'But perhaps it was only vaguely related to his illness. I don't know much about medical research, if you must know.'

The line was silent.

'What's the matter?' Marianne dug deeper. She sensed that her web of lies was about to snap. 'The fact that he read me the reports, is that it? Should he not have done?'

'No,' said the voice after a while. 'He couldn't. Ernst Hottiger couldn't have read to you.'

'Why not? He wasn't illiterate, was he?'

'No, he wasn't. He couldn't read because he was almost blind.'

Marianne swallowed.

'Even with a magnifying glass, he would barely be able to see anything. Just light and shade; it's a shame that we couldn't help him.'

A moment later the line went quiet and Marianne hung up.

Chapter 35

Eschenbach was enjoying his few days' holiday and was sitting on the small terrace of his old-style apartment in Zurich. He stretched his arms. The sky was clear and the inspector knew that the sun was already shining in the east behind the old building complex. Just after eleven o'clock the first rays would make their way towards him over the dark tiled roof. It would be happening just a few minutes later from now on, he thought to himself; in August the day began to idle.

Although he had set it for three, he found himself alone at the breakfast table. Corina was at her morning yoga class and Kathrin was still asleep. Yesterday, they had gone to the cinema together to see *Master and Commander* with Russell Crowe. 'Another man's film,' Corina had whispered in his ear when Crowe's frigate was attacked and almost destroyed. 'Now you know what a real broadside is,' he said to the two women in his life. During the intermission, there was popcorn and cola, and ribs. 'Yet again, not a single woman,' Corina complained. Still, the big screen with Dolby surround sound more than made up for it, thought Eschenbach. His contented grunt was lost amid the noise of the battle.

He had taken the cordless telephone onto the terrace and answered with his mouth full.

'Is that you, boss?' Rosa Mazzoleni sounded hesitant.

'Yes, it's me . . .' He swallowed.

Rosa wanted to read him the story at once: *Zürcher Tagblatt,* front page, domestic news. 'It's almost a whole page, boss.' But she didn't get further than the headline. The inspector took the last croissant, which he had been saving for Corina, and said that he would come into headquarters straight away.

He left the house and bought himself a copy of the *Daily* at the kiosk on Paradeplatz, before taking a seat opposite at the Mövenpick wine bar. There it was: 'GOLF COURSE SHOOTER REVEALED TO BE BLIND. WHO REALLY SHOT BANKER PHILIPP BETTLACH?' By the time he had read the article, his espresso was cold.

The article had dropped like a bombshell.

Eschenbach sat in the black leather armchair in his office and put the receiver back in its cradle. He had had a long conversation with Elisabeth Kobler; she had done most of the talking and he had listened. She talked about sloppy police work and said he could forget about his holiday. The cigarillo between his lips had gone out, one end chewed thin. He looked out through the half-drawn blinds; it was midday and the sun was shining, oblivious to everything that was going on. 'Call Jagmetti and Lenz!' Eschenbach thundered through the intercom. He fiddled with his lighter, trying to relight the Brissago. 'I want them in my office in half an hour . . . this bloody thing!'

'Do you need anything else?' Rosa's voice cooed through the speaker.

'I think it's . . . blocked or something . . .' The inspector tapped the red plastic lighter on the desk top. 'Damn it! Or maybe it's the gas . . .' He held it up to the light. 'Ms Mazzoleni?'

'Yes?' she replied calmly. 'I've got some matches, if you'd like them?'

'Yes, yes, I would.'

The eye clinic at Zurich University Hospital is proud of its 150-year history of treating patients with eye-related ailments. Over the years, ophthalmology has made great advances . . .

Eschenbach read about the history of the hospital while they waited for Professor Randolf Madulan, the head of the clinic's research department. Jagmetti was flicking through a fashion magazine.

Then they were called in.

When they stepped out of the university building an hour later, they looked like beaten dogs. The sun was low and blinding and Eschenbach felt in his shirt and jacket pockets for his sunglasses. Nothing. Jagmetti plodded along next to him, saying nothing. Unlike his boss, he concealed his low spirits behind a pair of angular glasses that developed a dark-blue tint in the light.

'He was the perfect murderer,' said Eschenbach, wiping the sweat from his brow with one hand. 'And now the arsehole's blind.'

Jagmetti sucked air through his nose. 'Looks like it. As good as, anyway.'

When they reached the tram stop, they saw the back of the number 9 tram trundling off, before braking and stopping at the lights just a hundred metres down the road.

'Look at that, it left early and for what?' growled Eschenbach quietly.

'If we had run, we could have caught it,' said Jagmetti. He shrugged his shoulders and buried his hands in his trouser pockets.

'Maybe,' came his moody superior's listless reply. 'I don't run after trams any more. Seven minutes aren't worth having a heart attack over.'

Jagmetti said nothing.

They crossed the street and sat on a low wall in the shade of a block of houses.

'I only saw the guy in dim light, in his house on Lake Sihl. And then when he went down to the boathouse ... Christ, it didn't look like he was struggling to find the path.' Eschenbach propped his arms on his thighs. 'I should have summoned him to headquarters, then I would have noticed ... It's my fault. Goddam it!'

Jagmetti sat next to him in silence, trying to nod sympathetically from time to time, or stroking his finger through his thick hair – more out of awkwardness than anything. The inspector seemed hardly to see him at all. Eschenbach sat bent over, his elbows pressed against his knees, speaking between his legs to the tarmac, or maybe to himself. He was full of self-doubt and fury. When the tram arrived at their stop, they got up, wandered over to the other side of the road and got on it.

'Was he really blind?' asked Rosa Mazzoleni when Eschenbach walked past her desk half an hour later.

'Yes,' the inspector snarled. 'If the doctors are to be believed.' He shrugged.

'Better the doctors than the press,' she sighed. 'It's mayhem in here, I'm telling you . . . so I'll be happy when it's home time.'

'Me too,' blustered Eschenbach. 'Or Christmas, that'd be good too.' Furious, he slammed the door behind him, sat down at his desk and called the department for media relations. The press conference had been scheduled for half six that evening, an hour away; then he spoke to Kobler and called home. He thought about their plans: the visit to Corina's parents at Lake Zug that day, hiking in the Maderanertal . . . his whole holiday was ruined. He stood up, went to the window and looked through the skewed blinds to the street below. He took a couple of hurried drags on his cigarillo, pulled down one of the slats and threw the burning stub outside.

'Now we have to do our homework,' was the last thing that Eschenbach said before ending the press conference. It wasn't really an answer to the question he had been asked, whether the sloppiness in police operations would continue or whether, perhaps, it was the police who were blind. He hadn't really ended the conference at all. At times, it had felt more like a hearing and he had decided to stop it. He had been taking punches for over an hour. Marianne Felber from the *Zurich Daily* had smiled the whole time without asking a single question. Unlike the others in the room – including the police – she had done her homework.

By the time Eschenbach finally managed to leave headquarters, it was ten to eleven. As he walked, he thought about the conference they had held a month ago, when the murder was still fresh, lying before him like a white sheet of paper. Now he felt like a painter who tears up a sketch for the ninth time because the perspective is off or the sky is too dark. If you tinkered about with it too much, the genius of the thing would be ruined. He was hungry.

The Sheep's Head was still full, except for three tables. The large sliding windows that looked onto the street stood open and well-fed, cheery punters milled around outside. The inspector nodded as Estefan waved to him from the counter, then he sat down at the table in the corner and stretched his legs.

After a while, Gabriel came out of the kitchen with his monogrammed apron and unkempt hair: 'I've still got some paella, or do you want the jumbo prawns on the grill?'

'Maybe some meat, if you've got it . . .' Eschenbach looked at Gabriel and winked. 'Proper meat, I mean.'

Gabriel laughed. 'How about a fillet of beef, medium rare, with steamed tomatoes and *rösti*?'

The inspector nodded and took a copy of the *Zürcher Tagblatt* from the windowsill while Gabriel disappeared back into the kitchen. He read the sports and weather pages, the article about the new theatre director at the Schiffbau and the gossip column at the back. The domestic news section was missing.

'Voilà, beef *à la* Eschenbach,' Gabriel joked, shooting out of the kitchen like a happy comet with the plate and a bottle of wine. 'Hope you like it,' he said, placing the plate carefully on the white tablecloth. Then he filled two large glasses with wine and sat down.

'A Nebbiolo from Gaja . . .' Eschenbach murmured with his mouth full, studying the label on the bottle. 'You're bonkers.'

'Oh, come on, it won't hurt. To us! To those of us with eyes in our heads!'

They swirled the full-bodied red slowly for a moment or two then brought it under their noses; strong notes of oak, a faint hint of ripe redcurrants, a morning in Piedmont. The friends toasted, drank and looked at each other for a moment in silence.

'Are you sure he was really blind?' Gabriel was playing with the table decoration, a white and purple posy. 'I mean, you can't always believe what you read in the papers . . .'

'Yep, he was blind. Almost, anyway.' Eschenbach poured himself some more wine. 'He wouldn't have been able to tell a sparrow from a raven. Not even with a riflescope. He can't have been the shooter.'

'Hmm, so he couldn't actually have done it?'

'Nope.'

'And now what?' As he asked this, Gabriel pulled the little white rose out of the table decoration. It was wilting.

'No idea. I'm going to . . .' He chewed thoughtfully and looked past Gabriel to the large picture on the wall. It showed a lonely street with a rotting tree trunk, swept there by floodwater. Flotsam and jetsam.

The inspector did not feel ready to speak at length again until he had finished eating, wiping up the dregs of the sauce with a piece of bread and placing his knife and fork neatly next to one another on the plate. He wiped the napkin across his mouth several times. 'I went to the eye clinic at Zurich Uni today. They told me everything.' He took his black notebook out of his jacket pocket and turned the pages. 'Age-related macular degeneration – AMD – that's what they suspected at first. It seems to be quite common as you get older. You mostly notice it when reading. A blurry speck in the middle of the page, or a grey shadow.'

'Cataracts?' Gabriel interrupted him.

'No, I asked that too. AMD is different. The shadow grows larger and leads to a "deterioration in visual acuity".'

Gabriel held the empty wine bottle in front of his face. 'Can you read the small print under Gaja if you hold the bottle like this?'

'Now stop it, you're just long sighted – but who isn't? It wasn't AMD anyway.' He leafed through and found the term that he had forgotten. 'It was Sorsby fundus dystrophy.' Eschenbach sighed. 'I'm telling you, I think my memory's going. It's getting worse and worse.'

'What? I wouldn't be able to remember this Sorsby fundus . . . thing either.' Gabriel lit a cigarette and took a puff.

'Smoking is really bad according to that researcher, Madulain . . . Dr Madulan.' He looked at his notebook again.

'For what?' asked Gabriel.

'For everything.'

'I don't inhale any more,' said Gabriel with a mouth full of smoke. 'I just puff away on it out of habit.'

'It's really bad for your eyes, he said.'

'So, I might as well be inhaling, is that what you're saying?' He laughed and then coughed.

'I'm not joking. I think I might get my eyes checked. Just as a precaution, I mean.' Eschenbach took a sip of water.

'Have you stopped smoking, then?' asked Gabriel. It occurred to him that the inspector had left his cigarillos in his pocket.

'I'm smoking less,' said Eschenbach. 'Trying to, anyway.'

'Since your visit to the clinic today? Oh, give it a rest! It'll get better. You're not going to get this fundus thing.'

'Sorsby fundus . . .' The inspector was reading his notes. 'Sorsby fundus dystrophy – is extremely rare and is genetically determined, based on a mutation in the TIMP3 gene. Not a lot is known about it.'

'And the murderer had it . . . I mean, Hottiger had it.'

'Yes. It affects the eyesight very quickly; your vision deteriorates rapidly, mostly in your forties.' And after a short pause, he added, 'There's no effective treatment for it – not yet.' Then he shut his notebook. He hadn't written any more.

'I'm turning fifty next year,' said Gabriel, mostly to himself, bringing over a bottle of grappa with two small glasses. 'It's a Barolo. Life is too short for bad schnapps.'

Chapter 36

It didn't bother Eschenbach that he hadn't slept enough and had a hangover. It was a condition that he felt well able to live with, one that he sometimes even enjoyed. He imagined that a similar feeling would set in after the thirtieth kilometre of a marathon, when the runner could no longer feel their legs and everything around them seemed to grow further away.

He went through the Hottiger file again in the hope that he'd overlooked something significant. There was the tragic solitude of his youth and the support he had found in shooting. The 1960 Olympic Games in Rome, the army and then his career as a security adviser. It was a life lived in the service of others, as a protector and a guardian. Eschenbach wondered whether Hottiger could have laid down his life for someone else, sacrificing himself in the knowledge that he would never see again? It was a possibility, one he had to bear in mind.

Perhaps the truth lay in the photos in front of him. There was Hottiger posing in front of an Olympic flag with his medals: unsmiling, serious, his eyes dark and sharp. Perhaps it was simply something to do with how he was feeling, but Eschenbach thought of the marathon runner Abebe Bikila, a lanky black man from the northern uplands of Ethiopia, who, like Hottiger, had also won gold at the Olympics in Rome. Forty-two kilometres in two hours, fifteen minutes and sixteen seconds. The former guardsman to Emperor Haile Selassie had run the fastest time ever recorded back then, barefoot and seemingly effortlessly. In Tokyo, four years later, he won again. It was his last big win before he had an accident in the car that he had been given and was left quadriplegic. Abebe, the lame runner, and Hottiger, the blind marksman – the guardsman and the security fanatic.

Eschenbach was still rubbing his eyes when Elisabeth Kobler stormed into his office without knocking. He threw the Hottiger file on top of a pile of other papers. 'What is it?' he asked, without looking up.

'We've got to deal with this,' said the police chief.

'Oh yeah, and what's that?' He looked at her.

Kobler pulled a chair up to Eschenbach's desk and sat down. 'We've got to give them something.'

'Sorry, who do we have to give something to?' Eschenbach stayed calm.

'This article . . .' Kobler paused briefly. 'It shouldn't have been printed. It was a mistake . . . because of the holidays.'

'Oh really?' The inspector leant back and raised his eyebrows. 'And why's that?'

'Councillor Sacher is seriously pissed off. Someone called her about it and couldn't get through. The administration and editor-in-chief wanted to hold the article. Somehow it slipped through the net.' Kobler spoke quietly, swinging one foot.

'I still don't understand.' Eschenbach rocked forward and propped his elbows on the desk. 'Everything she's written in the paper is true. For once. Hottiger did have this condition. He was actually blind – mostly, anyway. There's no way he could have

committed this murder. It's shit, but it's true. And to be honest
. . .' He paused. 'To be honest, we should be grateful to Marianne
Felber for doing our job for us.'

'Do you know this journalist?'

'No, for God's sake.' Eschenbach raised his voice. But it's a
name that we should pay more attention to in future.'

'Councillor Sacher sees it differently,' replied his boss, cuttingly.

'I don't give a toss how Sacher sees it. We didn't do our job
properly; we stopped after thirty kilometres instead of keeping
going. Now we've got to deal with the shit.'

'*Rookie mistake*. Back to square one, then,' she sighed.

'No, not quite,' Eschenbach countered. 'But this isn't the end,
either.' Kobler's Americanisms were getting on his nerves.

'Now what? I mean, we've got to do something.' Kobler
gripped her knee in her hands and raised her shoulders as if she
were about to take a run up. Then she said, 'Doing nothing is not
an option, Eschenbach!'

The inspector nodded as if he had been expecting this. It
was Councillor Sacher's favourite phrase; empty and useless, he
thought. They could wait and let the killer make his next move
– that was always an option, and Kobler knew it. But it required
nerves and a thick skin, and he couldn't rely on either.

'I don't expect any kind of rapid response but doing nothing isn't a solution either . . .' He was obviously getting on her
nerves.

'Yes, I know!' cried Eschenbach, looking at the clock irritably. He couldn't listen to that stupid phrase any more. 'I'll think
about it.'

It was just before twelve midday.

'Make sure you do,' murmured Kobler, getting up. 'You know that I have every confidence in you.'

The inspector spent the afternoon in meetings and on the phone. He would have liked to speak to Johannes Bettlach in person, but getting hold of him was like getting blood out of a stone. This time, however, the inspector was not giving up. Apparently, Bettlach was abroad and he wanted to know which plane he had taken and what hotel he was staying in. His secretaries would know, and they were bad liars when it came to the details, when you wanted precise information. Eschenbach had the feeling that Bettlach wasn't aborad at all, that he wasn't really sitting on a SWISS plane, which had left Zurich at 12.30 and which would be landing in New York eight hours later. He simply sensed it; Johannes Bettlach was still in Switzerland, perhaps at his bank or in his old villa above Herrliberg, taking cover like a crane on its nest.

Even if Bettlach's secretary's humming and hawing over her boss's plans suggested that Eschenbach's suspicions were right, the inspector wanted to be sure. He had the information she had given him checked by Max Kubly and his people at Info Services.

'SWISS flight to New York at 12.30 today, I'll give you the number . . .' It took a moment for Eschenbach to find the note-pad with his notes and relay the information. 'Passenger lists, you know the drill . . . and also the reservation at Hotel Mercer in Manhattan.'

The officer at the other end of the line repeated each piece of information word by word. He had a bright voice and his name was Yves Bechstein. Eschenbach confirmed or countered each name and number with a 'Yes!' or a 'No!' On the one occasion that the inspector replied with an 'Mmm', Bechstein repeated his query, following it with a shrill 'Yes?' Eschenbach was thinking about how good it would be if this type of conversation was fully automated. With an automated baritone, he thought. Bechstein sounded like a trumpet.

When the conversation came to an end, the inspector asked if he could contact the US Immigration Office. 'Even if he's not booked in anywhere.'

'Of course,' said Trumpet, soliciting another 'Yes!' for John F. Kennedy and Newark International Airport.

The next morning, Eschenbach spent several hours translating the unanswered questions in the Bettlach case into an interim report. Kobler needed the report for Sacher. Urgently, she said.

Hottiger's plan had required an enormous bluff. But it was his last option. Ernst Hottiger had known that he would soon be completely blind, which must to him have seemed like a fate worse than bankruptcy, perhaps even worse than death. But it was unlikely that he would kill himself for that reason alone, and not just because his father had done it and he had hated him for it, or because it was a coward's way out, anathema to his values. But what if he could have used his suicide to protect others? Someone close to him, someone whose life mattered more to him than his own? Then there would be a purpose behind his suicide. For a man obsessed with security, this final act would be like turning the key in an open lock.

Chapter 37

'What is this?' Jagmetti threw the arrest warrant onto Eschenbach's desk and stood in front of him, looking like his house had just been burgled. 'Tell me you're not serious!'

'Yup,' replied Eschenbach. 'She was arrested at seven this morning. Finally, the show's over.'

'Doris is innocent,' Jagmetti hissed. Disappointment and rage burned red on his forehead.

'That's for the judge to decide, not me.'

'And this?' The young police officer hammered his index finger on the paper which was written in French. 'Why didn't I hear about it?'

'Surely I don't have to explain it to you?' Eschenbach raised his eyebrows. 'I was just about to come and tell you.'

'You don't trust me ...' Jagmetti paused for a moment before continuing his rant at the inspector. 'It's so ... rotten and underhand. If you had any balls, you'd say it to my face. Tell me that I'm no good at this job. That I'm a liability, a hindrance.'

Eschenbach wanted to say something but couldn't. Accusations and self-pity rained down. The inspector resisted the urge to light a Brissago. He simply sat there with his hands on the armrests, in silence, as if he were at a concert. After a while, once Jagmetti seemed to have run out of steam, he said, 'Are you finished?'

'Yes.' And after a brief pause, he added, 'Boss, I quit!'

'Listen to me, I'm not your sodding boss.'

'I don't care, I'm quitting anyway,' said Jagmetti before walking to the exit. His footsteps were hesitant, and it seemed as if the force of his anger had left him.

'Then do so in writing and send it to the head of training!' shouted Eschenbach behind him, before the door quietly swung shut.

The inspector leant back for a moment, folded his hands over his neck and thought about whether he should have told Jagmetti after all. He wasn't a suspicious person, quite the contrary. Respect for one another and mutual trust were the most important foundations for successful police work. Those were his principles; ideals he believed in and preached on every police training course. And yet, he had decided against them. *Contre coeur.* It hadn't been easy.

'You went too far with that last bit.' It was the voice of Rosa Mazzoleni, rattling through the intercom.

'Which bit?' grumbled Eschenbach, though he knew exactly what she meant.

'Don't be like that, boss.' She paused for a moment. 'It was a horrible way to find out, and now he's on his way to Sepp Kohler! Sepp's so stupid, he'll let him quit.'

'I don't think so.'

'Just a moment.' The phone rang in the background, then there was a click from the loudspeaker and the sound cut out.

Eschenbach looked at the clock and was about to get up when Rosa walked into the office.

'It was just a short call,' she said, looking cheerful.

'And?'

'Just a private call, nothing important.' She smiled. Her rose-pink trouser suit looked marvellous and her short black hair was combed back – held in place with plenty of gel.

'Nice colour – you're living up to your name,' said the inspector, gesturing to the empty seat opposite.

She stayed standing. 'I just wanted to say ... about before. I don't want you to think I've been eavesdropping on you.'

'I'd never think that.' Eschenbach laughed loudly.

Doris Hottiger's arrest was a media event, Eschenbach made sure of that. The arrest in Paris, the two-week extradition period at the airport detention centre at Charles de Gaulle and then the transfer to Switzerland on a scheduled Air France flight, arriving into Zurich-Kloten at half nine in the morning on 12 September.

Swiss citizens who were returned to their home country in this way – and it was very rare that they did so of their own free will – were immediately accommodated in a remand centre at Zurich airport, where they remained until the beginning of their trial. Typically, they would be there for up to a year – seldom longer than two. The prison was also home to people who were not Swiss citizens. These were in the majority, and were waiting to be returned to where they had come from, often against their will.

The only reason Doris Hottiger was not placed in the remand centre was because it had no cells for women. For this reason, she was imprisoned at Dielsdorf county jail, in a small cell in the west wing of the building.

The Philipp Bettlach case rolled on, chapter after chapter. The story of sexual deviance and revenge in a high-society family seemed to be made for the tabloids, and Doris Hottiger was transformed into a media star against her will for the second time in her short life: pretty and blond, with her finger on the trigger.

A short video clip was shown, interviews were conducted, admittedly with victims who had nothing to do with the case. Doris became the avenger of a seemingly huge number of tragic victims. The reports about her became as much a part of the daily news as the weather or the crisis on the Gaza Strip.

Dielsdorf county jail, where Doris was living in twelve square metres of space, was soon on everyone's lips and enjoyed a degree of notoriety previously enjoyed by the Swiss Federal Palace that housed the Government.

The warden Martha Imhof, who had been in charge of Dielsdorf for seventeen years, unsurprisingly suffered a nervous breakdown. Following an ill-considered statement on her part, the country's most highly circulated newspaper turned the committed Christian into a cold-hearted dragon.

Eschenbach sat in his office reading through the press reports. His plan had been to use the media to ramp up the pressure. Pressure on Doris and – if she really was innocent – pressure on the murderer, who was still at large. In the three weeks that Doris had been sitting in the remand centre, the case had developed its own steam, which the inspector found increasingly unpleasant as the days passed.

He had woefully underestimated the matter: the inner conflict, turmoil and tension that he had hoped would coax the killer into the open had all come back to haunt him. And because of the ongoing reporting in the tabloids and on TV, people were confessing to the crime every day, leaving the police force struggling to cope.

'When are you expecting a confession?' This was Elisabeth Kobler's usual question. It was the second time she had called to ask this in the past twenty-four hours.

'I don't know . . . I don't actually think we're going to get one.'

'Isn't that a bit pessimistic?'

'Confessions usually come at the beginning or not at all.'

'That's true . . .'

'See?'

'Then let's prepare ourselves for a trial without one,' said Kobler. 'That's fine by me. There are obvious grounds for arrest, after all. We can't be accused of anything.'

'No, it's not that.'

'Have we found the murder weapon?'

'No. The Blaser R93 Tactical that we suspect was used has disappeared. We found the serial number, firearms licence etc., at Ernst Hottiger's house. It was registered as part of his collection.'

'And it's well known that Ms Hottiger frequently visited there.'

'Yes. She had a key and would check in when Ernst Hottiger was at home or abroad. Delivery workers and neighbours have confirmed it.'

All of this had already been noted by the media several times, featured in many newspaper articles.

'And Hottiger's lawyer . . .'

'Alex Kalbermatten,' offered Eschenbach.

'Yes, him. From Kalbermatten & Dormann – one of the best firms for criminal cases, by the way.'

'I know.' Eschenbach rolled his eyes. 'His release request wasn't granted. It's hardly surprising when Doris has already done a runner abroad once.'

'Everything's as it should be, then.'

'Yes.'

Once they had said goodbye, Eschenbach looked at the clock and wondered whether he would still be able to catch the tram.

Once a week he would take the S5 to Dielsdorf to visit Doris in the hope of getting something sensible out of her: a confession or some information that would further the investigation or clear her name. He did this every Tuesday, unofficially, as a civilian. Otherwise he would have had to follow protocol by summoning her to headquarters for an interrogation, with a host of police officers accompanying her, standing around in awkward silence.

Even though he had only been making his brief visits to see her for three weeks and even though she spent most of them sitting opposite him in silence, it had become a habit of sorts. He would leave headquarters just before five, stroll along the Sihl to the station and order a doner kebab from the Turks on the station concourse. And every time he was lucky enough to find a free window seat on the tram, facing forward.

It irritated Eschenbach that it was Wednesday already and he hadn't managed to find time for his visit the day before. Corina insisted that they go to the Schiffbau to watch a popular production by Christoph Schlingensief. The cast had roared at one another for two hours and Eschenbach had resisted the urge to fall asleep.

Had Doris been expecting him? He liked the few routines that his job allowed: the walks through Zurich, the morning meeting where he would gather his closest colleagues, the chats over coffee with Rosa. They were like little toeholds for him, small islands resisting the constant flow of change. It was ten past five and Eschenbach decided to take the car.

As he drove his old Volvo back into the city – through the Milchbuck Tunnel at walking pace – an unusual feeling came over him again. He had it every time he came away from seeing Doris. But this time, he was able to pinpoint it: it was a heaviness that cocooned him like the exhaust fumes from the cars that waited in front of him and slid past him. It was a bad feeling.

It occurred to him that in the three weeks that he had been visiting Doris, she had lost weight. It was not the kind of weight loss that suited a person, the kind achieved by the occasional salad. It was completely different, as if some sallow greyness had stolen away the sensuality of her mouth. Her cheekbones stood out more clearly than before, replacing the apples of her cheeks altogether.

The colour just goes, he thought. It had been the same for his father who had died four years ago of stomach cancer. As he crept forward along the N1, he remembered his visits to the Paracelsus Hospital in Richterswil. He remembered the old man's good-natured brown eyes, how he believed in life until the very end and the jokes that they had made to distract themselves from the spectre of death.

Eschenbach was stuck in a traffic jam for over an hour. With the windows open, he crept through half the city, heading west.

By the time he merged onto Langstrasse, he had already listened to Daniel Barenboim's recordings of Beethoven's Second and Fourth Symphonies and, as he only had the two cassettes, he wondered which one he wanted to play again. He abandoned them for the radio, where selected guests were discussing the Hardturm building project. It would be big and expensive – a temple to football, worthy of the city, with a shopping paradise to boot.

At the top of Badenerstrasse he turned right, and a hundred metres later he spun the car around a tram island and onto the opposite lane. A hundred-franc fine, he reckoned, then he turned right into Marta-Strasse and searched for a car park. Rosa Mazzoleni had given him the house number when he rang her from the car.

The name C. Jagmetti was written by hand on a small piece of white tape. Eschenbach pressed the bell and counted three floors. There was no lift. The stairwell was poorly lit and run-down. Eschenbach avoided touching the handrail.

The door stood open when he arrived on the third floor, gasping for breath. 'Hello,' said Claudio Jagmetti, walking towards him from inside the apartment. Barefoot, wearing jeans and a white T-shirt. 'Basle–Liverpool, three–nil,' he said, stretching out a hand.

Green turf flickered on a small screen in the background.

'Half an hour in and three goals for Basle already.' He seemed to have repeated this because he assumed that Eschenbach might otherwise assume Liverpool were in the lead. He wasn't wrong.

'Should I come by later?' The inspector gestured to the TV with his chin.

'No, come in, I'll get us a beer.' He switched the television off and went into the kitchen. 'I assume Corona's OK?' he said as he came back into the living room with two bottles in his hand.

Eschenbach nodded. He was sitting on the low sofa; he had stuck a cushion behind his back and stretched his legs out. Aside from the sofa on which they were sitting, the only other furniture in the room was an aluminium bistro table and two chairs. Two black boxes took up the corners – speakers for the stereo, which stood on the same wooden unit as the television. The walls were bare.

'What a match . . . who would have thought?'

The inspector nodded. He assumed Jagmetti was still talking about the game. Then he put his bottle down.

'Sorry, I didn't think. Shall I get you a glass?'

'I'm all right, thanks.' He laughed and shook his head.

It must have irritated the young police officer to see him drinking out of the bottle. 'As far as I know, you drink Corona without a glass.'

The two officers sat next to one another for a while without speaking, and because neither of them spoke, they kept lifting their bottles to their lips, drinking and then setting them down.

'Still got your heart set on rebellion?' It was Eschenbach who took the first step.

'Josef Kohler's assigned me to the IT department . . . it was my idea.' And after a brief pause, he added, 'I never gave in my notice.'

'Mmmm,' Eschenbach mumbled, sucking at the bottle. 'I don't know if it was right not to tell you . . . somehow I hoped you would come and see me.' He took another sip.

'I thought it was better this way. The whole media frenzy and everything . . .' He rubbed his hands on his jeans. 'Now I'm tinkering about with the cantonal police website.'

'And is that exciting?'

'It's a change.'

The inspector wrinkled his nose. He had always thought the same about IT. 'But you don't really want to stay there, do you?'

'Yes, until it's all over.' Jagmetti looked at the television even though it wasn't on.

'Until the trial is over, you mean?'

'We'll have to see.'

Eschenbach rearranged the cushion at his back and turned to Jagmetti. 'Did she say anything to you?'

'No.' The answer was short and sharp. And when Eschenbach didn't speak for a while he added, 'Doris is innocent.'

'I know you think that. But unfortunately, the evidence suggests otherwise.'

Jagmetti said nothing.

The inspector had seen the list of people who had visited Doris and knew that the young police officer went to see her regularly. As a civilian, it wasn't against the rules and, as someone with genuine feelings for Doris, it was entirely natural. After Eschenbach had finished his beer, he tried again; heaving himself onto the edge of the sofa, he placed the bottle on the wooden floor. 'I want to be honest with you and present the matter to you as it currently stands.'

Jagmetti nodded.

'I am as in the dark as you are when it comes to whether Doris shot him or not.' Eschenbach paused, waiting for a reaction. Nothing came; no outrage, no temper, not even an angry look. The young police officer simply sat there, looking at the wall.

'She hasn't confessed yet – actually she hasn't given us anything useful at all.' Eschenbach was speaking more slowly than usual, hoping to give Jagmetti the opportunity to say something. 'At the moment, there are six investigators taking another look at Hottiger's background. The shooting association, the army . . . same old story – you already know it all.'

Jagmetti still said nothing, but picked up his bottle and, noticing it was empty, placed it back on the table.

'We have to assume that Ernst Hottiger knew the murderer,' Eschenbach continued. 'Perhaps he even ordered the killing of Philipp Bettlach. That's our theory, anyway.'

'*Your* theory,' Jagmetti interjected.

'Yes, my theory. Either way – and here's the second point – with his suicide, he was trying to cover it up and hide the real killer.'

'And he nearly managed it.'

'Exactly.' Eschenbach was pleased that Jagmetti had been prompted out of his lethargy. 'The whole thing was perfectly staged. The dimly lit room where we talked and the fact that I had never met him before. The way he walked so confidently down the gravel path to the boathouse: a masterpiece. He must have been familiar with every stone beneath his feet so that, even when blind, he could walk like a sighted person. And then the explosion destroyed any trace of his eye condition. An ingenious move. And yet . . .' The inspector ran a hand through his hair and paused for a moment. 'It was too simple, we didn't think about it properly.'

'What do you mean?'

'A security professional like Hottiger never would have blown himself up so spectacularly – it just wasn't his style.'

'I read once that people high up in the army shoot themselves – put a pistol to their heads. It's the only reason they carry guns.' Jagmetti laughed. 'But I assume that's more urban myth than fact.'

'Not necessarily. It's a very efficient way of killing yourself; it's quick and easy. Every high-ranking officer is entrusted with confidential information – and for this reason they will always avoid capture. Ultimately, it's self-protection, or a reflex, call it what you will.'

'Did you learn that in the army?' asked Jagmetti, who had only been a private and owned a rifle but not a pistol.

'Yes, and I'm convinced Hottiger would have done exactly that, if he had only been concerned about his own life. But the risk of his blindness being discovered was too great. So, he put his trust in a crate of dynamite and accepted that he might hurt or even kill someone else. The fishing boats come close to the shore . . . he wouldn't have been able to rule it out.'

'He might not have cared,' said Jagmetti, who wasn't convinced by Eschenbach's argument.

'Ernst Hottiger spent his life protecting other people. He would never have endangered an innocent human life out of recklessness or despair. Everything he did was part of his plan – even his suicide. He put himself in the firing line, in front of the murderer, to protect them.'

'You're right. Then he must have known the murderer.'

'Or, the murderess. I don't know how else to explain it.'

'And you think it's Doris?'

'The evidence is against her, that's the clincher. What I think is irrelevant.'

'And what if she's protecting someone, like her foster father?'

'Then it's up to her to come clean.'

'Blood is thicker than water, she said.'

'In those exact words?' asked Eschenbach.

'Yes. She has a really strange sense of family . . . and a father complex.'

'I know.'

'It's pointless, I've tried everything. She just switches off, then she's as silent as the grave.'

'I see.'

They sat next to one another for a while without speaking, staring at the bare white walls and the television that Jagmetti had switched off an hour before.

Eschenbach stood up and made to say goodbye. 'Keep in touch, all right?' he said. 'I think Rosa misses you.'

Jagmetti walked him to the door and pressed the light switch.

The stairwell was still dark.

'Doesn't matter . . . it's OK,' shouted the inspector after the first couple of steps. And as he reached the bottom of the first flight, he called up over his shoulder, 'And I miss you too, by the way!'

Chapter 38

The next morning, nothing was as it had been. Rosa Mazzoleni was at home with an upset stomach after being rushed to Triemli Hospital the night before. Suspected salmonella, she said. In the end, it turned out to be the mussels, *cozze* in Italian. Eschenbach wasn't surprised; he had never been a fan of seafood. He wished her a speedy recovery and told her to get some sleep. A quarter of an hour later he called back because he couldn't find the key to the cupboard, then ten minutes after that with a question about the coffee machine. He didn't want to disturb her a third time, especially now that he had managed to erase the messages on the answering machine while trying to play them back. He left headquarters disgruntled.

He walked up Gessnerallee towards the Sihl Bridge and took a seat at the little café on the corner. In summer he would some-times come here to eat ice cream – homemade stracciatella, one of Rosa's recommendations. Now it seemed too cold for that and he picked a salami sandwich instead. He stood next to a high marble table, chewing his sandwich, and looked through the frameless window at the traffic outside, trundling along from Stauffacher junction towards the centre of the city. It was the second wave of traffic that morning, just before nine, before the big shopping centres opened their doors and life on Zurich's roads really got going. Before that there were the tradesmen and employees who left for work between six and eight, most of them with their phones to their ears or – in their cars – speaking into their hands-free kits. From A to B, from one underground car park to the next. Eschenbach sometimes wondered whether these people would be able to find their way to work in the morning if the roads were suddenly clear and there were no cars to follow in front of them.

Eschenbach could hear a *Pink Panther* ringtone. It was a while before he realised that it was his and that Kathrin had changed his ringtone again.

'Who am I speaking to, please?' he asked a second time after the caller failed to understand him. It was unusual for a stranger to call him on his mobile phone.

'Corporal Schubiger, Bellevue police station.' The voice sounded female; it was very loud.

The inspector had rushed out onto the pavement in search of better reception.

'Am I speaking to Inspector Eschenbach?' asked the stranger.

A lorry rumbled past him.

'Yes,' he shouted, holding a hand to his other ear.

'Hello?' yelled the voice.

Eschenbach went back to his window seat in the café and looked at the three small bars on the phone screen. Apparently, this was good reception.

'Yes, Eschenbach here!' he growled, stuffing the last bite of his sandwich into his mouth.

The corporal, who was a woman, shouted the name of the police station again, as well as her name and rank. Then she said, more quietly, that no one was answering the phone in his office and that she had got his number from Max Kubly at Info Services.

Eschenbach washed the rest of the sandwich down with a glass of water. 'So how can I help?' He felt his teeth with his tongue and looked to see if there were any toothpicks.

'There's a Ms Marchand here, Eveline Marchand. She wants to speak to you, says it's urgent.' And after a short pause, she added, 'She says she's killed someone.'

Eschenbach stopped for a moment, then said, thoughtlessly, 'Don't let her go anywhere, I'll come straight there.'

The young woman at the bar followed him out onto the pavement with the bill in her hand. He only had a one-hundred franc note on him, so they went back into the café. To Eschenbach, it seemed to take a lifetime before he was back outside, walking the five hundred metres to Paradeplatz.

He fidgeted constantly throughout the short tram ride down to Bürkliplatz and then past another station to Bellevue. He couldn't think when he was sitting down, so he walked from the back of the carriage to the front and back again. He walked the entire length of the wagon several times, making sure that he didn't bump into the few passengers who were sitting down.

Eveline Marchand was sitting at a broad wooden desk in the corporal's office at Bellevue police station. When Eschenbach entered, she greeted him with a shy nod and stood up.

'Ms Marchand has already made a confession,' said Corporal Schubiger, a slightly chubby woman with blond hair. 'She just has to sign it.' She carefully pulled the sheet of paper out of the old IBM and passed it across the desk. 'Just at the bottom here, please.'

Eveline stood up and signed her name.

Schubiger took the sheet of paper and placed in the photocopier. 'I'll make you a copy . . . and then I'll need another signature for the transfer.'

'Yes, yes, I know,' said Eschenbach, pulling a ballpoint pen out of his jacket pocket.

At the counter, a police officer was talking to a woman reporting a mugging. She was describing the contents of her stolen bag to the officer.

After all the formalities were dealt with and Eschenbach had thanked the corporal, he left the office with Eveline. They took the service gate which led into a small courtyard. A patrol car was standing in a marked parking space; two girls were playing hopscotch nearby.

'I didn't know where to find you.' Eveline smiled. 'The police station at Bellevue is the only one that I know. When I was a girl, I got my bicycle tags here . . . I think they were red. Do they still have them?'

'No, only tags now, you have to attach them to your bike. I think they even give them away free.'

'Do you have to know that . . . I mean, as a police officer?'

'You do, actually.' Eschenbach sighed. 'It's been a long time since I last rode my bike.'

As they walked along side by side, the inspector made a brief call to Ivo Fröhlich, a friend he knew from a sports outing with work. 'Can you get me a booth, with an Stg. 90? I'll tell you the rest later. I'll be with you in twenty minutes.'

At Sechseläutewiese, they got into a taxi and the driver nodded when Eschenbach told him their destination. An address in Oberrieden, obviously one which was familiar to the old man at the wheel.

'I still have a few things at the hotel,' said Eveline after they had been sitting next to one another for a while in silence. 'Perhaps we should go and pick them up. I mean, before we . . .'

'We'll have time,' said Eschenbach. 'We're not going to the detention centre . . . not yet.' He took his pad out of the inner pocket of his jacket. He scanned it and looked at Eveline from the side. 'You must be a good shot if you really did this.'

'I learnt from Ernst . . . he showed me everything.'

'That's as may be. Still, Philipp was shot from a considerable distance.'

'I know,' she nodded to herself without sparing Eschenbach a single glance.

The Oberrieden shooting range lay on a slope with a wonderful view of Lake Zurich. Ivo Fröhlich was waiting for them. He was tall and slim with snow-white hair. A pipe hung from the corner of his mouth and the olive-brown jacket that he wore open over a light jumper had seen better days.

'If you're here then I guess hell's about to freeze over.' He took Eschenbach's hand in both of his and shook it. He turned to Eveline and said, with a wink, 'You can't imagine how patient I've had to be with him. A terrible shot, but he's a good chap.' Then he held out his powerful hand to greet her.

Eveline laughed.

Eschenbach used the brief interlude following the introductions to take the old man aside and explain to him in a few words what was actually happening.

'Very good!' said Ivo Fröhlich. 'Now come on over! Get yourselves inside – I've got everything ready.'

Inside, the shooting range was lit with fluorescent tubes and the individual booths were separated by wooden panels like stables. There were grey gym mats for the shooters to lie on.

On the wall mount, which had space for several guns, was a black rifle. Ivo took it down.

'An STG-90 – fifty shots, loaded and safety on.' He gave it to Eveline and they could see that she had underestimated the weight of the gun. 'I've set it to single fire.'

'I think we'd best take one of the middle booths,' said Eschenbach calmly, exchanging glances with Ivo Fröhlich.

Fröhlich brought two pairs of orange ear defenders. 'You'll be needing these . . . they're no good to me any more.'

Eschenbach clamped them around his neck like a disc jockey and went to help Eveline. She was wearing black jeans without a belt and light trainers with red stripes. She was holding the barrel like a walking stick. Eschenbach was reminded of his first days of military training school, when he held a gun in his hands for the first time. He smirked.

'Do you really want to do this?'

'I can do it,' she said, dragging the gun along the mat.

'OK, then,' muttered the inspector. 'If you really want to . . .' He took the rifle, folded out the metal supports and set it down so that the barrel was facing the target. When he noticed that she couldn't find the safety catch, he knelt down next to her. 'You have to close one eye and then, with the other . . . look here: rear sight, front sight, target. The target is over there . . .' he pointed to the small, white square three hundred metres away. 'That's the target.'

Ivo Fröhlich had sat down on the bench a little way behind the wall. He sucked on his pipe and watched the inspector – a terrible shot himself – teach another person to shoot for the first time.

Chapter 39

The shot rang in Eschenbach's ears; he had forgotten to put on his ear defenders. Perhaps that was why it took him a moment to realise that Eveline was crying. She lay behind the rifle on the mat, her hands over her face. He sat down next to her while Ivo carefully took the gun away.

Neither of them mentioned that the target remained untouched.

Often, in situations such as these, moments of speechless desperation, the inspector found himself with an upset stomach.

'Shall we get something to drink?' he asked.

She nodded and Ivo filled the silence by talking about how urgently he needed to make repairs to his shooting range.

'I'll drive you both to Buchmühle, we can get something there,' he said.

Eschenbach mumbled a thank you and got into Ivo's old Land Rover with Eveline Marchand. They descended the slope via a steep road and went through a short underpass over which the motorway rumbled towards Chur. The heavy grey blanket of cloud that had darkened the sky all morning revealed cracks of blue and the radio was playing Swiss folk music.

'It's Vreneli-Schottisch,' said Ivo Fröhlich. He hummed along and fiddled with the volume dial on his radio. And, as if obliged to liven up the subdued mood of an entire troop of riflemen, he let the car trundle along to the restaurant in time to the bouncing bass of the Heirassa band.

When the inspector noticed that Eveline's hands were no longer shaking, their movements calmer and more assured, he began to talk. About the Bettlach case and about how, over the last seven weeks, it had become the case of Doris Hottiger.

'I understand that you would have liked to take the blame.' He smiled and added, somewhat clumsily, 'I think that's what mothers do.'

She looked at him briefly, then back down, stirring her camomile tea.

'Ernst wanted to as well – and it's just a stupid mistake that he didn't manage to.' The inspector bit into a dry piece of *Linzertorte* and washed it back with a large gulp of Fernet-Branca. 'He wanted to cover it up because he knew it was Doris who shot Philipp.'

Eveline looked at him in disbelief.

'He had failed as a father, failed in his duty to protect her; that's why the murder came just at the right time and he believed that he could straighten things out with a single, daring feat.'

'No, that's not true!'

'Yes, it is.' The inspector ran his finger over the rim of the schnapps glass. He did it without thinking; it was a tick that drove Corina mad. 'Why else would he have taken his own life? Doris was the most important thing in the world to him, the one reason he could justify killing himself. The one way he could justify doing something he despised.'

'You know nothing,' she hissed.

'Oh, come now, believe me, it's too late for that.'

'Doris won't say anything.'

'Doris can keep her silence as long as she likes. It's her right. And you can too. You all can, for all I care! It won't be the first murder trial to go ahead without a confession.'

'She's not saying anything because she doesn't know anything!'

'That's for the judge to decide. It's not up to me, Ms Marchand; my investigation is over.'

'You're making it very easy on yourself.'

'I've done what I could; it's no longer in my hands. All I will say is this: the lawyers that Johannes Bettlach has hired might be good, but they've got a very poor hand.'

'They will win the trial.'

Eschenbach shrugged his shoulders. 'Anything's possible, I suppose . . . but I don't think they will, to be honest.'

'Then we'll lodge an appeal.'

At this point Eschenbach hesitated, and the corner of his mouth twitched with the urge to laugh. 'I'm sure you will.' He took a hearty gulp of Fernet and felt its warmth spreading through his chest. This wasn't Eveline talking; these were the words of an anxious mother. They were the words of someone seeking the upper hand. Suddenly, a strange certainty dawned on him. Eveline had discussed the case with Johannes Bettlach. He continued to goad her: 'An appeal? Even then she'll end up spending three or four years in a hole – despite being innocent, as you claim. Twice a week, I check the list of the names of the people visiting Doris. You're on there – so you must know how pleasant it is.'

She nodded.

'Your twenties count twice as much as the rest of your life, Ms Marchand. I'm sure you'll agree with me on that. And if you spend them in prison, perhaps they count for even more ... I don't know.'

'We'll sue ... for damages.' It sounded helpless and the inspector saw that she was close to tears.

'You'll have to win the trial first ... and even then, what will it get you? Money?'

Eveline said nothing but stared intently at her tea; she hadn't drunk a single sip.

'If Doris gets out of Dielsdorf,' the inspector went on, 'guilty or not, she will have lost her youth. And believe me, in the end it makes no difference whether it's two years or five. She won't be the same woman any more. If you chop off the top of a young pine tree, it will never reach the sky.'

Eschenbach was weaving a sorry tale, like a factory worker turning the screws in a VW Lupo.

When ten minutes had passed, Eveline stood up and asked the landlord to call her a taxi; she left without saying goodbye, and without a single glance back at the restaurant.

The inspector cradled the empty schnapps glass in his hands, stared at a row of antlers attached to the wall and at the empty, wooden tables around him. Then he ordered a second schnapps and, shortly after, a third.

The most difficult part of his simple plan was behind him. Now all he had to do was wait.

Chapter 40

The call came the following day, just before eleven in the morning. And when Johannes Bettlach stepped out of the lift at HQ just an hour later, supported by Eveline, the inspector barely recognised him.

His wrinkles had become furrows and his pale eyes were encased in deep, sad, cavernous sockets. His silver mane, which the inspector remembered resembling a halo, looked dull and much too large for his hollow face. It was an old man who stood before him.

'He would like to speak to you in private,' said Eveline after helping Johannes Bettlach to his seat in Eschenbach's office. Then she went out and closed the door behind her.

'I shot Philipp,' Bettlach began, unprompted. 'The Blaser . . . R93 Tactical. Ernst gave it to me.'

Eschenbach leant back in his chair. 'Could you take a shot like that? I mean, it was over half a—'

'I have the same military training that Ernst had.' The old man interrupted him curtly. 'You don't need a gold medal to kill someone.'

'Where's the gun now?'

'I buried it . . . next to my mother's urn in my garden, by the old plane tree.'

'We will check that,' said the inspector plainly.

'It's there, believe me. You'll be able to find it . . . if you use a metal detector. I assume the police have access to such things?'

'No,' replied Eschenbach, but the sarcasm escaped his guest. 'Then the business with Ernst was a put-up job?' he sighed.

'No, I wouldn't say so . . .' Bettlach spoke quietly again and thought for a moment. 'Since his eyesight had begun to deteriorate he often spoke about death, saying there was no point in it all any more. After he gave me the gun, he had to assume that it was I who shot Philipp.'

'Did you speak to him about it?'

'No.'

'And still he covered for you?'

'Ernst was like that.'

Eschenbach frowned.

'The only thing he cared about was the mission at hand. He spent his whole life in the service of others. Whatever he did . . . it always had a purpose. I think, with his suicide, he made sure that even his death served a purpose.'

'For his friend?'

'No, not me.'

'Who, then?'

'He did it for Doris.'

'But you two were friends.'

'Yes, that's true . . .' Bettlach hesitated for a moment, before going on. 'Ernst had retreated somewhat in recent years . . . there were nasty scenes because of Philipp.'

'Because of Doris?'

'Before that. He could no longer stand by and watch innocent people fall apart . . . it's terrible. I had no idea who . . . or how many . . .'

'You could have prevented it . . .'

'Perhaps . . . We've already talked about this, haven't we?'

Eschenbach nodded.

'I always hoped and prayed that it would stop one day. The doctors fed my sense of hope, without really promising anything . . . and without really sharing it.' He wrung his hands and looked at Eschenbach in desperation: 'Hope's a bitch, Inspector. I tried to deny it, I didn't want to believe it, until Doris showed me the videos.' He gripped the armrests of his chair and pulled himself closer to the table. 'Did you see them?'

Eschenbach nodded.

'My son is . . . he was a monster, wasn't he? I never realised . . . To me, he was always just my son.'

'Your son? You mean your brother, surely?'

'No. He was my son, my own flesh and blood.' He looked at the inspector. His eyes were moist. 'Don't you understand? I'm Philipp's father.'

Eschenbach faltered. 'And the border guard . . . your mother's lover?'

'There's no Swiss officer, there never was. My mother and I invented that later. It was me. I took the refugees across to the other side of the lake in a rowing boat. In the morning, when the mist lay over the water and you couldn't see your hand in front of your face. It was me . . . I was my mother's lover.'

'Philipp was your son . . .' Eschenbach repeated, as if hoping to be better able to believe it if he said it out loud.

'My only son, yes.' Bettlach shook his head, as if he meant the opposite. 'It's in my damn genes, do you understand? I had to stop them, I had to make sure that it didn't just carry on.'

Eschenbach nodded, though he wasn't sure he had understood.

'When this disaster began . . . with Philipp and Doris . . . and the whole story threatened to repeat itself again, I had to do something about it.' He clenched his fists in despair. 'When a record keeps skipping, you take it off the turntable.'

The inspector remembered that Ernst Hottiger had said the same thing. 'What about a secure institution . . . I mean, couldn't that have been a solution?'

'Of course. All of these institutions . . . hoping all over again . . . and having my hopes dashed.' He shook his head as if he had already considered it a thousand times. 'I'm getting old, Inspector, and after I'm gone, who would look after Philipp?'

'Did he know that you were his father?'

'No, I never told him . . . Adele kept it a secret too; she took it to her grave. We both wanted to. Now I'm the only one who knows.'

'Eveline knew, of course.'

'No! She didn't know anything about it.'

'Really?'

'Until yesterday . . . then I told her everything.'

Eschenbach raised his eyebrows in surprise.

'Even you, Inspector, you never would have known if I hadn't told you. But I know that you won't tell anyone. It doesn't matter any more, does it?'

'No, not now.' Eschenbach looked into the old man's watery eyes. 'And Hottiger, did he know?'

'Ernst? I assume he did. We knew a lot about each other without having ever spoken about it. I think he would have done the same in my place.' Bettlach paused for a moment. 'Yes, I think Ernst knew.'

'And Doris? Does she . . .'

'Yes. Eveline and I told her this morning. Now she knows that I'm her father . . . and Philipp's father too.'

'And?'

'And nothing. She had to know. It's important for her, do you understand? I kept my silence too long; I swept it all under the carpet.'

'Don't you think this admission has come a bit late?'

'Maybe . . .' The old man was gripped by a sudden fervour. 'But we have to know who we are . . . and where we come from. It's important for us, for our peace of mind, believe you me.'

They both sat there for a while before the inspector called two officers to accompany Johannes Bettlach to his cell. Somehow, he felt sorry for the old man, the way he trudged away, bent forward and supported by the two men. Like a gambler who had spent his life trying in vain to beat the cards that fate had stacked against him.

Eschenbach sat back down, just for a moment, and made a note of the key words that he would type up in his concluding report later.

'Ms Marchand is still waiting,' Rosa Mazzoleni warned over the intercom. 'Can I send her in?'

'I'll be right there,' he called and stowed the notepad in the drawer. As he went to close the window, which he always kept open a crack because he smoked, Eschenbach saw the police car depart. Through its dark rear window he thought he could make out Johannes Bettlach's silver mane. The car carefully merged with the traffic and drove away.

Although it was just a short distance from headquarters to the county jail in Rotwandstrasse, for the old man it would be like a journey to another world.

'He won't survive it,' said Eveline, suddenly by his side. 'His pictures, his music . . . he'll miss it all.'

'Probably.'

'He'll miss the world outside.'

The inspector nodded.

They stood at the window in silence for a while, watching the evening twilight as it sank slowly over the city.

Epilogue

For two days, it had snowed without stopping. Thick, wet flakes tumbled over the roofs of the houses and onto the cars which stood abandoned on the side of the road, their journeys cut short by the snow and the ice. Everything slowed down at this time of year, when the roads were blocked and the power lines that served the trains and trams were iced over. People arrived in the office late and left early to make their way home. Only the cleaning staff were as punctual as ever. At half seven in the evening, they would be there: Turks, Tamils, people from Kosovo, Moldova, Chechnya and who knows where else.

They would greet Eschenbach with a smile as they came into the office, before running fluffy rags over the desks, chairs and the telephone, tinkering around with the vacuum. The security guard who accompanied the gaggle of cleaners and checked that nothing unlawful was going on, saluted him. Eschenbach waved.

A few Christmas cards stood open on Eschenbach's desk: homemade cards as well as photos and corporate cards. Festive greetings from his friend Christian who had gone skiing in Klosters with his children, and Gabriel, inviting him for an aperitif. One of the cards showed the Champs-Élysées bedecked with Christmas trees: 'I passed my exams and am spending the New Year with Doris in Paris.' Some words had been scribbled underneath the printed greeting '*Joyeux Noël*': 'Huge thanks once again, I'll be in touch in January.' It was signed Claudio Jagmetti.

Some distance from the happy muddle of cards lay a letter. The handwriting, looping in blue ink, would have been better suited to fine, deckle-edged paper than the grubby, squared paper on which it found itself.

Dear Mr Eschenbach,

I have written you a letter every day since I was admitted here on 9 October. Usually I do this in the afternoons at half three, after a short one-hour nap or a lie-down. You don't know this – you couldn't, because I always tear up the previous day's letter as soon as I have written the new one. Writing comforts me and makes a change from reading all the time.

I began the first letter 'Dear Inspector'. At some point, this became 'Dear Inspector Eschenbach' and perhaps at some stage I will arrive at 'Dear Eschenbach'. I don't know your first name, and I can't remember ever hearing it or reading it anywhere.

Zurich County Jail is a hole behind the courthouse, but you know that better than I do. Nevertheless, I wish to stay here – even though you are trying very hard (I assume it's you) to have me moved to a luxury bunker. It is the only jail in the city – my city – and it means more to me than the prison Pfäffikon or any other dump outside. This might sound strange to you, but that's who I am now. And it's the same here: old, with little barred windows beneath the roof. They aren't made for you to see out of – only if you stand on the bed – and I'm much too old for that now.

In short, this is the perfect place to die. One already feels half buried, so the next step can't be far away.

At night, when I lie in bed and read a little [in brackets he had written and crossed out *'Anton Chekov' and written 'Jane Austen'*]*, I test it out: the matter of dying . . . At the moment, I'm still practising; I think what I lack here is not the peace and quiet but the courage with which to do it. My trembling knees and occasional arrhythmias are my allies. I think that we will make it to the anniversary of Philipp's death. A death in summer – now that has a certain romance to it.*

The one thing that keeps me, temporarily, from doing it, is food. I don't know where it comes from (maybe they actually cook it themselves as they claim to do) – anyway, it's excellent. It's as if they want to make up for the dilapidated setting with culinary finesse.

Eveline comes to see me regularly; Doris also comes from time to time, as does Ms Saladin – my loyal secretary. It's not easy with them. They want to cheer me up, but ultimately, it's me who ends up comforting them. Sometimes I'm even glad when they leave, and I can go back to my cell. When you're old, there comes a point where everything has been said – even the unsayable.

In two days' time it will be Christmas, and I have been trying to bribe Mr Donat In-Albon for over a week to get me a candle (Strictly forbidden – they're a fire hazard!). I think I'm the only Christian here – except for the staff.

In-Albon is thirty-five and my warder (he insists on this description) – I call him my keeper, which annoys him no end. You only get keepers in zoos, he says (to which I respond by saying that I'd be happy to move into the elephant enclosure). I've been nice to him (which is to say, I've stopped poking fun) because I want a candle and, if I succeed, I'll give him a copy of Goethe's Werther *and two tickets to the Conelli circus (I often used to go with Doris at Christmas). If not, then I'll give him the Goethe, but no tickets.*

The walls here are covered in scribbles of all sorts of mad stuff (languages that I don't even recognise). I had always thought that it was only like that in films. Recently, I caught myself searching for a suitable quote of my own. Perhaps something by Oscar Wilde. I still haven't decided.

Best wishes,

Johannes Bettlach

Eschenbach picked up the loose sheets and folded them twice along the existing crease. It was exactly how they had been folded when they were brought to him that morning, along with the news that Johannes Bettlach was dead.

The prison doctor's report would later record that he died on the night of 24 December. Probably around six in the morning and without any indication of external trauma.

Turn the page for a sneek peek at

WHEN TIME RUNS OUT

by Elina Hirvonen

Available in paperback and ebook now

1

When he was a child, he responded to smiles with a smile. He had two front teeth in his lower jaw and a dimple in his left cheek. When someone smiled at him, his face melted into sunshine and his dimple appeared so soft and delicious that it was tempting to press a finger into it and tickle gently, just to hear the laughter that shook his entire body.

When he sat in his buggy on the tram, strangers would lean over him, smiling and chatting as if they had always known him. He would smile back and point with his chubby fingers at the trees, buses, diggers and street lamps that were visible beyond the windows and say: 'Dat!' And people looked in the direction in which he was pointing, smiled and said: 'What a lovely tree. What a lovely digger. What a lovely motorbike. What a lovely child.'

When the people got off the tram, shielding their faces from the cold wind and the rain, they smiled for such a long time that they no longer remembered why.

2

Helsinki, some time later

He listens again to Pink Floyd's 'Nobody Home' – a song
which he has listened to many times each day, for years.
When the music ends, everything in him feels light. This is the
last time.

His smile is light, his fingers lighter than a fly's wings. He
stands in the middle of the city, on a roof which he has always
wanted to climb. In his left hand is a semi-automatic small-bore
rifle. It was astonishingly easy to steal it from the boot of a car
parked beside the shooting range. Ever since he decided to put
his plan into action, everything has been astonishingly easy.

This is something I'm good at, he'd thought as he filmed his
message and posted it online, packed the rifle into its bag and
dressed in a black windcheater, black trousers and soft-soled
trainers in which he would be able to climb well. The music
moved his body; as he left home he felt like taking a couple of
high leaps, leaving the mark of his knuckles in the ceiling with
his fist, smashing a hole into the ceiling and marking the wall
with the sole of his shoe, running nimbly over the cars, blowing obstacles from his path, like dandelion seeds, feeling so

intensely in the moment that nothing could check his speed or his strength.

Now his movements are slower than usual, as if everything were happening underwater. The city is his dream and the sounds of police cars, ambulances and escaping people come distantly, from the other side of the water's surface.

The only thing he can see clearly is the woman he is aiming at. The woman is younger than his mother and so ordinary-looking that she could be anybody. Beside her is another woman, so old that she will probably die soon in any case. He rests the weapon against his shoulder and zooms in on the younger woman's head with the variable scope as if he were making a movie.

The weapon fires when you press the trigger. After the first shot you can fire again without reloading. The trigger is cool beneath his finger. Only a small movement is necessary. The click of the trigger and the kick of the rifle butt against your shoulder. His finger is not trembling. He narrows his eyes. The old woman is shouting something at the younger one, who turns her head away.

They may be mother and daughter, he thinks, as he sets the rifle down for a moment, shaking his arms and taking a deep breath as if after a long dive. Then he raises the rifle again and takes aim at the woman, who is holding her hat as she runs for safety.

3

Laura

I pour some sea salt into an oven dish, scrub a swede clean and set it in the middle of the bed of salt, a round swede-moon. *This will be a good night*, I think. I have studied the art of positive thinking. Eerik, my husband, would laugh if he knew. Everyone who knows me would probably laugh at me. I have always considered that kind of thing stupid, and said so. But now I have decided to fill my mind with positive thoughts, to smile until my brain begins to feel pleasure, and to love myself so much that it will be easy for others to love me too. Otherwise I won't manage. I am fifty-eight years old and completely healthy. I do yoga in the mornings and lift weights in the evenings. I very probably have decades of life left and I have decided to learn to enjoy them.

I am on my way to the university to talk about the climate catastrophe. After that I will fetch Eerik from the airport. In the evening our son Aslak is coming round for dinner.

I lay the table with mismatching plates and put a tall red candle in a wine bottle. It makes me laugh a little: in almost forty years together Eerik and I haven't acquired proper flower vases, candlesticks or complete sets of crockery. Whenever I put a flower or a candle in an empty bottle I remember what it was like when we had little money and plenty of time, what it was like to go to parties thrown by people we didn't know, to wake up to languid Saturday mornings with friends, to order pizza and watch movies whose words we all knew by heart.

I am making Aslak's favourite dish, swede braised until it is soft, then fried until it is sweet and crispy. With the exception of a short period in his youth, Aslak has been a vegetarian all his life, and I am extraordinarily happy about this. As a child he would begin to cry if he saw newspaper advertisements for marinated chicken strips or wafer-thin slices of ham.

'How can anyone live in a world in which living creatures are made into *strips* and *slices*!' he said, his tears falling from his cheeks onto the newspaper. I took the paper from the floor and folded it up, stroked his head and said: 'My love, the world is always changing. You can be part of making it a better place.'

I put the swede in the oven, set the timer for two hours and pull on the clothes that I nearly always wear when I am lecturing to young people: a simple dress, thick tights and high boots. I glance at the mirror. I have short hair whose iron-grey stripes gleam, depending on the day, bravely or sorrowfully, and there are wrinkles around my eyes – wrinkles I haven't got used to. I hardly use any make-up, but nevertheless, occasionally at the chemist's or in an airport tax-free shop, I find myself reading the label of a new cream and hoping that the cream might be the solution. That it might return me to a time when everything was supposed to be possible.

Soon we are sitting at the sturdy, wooden kitchen table. When Eerik and I moved into this flat, we wanted a long table for a large group of friends. Through the years I often planned dinner parties which we would hold when we had time, when everyday life loosened its grip, when Aslak was going through a better period. I came up with complicated dishes and thought about how to invite friends who didn't know each other. We would eat for a long time and open one bottle of wine after another, the children would say goodnight to everyone in their pyjamas, the evening would continue on into the night and we would talk and laugh and in the morning we would wake up having had too little sleep, but full of energy after a happy evening. Those dinners never happened, and we sat around the big table, a long way from one another.

At that table Aava and Aslak, in their high chairs, ate their first solid food – half a teaspoon of mashed sweet potato. At that table they blew bubbles in their milk glasses and giggled when we told them not to. Years later they sat silently in their places, I talked too much to sustain the conversation, both Eerik and the children chewed their food with glum faces and I was sure that he was thinking of grinding me with his teeth.

I imagine our conversation.

'Aslak. You can't go on like this.'

I say it out loud. The words thud into the room where there is no one but me; they take with them the weight that has spread within me. It has made my breathing laborious and my steps heavy.

'We won't abandon you. We want to help you find somewhere where you can work out what is weighing you down. You're young, sensitive and intelligent and you have a lot to give. We hope that you will have a good life and be able to do the things that are important to you. Don't you want to do that too?'

I think of Eerik's so very familiar posture, which over the years has become ever so slightly stooped, as if he were carrying a burden that was too heavy. Eyes the colour of a winter sky and a gaze that, even in the happiest of moments, has a trace of disquiet. Fine wrinkles at the corners of his mouth, and a chin, covered in grey stubble, which he always rubs when he hears something he doesn't like. I think of Aslak's head, sunk between his shoulders, eyes hidden behind his heavy eyelids, teeth biting his lower lip. I think how everything in him could withdraw still further inside, how his whole body could look for a tortoise's shell to protect it, under which it could hide.

4

A cold wind penetrates my cape-like coat. I wrap it more tightly around my body and try to ring Aslak. I want to make sure that he really is coming, that he is not planning to cancel our arrangement on some pretext whose implausibility would show clearly how little he values me and Eerik.

This happens often. We ask Aslak round, he promises to come, but he does not come. We pretend to be disappointed and suggest a new time, feeling guilty about how relieved we are. Meetings with Aslak are complicated and awkward. I hope for something that will never happen, and Eerik is desperately correct. Even Aslak tries, when he is in the mood, to play the part of a grown-up son. After such occasions Eerik rolls a joint, although he has been trying to give up smoking for almost thirty years. I go for a run, running such a long way in the forest that the world grows dim as if I were drunk.

All the same I go on arranging get-togethers whose spoken aim is to cheer Aslak up and to show that we care. The unspoken aim is that something should finally change.

On Mother's Day I persuaded Aslak to come into the centre of town for brunch. I had booked a table in a restaurant in a renovated banking hall; in front of it seagulls strutted and inside it sat well-dressed families in which even the small children behaved well.

I was wearing a sea-green silk dress, Eerik straight trousers and his best shirt; I had also bought Aslak a new sweater. He arrived with his hair greasy and his skin pale and waxy, dressed in a bobbly T-shirt that smelled of sweat.

'He can't come looking like that,' whispered Eerik, but I hugged Aslak. That day the sky was bright, the smell of the sea was in the air and I had decided to be a happy mother.

I grasped Aslak by the shoulders and piloted him into the restaurant. Eerik paced past me, his eyes on the floor, and the waiter directed us to the table with a smile despite the pungent smell emanating from Aslak.

We ate many tiny starters, a hot main course, cheese and a dessert. Eerik was silent throughout the entire meal and I talked constantly, smiling until my cheeks ached. I passed food to Aslak and ordered drinks, champagne in honour of the occasion, although Eerik raised his eyebrows: in his opinion it was better to drink water with Aslak. I put my arm around Aslak and talked about books and movies he knew nothing about, bands that he had listened to years ago, and memories, the few we had in common that I dared speak about.

'Do you remember when we were on the cycling holiday in Copenhagen? You and Aava sat in a box bike eating melon?

'Do you remember when you learned to skate – you let go of the support and suddenly raced round the rink?

'Do you remember when you programmed your first robot . . . when you wrote an essay and the teacher gave you full marks?'

After the meal I paid the bill, got up with a smile and went to the toilet, locked the door and burst into tears. When I returned, Aslak had already gone. Eerik stood silently by the cloakroom waiting for me, then walked silently out before me.

Aslak doesn't answer. This often happens. When I try to let Aslak take responsibility and don't pay his bills, I cannot reach him for weeks and finally I become so anxious that I take it upon myself to look after all his expenses. I don't tell Eerik about this. He thinks I treat Aslak like a child and that is why he seems stuck in the nest, a fledgling grown enormous who doesn't know how to fly. I leave Aslak a message and run to the metro station.

Beside the entrance is an old beggarwoman on her knees; I turn to give her money and she says thank you in Finnish. I'm startled.

'What a sentimental nationalist you are,' Eerik would say if he was with me. He feels it is perverse of me to avoid gypsy beggars as if I did not see them but to stop whenever I see an elderly Finnish person with a cup in their hand.

When I look more closely at the woman, I notice that she has applied rouge under her sharp cheekbones and wound her scarf around her neck in the manner of French women twenty years ago. For a moment I see myself in her place, in a too-thin coat with a cardboard cup in front of me, trying in spite of the circumstances to look dignified.

I want to speak to my daughter Aava. She lives in Mogadishu and never calls me. Not even when the place where she lives, a small island surrounded by a wall and high watchtowers whose barracks are home to foreign workers, was bombed and her neighbour died.

I am always the one that makes the approach, Aava the one who ends the conversation. Aava leaves and doesn't come back for a long time, pays a quick visit to Finland and only has time for one meeting, even that a brief one, during which she glances around her as if checking for an escape route. When I suggest another meeting, a joint day out or trip, a couple of days when we could get to know each other again, Aava leaves again. She goes to countries where there is too much blood and too little water, to camps quickly jerry-built amid wars, their dry streets swarming with children whose parents were born in the same camp.

I am proud of Aava. My daughter has the courage to go wherever she wants, to survive anywhere. I would like to say this to her. I would also like to say that you don't always have to cope, and when you can't bear it any more, you can come home. I tried once.

'Do you really not get it? It's home I want to stay away from,' Aava said, and I smiled as I learned to do when I was a child and something inside me was crushed.

I love Aava, of course. And admire her. But my admiration is not as pure as I would like it to be. Aava is a better version of myself. She does important work all over the world and lives a life that I thought for years that I would live sometime. Aava doesn't have to negotiate her decisions with anyone, and she doesn't know what it feels like when passion fades. When she comes home, she can close the door and be quiet; she can go whenever she wants to and mourn her own sorrows alone.